"A haunting love story. . . . With beautiful prose and picturesque descriptions, Amanda Barratt draws on the true life events that shaped the romance between Dietrich Bonhoeffer and Maria von Wedemeyer. . . . Infused into every page is a faith that not only Dietrich but Maria was willing to stand on, no matter the cost."

—JAIME JO WRIGHT, author of *The Curse of Misty Wayfair* and Christy Award winner *The House on Foster Hill*

"An extraordinary story, richly researched and beautifully told. Within these pages is a treasure lost to time and now returned to vivid life through Amanda Barratt's gifted pen."

—LAURA FRANTZ, Christy Award–winning author of *The Lacemaker*

"As beautiful as it is brave, *My Dearest Dietrich* is an illuminating novel that exposes the darkness and chases the shadows away. This is a multi-faceted story of the highest stakes and the deepest loves, and Amanda Barratt has proved herself worthy of its telling."

—JOCELYN GREEN, award-winning author of *Between Two Shores*

"Every once in a while a novel so captures my heart that it feels like a gift from the author. *My Dearest Dietrich* is that kind of book. Barratt has taken a true love story, weaving it into a narrative which is endearing, heart-wrenching, and tender. I savored every word of this novel, reflected on the wisdom infused into each chapter, and allowed hope to fill my heart even to the very end. This is a story we so desperately need now."

—SUSIE FINKBEINER, author of *All Manner of Things* and the best-selling Pearl Spence series

"It is not often I have the sublime pleasure to read a novel that lingers with me long after I've finished the last page and closed the book. Amanda Barratt's stellar writing creates a world that, based on truth, also demonstrates such intimate knowledge of her characters as to make them living, breathing, thinking human beings. This is a kaleidoscopic emotional journey through heart-stopping moments of danger and risk faced by two star-crossed lovers. Their tale will take you from weeping over war's futility to awe at one man's unwavering faith and conviction.

"A tribute to those who sacrificed greatly to try and bring peace and lasting freedom to a nation ruled by war, *My Dearest Dietrich* is that rare and beautiful body of work that will appeal to a broad range of readers, including fans of historical fiction and Christian romance."

—KATE BRESLIN, best-selling author of *For Such a Time*

My
Dearest
Dietrich

My Dearest Dietrich

A Novel of Dietrich Bonhoeffer's Lost Love

Amanda Barratt

KREGEL
PUBLICATIONS

My Dearest Dietrich: A Novel of Dietrich Bonhoeffer's Lost Love
© 2019, 2022 by Amanda Barratt

Published by Kregel Publications, a division of Kregel Inc., 2450 Oak Industrial Dr. NE, Grand Rapids, MI 49505.

Many of the letters quoted in this work are genuine correspondence taken from *Love Letters from Cell 92* by Dietrich Bonhoeffer, Maria von Wedemeyer. Copyright © 1992 by C. H. Beck'sche Verlagsbuchhandlung. Translation copyright © 1994 by HarperCollins Publishers, Ltd., Used by permission of Zondervan. www.zondervan.com

Other letters taken from *Letters and Papers from Prison*, revised, enlarged ed. by Dietrich Bonhoeffer, translated from the German by R. H. Fuller, Frank Clark, et al. Copyright © 1953, 1967, 1971 by SCM Press Ltd. Reprinted with the permission of Scribner, a division of Simon & Schuster, Inc. All rights reserved.

All photos used with permission: *page 8* courtesy of Wikimedia Commons and the Deutsches Bundesarchiv, Bild 183-R0211-316 / CC-BY-SA 3.0; *page 11* in the public domain; *page 346* courtesy of Casarsa, iStock by Getty Images, 180847842.

Scripture quotations are from the King James Version.

ISBN 978-0-8254-4763-1, paperback
ISBN 978-0-8254-7579-5, epub

Printed in the United States of America
22 23 24 25 26 27 28 29 30 / 5 4 3 2 1

To those who spoke out for the voiceless
and paid the ultimate price.

*"Blessed is the heart with strength to
stop its beating for honor's sake.
Blessed is the match consumed
in kindling flame."*
—HANNAH SZENES, 1921–1944

For Your glory, Lord.

Acknowledgments

Bringing Dietrich and Maria's story to the pages of this novel would not have been possible without the outpouring of love and support I received. This story captured my imagination in ways as unique and heart-wrenching as the lives of these characters, and I could not have walked this road alone.

I am deeply grateful to . . .

The authors and publishers whose works on Bonhoeffer I painstakingly pored over, particularly Eric Metaxas's *Bonhoeffer: Pastor, Martyr, Prophet, Spy*. I'm especially grateful to Eric's biography for introducing me to the love story of this great man of faith. Also to Ferdinand Schlingensiepen for his impeccably researched *Dietrich Bonhoeffer 1906–1945: Martyr, Thinker, Man of Resistance*. Without the happy hours I spent with these treasure troves of knowledge, this book would never have been written. I'm also profoundly grateful to the late Eberhard Bethge, and his wife, Renate, for being the first to share the story of their beloved friend with the world.

The amazing team at Kregel Publications who labored with me to bring this novel to print. To each and every one of you . . . thank you, thank you. A special shout-out to Janyre Tromp, my brilliant developmental editor. Working with someone who shared my passion for Bonhoeffer's life and legacy was truly an answer to prayer!

My wonderful agent, Rachel Kent. Your wise encouragement makes the writing life all the more joy-filled!

I owe a debt of gratitude to Bishop Kenneth Kinner, who shared with me his memories of Maria von Wedemeyer-Weller from the 1960s. To have the privilege of speaking with someone whose life was touched by Maria's is an experience I will always cherish.

Emily Putzke, who read this story in the midst of a jam-packed summer of World War II research trips. Your willingness to take time out of a busy schedule to help make *My Dearest Dietrich* as accurate as possible was a true gift!

My beloved friend and critique partner, Angela Bell. Thank you for critiquing this story on a tight deadline and offering great feedback. Reading your encouraging comments brought tears to my eyes!

Schuyler McConkey—for loving this idea when I shared it with you, and walking this journey with me every step of the way. Thank you for your readiness to talk Bonhoeffer and theology, taking me to the most amazing coffee shops, and always being there to listen. You're a gem, dear friend!

A special thanks goes to Adriana Gwyn, who translated an entire book from German to English during a nine-hour Skype call. Working with you was definitely one of the highlights of the research process. Thank you so much for sharing your gift of languages with me!

My PIT Crew, for praying me through the process. The time, dedication, and love you invest in interceding as I write are gifts I do not take lightly. Thank you!

My dad, for taking me to Holocaust museums, watching World War II movies with me, and listening to me talk about Dietrich for months on end. I love doing life together!

My beautiful and amazing sis, Sara. There are not enough words to describe what you mean to me. You're the first person I shared this idea with, and the love you shower over me and this project continues to blow me away. Without a doubt, you are my "Eberhard." The invaluable time you invested in brainstorming and editing in the midst of your own work shaped this story into what it is today.

My mom. Thank you for that dinner conversation so many years ago, when you happened to mention, "I've been reading this incredible biography about a guy named Dietrich Bonhoeffer." You encouraged me to keep going when I wanted to give up, prayed for me, invested valuable time in helping me research, and read and edited this project more times than I can count. You're the truest example I know of a strong, godly woman, and my love for you is beyond measure!

Lastly, I'm forever grateful to my Lord and Savior Jesus Christ. You are my Abba, my Strong Tower, and the breath in my lungs. Thank you for the sweet assurance that whoever and wherever I am, I'll forever belong to you.

Character List

The Bonhoeffer Family

Dietrich Bonhoeffer—A thirty-six-year-old theologian who now works as a double agent in the conspiracy against Adolf Hitler.

Dr. Karl Bonhoeffer—An eminent psychiatrist and Dietrich's father.

Paula Bonhoeffer—Dietrich's mother.

Klaus Bonhoeffer—Dietrich's older brother. A lawyer and a member of the conspiracy against Hitler.

Emmi Bonhoeffer—Klaus's wife.

Children—Walter, Thomas, and Cornelie.

Ursula Schleicher, née Bonhoeffer—Dietrich's older sister.

Rüdiger Schleicher—Ursula's husband and part of the conspiracy.

Children—Renate and Hans-Walter.

Christel von Dohnanyi, née Bonhoeffer—Dietrich's older sister.

Hans von Dohnanyi—Christel's husband. Lawyer in the Abwehr (German Military Intelligence) and key member of the conspiracy.

Children—Klaus, Christoph, and Bärbel.

Sabine Leibholz, née Bonhoeffer—Dietrich's twin sister. Was forced to escape Germany due to her husband's (**Gerhard Leibholz**) Jewish ancestry.

Children—Marianne and Christiane.

Lotte—The Bonhoeffers' maid.

The von Wedemeyer Family

Maria von Wedemeyer—The eighteen-year-old daughter of a Prussian landowner whose family is anti-Nazi, though both her father and brother serve in the Wehrmacht.

Major Hans von Wedemeyer—Maria's father.

Ruth von Wedemeyer, née von Kleist—Maria's mother. Sometimes called "Ruthchen."

Ruth-Alice von Bismarck, née von Wedemeyer—Maria's older sister.

Klaus von Bismarck—Ruth-Alice's husband.

Max von Wedemeyer—Maria's older brother and a soldier in the Wehrmacht.

Hans-Werner von Wedemeyer—Maria's younger brother.

Christine von Wedemeyer—Maria's younger sister.

Lala von Wedemeyer—Maria's younger sister.

Peter von Wedemeyer—Maria's younger brother.

Ruth von Kleist-Retzow—Maria's maternal grandmother.

The Conspirators

Admiral Wilhelm Canaris—Head of the Abwehr. Working closely with Hans von Dohnanyi to overthrow the Nazi regime.

General Hans Oster—Member of the Abwehr and leading figure in the German resistance.

General Ludwig Beck—Leading figure in the resistance against Hitler.

Wilhelm Schmidhuber—Member of the Abwehr who participated in the Operation 7 plot to smuggle fourteen Jews into Switzerland.

Henning von Tresckow—Maria's uncle. Heavily involved in the plots to assassinate Hitler.

Fabian von Schlabrendorff—Maria's cousin. Involved in the plots to assassinate Hitler.

General Paul von Hase—Military commandant of Berlin, Dietrich's uncle, and conspirator.

Other Characters

Eberhard Bethge—Dietrich's best friend.

The Vogel family—Maria completes her required national service by working as a nanny for this family.

Manfred Roeder—Judge in charge of interrogating Dietrich and other arrested conspirators.

Oskar von Scheffler—Gestapo police detective and acquaintance of Maria.

Corporal Knobloch—Guard at Tegel Prison.

Prologue

O verhead, there was no sky.
Or rather, it was unlike any sky Maria had glimpsed before. Unvarnished gray, almost white. If the sun ever existed, it had long since fled, leaving rays void of color and cheer in its wake.

The road ahead stretched long and straight. At its end, a great brown building squatted, bricks and roof providing the vista's only color. Everything else . . . white. Endless white. Snow on the ground. Billowing smoke. Swirling flakes raining down.

What those papery flakes represented, what they had once been, Maria couldn't bear to think of.

Nein, she must keep to her purpose. Any deviation would be fatal to her sluggish mind, her leaden feet.

"Dietrich." The word whispered from her half-frozen lips. "Dietrich."

Just keep thinking of him. That would keep her warm.

It had started as a girlish game of hers, running his name over and over in her mind, turning each syllable, toying with the letters, as she went about her daily duties.

Now it was the cord that kept her body upright, her limbs moving, and her numb fingers clenched around the handle of the heavy suitcase. With each step, the case jostled against her shin.

"Dietrich . . ."

Just a few more steps.

"Dietrich . . ."

Finally she reached the half-moon-shaped entrance. A guard—weathered face etched with severe lines, black SS cap straight upon his close-shaven hair—looked her over as if she were an apparition. To him, she probably was. A fraülein of only twenty, approaching the gates of a concentration camp on foot. Only she didn't feel twenty. The weight of these past months, years, had bestowed upon her the mind of a woman three times that.

"*Guten Morgen*, Fraülein." He gave a stiff nod, his shoulders broom-handle straight.

Oh, honestly. They weren't in a ballroom, for pity's sake. It was cold enough to turn water into icicles in seconds. Her fingers had become claws around the case's handle. Her hair was in tangles, her nose redder than the armband wrapping the man's right bicep.

Still, she needed something from this man. And it was better to smile than to make enemies. Hadn't the Tegel months shown her that?

"*Guten Morgen*, Herr Officer. I'm here about a prisoner."

His gaze sharpened into even grimmer lines. Undoubtedly, this specimen of SS training had at one time been some mutter's little boy, some sister's playmate. Given the girl fits of exasperation, as Max had in their childhood days. Brought a whole new meaning to the word *dummkopf*, yet done it all so charmingly that she could only throw her hands up . . . then laugh and ply him with *kuchen*.

She'd have to appeal to that, the little boy hidden beneath the skull and crossbones insignia.

"You've got to help me." It was all too easy to weave desperation through the fabric of her words. Desperation, something Germany—mighty, Führer-led Germany—did not condone, yet its people made bedfellows with. "I've walked seven kilometers here, and I'll have to return on foot. Please, Herr Officer. I need answers. The man I'm searching for . . . he's my fiancé."

Success. He'd softened somewhat, perhaps at the memory of his own sweetheart. Of happier days when love was a thing to rejoice in, laughter an everyday sound.

"*Ja*. You have a name?"

She nodded. "Bonhoeffer. Dietrich Bonhoeffer."

"Wait here." He moved, as if to turn. Then snapped a glance over his shoulder. "Come inside." A stiff motion with his black-gloved hand. "You look cold."

Forcing her feet to move was accomplished only by sheer willpower. They made their way inside a large and dark room. A fire—color and warmth at last—lit a large stone hearth.

"You . . . um . . . can warm yourself over there. I'd offer *kaffee*, but we're low at present."

The warmth beckoned, and she crossed the floor, her boots leaving a watery trail in their wake. She crouched in front of the flames, much the same way the family dog had during long winter nights at Pätzig. For what seemed like an hour, she sat there. Finally, blessed warmth returned to her hands, and she pried them from around the leather handles. Though the tingling and burning that ensued made tears prick her eyes, at least she wasn't frostbitten.

The presence of warmth made another of her needs starkly apparent. When had she last eaten? Her hollow stomach—where had the rosy-cheeked girl who devoured plateful after plateful of strudel, gone?—gurgled in protest.

Yet this need of hers, so weak and human, could wait. It was Dietrich—not theologian Dietrich, or brilliant Dietrich, nor even Tegel Dietrich, but the Dietrich she loved with full and startling intensity—who mattered most at this moment.

She sensed someone watching her and turned. The guard stood beside the cluttered desk, one hand resting on its top, looking at her, not with detachment, but with something else altogether in his eyes. It couldn't be pity. Not from a member of Hitler's trained, lauded, and equipped forces. Not from a man who viewed death as often as a scullery maid saw dirty dishes. Yet . . . yes, there was pity in those veiled eyes.

Somehow she managed to force her legs to stand.

"Well?"

"I'm sorry, Fraülein. I have no record of anyone by the name of Dietrich Bonhoeffer."

"Are you sure?" Where else could they have taken him? They gave her no word in Berlin, no one knew here. How could one man simply disappear, even in the chaos engulfing war-torn Germany?

"I checked. Our records are meticulous." He stiffened, as if challenging her, a red-nosed, disheveled fraülein, to question him. Then, softening again, added, "I'm sorry your journey has been wasted. These days . . . it is easy to misplace people."

The hours of walking, the cold, the frustration bordering on despair, boiled within her like a kettle left on the stove much too long. "I didn't misplace him." She spat out the words, quick bursts of rage, before regret could worm its way in. "Your kind took him. An innocent man and the best that ever breathed air." Snatching up the suitcase, she spun on her heel, strode from the building and down the road, before the man could follow and arrest her for unpatriotic talk. They seemed to be arresting everyone these days for the slightest offense—Hans, Rüdiger, Klaus.

Dietrich.

The road ahead seemed to mock her, each step one that must be fought for, triumphed over, before she could reach shelter. Frigid air bit through her threadbare coat, slashed across her thin stockings. Tears, those renegade signs of weakness, flooded her eyes and sped down her cheeks. She swiped them away with an impatient hand. Nobody cried anymore. There was just too much sorrow and not enough time.

She slipped her numb fingers into the pocket of her coat, fingertips brushing a folded piece of paper. One of Dietrich's letters to her. Its words echoed in her mind:

> *The thought that you are concerned would be my only concern. The thought that you're waiting with me, lovingly and patiently, is my daily consolation. All will come right at the time appointed by God. Join me in looking forward to that time. . . .*

"I'm trying, Dietrich. I'm trying to believe that there *will* be a time. That one day we'll again sit in Grossmutter's parlor, and you'll play the piano, and we'll be happy. Happy not because there's anything in particular to be glad about, but because we're together. That's all that matters. We'll be together."

There. Think of that. Though she hadn't succeeded at the camp, the war would soon be over. This horrible, godforsaken war that had claimed the lives of one too many good men. But the memory of Dietrich and his words rose in her thoughts again: "*Nein, Maria. Nothing is ever godforsaken. He is in everything . . . In the giving and taking of life. In all of our moments, even this one.*"

She kept talking aloud, if only to keep her senses alert.

"*Ja*, Dietrich. You're right. You always are, you know. It still amazes me that you chose me, the silly girl who couldn't understand theology, who coaxed you into playing American music. I'm not that girl anymore, you know. How can I still be? After all these years have brought, I've changed, you've changed. But know this. Wherever you are . . ."

The exertion of her pace, the cold scraping her lungs stole her last words. But as she trudged down the endless road, the suitcase heavier than ever, the sky above gray and lifeless and empty, she let them fill her heart.

I love you.

Chapter One

A dictatorship is like a snake. If you step on its tail, it will bite you.
The words played through Dietrich Bonhoeffer's mind as the taxi trundled through the streets of the ancient Swedish royal city. He stared out the sun-streaked window, his reflection an overlay. Nausea churned through him. But it was no longer due to yesterday's turbulent flight from Berlin to Stockholm. Nein, he'd recovered from that quickly enough.

The sensation of being observed, followed, occasioned a queasiness of an entirely different nature. One not easily shaken away.

The cramped taxi interior was rife with stale cigars and desperation—the former belonging to the profusely sweating driver, the latter his own, albeit concealed.

He'd worked too hard over the past few days for some hitch to prevent this meeting from going off according to plan.

The taxi jolted to a halt in front of the Nordic Ecumenical Institute. Dietrich paid the driver—who barely nodded—grasped his suitcase with one hand, and opened the taxi door with the other. Afternoon sunlight warmed his face, the air pure and fresh.

With practiced calm, he scanned his surroundings, taking in the several-story, stone building, the manicured lawn, and wide steps leading to the front door. Had he been followed? Or was the sensation of a spider crawling up his neck due to pent-up nervous energy? A figure ambled around the back of the building, wearing a worn cap and carrying a toolbox.

Only a handyman.

Not the Gestapo.

Dietrich strode toward the door, black oxfords crunching on the gravel. He climbed the steps and gave a firm rap to the tarnished gold door knocker.

Would Bishop Bell still be here? Or would the hour trip from Stockholm to Sigtuna to see the Bishop of Chichester have been undertaken for nothing?

A fresh-faced maidservant opened the door.

"Yes?"

"A visitor here to see Bishop Bell and Harry Johansson, if I may." Dietrich shifted the suitcase in his palm, posture erect, conscious of the clipped syllables that marked him as bearing an accent from the Führer's country.

There were few reasons for a German not in uniform to be visiting neutral Sweden. The last thing he needed was undue attention.

"Follow me please." The girl opened the door, motioning him down a narrow, dimly lit hall. Thankfully, she hadn't inquired his identity.

Though the papers within his suitcase didn't weigh much more than a loaf of bread, the knowledge of their existence made the case seem lined with lead.

The girl opened a door, revealing a room paneled in wood and cluttered with bookshelves and a well-used oaken desk. But what drew Dietrich's attention was the gray-haired gentleman sitting, large hands loose between his knees, in a wing chair near the window. The conversation between him and the lanky blond man sitting on the edge of the desk drew to an abrupt halt. Both gazes swung in Dietrich's direction. Bell's eyes widened in shock.

"Hello, George." Dietrich smiled. He hadn't seen his friend since the spring of 1939. Much had changed in his life—and in Germany—in the interim.

"Dietrich!" Bishop Bell rose to his feet. He opened his mouth, as if to exclaim over the unexpectedness of his arrival, but Dietrich spoke up first.

"You haven't changed a bit." Though nearing sixty, Bell looked in robust health, the space of years adding a few lines around the eyes, a few inches to his girth, but little else. Pressing on, Dietrich continued. "And this must be Mr. Johansson. Dietrich Bonhoeffer, at your service." He held out his hand to the Swede, and the man shook it heartily.

"Pleasure to make your acquaintance, sir." Johansson's smile was equal parts congenial and curious.

After a few minutes of pleasantries, Johansson left the room, leaving Dietrich and Bell alone. The second the door clicked, Bell's facade changed into stark astonishment.

"Whatever are you doing here? I heard you were in Norway on your way to the front lines." He sank down heavily into his chair.

"You mean what other reason would I have for being in Sweden, now of all times?" Dietrich took an unoccupied seat, placing his suitcase beside it.

In another time and place, he'd have relaxed in the comfortable easy chair, stretched out his long legs, and settled in. Not today. The pressure of what he'd come to relay made him sit stiff and straight. "It's a long story. In short, I'm officially employed by the Abwehr."

"You work for Germany's Military Intelligence?" Bell leaned forward, gaze darting to and fro, as if unable to grasp the weight of Dietrich's words.

"In a word, *ja*, I do." There wasn't much time. Someday after the war, when he and Bell could meet again, he'd explain everything. Right now, he need only hit the high points. "My brother-in-law, Hans von Dohnanyi, is at the heart of my involvement. And the conspiracy." It was only a word.

But a weighted one. Laden with so many implications . . . so many lives.

On instinct, he scanned the room, checking for telephones that could be tapped, open windows where anyone could overhear.

Under the Malicious Practices Act, communication with England or any enemy government wasn't only dangerous. It was treason. Punishable by execution.

A treason he committed with all his might and main.

Heart pounding, he leaned forward, voice cut to a whisper. "It's not just a conspiracy. There are plans . . . plans in place for the overthrow of the German government and the assassination of Adolf Hitler."

Bell's sharp intake of air sliced the atmosphere like the whistle of a bullet. "It's true then," he breathed.

"Never more so," Dietrich said. "And we need you, George. I traveled from Berlin with the express purpose of meeting with you to ask—beg— you on behalf of my friends in Germany to aid us in getting word of our plans to the British government. When—if—the coup succeeds, those involved want to know that Britain will be willing to negotiate peace. With your contacts in the House of Lords, you can speak to Anthony Eden. As foreign secretary under Churchill, Eden can help us, if only he can be convinced." Dietrich's words came faster now, rushing out of him. "Hans and General Oster believe that many more officers under Hitler could be convinced to join us if they could be certain we had the support of the British government. In the way of gaining such support, you could do a great deal for us."

Bell pressed a hand against his lined forehead. "Of course. Of course. I'll do my utmost. But the secret memorandum you sent to me last year . . . none of them took it very seriously. They reject the idea that anti-Nazi forces in Germany could have any effect, except after complete military defeat."

"Field Marshals von Bock and von Kluge don't agree. They're determined, along with General Beck and General Oster and others, to see the government overthrown after Hitler's assassination. Until that event takes place, we cannot gain much headway."

"Field Marshals von Bock and von Kluge," Bell murmured, as if committing the names to memory. He nodded. "Give me all the names and information you can, Dietrich. I'll use it to the best of my abilities. You know as well as I that Churchill is vehemently opposed to any discussion of peace. He wants the war won, and at all costs. After these long years of fighting, the lines between Germans and Nazis have become blurred. Almost to the point of being indistinguishable. And can you blame them? London has been ruthlessly bombed . . . hundreds of civilians killed. They've endured great losses dealt by the hands of Hitler and his generals. It's little wonder they're cautious at the idea of this 'resistance.'"

Dietrich stood and paced toward the window, staring out but seeing little of the vista of blue sky and sunlight. Instead, the faces of the hunted and defenseless rose before him, an endless line of specters who would forever haunt him. Those Germany had ordered euthanized because they believed their state of health decreed them unworthy of life.

And the Jews. God's chosen ones. No matter he stood in a room in neutral Sweden, he could not ignore the fact that, by order of the Führer, millions of them were being systematically murdered, crammed into railcars like cattle shipped to the slaughterhouse. Women. Children.

Souls.

He swung back around, facing Bell. A swirl of dust motes floated in the sunlight, the rays landing on Bell's thinning gray hair. His friend would aid their cause, get the truth to those at the top. But would he succeed at convincing them?

"Only a few know of my involvement," he said quietly. "Many believe because I'm part of the Abwehr that I've deflected, turned away from standing with the Confessing Church." He swallowed. "Germany has sinned, George. We must all pay the price of bringing the nation to repentance. Christ calls us to suffer on behalf of others. My suffering involves putting aside qualms of conscience. I lie. I create falsified memorandums to disguise the true nature of my journeys."

"And participating in plans that involve murder?" Bell met Dietrich's gaze. There was no censure in the man's eyes. Only a demand for honesty.

Dietrich nodded. He would not allow himself to squirm beneath such talk, however uncomfortable it made him. "Perhaps that, too, is part of Germany's punishment. That we are forced to resort to such means." He resumed his seat, drawing out his suitcase to gather papers for Bell to take with him. "We've gone too far for any other course of action. It must be done."

His brother Klaus's words resurfaced, their refrain an eerie cadence in his ears, as Dietrich prepared to expound on details of the conspiracy, relaying things that, if known, could lead to deadly consequences as fast as the time it took for a Gestapo finger to squeeze the trigger.

If you step on its tail, it will bite you.

Chapter Two

June 8, 1942
Klein-Krössin Manor
Pomerania, Prussia

A h . . . the memories he had of this place.

Dietrich approached the cottage, afternoon sun warm on his face, the twitter of birdsong high on the air. Klein-Krössin had always been a haven for him, a small corner of serenity. A place for thinking and writing, long conversations accompanied by *kaffee* and firelight.

After the wearying travel to and from Sweden, he needed this respite more than ever.

He'd have knocked—had Ruth von Kleist-Retzow not thrown open the door first.

"Dietrich. How good to see you!" Though Ruth's hair had long since turned white as the snowy alps, and her skin boasted more than a few lines and furrows, the brightness of her smile put to shame a hundred electric bulbs.

"Ruth." He embraced the woman, then held the door for her to reenter the house. Inside the small foyer, it smelled just as a home ought. Clean, like soap and polish. Welcoming, like strudel and sauerbraten.

"You look tired, Dietrich." The woman's keen eyes missed nothing.

"The Abwehr keeps me busy." Though Ruth had more than a slight inkling about the true nature of his activities, such things weren't spoken of in broad daylight, even in the relative safety of Klein-Krössin. "And besides, who isn't tired these days?"

"Well, you're free to stay as long and often as you choose." Shoes tapping on the gleaming wood floor, Ruth led the way into the parlor. It was a room used and loved; its state both tidy and disordered. Though everything was spotlessly clean, photographs cluttered the mantle—Ruth's many children and grandchildren, and pillows and throw-blankets adorned the two floral-upholstered sofas. A window set ajar let in summer's fragrance and the sound of muted honking—Ruth's beloved geese.

If he hadn't already come to terms with the *why* of his lifestyle—what man of his age and capabilities was exempt from use in battlefield service for the Fatherland?—enjoying such luxury would have brought with it a hefty measure of guilt. But he was being used by God, a task a thousand times more important than any job dictated by the Führer. Used to minister, to write, to conspire.

The last he could never forget, not even at Klein-Krössin.

"I can only manage a week at the most, this time. But I hope to get plenty of work done while I'm here."

"You're still writing *Ethics*?" Ruth motioned for him to sit on the sofa opposite her.

"*Ja.*" Whenever he had the time and God provided the inspiration. Dietrich always made good progress in the writing studio Ruth had fixed up for him in her attic. It was there he'd finished *Nachfolge*, a book that had received more acclaim than he'd expected, even in America where it was known by the title *The Cost of Discipleship.*

Of course, nothing bearing the name of Dietrich Bonhoeffer was printed in Germany these days.

"So tell me, Ruth, how are you doing?"

The lady opened her mouth to respond. But footsteps, quick and clattering, cut her off.

A girl stormed into the room. *Ja*, stormed was the only way to describe it. Mud splattered the front of her skirt and blouse, dotted her nose. She wasn't tall in stature; neither was she particularly petite. But what she didn't own in height, she made up for with indignation.

"You wouldn't believe what that *dummkopf* Friedrich Schiller did! Remember those strawberries I gave to Greta just this morning? I found him in front of the butcher's, attempting to take them from her. I tried to get the basket away from him, but he pulled and pulled. And you once said he was such a *Liebling. Liebling!* If that boy is this much trouble at nine years old, I shudder to think of what a terror he'll be at fifteen." She planted both fists on her hips.

Dietrich sat motionless, trying to suppress a chuckle. Of course the situation wasn't at all humorous—a boy stealing a girl's fruit. But the way this fräulein, whoever she was, looked so royally indignant warranted a bit of mirth.

"I see." Ruth's smile was almost too patient, as if she'd witnessed such outbursts before. "I'm sure you gave him what he deserved, dear. In fact, I pity Friedrich Schiller for having the misfortune to meet with your wrath. I doubt he'll come back for another helping anytime soon."

The girl nodded. A strand of honey-colored hair dangled down her cheek.

"But, Maria, it isn't good manners, as you well know, to barge into the room in such a helter-skelter fashion. Especially when we have company."

It was as if she suddenly noticed his presence. The girl—Maria—clapped both hands over her mouth. Shock and mortification raced through her eyes in rapid succession.

For a moment, no one said a word. Maria stared at him. He looked steadily back. Ruth glanced between them both, hands folded in her lap as calmly as ever.

Finally, Maria pried her hands away from her mouth.

"Grossmutter, who is that?" She pointed at him as if he were some sort of unwelcome spider.

Ruth laughed in that silvery way of hers. Before she could make introductions, Dietrich stood and crossed to where the girl was.

"Allow me to take the liberty of introducing myself. I'm Dietrich Bonhoeffer. And you are?" He smiled, wanting to ease her discomfort. After all, it wasn't her fault she'd fallen in the mud or been unaware of his arrival.

Her chin angled slightly. She had an arresting face, almost girlishly round in its angles and planes, yet proud and startlingly lovely. "Maria von Wedemeyer."

Now it was his turn to be shaken. Gone were the long braids and shapeless pinafores he remembered about the little girl he'd attempted to take on for confirmation classes. The Maria before him, with her expressive blue eyes and upswept, albeit tousled, hair, was twelve years old no longer.

He cleared his throat, realizing she expected him to say something along the lines of polite conversation. "It's . . . um . . . very nice to meet you. Again."

She held out her hand, though it, too, was a bit muddy. He took it anyway, unable to unglue his gaze from her face. She appeared recovered from her earlier outburst and gazed back, unblinking. Her fingers clasped his, not hesitating or limp, but warm and decisive, and it was probably longer than necessary before he found his senses and pulled away.

Maria faced her grossmutter. "Why did you not tell me Pastor Bonhoeffer was arriving this afternoon?"

Ruth laughed again, as if the whole situation were as entertaining as a comic opera. "Why? Would you have made more of an effort in your appearance?"

Maria shrugged, a flash of laughter in her gaze. "Oh probably. It's a good thing I refrained from dragging Friedrich Schiller in here by his ear. He's a good deal muddier than I at the moment." She grinned, as if accustomed to giving her grossmutter what for.

"Why don't you go and change, Maria." Ruth inclined her head toward the door.

"Of course." Maria turned her attention back to him, a flush suffusing her cheeks. "My apologies for my sudden entrance, Pastor Bonhoeffer. It's a habit of mine while here at Klein-Krössin."

He couldn't help but smile—nein, grin. It loosed something inside him, giving into the impulsive urge that made his lips tug upward. "It's quite all right, Fraülein von Wedemeyer. It was a good attempt you made, trying to help Greta."

"Even if it didn't work out the way I wanted. But as Goethe says, 'He who goes not forward, goes backward.'" With a little wave, she turned and left the room. Dietrich stared after her, this muddy, Goethe-quoting girl who'd swept into the room, disordering it—and him—in a matter of seconds.

Once Dietrich resumed his seat, Ruth began, "You must excuse my granddaughter. I realize now that I neglected to tell her you were arriving this afternoon. She's so high-spirited, that one. If she weren't leaving tomorrow, I fear your days here would be anything but peaceful."

Dietrich held up a hand. If he let himself listen to more of Ruth's elaborations on her granddaughter, he would be foolish enough to admit just how diverting he'd found the past moments of conversation. He produced a properly pastoral, though entirely truthful, reply. "I admire anyone seeking to defend the defenseless. Even if she did go about it in a rather . . . interesting manner."

Ruth laughed. "That's one thing our Maria is. Interesting. She just graduated from school, you know. Elisabeth von Thadden's academy in Wieblingen. I expect they tempered her antics somewhat. But she'll be company for the both of us tonight. Now, if you'd like to bring your cases in from the car, I can show you to your usual room."

"Please don't trouble yourself." Dietrich stood. "I hope I've stayed here often enough to dispense with the formalities. You rest here, and I'll see to my own luggage."

Ruth acquiesced, and Dietrich left the room. As he collected his bags and carried them upstairs, he couldn't deny the smile that crossed his face at the thought of an evening spent in the company of a fraülein who got covered in mud while defending little girls and sassed her grossmutter with laughter in her eyes.

Well, she'd certainly presented herself as a grand, grown-up lady. All elegant attire and polite how-do-you-dos.

Maria's cheeks still flamed with mortification. She'd embarrassed herself in front of Pastor Bonhoeffer as a child. Now she had to go and repeat the mistake.

She gave a critical glance at her reflection in the guest bedroom mirror. Mud no longer speckled her nose, thank goodness. But her face was still round, her hair such a straight, unremarkable shade of blondish-brown. At least the lavender dress with its white lace collar was presentable. And she'd managed to braid her hair and coil it into a bun, the way her friend Doris always styled hers. Of course, forever-daring Doris had since bobbed her own effortlessly curly locks.

Oh, for goodness' sake, Maria. This is your grossmutter and her theologian friend. Pastor Bonhoeffer's no American film star.

Nein, but there was something . . . interesting about him. Different. She'd noticed it, even as a girl. And when he'd greeted her this afternoon, with that half smile playing across his features . . .

You're being a dummkopf, *Maria. Pastor Bonhoeffer has to be over thirty-five.*

And a thoroughgoing academic in the bargain. The history Grossmutter once relayed to her recalled itself to mind. He'd earned his doctorate in theology at the age of twenty-one and gone on to pastor in Spain, complete a postdoctoral degree, study in America, lecture at Berlin University, and actively participate in maintaining ecumenical communication between foreign churches. After the Führer attempted to dissolve any church not consistent with National Socialist ideology, Pastor Bonhoeffer became one of the foremost leaders in the Confessing Church—a group that fought desperately both to counter the false teachings of the Reich Church and to keep alive a church founded on Scripture's doctrine rather than Herr Hitler's. He'd taken advantage of the isolated backcountry of Pomerania to train young pastors in the truth of the Bible instead of the widely accepted heresy of Hitler's Reich Church—an illegal practice that could have been shut down by the Gestapo at any time. Eventually that was what had happened.

Ja, the man kept a hectic schedule. And was, come to think of it, probably older than thirty-five.

Her grossmutter's connection with Pastor Bonhoeffer had come about when he'd transferred his group of young Confessing Church pastors-in-training to a rambling manor house called Finkenwalde, near Grossmutter's second home in the town of Stettin. The two formed an instant bond forged by similar ideas. Grossmutter consequently took up regular attendance at the Finkenwalde chapel. She'd seized every opportunity to bring along her many grandchildren, which had led to "the confirmation class incident." Maria winced.

Flicking a final glance at her appearance and dismissing her thoughts with as much haste, she smoothed down the front of her dress and made her way downstairs, careful not to skip—a rather bad habit of hers.

Pastor Bonhoeffer stood in the parlor, hands behind his back, gaze on the window.

He turned at her entrance. Doris would probably call what he did next a "double take." Had she altered her appearance so drastically he didn't recognize her? She hadn't been covered in *that* much mud.

Because he couldn't possibly be looking at her the way men did at Doris. They always stared at her friend with unabashed admiration. Those same men usually spared Maria all of three seconds of their attention.

Since he stared at her, she decided to peruse him. Light blond hair. Dark gray suit and navy pinstripe tie, his tall, solid frame filling the well-made coat. To be honest, he didn't look at all like a stodgy theologian, but rather like the sort of man it would be difficult to best on a soccer field. Though his gold-rimmed glasses were perhaps at variance to that, giving him a somewhat scholarly air. Like the kind of man who pondered deep topics one moment, but wasn't afraid to laugh the next.

"*Guten Abend.*" He gave a crooked smile.

She dipped a nod. "Likewise. Where is Grossmutter?"

"Having a word with the cook. Apparently, whatever it was we were having for dinner wasn't put in the oven on time." He said all of this with a smile, as if minor inconveniences didn't annoy him in the least.

"So what are we to do till then?" What exactly did theologians do for fun? She wasn't sure she was up to a discussion of some weighty tome.

His glance—he had such intense, almost startling, blue eyes—turned toward the window again. "It's nice outside. We could . . . take a walk?"

"I'm not sure Grossmutter is up to long distances." Though it did look inviting out of doors. The sun had reached the point where its honey warmth turned to streaks of gold and umber. And she could smell the clean sweetness of the air coming in from the partially open window.

"She already told me she had other matters to take care of. She said she wasn't up to much entertaining tonight, but that we were to join her for dinner in an hour or so and occupy ourselves until then."

"So she suggested just we two go?" Maria couldn't help the laugh that escaped. So like Grossmutter to give her granddaughter the company of a theologian for entertainment. Of course, this *was* Grossmutter, a born-and-bred Prussian aristocrat who'd named her guest rooms Hope, Joy, and Contentment.

"If you'd rather not . . ."

"I didn't say that," she hastened. Perhaps a bit too quickly. "That is"—she added a smile—"a walk would be lovely." There. Wouldn't Doris be proud?

He motioned for her to precede him, and they made their way into the garden—a bower of neat paths, shrubbery, and blossoms in bloom. War or no war, Grossmutter loved her flowers. She'd attempted to pass the interest on to her granddaughter, but even now, Maria couldn't tell the difference between one variety and another. Except that some were purple, others red, some smelled better than the rest, and whenever she gathered a rose—her favorite—she invariably pricked her finger in the process.

He fell into step beside her, hands behind his back. "So did you ever take confirmation classes?"

She nodded. "A year later. Not with anyone as well-known as you, of course. I think Grossmutter still cringes upon remembrance of the occasion. Her twelve-year-old granddaughter making an idiot out of herself in front of the celebrated Pastor Bonhoeffer." She gave a rueful smile. "I'm glad I can't recall all the stupid things I said."

"I don't remember anyone making an idiot out of themselves. Except, perhaps me." His smile was earnest. "As I recall, some of your answers to the questions I posed were quite interesting."

"I can assure you I've learned a few things since then. Although you probably couldn't tell, based on my performance this afternoon." She picked a tiny purple flower, twirling it in her fingers.

"Really, Fräulein von Wedemeyer. Depreciation isn't becoming. I thought what you did today was . . . very fine." He met her gaze, and she marveled again at the depth of his. Full of purpose, clarity, and, even rarer, hope. These days, hope seemed to be more rationed than *kaffee* and sugar, despite the impassioned speeches people made on the radio and the lavish victory parades they threw.

Pastor Bonhoeffer had always been different. She remembered the earnest way he preached from Sunday services at Finkenwalde. Once, rather bored by the lengthy sermon, she'd sat absolutely still and counted how many times he said the word *God*. Sixty-eight in all. Of course, following lunch that afternoon, that same serious pastor had proceeded to cheerfully trounce everyone at table tennis. She'd always been too intimidated to play.

She tilted her head to look at him. How different he seemed now, simply a man walking beside her instead of the great pastor in the pulpit. And she, no longer the little girl relegated to playing with her brothers and sisters, could be free to converse with him on equal terms.

Tonight had the texture of hope in it, brought on perhaps by the presence of this man who seemed to emanate it. As if the fragrance in the air and the shades of the sky gave them permission to temporarily forget about all that went on in the world outside Klein-Krössin.

Maybe . . . even gave a theologian permission to have some fun.

"I've never met anyone who's been to America. What was it like?"

"Who told you I've been to America?"

"Grossmutter did. She's always talking about you."

"Is she now?" Pastor Bonhoeffer's gaze flickered with amusement. "Doesn't that get rather dull?"

He was teasing her. Maria grinned. "*Ja.* It does rather."

He chuckled. "I'm sorry I'm not a very interesting person."

"Oh, but you are," she hastened. "Your trip to America interests me a great deal. What did you do there?" She couldn't help the burning curiosity. Though most would think it unpatriotic to be so interested in a country that fought against their own, fascination filled her whenever she heard the name.

"Well, I studied." Their steps slowed, until the pace they kept could hardly be called a pace at all. "At Union Theological Seminary."

"Did you enjoy it?"

He hesitated, as if choosing his words with care. "It was different. Of course, that's to be expected, considering they are separated from us by an entire ocean, speak a different language, and live in very different ways. But as more time went on, I found many things to admire."

"Did you hear any of their music? Swing, I think they call it?"

She learned then that theologians could do more than smile politely. He grinned like one of Doris's boyfriends, as if she'd said something altogether delightful.

"Many times. It was all rather . . . exhilarating. But do you know where I found the music I enjoyed most?"

"Where?" They reached a small stone bench, and sat down at almost exactly the same time.

"There was this church I attended. Abyssinian Baptist. Church in America is an entirely different experience than here in Germany. At least at that church it was. The rest of them, well, most of what I heard could hardly be called a sermon at all. But there . . . ." His words trailed away, and he gave a self-conscious shrug. "You don't want to hear all of this, I'm sure."

"Oh, but I do. Tell me about it." Honestly, there was something very attractive about conversing with someone who had done and been to places she'd only heard of. Someone who *knew* so much.

"I think it had a lot to do with the excitement of the congregation. People looked forward to coming; it wasn't just something they did for social reasons. And the preaching. It was there that I learned, perhaps for the very first time, what it was to be not just a theologian but an actual Christian. Someone who took the gospel out of dusty pages and ancient cathedrals and applied it to day-to-day life and everyday people, while still maintaining the truth of that gospel without attempting to dilute it into something weak and popular." A fire of enthusiasm lit his eyes, and he leaned toward her as he spoke.

"We do that at Pätzig, I think. When one of our tenants is ill, we don't just pray for them at morning devotions, but we take them soup in the afternoon." She spoke quietly, lowering her gaze to her clasped hands, still holding the limp flower. She let the flower fall to the ground, feeling foolish. He'd probably think her analogy silly.

"Exactly! That's just my point. It's taking the Sermon on the Mount and not simply reading it as if it were a novel or any other book but living it out in all circumstances and with all people. Of course we can't do any of it in our own strength."

His words . . . they weren't theology as usual. Maybe if she listened to him more often, she'd have a greater appreciation of the subject.

The sun had turned to a ball of crimson, a chill finding its way onto the evening air. She must have rubbed her arms to stave it off, as he instantly stood.

"You must be cold wearing that summer dress." He looked her over, then gave an embarrassed smile, as if he'd admitted something scandalous. Was it the dress? Did he find her pretty in it?

The notion made her stifle a laugh. "You sound like Max. He insists whenever we go on a particularly arduous ride or walk that I wear what he calls 'proper clothes.'"

He held out his hand. She placed hers in it and stood, her fingers enveloped for the briefest of moments in warmth and strength, leaving a trail that lingered long after he let go.

"You must miss your brother very much."

Her throat tightened. She pressed her lips together, gazing out at the vista of gently rolling hills of green. Perhaps one could never fully erase reality. There was a war going on, and it was ridiculous to pretend, even for a little while, that there wasn't. "*Ja*, I do. But isn't that what every woman does these days? Misses the men in her life? Living for the mail delivery, wetting her pillow with tears, praying and begging God that they may be restored to her?"

He nodded, slowly. And she wondered vaguely why he was here when most others of his age and abilities were being used in service of Führer and Fatherland.

"I know it's hard, Fräulein von Wedemeyer. It's always difficult to be parted from those one loves most."

She forced back the knot in her throat and gave a small smile. There would be time enough for sorrow and missing in life outside Klein-Krössin. Right now, she wanted to stay in this special world, if only for a few more hours. "I remember from when I was a little girl that you were good at music. Would you . . . that is, I would like very much to hear some American songs. If you can play any, that is." The moment after she made her request, hot embarrassment filled her cheeks. Now what would he think of her?

But he only laughed and motioned her to precede him inside. "I'll play for you. One song, at least."

Grossmutter sat in the parlor, glasses perched upon her nose as she read in the dusky lamplight. Maria hesitated. Would he still play for her with Grossmutter looking on? But Pastor Bonhoeffer immediately crossed to the piano and opened the lid.

"You like music, don't you, Ruth?" he called across the room.

Her grossmutter gave her a wondering glance, but Maria only smiled. Steps light, she hastened toward the piano. He took a seat, fingers lightly resting on the keys. She waited, almost breathless, as he gently touched one, a low, soft note filling the stillness.

Then he began to play. From memory, it seemed, the notes taking wing from his fingertips and soaring high onto the air. Maria breathed them in, letting her ears feast upon the sound, the way one savored the scarcest scrap of strudel, or the last drop of *kaffee*. It was the sort of song a girl could dance to, and she almost did just that. Would have, had it been a record on the gramophone and her grossmutter not present.

She did sway back and forth, eyes closed, humming along softly. In this music, there was no war, or sorrow. A bit of unhappiness, perhaps. And longing. For joy and love and other things forbidden.

Did Pastor Bonhoeffer, man of brilliance and theology, hear the same cadence to the notes as she? Somehow, though she couldn't be sure, she sensed he did.

The tune died away. He turned, met her eyes. Smiled—something wonderful in it. Though the song had been a gift given to her, perhaps he'd taken equal pleasure in the unwrapping.

Nein. Not perhaps. He truly had. The smile proved it so.

And as Maria lay awake that night, staring out her window at the inky sky, she let the moment linger. Replaying the music and his smile over and over in her mind, until the familiarity of each second became as real and ever-present as her own breathing.

Chapter Three

The trip had been for naught. Or rather, the answers they hoped to receive had not accompanied their arrival in Italy.

Hans was getting frustrated. Dietrich sensed it in the way his brother-in-law paced back and forth across the faded carpet in their hotel suite. They all were. They'd traveled first to Venice and met with Wilhelm Schmidhuber, legally part of Munich Military Intelligence, illegally a fellow conspirator. Then the three of them headed together to Rome. They'd been awaiting news from London and Bishop Bell for days now. It still had not arrived.

It was maddening—this reticence. After all the work they'd done, the lists of names they'd provided. Why couldn't Bell convince those in Britain that there were men in Germany who loathed what was being done in their country? People who longed for peace and restoration, even at the cost of working against the Reich.

People like himself and Hans.

"I don't understand." Hans fingered his cigarette, his usually meticulous light brown hair rumpled from the many times he'd run his hand through it. "Bell assured us he'd make progress. He was optimistic. Well where's that optimism now? That's what I'd like to know."

Dietrich crossed the room and opened the window. At the rate his brother-in-law was going through cigarettes, soon neither of them would be able to gulp a decent breath of air through the haze of smoke.

"Bell didn't make any promises he couldn't keep. He only said he'd do his best." Earlier in the morning, the streets had been fairly empty. Now they teemed with activity—cars, pedestrians, all the noises of humanity going about the business of living.

"His best?" Hans chucked the cigarette in an ashtray and shoved his hands in the pockets of his navy blue suit. "His best isn't good enough. Not when Uncle Rudy"—even here they used code names, Uncle Rudy being Hitler's—"is doing *his* best to make the situation in Germany more treacherous by the day. Soon it'll be too late. No one will want to help us, because they'll believe—most already do—that all of his countrymen are part and parcel with him and the evil he perpetrates. The world will cease to recognize the existence of a good German. The writing's already on the wall."

Truer words were never spoken, but they'd already dwelt on them month upon month.

"Don't despair, Hans." Dietrich placed his hand atop his brother-in-law's shoulder. How thin Hans had become. He'd always owned defined features and a fair complexion, but even the grueling work of finishing law school hadn't taken as much of a toll as the years of conspiratorial activities. "There's still time. Bell is working just as hard as we are on the British government case. We'll return to Germany, you'll see Christel and the children again. Meanwhile, Bell will keep us informed of the proceedings as they unfold."

"*Ja*, Dietrich, you're right." Hans heaved a weighty sigh. "We'll go home."

"And our trip wasn't a total waste. We made contact with friends." They'd had lively and motivating discussions about how the German church should function in the wider world after the war. "That was a good thing, *ja*?"

"You say that about every trip. Maybe that should be your new name, 'Good Thing Dietrich.'" Hans cracked a smile, a sign of youthful vitality beneath weary features. "You wrote to Sabine?"

Dietrich smiled at the mention of his beloved twin sister living in England with her Jewish husband and young daughters. The Bonhoeffers had smuggled them out of Germany at the beginning of 1938, mere months before Kristallnacht. If they'd delayed, Sabine and her family would have joined the thousands of others shipped to labor camps, all because Gerhard Leibholz, a baptized Christian, had the blood of God's chosen people in his veins. Sabine and Gerhard would have been worked to death in Poland. The children, beautiful Marianne and Christiane, gassed . . . never to return . . .

Dietrich shoved the thoughts aside. Sabine was safe. Marianne and Christiane, happy and well with their new schoolmates in England.

Hans pulled his spectacles off and cleaned each lens with a handkerchief. "Well, there's nothing left to keep us here. I'll go down to the telegraph office, then check our mail and see if there's been any news. If not, we'll leave for Berlin on the next available flight."

"Always thinking ahead, you are. Maybe that should be *your* new name, 'Good Plan Hans.'" Dietrich picked up the overflowing ashtray and dumped it in the wastebasket, while his brother-in-law donned his fedora and headed for the door.

He situated himself on the couch to wait for Hans's return. Everything had already been packed. They traveled light on these trips—one suitcase each and a late-night flight into Germany. Made things easier that way.

Since his return from America in 1939, his life had been a paradox. Stretches of study, writing, and solitude, followed by thunderbolts of travel and activity. Both had taken him places he'd never dreamed he'd go. In his writing, he explored new themes and printed new materials until the Gestapo put a stop to the latter last year. Now he found himself in the interesting position of a pastor forbidden to preach, and an agent fighting against the side he was supposed to be working for.

He pondered the words he'd written only a few weeks ago. "It is worse for a liar to tell the truth than for a lover of truth to lie." Years ago, if he'd written the same sentence, it would've been simply that: a sentence. These days, the words weren't mere letters, but a living reality that demanded, fairly screamed, to be acknowledged. A reality that could extract from all of them, from him, the heaviest and most final of costs.

Somewhere in the hotel, a pianist sent music drifting through the air, bringing with it a wave of memories. Of playing the piano as Fraülein von Wedemeyer looked on with an expression of unparalleled joy. Listening to her expound over dinner on her decision to study mathematics. Though neither of them knew a great deal about the subject, they managed to discuss it for over an hour. Probably not making much sense.

She occupied his mind these days, did Fraülein von Wedemeyer. He would have attributed it to the long hours spent traveling with nothing to do but think. But he knew himself better than that. And in a letter to his friend Eberhard, he'd revealed more than he should have.

I haven't written to Maria. It really wouldn't do, not yet. If another meeting proves impossible, the delightful memory of those few, highly charged minutes will doubtless recede into the realm of unfulfilled fantasies, which is amply populated enough already. . . .

There were some disadvantages to having a friend one could tell anything to. Sometimes, one ended up revealing too much. Since he'd written the letter on a train that was far from a smooth ride, maybe he could blame the bumps for jarring his brain.

Unfulfilled fantasies. What kind of a phrase was that?

One from a man who wanted something more in his life than platonic friendships and close family. He'd been content with those relationships for so long, how could it be possible that one evening, a few hours could birth in him a longing he couldn't seem to shake?

He'd taken the matter to prayer, seeking answers. Somehow it seemed easier to forget about her. There was the timing, for one thing. But that was only the start of it.

At any rate, he'd be heading back to Klein-Krössin upon his return. Though the Gestapo had forbidden him from publishing further works, they hadn't said anything about writing them. And ideas simmered in his mind that he longed to delve into. Of course, there wasn't any point in hoping Fraülein von Wedemeyer would be at her grossmutter's. By now, she had probably begun her requisite term of national service. It would be forward, more so than he wanted to be right now, to attempt to contrive another meeting.

A key turned in the lock. Hans opened the door, hands bereft of any letter or telegram.

"So there's our answer. Silence." He flung his hat on the end table and strode into the bedroom.

"Perhaps this time." Dietrich followed and picked up a suitcase that waited by the door of the empty hotel room. He well understood Hans's frustration. They, and those who believed as they did, were working on all fronts. Infiltrating. Conspiring. Even attempting assassination. Attempts that had so far been a shocking failure. "But time hasn't run out yet."

"Nein?" Hans hefted his suitcase toward the door, as if hauling Britain, Bishop Bell, and Prime Minister Churchill right along with him. He flicked a glance over his shoulder, gaze impervious as steel. In Hans's eyes, raw and stark, lay mirrored the despairs of many. "But it is *running* out. Darting away from us like a kite left untended in the wind. And the day is coming when it will be too late to grab hold of the kite and pull it back to safety. Mark my words, Dietrich. The day is coming."

Chapter Four

July 20, 1942
Pomerania

Though she'd traveled but a day's drive from Klein-Krössin, the Vogel house—the Vogel family—seemed a universe away. Or perhaps the sphere of Klein-Krössin was the other world, and the one she dwelt in now, the way everybody else lived.

Maria's back ached with the weight of carrying six-month-old Freida for hours on end. She'd warmed to the younger Vogel children; they were sunny enough, if a bit mischievous. But Gottfried, at only eight, was already being molded into an image of his vater, the great Standartenführer.

Softly shutting the bedroom door, where she'd laid Freida, four-year-old Lisa, and six-year-old Helga, Maria hurried in search of Gottfried, who'd recently declared himself "too important to take naps."

Fulfilling her stint of national service—required of all German young women after graduation—hadn't seemed like a difficult task after the laborious work of passing her exams at Wieblingen Castle School.

She hadn't known the half of it.

Forcing away a wave of crushing homesickness, Maria patted the pocket of her burgundy skirt, just to make sure Grossmutter's letter still rested within. She turned the knob of the front door and let herself outside.

Hopefully, she could occupy Gottfried with a book and gain a few moments to herself to read Grossmutter's words.

Along with his impressive rank, Standartenführer Vogel also owned a large manor house and farm, the latter worked, these days, by Russian prisoners of war. Maria shivered to look at them. Haunted circles ringed their eyes, their features a mix of defiance and defeat. More than anything else, they seemed hungry.

She brushed fingertips across her other pocket, where a half slice of bread rested. One of the young Russians had eyes so like Max's, his frame gaunter than the others. She'd risked the wrath of the Vogels and the detection of the soldier guarding the prisoners to smuggle the young man—Boris, his name was—something to sustain him, since he'd vowed not to escape until he could safely return to his family in Russia.

Shading her eyes against the glare of the sun, Maria scanned the front yard for any sign of Gottfried. The air smelled summer-ripe and fresh, the sky unadulterated blue. She opened her mouth to call for him when he appeared from behind a bush. He carried a stick in the manner of a rifle and goose-stepped down the avenue, chest puffed out, singing lustily.

> When Jewish blood splashes from the knife
> Hang the Jews, put them up against the wall
> Heads are rolling, Jews are hollering.

Icy cold soaked Maria. Such a stream of vileness coming from the mouth of a towheaded, pudgy-cheeked child.

Hate. When modeled for the impressionable, it was a sword too easily taken up.

"Gottfried!" she shouted. "Come here. Now."

He turned, midstride. Still carrying the stick, he sauntered over. She crossed her arms, breathless with horror and shock. Of course, Gottfried's favorite game was "playing soldier." But never . . . this.

"Fraülein Maria." He smiled up at her, showing a gap between his front teeth. His smile made her outrage bubble all the more. She bent down, gripping his shoulders with both hands.

"I don't ever, *ever*, want to hear that song again. Is that understood?" Her gaze bore into him.

Had she uttered those words to any of her own siblings, they'd have hung their heads, shamefaced and apologetic. No apology or shame evidenced itself in Gottfried's gaze. He lifted his head, eyes defiant, challenging.

"Why? Why do you forbid me from singing it?"

She tightened her grip around his fleshy shoulders. "Because it's vile and evil and wrong. And I won't have it while you're under my care."

"The Jews are our enemy." He spoke the words slowly, as if she were an imbecile in need of learning the simplest fact. "Vater says so. Who do you think taught me the song?"

She shivered. She'd not met Standartenführer Vogel, off fighting on the Russian front. She'd glimpsed his photograph from its pride of place on the mantle, a brawny man bedecked in uniform, sporting a severe gaze and a mustache much like the Führer's. But surely he couldn't have transferred this much hate to his child.

Surely he could.

"Well, he's not here. I am. And if I catch you singing that ever again, I'll wash your mouth out with soap." Her hands ached, perspiration beading her forehead.

He smirked, half laughing. "Nein, Fraülein, you won't. Because if you do, I'll tell Mutter I saw you with that Boris. I'll tell her I saw the two of you *together*, if you know what I mean. And even birdbrains like you know what the penalty for *that* is. So I can sing that song anytime I want."

She took a quick step back, like one who'd been slapped. With another triumphant grin, Gottfried darted away, marching with his stick. Singing all the louder.

Shaking, she made her way toward the house, until she reached the front steps. She sank down upon the warm stone, pressing her fingers against her eyes.

She was trapped. Gottfried's words rang in her ears. She had no doubt that the boy would tell tales and delight in doing so. The edicts they lived under had sapped many things, loyalty foremost. Children were encouraged to report parents for listening to illegal broadcasts, speaking in a derogatory way about the government, and on the list went. Those who did were lauded as good citizens of the Fatherland. Neighbors turned in neighbors. Friendship held no weight. It was all duty, duty, and Germany forever.

Their country was being destroyed. Not only by battle and bombs, but by an all-encompassing allegiance to a regime that spread its poison like a toxin through the country's veins. Lethal.

She didn't want any part in it. Though she may be forced to continue her national service, she'd not let the Vogels rule her. She'd continue to feed Boris, tell the little girls bedtime stories about a Lord other than Adolf Hitler.

She'd resist. Even in the small ways.

Dreading the thought of an evening with Frau Vogel, listening to her grating voice laude the merits of this young officer or that—the woman's fondness for her seemed sincere, but only as far as parceling her off to a Nazi like her husband, Maria fingered Grossmutter's letter. A woman's place was to run a proper German home, look pretty for her husband, and bear good, strong Aryan children for the Fatherland. Frau Vogel had said as much, when Maria happened to mention that she'd considered pursuing further education in mathematics.

Gottfried had either wearied or decided his singing wasn't getting him any attention. He sat beside a bush, legs stuck out in front of him, terrorizing some insect. Though her conscience pricked, she let him alone, and turned to the letter instead.

> *Dear Maria,*
>
> *I hope this letter finds you well and adapting to your work with the Vogel family. I think of you often, and imagine all you are doing and thinking, now that you have graduated from school.*
>
> *I had a good, long chat with your mutter on the telephone yesterday. She says she will write soon, but until then, wishes you to know she is thinking of and praying for you.*

She'd always been more Vater's daughter than Mutter's. They'd continually clashed, perhaps more because of their similarities than their differences. But of late, she'd welcome communication from any of her family. Eagerly, she scanned the next paragraph.

> *I know a visit from you will be out of the question for some time, but I still reflect, with fond memories, of your last stay at Klein-Krössin. Another person, I believe, also enjoyed your company. After your departure, your name happened to come up during one of my evening chats with Pastor Bonhoeffer. His expression spoke clearly how much he enjoyed your company, and the deep satisfaction he would find in a renewal of the time the both of you spent together. To be sure, his duties occupy him exceedingly, but if either you or he would simply say the word, I know I could arrange a meeting. An eventual understanding between the two of you would be a fulfillment of one of the dearest wishes of my heart—seeing two people I love joined together in that sacred union of hearts and lives. Do tell me your thoughts on this subject.*
>
> *I must close for now. But Lord willing, I will write again soon and trust to find a reply from my little Maria reaching me before long. Until then, I remain,*
>
> *With affection,*
> *Grossmutter*

Maria gasped. She'd expected a letter full of chatter and family news. Not this. It was incomprehensible. Grossmutter must be out of her mind to even write such words. Pastor Bonhoeffer and her? Why, he was Grossmutter's theologian friend, the author of *Nachfolge*, the man whose confirmation class she'd been deemed too childish to join . . .

To be sure, they'd enjoyed a lovely evening, twilight painting the night sky, the mesmerizing music that had caught her breath and lingered in her memory. But that was all it had been—an evening at Grossmutter's house with one of her highly intelligent guests. Not an uncommon occurrence, though it had been an uncommon meeting.

Right now, she wasn't interested in marriage. Her work and family left little time for such a thing. Besides, she had dreams of studying. Someday, perhaps even teaching. What place had a husband in all of that?

If she ever married, it would be to a man like she and Doris had dreamed of, lying awake at night in their bunks at boarding school, sharing whispered girlhood fantasies and giggles. A man who inspired a love strong enough to overcome all obstacles, to vanquish all difficulties. One worth donning a wedding dress for, one who elevated daily household tasks to something grand and fine. Because it would be *him* she kept house for, *him* whose children she bore and brought up.

Though Doris still held the attentions of plenty of boyfriends, she hadn't yet encountered such a man. Nor had Maria.

She stood, replacing the letter and striding toward Gottfried. He laughed, dangling the writhing insect midair. She squared her shoulders. Back to work.

Those days with Grossmutter, that evening with Pastor Bonhoeffer, were best forgotten. Not remembered.

Certainly not relived.

July 21, 1942
Berlin

Sitting alone in front of the radio wasn't a popular pastime of his. Dietrich usually had better things to do. But his parents had accepted an invitation to stay a few days at the home of an old family friend, and his mutter never liked to miss the BBC broadcast, the only trustworthy source for news anymore. One couldn't expect to believe anything that propaganda peddler Goebbels allowed over German airwaves. Of course, the penalty for listening to enemy radio stations was ten years imprisonment—or worse.

So Dietrich had drawn the curtains, closed the parlor door, and positioned his chair pressed up against their set. He always kept the dial tuned to a German music station until the very last minute, and he'd a few to wait yet. Strains of the hit song "Lili Marlen" crackled on the air, and Dietrich leaned back in the comfortable chair, the sticky summer heat prompting him to shrug off his coat and roll up his shirtsleeves.

A risk like this, though dangerous, had ceased to raise his pulse. Nein, it was the real risks, those of the conspiracy, that sometimes threatened to steal his breath.

How well he remembered the day when Hans had first revealed the existence of plans that would see Hitler overthrown and a new government put in place.

It wasn't that Hans had ever kept any secrets. Quite the contrary. He'd always been frank with his wife, Christel, and brothers-in-law about the dirty linen that the Reich Justice Ministry, where he worked in the legal department, preferred to keep off the public washline.

But it wasn't until Hans showed him the dossier that Dietrich realized how painfully little he had known. That evening, those memories, would never leave him. The sky above had been a fathomless canvas of pitch. The Dohnanyi house, still and silent, children asleep, Christel down the hall. Hans had ushered him into his study. Metal scraped against metal as he turned the key in the lock. He'd lit a lamp. Just one.

Dietrich had sat in the cracked leather chair—the Dohnanyis always believed in frugality—and watched as Hans fumbled with the file drawer of his desk. A thatch of his usually slicked back light brown hair fell over his high forehead as he placed four black files atop his empty desk. He brushed a hand over one, features tight.

"Take a look. It's all here."

More danger could lurk within a single leaf of paper than the deadliest Luger. As Dietrich turned through the files, reality embodied that statement. In explicit detail, the documents told stories, each more horrifying than the last. The corruption and thievery practiced by Nazi officials . . . the orders given to burn synagogues with the Jewish population of a village locked inside . . . mass murders in Poland where thousands upon thousands were gunned down, their lifeless bodies danced upon by their so-called victors . . . concentration camps . . .

Pictures accompanied the files. Naked men standing in front of a ditch, guns trained on their bodies. The same men lying in the ditch after being mercilessly shot, bodies woven together in a macabre braid of bullet-riddled humanity. Charred corpses . . . the emaciated body of a child . . .

Perspiration broke out on Dietrich's forehead. He closed the folder and met his brother-in-law's gaze.

"The information you have here . . ."

"Could get me killed," Hans stated, features grim in the swath of lamplight.

"Who . . . how did you get all this?"

Hans sank into a chair, resting both arms on its sides. "Admiral Canaris, the head of the Abwehr, asked me to compile it."

"But that's—"

"Dangerous?" Hans raised a brow. "Only when we use it against Hitler."

The enormity of the evidence and his brother-in-law's words covered Dietrich like a heavy, clammy hand. "Why are you showing this to me?"

"Because I thought it time you knew."

Dietrich had said nothing, staring down at the play of shadow and light flickering across the folders spread over Hans's polished oak desk. To possess such knowledge could only be followed with action. But what?

Germany had already forfeited its right to be called a Christian nation.

But this went beyond nightmares.

"Plainly speaking, Canaris and I, a few others, are putting things into place for a government overthrow. It's slow, of course. We'll need the support of high-ranking officers, and many of them are still fooled into believing Hitler is the country's savior. But the illusion will fade. As things grow worse, loyalties will turn."

"Worse?" How could things possibly become more so? But such a thought, even one born of the moment, was nothing more than bald naivete.

Hans only nodded.

A knock came low on the door. Hans jumped to his feet, sweeping the files up in one motion and locking them back inside his desk. He approached the door with a calm, measured stride and opened it cautiously.

"Oh, it's only you, Christel. Come in." He led his wife inside, gestured for her to take a seat in the chair he'd vacated. Christel wore a light summer sweater over her simple blue dress, her long, dark hair braided down her back, as she'd worn it when they'd been children.

"Did you tell him?" Christel glanced up at her husband. They were a unique couple and an ideal one. Despite the tension of the moment, Dietrich smiled to see the two of them, Hans behind Christel's chair, his hand against her shoulder. Between them lay no secrets. Hans relied upon Christel with no hesitation and total trust. And Christel proved herself worthy. Every time.

Hans nodded.

"What is he going to do about it?" The words were addressed to Hans, but Christel's gaze pierced Dietrich's. They were both Bonhoeffers, raised in a home where idle talk was forbidden, the solidity of ideas based upon how far one was willing to go to carry them out.

Carry them out . . .

He opened his eyes—he hadn't realized he'd closed them—the present returning. The seat beneath him again became the upholstered armchair in his parents' parlor instead of the cool leather in Hans's study. Dietrich checked his watch.

Time for the BBC. He turned the dial, keeping the volume whisper-low.

Faint, yet stronger perhaps for being so, came the *bumbumb* of Big Ben that heralded the beginning of the broadcast. Dietrich pressed his ear against the set, straining for what came next.

What had he done about it? Christel's question, spoken in her firm voice, came to him again.

He'd joined Hans, Admiral Canaris, and the others, using his church connections in England, Sweden, and Switzerland to attempt to make contact with the British government. Even helped to compile added information for the Chronicle of Shame. Since that momentous evening, the conspirators' plans had grown, other members added to their ranks.

Dietrich's forehead furrowed as he turned his attention to the broadcaster's words, his quiet breathing and the low English accent the only sounds in the empty house.

"This is the BBC . . ."

Chapter Five

Brushing a wisp of hair behind her ear, Maria gave the potato another vigorous scrub. Perspiration trickled between her shoulder blades . . . her face hot and no doubt an unappealing shade of red. She plunked the potato into the bowl of clean ones, where they awaited chopping. Around her, the kitchen servants employed by the Vogels—reduced to only two since the beginning of the war—bustled to prepare the evening meal.

Chop, chop went her knife as she sliced the potatoes into small discs to be added to the bubbling stew. The mixture of root vegetables and thick- ened broth would fill everyone's bellies tonight. Plain fare, compared with the mouthwatering schnitzel and bratwurst of the prewar days. Schnitzel and bratwurst washed down with real *kaffee*, thick and milky with cream, followed by *kuchen*, rich with sugar and raisins.

Bliss. Vater had always declared such meals "a little taste of heaven." While licking her fingers after the final bite of *kuchen*, she could not have agreed more. Or perhaps it tasted thus simply because her family—Vater— was sharing it with her.

"Fraülein Maria."

She started. The knife slipped mid-cut through a potato. Pain sliced her finger as she whirled to face the Vogels' son. Since the incident with the song, Gottfried and she had kept a tenuous distance. He obeyed her orders most of the time. But an undercurrent of resentment still lingered in his gaze.

"*Ja.*" The word came out in a breath.

"You're wanted upstairs." A sly grin slanted his mouth. "Mutter said to fetch you." He fingered the toy pistol strapped in a holster around his chubby waist.

Her heart pounded. Had he reported her for smuggling food to Boris? How would she answer? What would happen to her?

"It's a telephone call," Gottfried added, as if on afterthought.

An exhale of relief swept her lungs. "*Danke*, Gottfried." Maria glanced first at the potatoes still awaiting preparation, then down at her hand. Blood oozed red from the cut on the pad of her thumb. Her stomach twisted as a sudden wave of queasiness swept over her. But why? She was a country girl, well-versed in tending to her own cuts and scrapes and those of her brothers and sisters. Forcing aside the nausea, she pulled a handkerchief from her apron pocket and knotted it around her finger. Gottfried watched, gaze riveted, as if mesmerized by the red stain seeping through the snowy cloth.

Maria brushed past him and left the kitchen. As she approached the library door, her heart thudded dully in her ears. Strange. She'd always been able to dash across the fields at Pätzig for half an hour, scarcely losing breath. Why the sudden weakness? Had Gottfried shaken her that much?

Using her uninjured hand, she turned the doorknob. A cool breeze from the slightly open window stirred the curtains, bringing with it the scent of grass and sunshine. She inhaled, letting the fragrance steady her tight lungs and thrumming heart.

She crossed the carpet toward Standartenführer Vogel's desk. Papers skated across the polished oak, stirred by another breeze. They floated to the carpet like wings of a fallen dove.

Swallowing against another rise of nausea, she lifted the receiver.

Why are my hands shaking? This doesn't make sense.

"Hello."

Static on the other end. "Maria?" Her mutter's voice sounded far, far away.

"*Ja*, Mutter. I'm here." She punctuated her words with a nod, a foolish gesture since one couldn't see through telephone lines.

"My dear daughter."

The endearment gave her pause. Mutter rarely called her "dear daughter." Nein, it was Vater who gave her pet names. *Miesenmaus* had always been her favorite. Being called Missy Mouse by anyone else would have seemed more than absurd. But with dear Vater, the phrase, accompanied by one of his famous smiles, brought a rush of warmth that filled her for days after.

"*Ja?*"

Silence crackled. A silence that seemed to go on for so long she wondered if anyone was even there. Her fingers tightened around the receiver. Outside, the gardens beckoned in all their summer glory. How she longed to leave her shoes and stockings by the door and race barefoot through the grass, the blades tickling her toes, the earth one with her feet.

"Mutter, are you there?" Her voice seemed an echo in the room full of leather-bound books and fine furnishings.

"*Ja*, Maria, I'm here. There is something I must tell you."

"I'm listening." Her tone faltered, her throat suddenly dry.

Bad news. It couldn't be anything else, not with her mutter so quiet and strange. Who? What? Those questions remained. Begged to be asked. Was it a family friend? A cousin or uncle? They'd already lost several. So many serving by command of the Führer, scattered abroad like pieces of drift-wood. Floating.

Sometimes . . . sinking.

"Yesterday, the Russians launched an attack on your vater's regiment. He was already wounded by shell splinters, but he refused medical care, and stayed with his men. He managed to sound the alarm, before . . . before . . ."

Maria's eyes slid shut. Outside, a bird trilled a high, joyous melody.

A roaring, like the rushing of a mighty waterfall, began in her ears.

"He was killed by more shell splinters. They tried to get him to the hospital, but it was too late. He cherished you, *Liebling*. You were his pride and joy."

Nein.

It wasn't true. Couldn't be. Not Vater, her big, strong papa with his handsome smile and spectacles always tilting down his nose. Not Vater, her confidant, her hero. With others, she was the vivacious and bright image of her grossmutter. With him, she was the *miesenmaus* who brought a twinkle to his eyes and a grin to his lips.

Vati. It's not true, Vati. I won't believe it. Your little miesenmaus *shan't accept it.*

"Maria?"

"I'm here." Perhaps it was the remembrance of the pride Vater took in her that gave her strength to speak the next words with a modicum of assurance. "I'm coming home, Mutter. I'll be at Pätzig as soon as I can."

"*Ja*, you come home. I know the Vogels will help you make arrangements. I have other calls to make now. Auf Wiedersehen." Mutter's voice hovered on the edge of tears.

The mistress of Pätzig, the wife of Hans von Wedemeyer, did not often cry. Not in the presence of her children, certainly.

Yet on the other end of the phone, her mutter wept.

She should have spoken something. The sort of words Vater would say, ones that would make everything all right again, order a world turned upside down.

But she didn't. To her shame, she didn't.

"Auf Wiedersehen, Mutter. I'll be home soon." The words sounded like a whisper emerging from a mouth not her own. Had Mutter even heard them?

The line clicked.

Maria set down the receiver. How did one begin to look a loss like this in the face and reckon with it? How could she even begin to wrap her brain around the brutal truth? The finality? All that was and would never be?

What had his last moments been like? She stared down at her thumb, the blood that had seeped and dried on the handkerchief, its remnants a smear across her hand. The ugly redness . . . Vater's anguished face . . . explosions. Had he thought of her as life ebbed from his veins?

Her lungs tightened, each breath coming hard.

She couldn't think of that right now. She'd crumble into powder.

With an effort, she fixed her gaze on the window, losing herself in another place and time.

Wartenberger Lake near Pätzig. Fresh air. Sparkling sunlight glistening on the water's rippling surface. The squeals and laughter of her siblings clad in their bathing costumes, jumping and cavorting in the water. Vater, looking up at her from where she crouched on the springboard. No one was as strong as Vater. None could swim so well.

Ruth-Alice hovered in the background. Maria did not have to look at her to know her older sister's fear of the water. *Dummkopf.* What was there to fear?

She neared the edge of the diving board, keeping her gaze fast on Vater. He called out encouragement, spurring her to raise her arms above her head. Poised.

"Look out, Vater!" In the next instant, she was airborne. Plunging in, well out of her depth. The water closed over her head, but only for an instant.

There was never anything to fear.

Vater always caught her. Every time.

The memory faded, the wind over Wartenberger Lake blurring into the breeze swooshing into the Vogels' library. Maria swiped a hand across her cheeks, startled. She hadn't been conscious of shedding tears.

But there was reason to cry.

For who would catch her now?

Chapter Six

No matter that this was Berlin—a city bombed by the British less than a year ago. No matter that the Abwehr crept closer toward bigger, bolder plans with all the tension and stealth of hunters closing in on their prize. No matter that rationing had long since replaced *kaffee* with ersatz, strong tea with weak and reused leaves.

His mutter still drank afternoon tea in the garden behind her home.

And Dietrich, for one, was grateful to be joining her, witnessing her undaunted spirit amidst what everyone knowingly called "these days."

Vater too—Dr. Karl Bonhoeffer, eminent professor and psychiatrist— sat in one of the wicker chairs opposite his wife, Paula, cup and saucer balanced on one knee, a book in his hands.

"More tea, Dietrich?" Though the Bonhoeffer family never put much stock in royalty, with her hair braided into a coronet at the back of her head, posture straight, and dressed elegantly but simply in a navy housedress with white lace collar, his mutter looked finer than any lady of nobility.

"Nein, danke." Dietrich laid aside his empty cup and saucer on the wicker table. "But it never ceases to astonish me how you manage to put on such a spread every afternoon. And in Berlin, no less."

She only smiled. It was her hard work and ingenuity that made their abundance possible, but she was too modest to admit to possessing such traits.

His mutter stacked the empty cups and plates, piling the remaining aniseed biscuits onto the same plate as the squares of brown bread. "Later this afternoon, I'll take the leftovers to Frau Weber two streets down. Do you remember her, Dietrich? She used to live near us in Grunewald."

He stretched out his legs, resting one arm across the back of his chair.

The rumble of a far-off motorcar sounded, mingling with childish laughter, no doubt the Gruber boys across the way out chasing their hoops. Summer scented the air—freshly trimmed grass, flowering bushes, and the city undertone of motorcycle fumes and somebody's stale cigarette.

"Ah, Frau Weber. *Ja.* I used to carry her groceries home from market when she was expecting her first child. I never wanted payment, but she always had chocolate or a slice of *kuchen* for me. What a nice woman. Do you see her often?"

"More often these days." Mutter heaved a sigh. "Herr Weber was killed on the eastern front last month. Frau Weber's eldest son, Rudy, was conscripted earlier this year, and she has three little girls younger than him to care for."

Once "the weather looks like rain" had been a common phrase. Since the beginning of the war, the news most often on everyone's lips became: "Did you hear of her brother's death or his nephew's injury?"

"I didn't know." Rarely a week went by that he did not write a letter to one or another of his former confirmands, or Finkenwalde brethren, giving what encouragement he could when one was called up, or offering condolence on the death of a family member. He did his best to keep up with everyone's personal news and the latest from the front lines. Though it shouldn't have, saying he hadn't known felt like a failure. "I'll go with you. Do you know if we still have Sabine's wooden animal set? Perhaps we could take that to the little girls."

"That's a good idea." Vater laid aside his book. "I think it's in the spare-room closet. Let me see if I can go up and find it." He stood, crossing the grass and heading toward the back door.

The sky, radiant with sunlight only moments ago, took on an overcast hue, as if threatening rain hovered just around the corner.

Since his return from Rome and Venice, the only news from Bishop Bell about British government support had been negative. Anthony Eden had given Bell his answer, the gist of which ran diplomatically along the lines of, "Without casting any reflection on the bona fides of your informants, I am satisfied that it would not be in the national interest for any reply in the positive to be sent to them."

Polite, but an absolute no. Churchill and his government had shut themselves off to the belief that any German might be willing to wage war against the government of their own country. Thus Bell's influence with Eden proved as ineffective as trying to win at arm wrestling with both hands tied behind one's back.

If only the British could be made to understand the truth. If the conspiracy gained the support of the English, after it was over, Germany could be brought back to repentance. German Christians must be willing, desirous to show sincere grief and support to those whom they had caused to suffer. But with Eden's absolute refusal to sanction further communication, the power behind these ideas could not be kept alive forever.

Though this blow to the cause had proved a great disappointment, other plans were in motion. Ones that would only affect a few—fourteen in number.

But in the eyes of God, fourteen held the same value as a thousand.

Operation 7 was Hans's project. His brother-in-law's legal mind conjured greater schemes than any taught at university. Case in point: smuggling Jews—fourteen of God's chosen people—out of Berlin camouflaged as Abwehr agents. The Jews traveled to Switzerland for the supposed purpose of telling the Swiss how well the Germans were treating Jews. Instead, they'd reveal the truth to the Swiss authorities and then be free to secure what livelihood they could in Switzerland until the end of the war. The paperwork had to be managed just so . . . everywhere more and more paperwork.

It had taken countless hours of work—maneuvering the Jews off the deportation lists, making them official Abwehr agents. Dietrich had procured visas and arranged sponsors for the fourteen upon their arrival in Switzerland.

Little wonder Hans and Admiral Canaris wore looks of perpetual exhaustion.

Though Dietrich was the least overworked of the three, he'd be gaining a reprieve starting tomorrow. Ruth had written for his assistance in procuring a doctor to examine her for cataract surgery, and he planned to travel to Klein-Krössin to aid Ruth and work on his book. Berlin simmered with an electric undercurrent brought on by the war, a far cry from the days when families flocked to the Zoologischer Garten instead of to underground air-raid shelters. Klein-Krössin meant rest, if only for a little while.

"Dietrich."

He turned. Vater stood inside the open doorway, hands bereft of the wooden Noah's ark set.

"*Ja*, I know. Eberhard needed a place to store some things, and I put them in the spare-room closet." He stood with an apologetic smile. "In your next letter to him, be sure to hint around at finding a new location for his old skiing gear. That will make him laugh. For now, I'll help you look."

Vater shook his head. "I found the toys. As I was coming downstairs, the telephone rang. It's Frau von Kleist."

"Probably something she wants me to bring her from Berlin. I'll only be a moment. Pardon me, Mutter." He crossed the lawn and entered the house, closing the back door behind him. Footsteps clomped overhead. No doubt the maid, Lotte, busy at the daily dusting.

He moved down the hall and entered his vater's study, a room almost as familiar to him as his own upstairs. The family collection of books shared shelf space with photographs and mementos. A window overlooked the garden where his parents sat in companionable conversation. Dietrich picked up the telephone.

"Hello, Dietrich." Ruth's familiar voice sounded muffled.

"How are you, Ruth? Do you want me to bring you some of Mutter's strawberry jam? Or is there a book I could pack to read aloud?" The highly literate Ruth undoubtedly missed being able to read for hours on end, as in the days before her eyesight began to weaken.

"Nein, nothing like that."

The telephone service in Berlin wasn't that impaired. So he couldn't chalk up the tremor in her voice to any technical difficulty.

His heart sped. "Tell me."

"It's my daughter's husband, Maria's vater. We just received word. He was hit when the Russians launched a shell attack. He survived only long enough to warn his regiment of the impending danger. I just got off the phone with Ruthchen." Ruth's voice cracked.

"But isn't that what every woman does these days? Misses the men in her life? Living for the mail delivery, wetting her pillow with tears, praying and begging God that they may be restored to her?"

Maria's words. She'd spoken them less than three months ago, eyes so bright and clear. Fearful, perhaps, but no rocks had yet been slung into the lake to ripple the peaceful waters. How well he remembered from his time teaching her brother's confirmation classes the closeness between daughter and vater. How vivid the recollection of Herr von Wedemeyer discussing with him in earnest tones his desire for all of his children to receive good spiritual instruction.

No doubt the family had many memories of their own. Ones that would be held close and cherished. Because now, memories were all they had left to them. A few belongings left over in cupboards and closets, a favorite book, a well-loved chair. Memories.

And the hope of eternity.

"I don't know what to say." As a pastor adept at writing numerous letters of comfort and condolence, he should have. But the thought of youthful, smiling Maria reduced to tears over the loss of her vater twisted his heart into a ball of grief and pain.

"The Lord giveth, and the Lord taketh away. Blessed be His name." Dietrich could hear the strength in Ruth's words. He could also hear the tears.

He cleared his throat. "The children of Herr von Wedemeyer were fortunate indeed to have such a vater. They have received a fine spiritual inheritance. God will use that to give them strength, Maria and Max and the others." A prayer filled his heart even as he said the words.

Let Your grace and strength be their comfort, Almighty God. Show them how to rest in the assurance that they are Your children, never separated.

"Write that to Max. A letter from you will do much to encourage and strengthen him. And one to Ruthchen. My daughter is strong, *ja*, but she has been broken. We all have."

"*Ja*, I will." He swallowed past the knot rising in his throat. "I'll write once I arrive at Klein-Krössin. Then you can read the letters before I send them."

"I'll see you soon then." A calmer cadence infused Ruth's tone. She'd weather the storm. This wasn't the first loss she'd endured in her seventy-five years.

"Soon, Lord willing."

He set down the phone, braced both hands against the top of his vater's desk. For long minutes, he stayed there, head bent, heart crying out with fervent prayers. Death. A fixture on every street, etched into every face. War, the most adept of thieves, stole without respect of persons. The von Wedemeyers were not the first to suffer, nor would they be the last. Yet the normalcy of the situation did not make the facing of it any easier to endure. Pain was still pain, war or no war.

Though mile upon mile separated them, though not one word had been exchanged since that evening at her grossmutter's, the weight of Maria's grief pressed down upon him as surely as if he'd encircled her in his arms while she wept.

Chapter Seven

Like a rent in fabric formerly whole, the wake of her vater's absence yawned wide and gaping.

Maria lingered on the graveled avenue leading to her family's stone manor house. She'd stood in this very place as a girl of fourteen, on holiday from her studies, her little case in hand, heart beating with the anticipation of being home again. Fairly flying through the house, feet skating across the polished floors, she'd burst in upon them—her mutter setting aside her sewing with a start of surprise, the little ones running toward her with squeals of excitement in the hopes of finding a treat in one of her coat pockets.

Max would be standing beside the window, one hand leaning on the sill, and he'd turn and smile that crooked, brimful-of-mischief grin, as if to say: "What romps shall we get up to this time, Sister mine?" She'd roll her eyes at him, knowing full well he'd have her playing pranks before evening's end.

Then she'd hurry past the children with a quick hug to each and a promise of some small package in her case—and run straight into Vater's arms. He'd hold her close in his strong, cigar-scented embrace, softly saying against her hair how glad he was that his little *miesenmaus* had come back at last.

Then and only then would she finally be home.

Maria straightened her shoulders, swallowing past the ache in her throat. She must be strong for Mutter and the rest. She was not a little girl in the safety of tranquility anymore, but a woman of eighteen in the midst of war. A war raging in the lives of everyone, not only the soldiers fighting at the front. The palatial home before her, with its butternut stone walls and lush gardens, had once seemed a place set apart from the outside. Now it had joined the ranks of dwellings both humble and grand across Germany and around the world.

A home of the grieving.

She lifted her face to the warm rays of sun, breathing in the loamy scent of country air. Her low heels crunched against the pebbled drive as she crossed the remaining distance and climbed the set of steps leading to the double french doors. She turned the knob, the metal cool and smooth against her palm, and let herself in.

Silence rang in her ears, echoing off the high ceiling and polished parquet floor, reverberating off the paintings hanging in their frames, each in their designated spot on the salmon-colored walls.

If she hadn't received Mutter's phone call, she'd still have known something was amiss upon setting foot inside the entrance hall. A house that had seen seven children born was never silent for long.

She reached up and removed the hat ringed with cranberry-colored trim that had seemed so fashionable when she'd purchased it two years ago. Footsteps sounded on the stairs.

Mutter, one hand trailing along the railing, descended on fifteen-year-old Hans-Werner's arm. Thirteen-year-old Christine and ten-year-old Lala followed. Six-year-old Peter came last, clutching the hand of their eldest sister, twenty-two-year-old Ruth-Alice. The children's eyes lit as they saw her, but not in their usual way. No one ran, or squealed, or chattered. It was a silence as cloying as it was unfamiliar, and they were all squirming beneath its weighty hand.

"It's good to have you home again, Maria." Mutter clasped her hands and kissed her softly on the cheek, whelming Maria in her familiar rose fragrance. In a dark blue dress, gray-peppered hair pulled into a tidy bun, her mutter still looked every inch the wife of a respected landowner. Only the slight slump in her normally faultless posture, and the strain around her clear brown eyes bore witness to the desolation of the past few days.

"*Ja.*" Maria forced her lips to smile. "I'm glad to see you looking so well." She turned and knelt beside her siblings, giving each a hug in turn. Hans-Werner, growing taller by the day; Christine, home from boarding school; Lala, brown hair in thin, dangling braids and smelling of wind and horses; and little Peter, looking so like Max, who hugged her tight, as if doing so would bring their *vati* home on the morning train.

Last, she embraced Ruth-Alice. Ruth-Alice, who not only feared for the safety of their brother, but for her husband, Klaus, an officer in the Wehrmacht. Her oldest sister always seemed so brave and steady, and as the two clasped each other, Maria felt her sister's strength transmitted through her touch. A slender strength though. Maria had always been the sturdy one.

The sisters parted. "Any word from Klaus?"

Lips pressed together, Ruth-Alice shook her head, small silver earrings dangling under her curled, upswept dark hair. "He couldn't have been expected to receive the letter I sent so soon. I pity him, receiving news like that in such a way, all alone at the front. We, at least, have had the comfort of each other."

"It's an all-too-common circumstance." Maria sighed. "And he must be told." She looked down at Peter, hovering near her skirts.

"I missed you, Maria." He smiled, revealing a missing tooth.

"And I, you." She bent down and ruffled his hair. "You're much nicer than the *kinder* I look after. The little boy there has a frightening propensity for playing with worms."

"I like worms," Peter piped, prompting a laugh from everyone but Mutter, who smiled wearily.

"Why don't you go upstairs and tidy yourself up," Ruth-Alice suggested. "Lunch will be ready in the dining room in a few minutes."

"*Ja.*" Had this been any other visit, she'd have darted up the stairs, calling over her shoulder to Peter that he'd better not eat all the *kuchen* before she came down. Doing so now would've seemed out of place. And sweets were a rarity, even in the country where food was more readily available than in cities like Munich and Berlin.

Once upstairs, she opened the door to her second-floor bedroom, grateful someone had set out a basin of water and some soap. Kicking off her shoes, she let her aching feet sink into the thick rug, then padded across the floor to wash her hands and face. Her wrinkled, dusty traveling clothes she left in a pile on the floor to pick up later, exchanging them for a simple cotton blouse and gray skirt.

Pins in her mouth and a brush in one hand, she was attempting to comb her windblown hair into a presentable knot when she spied a package wrapped in brown paper lying on her writing desk. After securing the final hairpin, she crossed to where the parcel lay and picked it up. An envelope rested beneath, her name penned in Grossmutter's large and slightly uneven script. She opened the letter first.

> *My dear granddaughter,*
> *Words cannot fully express the sorrow I feel for you and your family at the passing of your dear vater. You, with your passionate temperament and extreme sensitivity, must be taking this harder, perhaps, than the*

others. Yet you have learned from childhood that God gives and takes away. We are not to question the sovereignty of His will, only to know and trust that it is sovereign.

I have already discussed with your mutter the possibility of your joining me in Berlin at the beginning of October. My old eyes have finally left me with no choice but to have the dreaded cataract operation, and I'd very much like for you to come and read to me during my stay in the hospital. It would be a great comfort to us both, I think, to be near each other for a few weeks.

I am enclosing a copy of a book that has been a great source of wisdom and encouragement to me since I first discovered it some years ago. I do not think you have read it yet, and during this time of trial, I hope you will find it of use. If you have any questions as you read, know you can always talk things over with me, as you have always done.

You are in my prayers, and in my heart, Maria.

With affection,

Grossmutter

With a sigh, Maria let the note fall onto the desk. So like Grossmutter to think a book would make everything better.

What use was one, when all she wanted was Vater home again, safe and well. Even just one more minute with him, one last embrace. One more chance to tell him how sorry she was if she'd ever been self-centered and disobedient, whisper how much she loved him . . .

A sob caught in her throat, burning like a live coal.

It would never happen. Vater wouldn't come back to her. Not even his body. That would remain in a military cemetery somewhere, or worse . . .

His booming voice would never call up the stairs for her to hurry to put on her riding clothes and go for a gallop across the fields. She'd never again hear his echoing laughter, nor clasp his strong hands in hers as he twirled her in a waltz. He'd been her hero in everything, the one who challenged her mind and answered the difficult questions that always exasperated Mutter.

She stared at the brown-paper wrapped book through a blur of tears. Grossmutter would want to know her gift was appreciated, and she'd have to include the title in a letter of thanks, even though right now she hardly thought her benumbed mind could grasp more than the simplest phrases.

With a swipe of her hand across her eyes, she picked up the package and undid the wrapping. A simply bound black volume stared back at her, the cover cool and smooth against her fingers.

Nachfolge by Dietrich Bonhoeffer.

Had that evening at Klein-Krössin really happened, or had it all been just a dream? How flippant and carefree she'd been, with her teasing and flirting and swaying to American music. The war had not yet fisted its cruel fingers around her family, ripping apart their lives.

Leaving them with a world growing more tenuous by the day.

Chapter Eight

October 2, 1942
Berlin

G ermany's capital had become infamy's headquarters.

Not that the thought came as any surprise to Dietrich—it had been going on for almost ten years, after all. But the truth struck him afresh as he made his way across the street heading to the Franciscan Hospital. A cadre of uniformed officers goose-stepped down the middle of the cobbled road, the few automobiles rumbling past giving them a wide berth.

As the months dragged on, everything in Berlin looked just a bit more faded—from the once-bright colors on the dress of the woman pushing a pram a few feet ahead, to the Nazi party flags hanging like birthday banners left out long past their welcome, to the faces of the people themselves. Men, women, children, all with eyes older than their years, their visages speaking of hardships their lips did not dare voice. Loss. Hunger. The dream of a glorious Fatherland slipping through their fingers like paper-thin ashes.

Reaching the wide, stone steps of the large hospital building, Dietrich motioned a young mother with two children on ahead, then made his way up and through the front doors. Inside, the vestibule echoed with activity—a trio of doctors with clipboards in hand, anxious-faced women standing in lines. After a quarter of an hour spent queuing, he requested the room number from the frowning woman at the front desk and made his way down corridors and up a flight of stairs.

With each step, an entirely foreign sensation swamped him. In his ministerial capacity, he was accustomed to visiting sickbeds. Ruth von Kleist was no exception, considering he'd even been the one to engineer the arrangements for her stay and operation, securing his vater's advice as to the best doctor to perform the cataract procedure. He wanted to visit Ruth as much as he could, though his upcoming trip to the Munich Intelligence Office to finalize travel plans for his Abwehr mission to the Balkans and Switzerland would probably only allow him this one opportunity.

Nein, this feeling of expectation and . . . dare he say anxiety . . . had nothing to do with Ruth.

Maria.

Never could he have imagined a woman could fill his mind so fully and with such strength. She'd lingered there as he'd written first to her mutter and then to her brother Max, following Hans von Wedemeyer's death. His very fingers had ached to pen a letter to her, but he didn't dare. It would've been too forward, too . . .

So he hadn't. Tried to forget any hope of seeing her again.

But she was here, in this very hospital, each step taking him closer to her side. It felt like a dream, though the squeak of his shoes on the linoleum and the pungent antiseptic in the air confirmed its reality.

Right now, he dearly needed one of his rational friends—like Eberhard— to talk some sense into his thick skull, because the very idea of another meeting made it difficult for Dietrich to draw a decent breath of air. He stopped in the middle of the hall.

A uniformed nurse, purpose in her step, cast a strange, medically questioning look in his direction before scurrying away.

Passing an orderly pushing a cart and two doctors engaged in focused conversation, he checked room numbers until he found the right one. He glanced down at the bouquet of purple flowers in his hands—a rather pointless gesture, since after her eyes were bandaged, Ruth wouldn't be able to look at them. Not to mention, their purchase had required an outrageous expenditure.

But Ruth loved flowers, and she would be pleased that he thought to bring her something. Goodness knew she'd done enough for him through the years.

And the color reminded him of the dress her granddaughter had worn that night in the garden.

Drawing a deep breath, Dietrich knocked on the door.

Footsteps.

He straightened his shoulders, brushed a hand down the front of his tailored, gray suit, and tried for a smile. The door opened.

He blinked.

The Maria of that evening in June and the woman who stood inside the doorway were akin to each other, perhaps, but not the same. Her simple, schoolgirlish frock had been exchanged for an elegant dark red suit. She'd previously worn her hair in a braided fashion similar to the styles of his mutter's generation. Today, her golden brown waves hung to just above her shoulders.

Then, her expressive oval eyes had sparkled with the radiance of rare gemstones. There was a glimmer in them today, albeit a small one, but that was all. Still, her lips turned up in a sort of hesitant gesture, almost in surprise, as she evenly met his gaze.

"*Guten Tag*, Pastor Bonhoeffer."

"Hello, Fraülein von Wedemeyer," he said softly.

"You're here to . . . um . . . see Grossmutter?" Her gaze darted to the flowers in his hands.

"If she's awake and well enough to see me."

She cast a glance into the room behind her. "She's sleeping right now. I could wake her, I suppose, but—"

"Nein, Nein." He held up the hand not holding the flowers. "I wouldn't want you to do that. Why don't we wait a while? I've heard it's hard to catch any decent rest in a noisy place like this. Come into the hall. There's a bench where we can sit."

She looked a touch reluctant but followed him out, the door clicking quietly behind her. Already, he regretted the flowers. What a *dummkopf* he must look, carrying them around. But he couldn't just abandon them in a rubbish basket either.

They continued down the corridor, the only silent people amid harried nurses, orderlies pushing wheelchairs, and an elderly couple half yelling at the nurse behind the desk.

They reached the unoccupied, backless bench, and he motioned her to sit. She did, ankles crossed, gaze straight ahead as if she were one of his confirmands preparing to be quizzed. He sat on the opposite end, both hands around the bouquet, the scent of antiseptic, carbolic acid, and flowers whelming the air.

He'd expected to sit at Ruth's bedside, chatting with her, perhaps leading them in prayer before he left. Instead, Ruth slumbered down the hall, and he was left in a situation growing in awkwardness with each passing minute. Young theologians, professors, family members, and the poor, he could converse with any day of the week. But he could count on one hand the number of times he'd been in comparative solitude with an attractive woman. Especially one who'd slipped her way to the forefront of his mind countless times over the past months.

He needed to redirect his thoughts. Think of her as a person like any other, one in need of his pastoral help and guidance. For doubtless she, like the rest of her family, still grieved the loss of her vater, despite the composed expression in her eyes.

"How is Ruth faring?" He shifted to better face her, and she turned toward him slightly.

"Oh, you know Grossmutter. In control as ever, wishes she weren't here in the first place. The doctors say she's doing well and the operation will take place within the next fortnight. She keeps me occupied, reading aloud."

"What are you reading?" Always a good topic, reading. A safe subject, unless of course one discussed any of the books banned by Herr Hitler for "the good of the people."

"The Psalms, mostly." She leaned toward him, filling his senses with a sudden sweep of fragrance altogether feminine. "And"—she cut her voice low—"a copy of your *Nachfolge*. Though always very quietly and never when the nurses are around. I've become quite adept at hiding it whenever one of them comes in." A touch of amusement traced her lips.

"A welcome skill these days." He answered her in the same quiet tone. "And what do you think of the book?"

She paused, head tilted as if in thought. Perhaps it had been vain of him to ask, as if he sought some accolade from her. Though he'd have asked the same had she given any number of titles. And he really did want to know her thoughts, or if she had questions.

"I must admit to having a difficult time understanding some parts. Grossmutter tries to explain them to me, but I want to know it for myself. Do you believe it? Everything you wrote in there?" She studied him, as if she were accustomed to seeking answers to all her questions.

He smiled. "A strange question to ask an author." He set the flowers on the farthest edge of the bench, resting both hands on his knee. "And my answer would be *ja*, for the most part. Though I suppose I've grown to see that things are not as straightforward as I thought them when I wrote that book. I still believe in the truths I laid out, but find that, above all, a Christian should read the Bible as if it were God speaking directly into each of our lives and individual situations. The Ten Commandments and the Sermon on the Mount will always be our standard, a measure which we must use to answer every question. But that is not always as easy as it sounds."

He could have stopped there, but the intentness of her expression, as if she were searching for something, made everything else fade into the background, leaving only the two of them. "Take, for instance, a schoolboy whose teacher asks him, in front of the entire class, if his vater came home drunk the previous evening. Is it better for the boy to tell the truth and answer yes, or lie and, by the falsehood, maintain his vater's honor?"

Her brow furrowed. Silence fell. He could have filled in the gaps by answering the question as he saw it but instead waited, letting her ponder for herself.

Finally, she gave a little smile. "It is an interesting thought. Especially now. I wonder if Vater ever . . ." Her words trailed away, as she looked down at her clasped hands, so small and fragile, clenched together in her lap.

The impulse proved too strong to ignore. He reached across the space between them and placed his hand over hers. She looked up at him, eyes brimming with tears unshed, her expression so raw and wounded it made him ache.

"You must miss him very much." He rubbed his thumb over her knuckles in slow circles.

She nodded, her grief all the more poignant for being wordless.

He cleared his throat, surprised at the emotion rising there. "A few days after I got the news, I . . . wrote Max a letter. Wanted to write one to you, but . . ."

"What would it have said, if you had?" Despite the sophistication of her appearance, her voice sounded small and vulnerable as a child's. A girl-woman still in need of a vater's love and protection. When that shell had exploded, obliterating Hans von Wedemeyer's earthly body, much more than a life had been lost.

He'd sent countless letters to the grieving wives and children of his fellow seminarians and friends. In each, he spoke about what the person had meant to him and how he hoped the family would take comfort from the legacy left behind.

None of the letters, even after penning so many, had been easy to write. But Maria needed his answer. For her, he'd do his best.

"I'd have said how much your vater loved you. When he came to Finkenwalde that day many years ago to discuss Max's confirmation classes, he spoke of all his children, but you especially. How you were the one who wanted to embrace life as a participant, not merely a spectator. He said, out of all his offspring, you were most like him. And that, though you may not have passed the initial test to enter my confirmation classes, it was because you were too smart for *me*, not the other way around. He laughed when he said it. He had such a fine laugh, your vater." Dietrich smiled, remembering.

Maria gave a little laugh that came out half like a sob.

"He was a true Christian, believing that living for God goes beyond the purely spiritual and works its way deep into our lives and actions. He would understand your sorrow, Fraülein von Wedemeyer. But he would want you to go on, fully and entirely."

She pressed her lips together, fingers squeezing his. There was a rightness in their clasped hands. He sensed it with the same certainty he'd known he was meant to study theology all those years ago, with the same assurance he felt when, after his second trip to America in 1939, he'd decided to return home to do what he could for his fellow countrymen facing the war.

Defining moments in his life. They'd altered his course, determined his actions, but they'd been right decisions. The path his future with Maria von Wedemeyer would take had yet to be charted, but a future there would be. Many would fail to understand how he sensed this so inexplicably, but each look into her eyes confirmed it. Years ago, he'd failed in his relationship with Elisabeth—the sophisticated and intelligent Fraülein Zinn. When he'd discovered her feelings for him went beyond her desire to discuss his theology, he'd fully acknowledged his failure. But there hadn't been rightness between the two of them, despite how perfect they'd outwardly seemed for each other.

There hadn't been *this* . . .

"Danke, Herr Pastor." Maria slipped her fingers from his, brushing away a tear hovering diamond-like upon her lashes.

And Dietrich sent a silent prayer heavenward that God and His perfect will would guide him, the two of them, in their future as in everything else.

Chapter Nine

"It won't be long now." Serenity infused Grossmutter's tone, but a waxy sheen of anxiety marked her pale face.

In the hard-backed chair beside the hospital bed, Maria did her best to keep her grossmutter's thoughts away from the imminent operation. She'd just laid aside *Nachfolge* after an hour of reading, in between interruptions from various nurses and the surgeon on duty.

"It's going to be all right. And I'll be waiting right here when it's all over." Maria squeezed her grossmutter's hand. The woman's skin was cold. She reclined in the hospital bed, a little island surrounded by an ocean of white sheets. Her gray hair had been pulled back into a loose bun, framing round features that told Maria what she would look like in another fifty years.

Her stomach burned with nervousness. The hospital was competent, but Grossmutter was not as strong as she'd once been. What if there were complications?

"I know it will be, dear." Grossmutter squeezed back, a smile on her lips. "Let's talk about something else, shall we? I must admit I'd rest a deal easier knowing Dietrich was here to wait with you. Tell me, Maria, what do you think of him?" She turned her head, gaze meeting Maria's, eyes clear and penetrating for one about to have a cataract operation.

The sudden question threw her off-balance. Grossmutter waited, hands clasped atop the blanket, a knowing smile tipping her mouth.

"I . . . I like him," Maria stammered.

"And?"

Maria wasn't about to answer sharply, not when Grossmutter was minutes away from going into surgery. She took a deep breath, inhaling the scents of pungent soap and sterile everything. "And . . . he seems to me to be quite remarkable. I find him intriguing."

A uniformed nurse wheeled in a white iron cot, shoes squeaking against the floor, effectively halting their conversation. "Time to go."

Fear fluttered into Grossmutter's eyes. Maria patted her shoulder. "I'll be praying for you," she whispered. "Think about something happy."

The nurse assisted Grossmutter onto the cot and moved to wheel it from the room. Maria smiled reassuringly from her seat next to the hospital bed.

"I'll think about you and Dietrich then," Grossmutter said, leaning against the pillow. "That would make me very happy indeed."

The nurse wheeled the cot from the room and down the hall.

Maria bit her lip. What had she meant by "you and Dietrich"? Perhaps Grossmutter simply wanted to dwell on two of her favorite people.

Maria stood and stepped to the window, opening the heavy curtains to let mid-autumn sunlight cast its rays across the well-worn floor. When they brought Grossmutter back, Maria would have to close the curtains again. But after over a week in this small, close room, darkened per the patient's request, she welcomed the sun's warmth. With shades drawn and stark furniture, the chamber put her in mind of a prison.

She resumed her seat, long hours stretching before her with nothing to do but wait. Her thoughts turned to Boris. How was he faring without her to smuggle provisions? She'd told him of her vater's death before leaving the Vogels, explained she had to be away for a time. He'd nodded and, in broken German, said how sorry he was. She'd return to the Vogels soon, after Grossmutter no longer needed her. But for now, she could relish the freedom of being away from the National Socialist atmosphere and enjoy the time spent with Grossmutter and her friends. Friends like Pastor Bonhoeffer.

"What do you think of him?"

The question rose to her mind, unbidden.

Even now, the strength of his hand around hers still filled her senses with startling power. When she lay awake on Tante Spes's lumpy mattress, she turned the moment around and around in her mind until she'd relived it more times than she could remember. Holding his hand had given her an undeniable sense of peace, yet at the same time an exhilarating kind of confusion.

There was no way to rationalize this, nor cipher it out as she would some complicated mathematic problem. Two times two always came out four, but each new memory of Dietrich Bonhoeffer brought with it a new dimension, more questions.

During his visit with Grossmutter, upon her awakening, Maria had remained in her chair, content to keep to the shadows. She'd listened to their intelligent talk, marveling at his giftedness—how he could speak in such a way that provided simplicity and clarity with her, then converse with her Grossmutter with such erudite wisdom. Sometimes one of them would lower their voice and whisper so quietly that Maria couldn't make out what they spoke. After leading them in prayer, Pastor Bonhoeffer had taken leave, his final remarks suggesting he'd not be in Berlin for some time. The nature of his business and reason for his departure, even Grossmutter didn't seem to know. Or if she did, she didn't let on.

Whatever he did, it was dangerous. Though by all appearances he seemed a loyal German, she knew enough of her own family's anti-Nazi leanings to believe him anything other than against the regime. Her own cousin and uncle were deeply involved in resistance work. Exactly how much danger did Pastor Bonhoeffer undertake?

A knock sounded on the door, and a nurse poked her head in.

Maria stood. The operation couldn't be over already . . .

"A telephone call for you, Fraülein von Wedemeyer. If you'll follow me." The nurse turned with such brisk precision, Maria was surprised the woman didn't click her heels.

Past ranks of doors, down to the end of the hall where a telephone sat atop a small desk for use by family members of patients. It seemed a civilized sort of thing to have in a hospital that bore the scars of wartime like many Berlin buildings—broken windows repaired in haphazard haste, signs providing instructions as to the location of the air-raid shelter.

The nurse marched away smartly. Maria took a seat on the wooden chair in front of the desk and picked up the receiver. Probably Mutter on the line, wanting to know Grossmutter's progress.

"Hello." She rested one elbow on the desk. The last person at the telephone had left behind a scattering of cigarette ashes. Maria brushed them onto the floor.

"Fraülein von Wedemeyer." The line crackled, and his voice sounded far away.

"Pastor Bonhoeffer. Where are you?" She sat up straighter, wishing for a silly, girlish instant that she'd worn a different dress and curled her hair, before remembering, warmth in her cheeks, that he couldn't see her.

"Where isn't important, but I'll be in Berlin tomorrow. A welcome change in plans, I hope?" As he said it, he sounded hesitant. Hopeful.

"*Ja*, most welcome." More heat filled her face. Oh, that sounded much too eager. Doris would have responded with something evasive and charming.

"How is Frau von Kleist? Her operation is today, is it not?"

"She's in surgery right now. But it should be over soon."

"When you see her, tell her I've been praying."

"*Ja*, I will."

Noises, like the commotion of a train station sounded in the background. Then another voice, quick and insistent. Pastor Bonhoeffer replied, something muffled she couldn't catch, then came on the line again. "I have to go now. But I'll see you tomorrow."

"Tomorrow then," was all she could get out before the line clicked.

She set the phone down, propping her chin in her hands, a ridiculous smile tugging at her lips.

It seemed the furthest thing from normal that the phrase "I'll see you tomorrow" could hold such expectation.

But it did.

October 14, 1942
Berlin

Danger stalked the Abwehr. A ravenous hunter seeking its prey.

Case in point—General Oster, Admiral Canaris, Hans von Dohnanyi—to name a few of the hunted.

Dietrich's preparations to travel on behalf of the Abwehr to the Balkans and Switzerland had been canceled with a speed that would have seemed surprising, if not for the nature of his journey. Though the Jews involved in Operation 7 had made it across the border and into freedom without incident, the large amount of foreign currency required for the trip had not gone undetected by the customs officer in Prague. Smuggling foreign currency out of one country and into another was a serious crime, one from which even the Abwehr wasn't exempt. Hans, through a coded message, informed Dietrich it would be best to return to Berlin, and lay low for a time. Attempting to travel could lead to arrest at a border checkpoint.

Head bent against the bracing October wind, Dietrich made his way toward the hospital. He didn't much like lying low. If only he could be put to more use. It seemed almost criminal to sit and do nothing when many of his fellow Confessing Church pastors were incarcerated in concentration camps—Martin Niemöller among them. Niemöller, a man who'd initially supported Hitler, who had at first shown hesitancy about speaking boldly on behalf of the Jews, now suffered alongside them.

A shiver that had nothing to do with the cold crept across Dietrich's shoulder blades. Unlike the majority of Germans, he knew the truth of what went on in those camps. Gassings, torture, mass shootings where bodies fell into ditches in piles of desecrated humanity. Martin was safe for the moment, but how long could anyone withstand the hellishness of that existence?

He turned the corner leading to the hospital, the street and its pedestrians colored in gray and brown, enlivened only by the Nazi flags hung at intervals. The grande dame Berlin had been stripped of many of her jewels by bombings, rationing, and lack of able men to keep up the streets. Her consolation prize for the loss of her beauty?

These moronic flags. Symbols of dictatorship and tyranny.

The hospital was before him now. Dietrich glanced up at the stone edifice.

Again, he'd see Maria. A prospect that probably filled him with too much enthusiasm. He couldn't possibly be developing feelings of a . . . romantic nature toward Ruth's barely-out-of-her-teens granddaughter? Why, at thirty-six, he was practically middle-aged. Not much of a catch, for all practical purposes. Still living with his parents, drawing only a limited income from the Pastor's Emergency League, and, well, last he'd looked in the mirror, he didn't quite fit the dashing, dark, and handsome type. None of these deficiencies had plagued him in the past.

Until Maria. Her smile, so sweet and bereft of guile. Her eyes, shaded with sadness, a sorrow he longed to alleviate.

He entered the double doors and climbed the stairs leading to the patient rooms. Skirting the usual nurses, doctors, and visitors, he found his way to Ruth's chamber.

A knock, then a pause.

Maria opened the door, letting herself out and closing it behind her with such speed she nearly knocked both of them over. He grabbed her arm, chuckling at the astonished expression on her face.

"Steady there. And where are you escaping to?"

"Grossmutter just fell asleep." She looked down at his hand against the dark green fabric of her sleeve. The lavender fragrance she wore mingled with the antiseptic scent of the hospital. Someday, if they ever had cause to be apart, he'd pull out this memory from the pockets of his mind, and smile over each little detail. Her hair, skimming her collarbones in soft waves of golden brown. Standing but inches apart, her foot bumping his. Her gaze fluttering up, then down.

He hastily took a step back, forcing propriety to eclipse the crazy turn of his thoughts.

"Ahem . . . How is Frau von Kleist?"

She straightened her shoulders, smoothing both hands down the front of her skirt. "In some pain since the operation. Her eyes are bandaged, and she mustn't move her head until it's certain the stitches will stay. She didn't get much rest throughout the night, so I'm hoping she'll sleep for a few hours. You might do better to come back for your visit later in the day."

"Will you return to your tante Stahlberg's for the afternoon?" he asked, scrutinizing her face. She looked a bit pale. No doubt the hours keeping vigil had taken a toll on her.

Maria shook her head. "I should stay here in case she needs anything."

While her dedication to her grossmutter was admirable, she ought to get some fresh air. And he was as good a person as any to play escort, considering he knew his way around Berlin.

"What about lunch? Will you eat?"

She shrugged. "They usually bring in a tray. If not, I'm sure I can scrounge up something. I'm an expert scavenger," she added with a half grin.

"Why not dine with me? The fresh air will do you good, and I'm sure I can find us some fare better than what's on offer here." He managed to sound nonchalant. After all, this wasn't what Americans called a date. It was simply a friend of the family offering to supply lunch to a hardworking young woman who didn't know her way around Berlin.

Simply?

Perhaps *complicated* was a better word.

Maria met his gaze, obviously not half as fazed as he by the notion. "Very well, Pastor Bonhoeffer. Since Grossmutter is asleep, I think I can spare an hour or two. Give me a minute to get my hat and coat." She disappeared inside the room, leaving him standing out in the hall like a schoolboy with his hands in his pockets.

Where ought he to take her? They shouldn't go far. Since rationing had increased, many establishments had closed down. And there weren't many places within the vicinity of the hospital.

Except, well, one.

She emerged a minute later, a light gray coat belted at her waist, a little black velvet hat perched atop her head.

"Smart enough for Berlin?"

"For anywhere, I should think." He motioned for her to precede him down the crowded hall. Ought he to have offered his arm? How had his sister Sabine and her husband, Gerhard, walked when they'd been courting? A pointless rumination, since he and Maria were certainly *not* courting.

Out into the crisp air of Berlin they went. Sunshine fell upon the city, adding color to the drab streets. A trio of young people zipped past on bicycles. All the Jews in the city had been forced to relinquish theirs. The wrongs of the regime hit him afresh. Discrimination—the same kind he'd seen displayed toward the African Americans in New York, only worse. A Jewish schoolgirl couldn't bicycle to school, while her German counterpart could. Of course, few Jews remained in Berlin anymore, and if they did, they daily ran the risk of discovery by the Gestapo.

His thoughts must have shown on his face, as Maria gave him a glance of puzzlement.

"Sorry, did you say something?"

"Several things. None of which you responded to." She gave a smile equal parts confusion and amusement. "You were far away just now, Pastor Bonhoeffer. Thinking of something sad, it seems." Her eyes, blue as the Danube, probed his.

"How well you read me, Fraülein von Wedemeyer." A sleek, black motorcar sped down the street in a rumble of fumes and exhaust. Probably someone on Reich business, since with fuel rationing, few used their cars if they could just as well walk.

"Let's not talk of sad things today." The pleading look she gave him was all the permission he needed to forget, for a little while, war and tension and counterintelligence. "Where are we going?"

He gestured across the street. Neon lights above the restaurant entrance spelled out the word *Alois*. Maria pressed her hand over her mouth, eyes wide.

She leaned toward him, voice cut low. "But . . . that's . . . isn't it owned by the Führer's brother?"

"*Ja.*" With the tide uncertain as to the Abwehr's loyalties, appearing in such a place with an attractive Fraülein could only help maintain the conspiracy's cover. And since everyone knew the restaurant's ownership, it was actually the safest place Maria and he could talk. "Alois uses his half brother as a marketing technique. But the two rarely have any contact with each other. We're quite safe."

She looked mildly reassured. Still, he cupped her elbow as they approached. Café-style tables lined the sidewalk, most filled by *bier*-drinking officers, several of whom turned and fixed Maria with long looks of appreciation. He caught her quick intake of breath.

What had he been thinking? He shouldn't have brought Hans von Wedemeyer's daughter here. Best to turn around and find somewhere else, even if it meant a longer walk. And while they walked, offer what apology he could to the woman at his side.

Before Dietrich could redirect their course, Otto von Hartmann, one of the SS officers who skulked around Abwehr headquarters in Berlin, unfolded himself from his seat at one of the tables, and headed their way, his boots snapping across the sidewalk. Hans called him a hungry dog sniffing for scraps.

"Heil Hitler." Hartmann executed a perfect salute. But his eyes focused on Maria.

Maria looked at him, uncertainty in her gaze. A chill slid through him. It was happening again, as it had so many times before. He'd never forget the first.

Time slowed, pulling him into the past.

June 19, 1940. Eberhard and he had been enjoying a break after a pastors meeting, lunching in an outdoor café. The sun warmed their skin. The strudel he'd bought for them both melted in his mouth, mingling with the familiar sweet and nutty taste of *kaffee*. Eberhard had mentioned a book. Dietrich stretched out his legs, reaching for his fork.

Trumpet fanfare blasted across the radio loudspeakers. Breaking news: France had surrendered! The crowd erupted. Several daring lads jumped onto chairs, a jubilant couple bounded onto the top of an empty table. Music swelled through the air, the familiar refrain of *"Deutschland über alles"*—Germany above all else.

Eberhard sat still as if he'd turned into one of the statues at the Tiergarten.

The crowd didn't just sing the anthem, they roared it, arms flung out in the Nazi salute, tears of patriotism streaming down ladies' cheeks, men with puffed-out chests and fervor in their eyes. The exact moment his own feet had moved, Dietrich couldn't tell. But he stood among the rest, arm out, mouthing the words of the song.

He turned to Eberhard, who hadn't budged. "Are you crazy? Stand up. We'll have to run risks for many different things, but the silly salute is not one of them."

Slowly, Eberhard got to his feet, his delay in reacting likely unnoticed by the rest of the crowd, now belting out the "Horst-Wessel-Lied." His best friend raised his arm, facing the loudspeakers, the melee of the crowd drowning the fact that the both of them only pretended to sing.

That day, they'd remained inconspicuous, two men feigning patriotism while inwardly plotting resistance.

Two years later, their involvement had deepened to levels even Dietrich hadn't foreseen.

And today, as he had then, Dietrich raised his arm in a perfect Nazi salute.

Free in conscience.

Full of revulsion.

Chapter Ten

October 14, 1942
Berlin

He could have been a member of the *Schutzstaffel*—the SS—with his perfect Nazi salute, his crisp "Heil Hitler." And this from Dietrich Bonhoeffer, a man who had been the head of an illegal seminary for the Confessing Church, who'd moved his students from one site to the next in an attempt to outwit Gestapo interference.

The two opposites didn't reconcile themselves.

Crisp autumn air blowing her hair away from her shoulders, Maria nodded politely to the specimen of Aryan manhood facing them. Close-cropped blond hair, broad shoulders encased in his gray and black uniform bearing the insignia marking him as an SS sturmbannführer—a major.

"Good to see you, Herr Bonhoeffer." The man's thick lips formed a smile some might have called handsome. To Maria they looked like two fat sausages curving upward.

"Likewise, Sturmbannführer Hartmann." Pastor Bonhoeffer's answering smile appeared friendly and at ease.

"And who is the lovely fräulein?" The sausage lips continued to smile, as the sturmbannführer's pewter gaze swept her from head to toe. As if he were a buyer at an auction, and Maria the current item up for sale.

Boarding school and life at secluded Pätzig had sheltered her from men, but she wasn't stupid. Real gentlemen didn't look at ladies with such unabashed admiration.

"Fräulein Maria von Wedemeyer." Pastor Bonhoeffer slid his fingers around her elbow once more. His warm touch couldn't completely allay the chill scrambling spiderlike down her spine, but it did lessen it. Some. "Her vater, Major von Wedemeyer, fell at Stalingrad at the end of August."

Maria looked down at her worn shoes, planted side by side on the crumbling cobblestones. She'd bargained on a quiet lunch with Pastor Bonhoeffer, not discussing a loss all too raw with this bratwurst-lipped minion of Hitler.

"Ah." Maria glanced up in time to see the sturmbannführer's smile fade, giving way to an expression of polite sorrow. "Then, my dear Fraülein, your vater received a great honor. To give one's life for the glory of our Führer and Fatherland is the greatest of privileges. You should be a very proud young lady."

His words and that patronizing expression . . . could there be any greater slap to the loss she felt? What happened to the days when an "I'm very sorry" sufficed as the response when someone suffered a loss? Why did their world have to turn everything into a patriotic tirade?

Maria lifted her chin. "I'd rather be a very happy one and know that my vater still lives." A surge of vindication shot through her at the sturmbannführer's astonished expression.

Beside her, Maria sensed Pastor Bonhoeffer tense.

Perhaps she'd been too rash. She'd always been one to let her words fly without thinking. Didn't her cousin and uncle—Fabian von Schlabrendorff and Henning von Tresckow—play the roles of adoring citizens of the Fatherland, all the while despising every second of it and plotting secret coups?

She plastered on a demure smile and dipped her chin. "Forgive me, Sturmbannführer Hartmann. I'm afraid my grief as a daughter threatens, at times, to overshadow the knowledge of the service *mein* vater rendered his country."

The sturmbannführer gave her the sort of look one would give a misbehaving pup who'd accepted its punishment with whimpers and wagging tail.

Next the oaf would be patting her head.

"It's quite all right, Fraülein von Wedemeyer. A slip of the tongue, and by no means a reflection of your heart, I'm sure."

Maria pressed her lips together.

"We only came out for a quick lunch before I return Fraülein von Wedemeyer to her grossmutter's bedside. She's over at the Franciscan Hospital, recovering from an operation. In light of that, you'll excuse us, I'm sure." Wherever had Pastor Bonhoeffer acquired such smooth manners? As if he were a country squire and the sturmbannführer his to command.

"Don't let me stop you." The sturmbannführer gave a perfunctory smile. "*Guten Tag* to you both. Heil Hitler!" Another smart salute, echoed promptly by Pastor Bonhoeffer. With a crisp click of his heels, the sturm-bannführer returned to the table where his uniformed comrades sat.

Pastor Bonhoeffer said nothing as they passed by the outdoor tables where officers, businessmen, and a trio of middle-aged ladies lunched on surprisingly luxurious dishes. The tantalizing scents of schnitzel and bratwurst made Maria's mouth water. Hospital food and Tante Spes's cooking paled in comparison.

The bell above the door jangled as they entered. Circular tables covered in plain white crowded the low-ceilinged room. Iron light fixtures illuminated the wood trim and walls bedecked with photographs and paintings of der Führer with a muted glow.

A smartly dressed waiter stopped in mid-stride and greeted them with flung-out arm, his other hand balancing a pile of napkins.

"Heil Hitler, how may I be of service?" The red-cheeked waiter belted out the sentence in one breath.

"Heil Hitler, table for two, please," replied Pastor Bonhoeffer.

Maria stifled an unladylike giggle. This ritual of greeting was laughable. Couldn't they all just say "hello" and "how do you do," as before? At boarding school, her teacher Elisabeth von Thadden had let the practice slide as much as possible—due to her own anti-Hitler leanings, Maria suspected. The same went for life at the von Wedemeyer and von Kleist homes. Despite her short time at the Vogels, she still noted the oddity of the practice, whereas most Berliners—like Pastor Bonhoeffer—had grown accustomed to it. What an alien world they lived in, where people risked arrest if they didn't fling their arms out like tree branches and salute a man taking their country down the quick road to tyranny.

It would've been funny had it not all been so serious.

"Very good. Right this way, please." They followed the waiter past clusters of tables, until he stopped at one near the furthermost corner. Depositing the napkins on a nearby table, the waiter pulled out her chair. She sat, smoothing her skirt.

"I'll be right back with your menus." The waiter hurried away.

The table was designed for four, and Pastor Bonhoeffer could have taken any of the seats. When he chose the one closest to her, Maria couldn't help the warmth that rushed to her cheeks—a not altogether unpleasant sensation.

Had he done so only out of habit, or did he desire to be near her? A question meant to be analyzed with giggling scrutiny over a long chat with Doris. Only the intimacy of this luncheon seemed a thing too special to share with her old school friend.

Pastor Bonhoeffer smiled slightly. "I hope the lunch makes up for any unpleasantness caused by taking you here. I'm awfully sorry about that. I didn't expect to run into any acquaintances."

"It's really all right." And it was. Despite the ridiculous salutes and the visage of Herr Hitler on every wall, they were here, together. In the corner of a Berlin restaurant, the scents of baking and spices in the air. Just a man and a woman sharing a meal and time together.

The waiter returned with the menus, each presented with another salute, before speeding off toward another table. Obviously, finding men for military service ranked above providing sufficient staffing at a restaurant. Not that she minded. The less anyone bothered them the better.

Silence fell as they each perused the menu. Maria's gaze fell on the prices. Ought she order the least expensive item? Could Pastor Bonhoeffer afford their lunch? He didn't seem to have any steady employment, so where did his income originate?

Doris would have paled in horror at the thought of asking such a question. But Maria didn't want to put Grossmutter's friend in financial difficulty because of his kindness to herself.

"Are you sure you can afford this?" she asked in a matter-of-fact tone.

He glanced up from where he'd been studying the menu, spectacles tilting slightly over his nose. For a moment, he looked rather taken aback. Then, a teasing smile edged his lips.

"Has anyone ever told you you're not an ordinary young lady, Fraülein von Wedemeyer?"

"*Ja.* Mutter has ever since I was old enough to walk," she replied, deadpan.

His smile deepened and his spectacles tilted down even farther. The gold-rimmed glasses gave him a scholarly aura that suited his personality. She resisted the urge to reach out and push them up, trail her hand along his jaw . . . She looked down at the menu, forcing away the impropriety of such thoughts.

"In answer to your question, *ja*, I can afford to pay for lunch. I'm rather good at footing the bill, or so most of my friends tell me. I remember one time, when I was teaching a class of seminarians, I was set to travel to Berlin the next day, and I asked them what they would like me to bring back—either chocolate or cheese. Almost in unison, everyone suggested I bring back both." He leaned back in his chair, hands resting atop the menu, eyes twinkling.

"So what did you do?"

"Brought back large quantities of both, with a particularly large portion for Herr Bethge, since I had it on good authority he was the one who put them up to it."

The waiter returned, and they placed their orders—schnitzel for him, potato pancakes and salad for her, along with ersatz *kaffee* and cream for both of them. When the waiter disappeared along with their menus, Maria resumed their conversation.

"Herr Bethge is a friend of yours?"

Warmth filled Pastor Bonhoeffer's gaze, the sort of warmth her own eyes might emanate when she spoke of Max or her sisters.

"The very best. Though we've known each other for less than a decade, sometimes it seems we've grown up together. Like brothers, I suppose. My parents would agree, since they've practically adopted him. Our running joke is that we're both so familiar with each other's experiences and feelings, we'd make terrific biographers. Though we'd have to decide beforehand which stories ought to be left out. He might resort to bribery to prevent me from telling the world about his terrible lack of housekeeping skills."

They sat laughing. She couldn't remember the last time someone had made her laugh like this. Months, undoubtedly, but it seemed a lifetime. In childhood, she'd thrived on fun and games. War had absented both from her life.

And as she laughed, she almost forgot the pain of losing Vater.

He'd want her to laugh. To go on living.

Their laughter faded, and they straightened in their seats like errant schoolchildren when the waiter arrived with their meal. They responded with suppressed smiles and hasty danke schöns.

Instead of turning his attention to their food, he leaned toward her. His scent—a mingling of soap, typewriter ink, and an essence that could only be described as *him*—swept over her with such comfort she was tempted to steal his handkerchief just so she could inhale the fragrance whenever she wanted.

"Tomorrow night, my sister is giving a send-off party for her son, Hans-Walter, who's soon to join up. Herr Bethge will be there, along with most of my family. I thought you might . . . that is . . . would you care to join us?" His smile turned tentative. Earnest. "It would make me very happy."

It already made her even more so, just by him asking. The rivaling trepidation and anticipation in his eyes as he awaited her answer. Was this how all courtships progressed?

Could what she shared with Dietrich Bonhoeffer even be called by that name?

Whatever the name, and whatever her uncertainties, she relished the way he made her feel when they were together—safe and joyful and a dozen other things she couldn't name. She wanted to know more of him, to meet his family and friends. Wanted suddenly, ridiculously, to make them her family and friends.

"*Ja*, Pastor Bonhoeffer. I'd love to come to your family party." She almost laughed at his relieved expression. As if he'd actually expected her to refuse.

"I'll look forward to it then." They turned their attention to their meal. Silverware clinked against china. A young lady plunked out a folk tune on a nearby piano.

Maria lifted the warm cup of ersatz to her lips, savoring the creamy drink. She lowered the cup, suddenly chilled, despite the steaming drink. Her lungs tightened.

On the opposite wall, a large painting of the Führer—brown-uniformed and modeling the swastika on his right arm—hung in gaudy splendor.

And his eyes . . .

They seemed to be watching . . . staring . . . directly at Dietrich.

Maria shivered.

Chapter Eleven

October 15, 1942
Berlin

*F*eet firmly planted on the ground, Bonhoeffer. No more thoughts of *unfulfilled fantasies.*

Like arriving at a family gathering with a woman at his side. One who made him smile when there was nothing really to smile about. Who, when she slipped her hand in the crook of his elbow, made him imagine outlandish things . . .

A church with a long aisle. Maria in a white dress, gliding to his side.

Walks in the Tiergarten, pushing a baby pram.

Ja, outlandish. Especially in wartime. Especially in Germany.

The blue sky of afternoon had given way to the dusky gray of approaching twilight as he and Maria made their way down the street. The party for Hans-Walter, the Schleichers' eldest son, wouldn't be a late one. No party was these days, what with blackout curtains and the threat of air raids.

But it was a party nonetheless.

Tonight, Maria wore the dark red suit that matched the roses in her cheeks. She'd added a few curls to her honey-brown hair. They bounced against her shoulders as she walked, like threads of purest gold.

Enough of this . . .

"It's getting cold." He wore a substantial overcoat atop his three piece suit, far greater protection against the wind than her knee-length skirt and light jacket. Should he offer her his coat?

"I don't think so." She turned those radiant blue eyes on him. "I like evening walks. At Pätzig, I used to adore staying out with Max well after dark. Whenever it rained, we would tear outside and run through the gardens, getting completely soaked and shrieking like mad. It was fun."

Well, she'd answered that question. She answered a lot of questions, did

Maria, in that fresh, unaffected way of hers. Some of the stories she told of her childhood years . . . It was little wonder her mutter's hair hadn't turned completely white, fretting over all the scrapes her *kinder* got into.

"It doesn't sound like it," he replied. Whenever it rained, he tended to use an umbrella or stay inside like any normal person would.

She spun to face him, walking backward along the sidewalk, curls swirling in the breeze. Twilight illuminated the laughter in her eyes.

"You wouldn't know, since you haven't tried it." Teasing filled her words. "You don't know if you'll dislike something until you've given it a fair go. If you ever visit Pätzig and it rains, you absolutely must go outdoors."

With that sparkle in her gaze, the list of places he wouldn't go for her had dwindled to nothing.

"If you say so." He chuckled.

They reached the Schleicher family home, situated next door to the Bonhoeffers. Both homes had been constructed in 1935, due to his vater's desire for a smaller residence to retire in, along with a consulting room downstairs to see his roster of private patients. The Schleichers—his sister Ursula and husband, Rüdiger—had built their house next door, which meant that both homes always had plenty of Bonhoeffers coming and going.

Dietrich opened the gate and motioned for Maria to precede him up the small, graveled path. She hung back once they reached the door, smoothing a hand across her skirt.

He turned the knob and entered the foyer, Maria following. Dietrich took off his overcoat and hung it up. Voices drifted from the living room, mingling with a Schubert piece being played on the piano—Renate, probably, since she'd been practicing it last time he'd been over.

Footsteps sounded, and Eberhard appeared, a glass in one hand, a plate in the other. A boyish smile spread over his friend's face. Though only two years younger than Dietrich, Eberhard, with his dark hair and athletic build, managed to look no older than his late twenties.

"I thought I heard footsteps." Eberhard set his empty plate and glass on the hall table. "Wondered if you were coming or not."

"You know I wouldn't miss this." The men shook hands. It was then Dietrich noticed his friend's attention wasn't on him, but on the young woman still by the door, hands clasped in front of her, looking less at ease than he'd ever seen her.

Eberhard quirked a brow.

"Come here, Fraülein von Wedemeyer. I want you to meet someone." Dietrich motioned her forward.

Maria came to his side, a shy smile on her lips.

"Fraülein von Wedemeyer, this is Eberhard Bethge. Eberhard, this is Fraülein von Wedemeyer." Dietrich smiled as he made the introduction. He'd written Eberhard about Maria, but the two had never met. What would Eberhard think of her? Knowing his friend, Eberhard always had an opinion.

And it mattered that these two thought well of each other.

Mattered for reasons he hadn't fully ciphered out, yet existed nonetheless.

"It's a pleasure to make your acquaintance, Herr Bethge. Pastor Bonhoeffer has been telling me a great deal about you."

"That doesn't sound promising. Did I suffer much in the translation?" Eberhard cracked a droll grin.

"Well, that would be telling, wouldn't it?" Maria's smile held her former ease.

"I'll take *you* to task later." Eberhard flashed Dietrich a look of mock severity. "For now, let's join the others."

They entered the living room just as everyone applauded at the end of Renate's piece. Eberhard headed toward the piano. The gazes of the rest of the room swiveled in their direction. Maria stood at his side, her shoulder almost brushing his, smiling tentatively.

"Everyone, I'd like you to meet Frau von Kleist's granddaughter, Fraülein von Wedemeyer. I invited her to join us for the evening since she's staying with her grossmutter in Berlin."

The assembled guests offered smiles and curious glances. Dietrich's older brother, Klaus, and his wife, Emmi, with their children Walter, Thomas, and Cornelie. Hans and Christel, along with their young ones: fourteen-year-old Klaus; Christoph, a year younger; and their daughter, twelve-year-old Bärbel. Rüdiger and Ursula, with their son, Hans-Walter, sitting beside them in uniform, a pretty young lady in the chair nearest to him. Their daughter, Renate, remained on the piano bench, Eberhard at her side.

"Welcome." Ursula hurried across the room, greeting Maria with a warm smile. "We're very glad you could come. Any friend of Dietrich's is a friend of ours."

"Danke schön. It's lovely to meet you."

"Where are Mutter and Vater?" Dietrich asked.

"They're a bit under the weather this evening. Vater thinks he's catching a cold, so they decided to stay home tonight. I took them over dinner a half hour ago." Ursula tucked behind her ear a wisp of gray-streaked hair that had escaped from its old-fashioned bun.

"I didn't know. I'm sorry to hear that." Dietrich tried to hide his disappointment. He'd wanted them to meet Maria, particularly his mutter. And the next time the family met together, Maria would likely be gone.

Hans unfolded his lanky form from his place on the sofa beside his wife and joined Ursula. "Very glad you could come, Fraülein von Wedemeyer." He offered a friendly but tired smile. With all the hours Hans put in at the Abwehr, it was a surprise his brother-in-law had been able to make the party at all.

If only Dietrich could be of more use. If only the currency issues didn't cast his name under suspicion at the moment, since he'd had a hand in procuring the passports for Operation 7. Were there any updates? He'd see if he could find a quiet moment alone with Hans later in the evening.

"Please, do come in and sit down, the both of you." Ursula motioned to a pair of empty chairs near the piano. "Eberhard and Renate are about to perform a duet. We never miss an opportunity to make music together, Fraülein von Wedemeyer. Dietrich is particularly good on the piano."

Maria tilted her head toward him. "I had the pleasure of hearing him play at Klein-Krössin. Both my grossmutter and I were quite impressed." Sudden sadness crossed her gaze.

When they'd been together at Klein-Krössin, her vater had still been alive.

The look vanished almost as quickly as it had come, as Maria listened to Ursula. As if she determined to remain cheerful by sheer force of will. A remarkable trait. He admired it.

They found their seats. Christel shushed everyone as Eberhard and Renate began to play, Eberhard on the flute, Renate at the piano. Music filled the room with strains of joy, each note a permission for everyone to think of nothing but the piece, dwell on no thought but that of melody and harmony. Even Hans relaxed, slipping his arm around Christel. Tall and earnest in his uniform, young Hans-Walter shared a smile with the girl at his side.

The Bonhoeffer family. Only a quorum tonight, but a family was still a family, even if parts were missed. Each individual couple a unit by themselves, but nothing compared to having them all together, men, women, children, united by blood, and something even stronger.

Love.

Dietrich glanced at his friend accompanying his niece on the piano. How fast time flew. It seemed like only yesterday Renate was a little girl in pigtails, running helter-skelter with her brother. Tonight, a poised young lady with pinned up hair sat elegantly on the bench. Renate glanced up at Eberhard, smiling as she played.

A look Dietrich had not noticed before passed between them.

Hmm. What have we here?

He turned to Maria, sitting at his side, a rapt expression on her face as she listened to the music. For years, he'd been the odd man out at family gatherings. All of his brothers and sisters had spouses. No matter that they always integrated easily with the rest, there was a certain separation that came with being a couple. One always knew whom they would sit beside at dinner. Whom they would partner at games, or play music with. Dietrich had never lacked friends, but when it came to family parties, he arrived by himself, and left the same way.

Tonight, he wasn't alone.

An almost irresistible urge to take Maria's hand overwhelmed him.

Eberhard and Renate finished the piece with a flourish. Everyone broke into applause. Eberhard took Renate's hand and lifted her to her feet. Hands joined, they took an over-dramatic bow, laughing.

"You played that piece beautifully, both of you," Ursula said when everyone had finished clapping.

Renate gathered her music. "Eberhard's been an excellent teacher."

Eberhard? Dietrich gave his niece a wondering glance. She'd always called him by the honorary title of Uncle Eberhard, like the other children.

"You really were excellent, Fraülein Schleicher," Maria said.

"Oh, please do call me Renate." Music in hand, Renate crossed to Maria's side.

"Then you must call me Maria. How long have you been playing the piano? I must admit to possessing little musical ability and always admire it when I hear others excel."

"Well, while you two share your entire life stories, I'm starving." Hans-Walter, the picture of vital young manhood, stretched out his long legs and winked at the girl next to him. "Dare I hope you made *apfelkuchen*, Mutter?"

"There's a large plateful in the dining room. I've been saving coupons for weeks." Ursula stood. "If everyone would like to go in, we'll have refreshments and more music afterward."

Dietrich stood and crossed to say a few words to the Dohnanyi children, while Maria chatted with Renate. When he returned to her side after the youngsters had scampered off in search of *kuchen*, he found the room empty save her. Ankles crossed, she sat in her chair, as if waiting for him.

"Aren't you hungry?" He smiled down at her.

"Not very. I'd much rather sit and talk to you." A flush suffused her cheeks.

"Then you're in luck, Fraülein von Wedemeyer, because I'd rather be with you too." Where was this coming from? That smile, his almost . . . playful tone. This was a Dietrich Bonhoeffer even he himself hadn't known existed, buried beneath the layers of scholarly theologian, weary double agent.

"Ursula won't think we're impolite?" A wrinkle knit her brow.

"With that crowd to contend with?" He laughed. "She won't even miss us."

For a moment, they sat in comfortable silence. Laughter and conversation drifted in from the dining room. Throw pillows rested askew on the two sofas, family pictures held pride of place on end tables. It wasn't a showpiece room, but a lived-in one. One that had seen many a cozy, family evening, with furniture that wasn't immune to children's messes and a broken lamp that someone had tried to glue back together with mixed success.

Would he ever have such a room, such a family? A houseful of noisy, mischievous children? A wife?

"Hans-Walter looks very fine in his uniform," she said at last.

"*Ja*, he does." Something about her voice . . . She wasn't merely making conversation.

"Seeing him dressed so reminded me of Max." Wistfulness filled her eyes. As if she saw not Dietrich, but the beloved brother off fighting for the Fatherland. "Why do you think Hans-Walter is joining up? Is it because he has to, or because he really believes in what he's fighting for?"

Who wasn't asking such questions? The foolish, perhaps. Those cheering for victory and signing up to fight simply because they were told to. But the wise, they were the ones grappling. Asking what a Christian ought to do when love for the gospel conflicts with a tragically compromised government, when crossing that government can lead one down an irrevocable path paved in sacrifice.

Forcing one to make the greatest of sacrifices, if need be.

Dietrich had chosen one path. Maria's vater and brother another. Both sought to make the right, the good, choice.

Dietrich weighed his words carefully. "I think in our country it's a long-held tradition that young men volunteer for military service, even lay down their lives for a cause of which they might not approve at all." He'd lived through the Great War; his older brother Walter had died fighting for Germany. He knew firsthand the horrors that ensued when one's country was plunged into all-encompassing conflict. Starvation. Fear. Grief. The shock of losing a family member . . . like having a part of oneself cut off.

"Vater didn't approve of the Führer and his war. Nor Max. They both went because it was the expected thing and hoped they might be able to serve their country in some way. Were they right?" Her tone was that of a mature woman, her eyes those of a little girl. Struggling, as he had so often done, with questions vast and far reaching.

He drew in a measured breath. "I think the question of 'right' can only be answered by the individual who throws themselves entirely upon the mercy of God. No institution or organization can make a choice of conscience for another human being." The Führer, in all his misplaced arrogance, had forced upon many what few, if they truly searched within themselves, wanted.

"And what does *your* conscience tell you?" Her clear gaze probed deep within him.

Maria had spoken boldly.

Dear God, what should I tell her?

He'd become far too adept at concealment, even with many of his formerly closest friends. It was better to let them speculate, than to endanger them, or himself, with the truth. He'd forfeited relationships because of this. Staunch members of the Confessing Church who thought he'd turned traitor because he worked for Intelligence. He'd accepted the loss as part and parcel of the sacrifice God had called him to make. But it still wounded.

Did Maria already know about the conspiracy? After all, two of her relatives, Henning von Tresckow and Fabian von Schlabrendorff, were deeply involved, even more entrenched than he. But her vater hadn't participated. And Max, though a reluctant soldier and doubtless serving only to avoid the penalty of conscientious objection, still fought on the front lines for Germany.

Dietrich believed he did too. For a future Germany, one where tyranny no longer held sway, where a dictator no longer grasped the reins. A repentant Germany. They couldn't move forward without repentance.

To Maria, he'd reveal some. Just enough. A thin and dangerous line to walk, but it was worth it to answer her question.

"There must also be people willing to fight from conviction alone. If they approve of the grounds for war, well and good. If not, they can best serve by fighting on a different front, in a different way. Perhaps . . . perhaps"—he swallowed—"even by working against the regime."

There. It was out. He'd given her something rarer than rare these days. The truth. She nodded, seemed to be absorbing his words. He'd been right to trust her; he sensed it in her eyes, understanding filling their cobalt depths.

"It would then, I think, be the task of those people to avoid serving in the Wehrmacht for as long as possible," she said slowly.

Remarkable. The daughter of a fallen Prussian officer speaking thus. There could be no doubt that she was Ruth von Kleist's granddaughter through and through and her own person altogether.

"Even taking a stand as a conscientious objector." Thankfully, because his Abwehr status deemed him "performing essential work," he hadn't been forced to come to that decision. The penalty for conscientious objection was severe—deportation to a work camp or outright execution.

She drew in a ragged breath, gaze on her clasped hands. "When you speak like that, it's so logically clear and obvious. But when I think of Vater . . ."

He nearly reached out, placed his hand over hers.

As if by the joining of their hands, they could together dispel all questions and confusions.

Brisk footsteps that could only belong to one of his sisters sounded in the hall. Maria lifted her gaze, put on a smile.

Christel came inside, arms folded, dark hair escaping from its upswept pins. "So this is where you two are hiding?"

Dietrich stood with half a smile. He'd known some curious family member would come in search of them. "You know me. Always hiding."

"And you've exiled Fräulein von Wedemeyer in here with you. For shame! Come into the dining room, both of you." She clapped her hands together. "You've been in here with this young lady quite long enough." Christel's face remained inexpressive, though Dietrich read a glimmer of amusement in her eyes.

"I do apologize." Maria's words tumbled over each other. "We got to talking and—"

"Not your fault at all, I'm sure. I know what it's like when one gets to talking with Dietrich." Christel and Dietrich shared a smile born of having grown up together.

"Come then, Fräulein von Wedemeyer. If Hans-Walter hasn't already eaten all the *kuchen*, we should be able to find some for us." Dietrich held out his hand. She placed hers in it, and he helped her to her feet. They hadn't finished their conversation, but it could wait.

Together, they followed Christel into the dining room for Hans-Walter's send-off to a war better lost than won.

The last *gute Nacht* echoing behind them, Maria fell into step beside Pastor Bonhoeffer as they left the Schleichers'. The past hour had been *apfelkuchen*, laughter, and music. A send-off for a boy who'd soon become a man.

The streets were empty at this hour, most preferring to stay inside rather than walk thoroughfares under blackout conditions. A few stars scattered across the fast-fading sky, pinholes of light stark against a backdrop of encroaching darkness. Stillness wrapped around them, broken only by their footfalls and the rumble of a motorcar somewhere far away.

Maria tilted her head to meet Pastor Bonhoeffer's gaze and found it already fixed on her. She smiled slightly, face flushing under his scrutiny, grateful for the almost darkness. Several times, she'd noticed his eyes upon her throughout the evening, as if he were seeing her for the first time. She couldn't help but wonder at it, marvel at his attentiveness. Marvel at so many things about him.

"It was a fine evening," he said quietly. He walked beside her, hands within his pockets, his shoulder almost, but not quite, brushing against hers.

"*Ja.*" She nodded. "Danke. For asking me to come."

"My pleasure." He smiled, creases forming around the corners of his eyes.

Their earlier conversation, broken off by Christel, filled her mind. She swallowed, the question inside her begging to be asked. His words about choosing not to serve in the Wehrmacht had given her a good deal to think about. But there was much he'd *not* said.

He placed a steadying hand on her arm as they turned down the next street. The total blackout imposed upon the city had made walking increasingly hazardous, despite the white paint on curbs, crosswalks, and intersections, making her more grateful than ever that she wasn't out at night alone.

"May I ask you something?" Wind stirred her hair around her cheeks. She tucked the strands behind her ear, looking up at him.

"Of course," he answered without hesitation.

She drew in a breath, letting the words come before she lost the courage to voice them. "How dangerous is it . . . for you?"

He seemed to start, as if taken aback. They kept walking, their steps shrinking the distance to Tante Spes's house. Silence hung between them, the air taking on that breathless quality it owns before the sky lets down a storm.

She shouldn't have asked that question. She wasn't entitled to an answer. They knew each other so little, yet the hours that lay between them seemed to encompass the space of years. As if they'd always been part of each other's lives.

Minutes passed without either speaking. She tried to read his expression, but he kept his face straight ahead, head slightly bent as if averted from her. Ought she to apologize?

"War brings danger to us all. Me as much as the rest." He looked at her for the first time since she'd asked the question, his face shadowed in the waning light.

They'd reached Tante Spes's street. He stopped near the side of a building. A drop of something cool and wet splashed her hair, followed by more in quick succession. Rain. Without warning, it came loose from the sky and fell upon them. But instead of taking cover, neither of them moved. She stood against the building, her back almost touching the bricks. His hands framed her shoulders, the touch light, but somehow intimate. She tilted her chin, heedless of the rain streaming from the sky.

"But yours is a different kind of danger, isn't it?" She scarcely noticed the cold, the warmth of his hands leaving room for little else.

He nodded. Sighed. "One all the more serious."

It was true then. Dietrich Bonhoeffer was part of the *Widerstand*. A resistance. A conspiracy. His words confirmed what she'd already suspected.

"What times in which we live," she said softly, the rain capturing her words. "So much at stake. So many things to consider. If only things were clearer, surer. When I was a child, everything seemed so . . . simple. But nothing is certain."

His hands fell from her shoulders, but he didn't step away. "Nothing was ever meant to be. Except God."

"Then how is one to face the future?" Rain cleansed the air, washing away the scents of a Berlin weary with war.

"With faith. Moment by moment."

"You live like that, don't you, Dietrich Bonhoeffer?" Her hair brushed her shoulders in damp strands, the bricks rough against the small of her back. Berlin in the middle of a rainstorm had never seemed so empty.

Her heart, so full.

"As much as I'm able." His earnest gaze met hers. His nearness, the simplicity and complication of this moment, sent a melee of emotions flooding her.

A smile traced her lips. "But you've never run in the rain." Her words came almost as a breath. "And there are other things you haven't felt, have never done. I can sense it when I look at you. Why?"

"Perhaps it's never been the right time. Or perhaps . . ." He left the sentence unfinished. His hesitancy emboldened her.

"The right time, Pastor Bonhoeffer, is always now. For living." She reached for his hand, twining their fingers together. "And for running in the rain. Come on."

As their mingled laughter blended with rainfall and footsteps, a breathless, bittersweet thought whispered through her mind.

There will never again be a night like this.

October 25, 1942
Franciscan Hospital, Berlin

Though the Gestapo had forbidden him from preaching, they'd said nothing about Sunday morning devotions beside Ruth von Kleist's hospital bed. And Dietrich enjoyed being able to preach again. Even if it was only to an audience of two—an elderly woman with bandaged eyes and her granddaughter, who sat beside the bed on a straight-backed chair, a Bible in her lap, gaze fixed intently on him.

With those Danube-blue eyes upon him, his mind took on the muddled consistency of congealed porridge. Amazing he could concentrate, to compile his thoughts enough to expound on Ephesians 5:15–21. He tore his focus away from Maria and turned instead to Ruth and his notes to finish out the sermon. He'd already been interrupted twice by nurses checking on Ruth—not the easiest way to preach.

"Always, we must be careful to give thanks for all things. Anything we do not thank God for, we reproach Him for. It's the mark of a true disciple of Christ when we're able to fully say with our whole heart and self, 'Not my will, but Thine be done.' In our own strength, we'll fall back on delusion—telling ourselves we are doing just that, while inwardly complaining about our lot and wishing it different. As we inquire the will of God, free from all doubt and mistrust, we shall discover it, and in the midst of that discovery realize the weakness of our own wants and desires in comparison with the superiority of His." He turned to Ruth. "We could end with a song. Are there any you know by heart?"

"I think I could manage 'A Mighty Fortress Is Our God,'" Ruth answered, her tone strong, despite how weak she appeared, swathed in white bandages covering her eyes and most of her face.

"All right. From the top then."

A mighty Fortress is our God,
A Bulwark never failing;

Our Helper He amid the flood
Of mortal ills prevailing.

Despite her weakened state, Ruth sang out loud and clear. Yet it was Maria's alto that caught Dietrich's attention and held it, as they went into the next verse. No one listening would have called her singing accomplished, yet the smile tugging the corners of her mouth and the rapt energy she gave to the song lent it a vitality lacking in many far more proficient. She sang, not in a way attempting to impress, but as if she truly meant the words. Their voices blended together, his and hers, in a joining greater than the simple meeting of melody and harmony. She met his gaze, held it in that direct way she had.

Music had played a part in many of his experiences. The song he'd performed for Walter the last night he'd spent with his brother before the lad— his brother had been so young—went off to fight in the Great War. The African spirituals that had so revitalized his discipleship journey during his year in America. The musical evenings with his family where they gathered under the guise of entertainment, plotted conspiracy to the notes of a Beethoven sonata.

From this day forward, until the Lord chose to call him homeward, this ancient Luther hymn would hold a special place in the annals of his heart and mind. They'd sung it together—united.

Oh, that they could be so in more ways than this.

The final verse ended. Dietrich concluded their small service with prayer, remembering the Wedemeyers and Kleists, the Bonhoeffers, those imprisoned for standing with the Confessing Church, and ending with a petition for those who, in the midst of this madness, sought God's will for their lives. Ruth and Maria echoed *amen.*

Was he mistaken, or did the young woman brush away a tear when she lifted her head?

If only he could do more to ease her sorrow. If only her vater had not been snatched from this earth. If only . . .

But God did not permit *if onlys.*

"Maria, would you go and ask the nurse if there's any tea to be had? I find I'm thirsty after all the singing." Ruth turned her head slightly in her granddaughter's direction.

"Of course." Maria stood and hastened from the room. As she passed, a trace of lavender filled his senses, lingering after she closed the door.

Dietrich moved his chair closer to Ruth's hospital bed.

"That was a splendid sermon, Dietrich. As always."

Had Ruth the benefit of sight, he would have responded with a shrug. Compliments always made him uncomfortable.

"I'm glad you enjoyed it," he answered.

"I think Maria did too." Ruth smoothed a pale hand down the front of her blanket. "You've been spending a lot of time with Maria. It's been good for her to have your company."

He smiled. "It's been a pleasure."

"She's grown into quite the young woman, has she not? Quite removed from the little sprite who used to play helter-skelter in my gardens." A fond smile creased Ruth's wrinkled cheeks.

"Not entirely removed, I think. She still possesses the same enthusiasm for life, completely lacking in artifice or pretense." Dietrich fixed his gaze on the bare hospital wall across from him, avoiding looking at Ruth, his own mind filled with memories of the moments they'd spent racing to her aunt's house, carefree as children. It had been a unique moment, a rarity for a man who'd traveled to half a dozen countries in his thirty-six years. A moment of freedom. Of being simply . . . alive.

"Admirable qualities. Most of the time." Ruth laughed. "I take it you admire many of her qualities." Her tone changed, turned almost probing. "She'd make you a fine wife, Dietrich. Despite the difference in your ages, your personalities suit each other well."

Wife. That word, like a chunk of flaming flak, slammed against him.

Dietrich held up a hand. "You can't be serious." *Ja*, in his innermost thoughts, he'd imagined her as his wife. Secretly, guiltily, like a little boy clutching fast to a treasure he knows his mutter will forbid him to keep. But he'd never even come close to sharing any of this with Maria.

"I'm perfectly serious." Ruth's tone couldn't have made her intentions any more clear. "Why do you think I've taken so many naps in the afternoons when you've been expected to visit? I'm not *that* old and weary."

Dietrich drew in a calming breath. He'd been friends with Ruth a long time. She was a strong-willed woman, but she'd never before manifested it quite like this.

"Please, Frau von Kleist, don't mention this to me again." He kept his tone firm. "I have a high regard for your granddaughter, it's true. But what you speak of . . . it's out of the question." Completely so. His dreams about Maria could extend no further than the recesses of his mind. In that realm, they would, must, remain. She was too young, his work for the Abwehr too dangerous. He couldn't ask her to share his lot if the worst befell him— imprisonment, even execution. He cared about her too much to subject her to that.

He cared about her, and so he must forget her.

The door opened. Maria stepped in, bearing a small tray. Dietrich stood, nearly knocking over his chair.

"I've brought tea." She beamed. He forced himself to look away from her smile. Too much radiance could inflict burns not easily salved.

"Danke, Maria."

"I'm afraid I must be going." Dietrich headed for the door. In light of Ruth's words, he couldn't remain here any longer.

"Show him out, Maria," Ruth directed calmly, as if, though she couldn't see, she nonetheless sensed the tempest their conversation had brewed inside him.

Maria followed him to the door, heels clicking across the hard hospital floor. He couldn't look at her. Physically, she wasn't what most would call startlingly beautiful. But she'd become that to him in a thunderbolt of time. So beautiful, in every way . . .

So unattainable for too many reasons.

"Auf Wiedersehen, Fraülein von Wedemeyer." His mind ordered him to utter the words, proper, polite, ever the pastor. But his heart, that renegade organ of fancy and feeling, beat with one refrain.

When shall I see her again?

War brought with it no certainties. None.

"Auf Wiedersehen, Pastor Bonhoeffer." Confusion flickered in her eyes. As if she wondered at the sudden change in him. For an instant, he almost wished her open nature would enable her to ask him why. But she said not a word. And he didn't trust himself to speak.

With a forced smile and nod, he let himself out. With determined strides, his feet ate up the space between Ruth's room and the front door. The faces of nurses and visitors blurred. His shoes squeaked on the linoleum floor. He was nearly there. Away from this hospital and the matchmaking Frau von Kleist and the woman whose presence made him feel things that could only cause pain.

He halted. The texts. He'd forgotten his notebook and Bible. Had it been another item, he would've just left it until later. But both books were among his most prized possessions, and he'd need them before the day was out. He had to go back.

He turned and traversed the path he'd just retreated. He stared at the door, the last place he wanted to enter. Or was it the first? The place he most wanted to be.

Ja. And for that very reason it was the last place he should be. Reluctantly, he knocked.

Seconds passed. Maria opened the door. She met his eyes, without speaking. "Why are you back," her gaze seemed to ask, "when you were so obviously eager to be rid of us?"

"My books." He stammered out the words. "I forgot them."

Wordlessly, she turned back into the room. With each step, her skirt swished, just a little, her steps even, shoulders straight. Her hair gleamed like honey in the morning light.

His throat went dry. He stared instead at his polished shoes against the backdrop of the linoleum. Stood there, head down, like a misbehaving child. She had reduced him to this.

"Here."

He looked up. She passed him the books. Their fingers brushed, her skin soft as summer twilight, just as warm. He took a step back, singed.

"Danke, Fraülein von Wedemeyer," he said quietly.

She nodded, didn't smile.

The door shut, stealing her from view.

Wood and metal. That's all it was. An inanimate object.

Yet so much more remained to separate them.

Chapter Twelve

Chill air seeped through her bedclothes, startling Maria awake. She shifted on the mattress, tugging the covers up to her chin. Early morning had always been her favorite time of day. It struck her as peaceful, hallowed, when nature woke, and humans remained hushed. A time for contemplation and Scripture reading. When her solitary thoughts could take priority over everything else.

This morning, she had plenty of those.

A change had taken place in Pastor Bonhoeffer when she'd returned with Grossmutter's tea. Or perhaps she'd just imagined it. How she'd wanted to speak to him, to tell him how his sermon profoundly affected her. But when she'd escorted him to the door, she'd been too tongue-tied to utter a word, and he'd looked as if he wished only to be gone. It had been such a confusing, muddled moment, and she'd probably behaved badly.

This morning, she was to pay one last visit to Grossmutter, who would be released before the end of the week, then begin the long journey back to the Vogel house. She'd enjoyed Berlin far more than she expected. The time spent with Grossmutter.

The visits with Pastor Bonhoeffer.

Maria pressed her hands to her cheeks, as if to stem the sudden rush of heat there.

He inspired something inside her. Something too powerful to dismiss, much as she tried. As if the both of them, despite all their outward differences, were two halves of the same whole. When he fixed his eyes upon her, as if she and she alone were the only thing worth gazing at, she couldn't deny the—

Downstairs, the telephone rang.

Maria sat up with a start. It couldn't be above seven. Her feet landed on the cold floor. Who could be calling at this hour? She grabbed her well-worn dressing gown and slid her arms through the sleeves. Had something happened to Grossmutter?

Out of her bedroom, down the hall and stairs. Every step made goose-flesh prickle her bare legs. The telephone continued to ring, each note jarring the stillness like a slap.

Tante Spes and her cousins probably hadn't stirred. If the call concerned them, Maria would have to waken them—not a task she welcomed.

The telephone sat on a table in the dining room, surrounded by bric-a-brac, Tante Spes's china collection in a well-stocked cabinet beside it. Maria wrapped the dressing gown tighter around her waist and picked up the receiver, careful not to jar any of the ornaments.

"Hello."

"Spes?" Mutter's voice—the crackly connection making it sound like she called from the opposite side of the earth.

"Nein, Mutter. It's Maria. Tante Spes is asleep." Why would Mutter think Maria was her aunt? They didn't sound anything alike.

The floor drove icy prickles into her toes.

"I've just received a letter." The connection sounded muffled, broken. Or was it her mutter's voice?

"I can't hear you, Mutter. Could you speak a bit louder?"

Footsteps sounded just behind her, too lumbering to be anyone's other than her aunt's. Maria turned. Tante Spes, curling papers splayed atop her head, a woolen sweater partially covering her thin nightdress, rubbed sleep from her eyes.

"Who's on the phone?" she mouthed.

"Mutter," Maria whispered. She turned back to the phone. "Sorry. Tante Spes just came down."

Silence met her ears. Not a comfortable, everything is all right, kind of silence, but a quiet that seemed to shriek. To shatter.

Max.

Her heart beat hard inside her chest like a prisoner scrambling for freedom. Air seemed poised to leave her lungs. She forced her voice to cooperate.

"Is it Max?" It was. Eerily, she sensed it. He'd been wounded. Only wounded. An arm or leg lost, but he'd come back to them. She'd stay by his side day and night, do everything to—

"He's dead, Maria. Our Max is dead."

She closed her eyes, the room, everything vanishing, leaving a black, gaping abyss that gulped her in. If only it would close around her completely, drown her in blackness. Anything to forget. Anything to disappear.

"I can't believe it." Her hands tightened almost painfully around the receiver. "I won't believe it." There had to be some mistake. Her brave Max with his laughing gaze and adventurous spirit was alive. He had to be. Only yesterday, she'd shut her eyes and lifted her face to the sky, keeping their appointed time. The space of minutes when both of them turned their faces toward the clouds and thought of the other. Smiled to know they both were together, though separated.

Max might be missing. Even wounded.

But he would come home. He must. She needed him. Without Vater, she needed him more than ever.

"I'm so sorry." Mutter wept, the agony of her sobs audible, even across the distance. "They said he died bravely. Until the last, he sought to inspire his unit by personal example."

Of course he did. Max would do no less. He'd taught her never to be afraid, not atop a horse at the age of five. Not of doctors' visits or of going away alone to boarding school.

Chin up and smile, Sister mine.

Brittle words without Max's presence to back them up.

"As soon as I can, I'll be home. Do you want to talk to Tante Spes?" She couldn't manage more. Just handed the phone to her wide-eyed aunt and fled the room like a coward. The frigid floor no longer mattered. Nor did the throb in her toe when it smacked against the edge of the stair. Already, she was numb all over.

She slammed and locked her bedroom door with shaking hands. Her feet gave out from under her and she fell, face pressed against the floorboards.

Reality shouldn't exceed nightmares. But it had. Brutally. Death was for others, those who hadn't already suffered loss. It wasn't meant for Max, so young and strong and brave.

Why couldn't she have taken his place? She'd have done so gladly—given her life to save his.

"Anything we cannot thank God for, we reproach Him for."

"Nein!" The scream ripped from her lungs. "Nein, Nein, Nein." She pounded the floor until the skin tore from her knuckles, sobs wracking her body. If death possessed such a voracious appetite, why couldn't it devour them all? Why must it leave some—seemingly the most vulnerable—behind? It was the worst kind of cruelty, even worse than death itself.

Spent, she sagged against the floor. The last time they'd been together, Max had hugged her tight, promising to come home soon. She'd believed that promise. And almost hated him for lying, promising something he hadn't fulfilled.

A selfish thought, but she wouldn't take it back. Her brother was in heaven, leaving her on an earth where bombs fell, men died, and phone calls shattered hearts.

The sounds of early morning traffic drifted in. Berlin going about the business of living. Voices. The whir of an engine. A gentle tap against her door. Tante Spes's worried voice.

Somehow, some way she must pick herself up off the floor and pack her things. This loss wasn't suffered by her alone. Mutter and the children felt their own grief. She needed to make arrangements to return to Pätzig.

To a house shaken by sorrow a second time.

"Oh, Max," she whispered, the words scraping her raw throat. "Did I ever tell you how I loved you? I can't remember now. Why can't I remember?"

She stood, feet leaden, moving only by sheer force of will. She didn't want to get up. She wanted to crumple back on the floor and stay there. Breath still flowed in and out of her lungs, but inside her body felt as dead as Max's. Only the thought of her family forced her exhausted frame into submission.

Ignoring her aunt's continued knocking, she moved to the washbasin and splashed the coolness over her burning cheeks. The water trickled down her scraped knuckles, mingling with her tears, now falling silently. In these droplets of salt and water lay a thousand unsaid words. Ones she wished she could have said, even written, to Max. To Vater.

But it was too late.

Always too late.

October 31, 1942
Berlin

Raindrops pummeled the glass outside Dietrich's bedroom window. It had rained most of the morning—the sky above slate gray, droplets falling like hundreds of Allied bombs. It wasn't a soothing rain, the kind Maria loved, but an angry pelting. As if nature vented its own fury upon Germany for all their misdeeds.

Dietrich glared at the crumpled sheets of stationery littering his desk. Five, to be precise. Five attempts to compose on paper what he would struggle to say in person.

Max von Wedemeyer was dead. Max, who less than five brief years ago had been a bright, young confirmand in Dietrich's classes. Max, who had been the joy of his parents, a brilliant student. Max—Maria's adored brother.

Maria.

It was to her he attempted to write. Ruth had phoned, saying that Maria had gone home to Pätzig as soon as she'd received the news.

How could he find the words?

Dietrich pulled off his spectacles and set them beside his discarded attempts. Scrubbing a hand across his eyes, he heaved a sigh.

When would the carnage cease? How many more must give their lives before an end was reached? Hundreds? Thousands?

Maria's smile floated through his mind, the smile she'd worn when speaking of her brother. They'd obviously shared a special bond. One now severed, at least in this life.

Dietrich stared out at the mottled glass. Losing a vater was heartache enough, but now a brother too? Longing rose within him. To see her, hold her close, ease her sorrow in any way he could.

He couldn't bring her brother back, but he could comfort her while she wept.

But he couldn't simply race off to Pomerania. Not when Hans had instructed him to remain in Berlin, at the ready in case it was deemed safe for a renewal of travel plans. So Dietrich must content himself with what he had—a blank sheet of stationery and a ready pen. Use these inanimate objects to the best of his ability to share what lay within his heart.

Winging a silent prayer for wisdom heavenward, he donned his spectacles and picked up the pen.

> *Dear Fraülein von Wedemeyer,*
>   *If I might be allowed to say only this to you, I believe I have an inkling of what Max's death means for you.*
>   *It can scarcely help to tell you I too share in this pain.*
>   *At such times it can only help us to cast ourselves upon the heart of God, not with words but truly and entirely. This requires many difficult hours, day and night, but when we have let go entirely into God—or better, when God has received us—then we are helped. "Weeping may linger for the night, but joy comes in the morning" (Psalm 30:5). There really is joy with God, with Christ! Do believe it.*

He added a few more lines, finishing with:

*May God work miracles in you, in those you love, in us all during these
days, and strengthen us for the life and work to which we return for
God's glory. Please greet your grossmutter in particular once more.*
  In heartfelt communion,
  Your faithfully devoted Dietrich Bonhoeffer

He stared down at what he'd written. Out of the five attempts, it was
the best, and the one he would send. Suitable enough that if her mutter or
the children read it, they'd not think it anything more than a kind pastor
writing to a family friend.

Right now, Maria's state of mind was in no condition to dwell upon
what—if indeed anything—had transpired between them.

He folded the letter and slid it inside an envelope. Sealing it gave him a
feeling of finality, but also of inadequacy. It wasn't enough. Could letters
ever be in such cases?

He penned the address, added a stamp, and swept the evidence of his
other attempts into the wastebasket. Hopefully, Lotte wouldn't take it into
her head to uncrumple and read them.

Sliding the letter into his jacket pocket, he descended the stairs, just as
the front door opened, and Hans—drenched from head to foot—burst in,
bringing a blast of bitter air with him. In appearance, his brother-in-law
looked as he always did, the same dark blue coat and gray fedora. But his
eyes gave Dietrich pause, sent a bolt of adrenaline through his veins. His
eyes bordered on frantic.

Casting a glance behind and around him, Hans yanked his dripping hat
from his head.

"Schmidhuber's been arrested."

Wilhelm Schmidhuber. The man highest on the suspect list for smuggling the currency needed to provide living expenses for their Operation
7 Jews in Switzerland. The Gestapo probably suspected the man of money
laundering, little knowing that their reasons for moving the funds had
nothing to do with avarice and everything to do with rescuing the people at risk of ruthless extermination. But though their motives hadn't been
found out, the Gestapo would dig. Question. No high-profile arrest ever
took place without an interrogation. When the time came for Schmidhuber,
would the man be able to refrain from mentioning Dietrich's and Hans's
names? Unlikely. The Gestapo were nothing if not thorough. Like a house-
wife making orange juice, they'd push and squeeze with ruthless abandon.

Turn him to pulp if necessary.

It was less a question of if and more a question of when the turn would come for the rest of them. They could only continue to gather evidence, contact enemy governments for so long. Already, they flirted with discovery on a daily basis.

Unless the Third Reich could be done away with first.

"Where has he been taken?"

"Gestapo headquarters Prinz-Albrecht-Strasse," Hans muttered.

Dread punched him low. Unearthly screams were said to echo from that place as victims were subjected to torture that had been honed to a science. Stepped-up questioning, the Gestapo called it.

Stepped-up to diabolical proportions.

"You're dripping all over the floor, Hans," Dietrich said quietly. "Let me help you off with your things, and you can sit down. You look in need of a rest."

Hans cracked a dry smile, as if Dietrich had just uttered the joke of the week. "Sit? When have I last had time for that? Nein, I must return to the office. I just wanted to tell you, to prepare you." Intensity flashed in his eyes. "You know how bad things are getting. Already, there's no doubt my correspondence is monitored, my telephone tapped . . ." He paused, swallowing hard. "I fear for Christel, the children. You."

"Don't worry about me." Dietrich placed a hand on his brother-in-law's shoulder. "That should be the last thing on your mind."

Footsteps sounded on the upper level. Both of their gazes flashed upward, then back to each other again. Only Mutter moving about in her bedroom. Nothing more. This house was still safe from prowling Gestapo. At least for now.

"But I do worry. Though, if our . . . other plans could go through first, all might still be saved." At the mention of these other plans, a shudder seemed to pass through Hans.

"God already knows the future, even if we may not always know what the future holds." The resonance of the words whispered over him. The past and the future were not theirs to manipulate, but God's to control.

Did Maria take comfort in such assurances? Or did she wander alone in a forest of questions and fears?

"Auf Wiedersehen, Dietrich." Hans gave a slight smile. "We'll talk soon." He opened the door, closed it after him, disappearing into the world of rain and angry sky and a Berlin writhing under the jackboots of the Third Reich.

Dietrich stood alone in the hall, gaze fixated on the front door. Lightning flashed, illuminating the dim house for less than an instant. Lightning. The prelude to thunder. The herald of a storm.

Was Schmidhuber's arrest the herald—the lightning—to their own storm? Or had that moment occurred the day Adolf Hitler first grasped power with both hands? Perhaps when Dietrich's radio broadcast, denouncing leaders who placed themselves above God, had been cut off midstream, a mere two days after the Führer's appointment to chancellor? Or when he'd first joined the Abwehr, helped with the plotting of Operation 7?

Whatever the date and time, they'd taken a hit today through Schmidhuber's seizure by the Gestapo. For now, they were still safe. Outwardly, at least.

Dietrich stared up at the ceiling, just as thunder growled, shaking the house.

Chapter Thirteen

Only work would keep her thoughts at bay. So Maria threw herself into her tasks with bruising vigor. She delivered food to those in the village suffering due to absent sons and vaters. Drilled her siblings in their studies. Cleaned the upstairs guest rooms that hadn't seen a duster or broom in ages. And every morning, she rose just as the first streaks of dawn tinted the sky, saddled her horse, and rode.

Only when she rode did she allow herself to think of Vater and Max—the ones who had taught her how to sit upon her horse, how to lead with the reins, how to jump without losing her seat. Both had schooled her in so much, these two men in her life. They'd shaped her, and oh, how willing she'd been to be molded.

Wind whipped her cheeks mercilessly. Her mount flew across fields, over hills, slackening its pace only when they entered the forest, their approach startling all manner of deer and birds. The ever-rising sun colored the sky, lending peach to the morning gray.

Maria drew up on the reins as they crested a hill, part of the acreage belonging to the estate. In a swift motion, she dismounted, swinging her trouser-clad legs over Sternenlicht's side, her boots sinking into the spongy ground.

Stillness. In her surroundings, in nature, in the absence of others. Even the birds had ceased their song.

Only in her heart did chaos reign.

In the week since she'd returned home, she'd avoided this very spot, though it had once been one of her favorites. Hers . . . and Max's.

On Max's last night before leaving to join his unit, they had come here. Twilight had dusted the sky, past time for returning inside. But still they lingered. Wind swept its sweet fragrance through their hair, across the hills.

"You're going tomorrow." Their horses munched on some low-growing foliage, and the two siblings stood, her hand around his arm as they faced the setting sun.

Max turned to her, blue-eyed gaze meeting blue-eyed gaze. A certain sadness, so out of character for her spirited brother, lingered around the edges of his eyes.

"And I'll come back." He spoke the words, fierce determination marking his handsome face. "It might not be for a while, but when I do, we'll come here again. Maybe then you'll not take so many tumbles off your horse." His smile revealed the gap between his two front teeth that his schoolmates had always teased him about. Whenever he'd relayed their antics to Maria, she'd itched to make the journey to his school, march inside, and inflict bodily harm upon the perpetrators—prevented only by the knowledge that if she did, Vater would shake his head and look sad.

Ignoring his remark about her riding abilities—she had, after all, fallen off eleven times in one day—she closed her fingers tighter around his arm. "Then I shan't visit here until you come back. I won't come here without you, Max."

"I won't come here without you, Max," she whispered into the silence, hugging her arms tight across her chest, fading memories replaced by the present. Betrayal, that's what being here alone was like. The breaking of a promise, the last one they'd ever made together. But she'd wanted to come, to feel close to him. Remember how he'd lifted her atop her horse as they prepared to return home, then snitched her hat and refused, laughing, to give it back. He'd never returned it, though it had been her favorite. Had he taken it with him to the front?

If she could only see him once more, tell him she didn't care whether he took her hat or anything else of hers, tell him she hadn't really minded his constant teasing. Tell him . . . oh . . .

She let her face fall into her hands, tears sliding down her knuckles, shoulders shaking. Mutter and her siblings had wept from time to time as they'd shared some memory of Max or Vater. Maria had steeled herself, found some excuse to slip away. But here, away from everything, only God could see her cry.

Finally, she lifted her face, drying her eyes with the back of her sleeve— Max's old hunting jacket. She'd taken to wearing it on her morning rides, the worn fabric on her shoulders almost as if he were somehow with her still.

"Guide me through this darkness, O Lord." She lifted her face to the sky as the sun continued to rise, the evidence of dawn and a new day all around her. "In You, there is still light."

The suffocating weight against her chest lessened some as she rode back to the house. Not completely, not even by half, but enough that she could freely breathe again, the fresh scents of dew and autumn wind filling her lungs with sweetness. Sternenlicht's hooves crunched the gravel as they made their way down the avenue toward the manor house. A sight near the front steps stopped her short. Mutter? Why was she awake at this hour?

Maria dismounted, holding her horse's reins loosely in one hand. The sight of her in baggy riding clothes, hair tousled, would only confirm Mutter's opinion of her as too wild for her own good. But perhaps, since Max's and Vater's deaths, such things didn't matter as much as they once had.

"*Guten Morgen.*" Maria tucked a wisp of hair behind her ear. "Why are you up so early?"

Mutter wrapped sweater-clad arms around her waist. In the gray light of morning, her face suddenly looked aged, as if lines that had not been there before had suddenly sketched themselves across her features.

"Waiting for you." A smile touched her lips. "You've been so busy of late, we haven't even spoken of your time in Berlin."

Those quiet days in the hospital, the hours spent with Pastor Bonhoeffer, that twilight walk to the Schleichers' when she'd teased him about running in the rain . . . They'd happened, but had it only been a few scant days ago? Years seemed to have elapsed since then.

"She did well. The operation was taxing, but she rallied, as she always does. I read to her, and we talked. It was mostly uneventful." Maria trained her gaze on the stone walls, the gardens nearby, sparse with winter's approach. Now that Vater wasn't here, she'd need to assist the gardener, prepare for spring . . .

"That must have been dull for you."

"We had visitors, from time to time. Some of Grossmutter's Berlin friends came by." Maria cast a critical eye over the shrubbery.

"When I talked to her over the phone, she mentioned her friend Pastor Bonhoeffer had been coming around quite often. That the two of you went to lunch and to visit his family." Mutter's gaze delved deep. As if she sought something. Though why would she be interested in the time Maria had spent with a friend of the family?

"We did. He thought I should get outside in the fresh air. It was very kind of him to be so thoughtful." Even now, the memory of his thoughtfulness sent warmth through her like the presence of a fire on a winter day.

"It was. I worried about you alone in Berlin. It's strange, though, for him to have so much free time on his hands." The rest went unspoken: *when most able men of his age are fighting and dying at the front.*

"He's not idle." Why did the need to defend him rise within her? She didn't know the answer, but the desire was there, suddenly. Almost beyond her control. "He works for Military Intelligence. He can't say a lot about what he does." He'd probably told her too much. But that he'd trusted her enough to do so sent more warmth traveling over her. "He writes a great deal. Right now, he's in the midst of a project about Christian ethics."

"Though he's been forbidden to publish anything? Why does he bother writing?"

Maria suppressed a sigh. This was how all of their conversations went. Why they tended to disagree upon so much was a question beyond her reckoning. She'd rarely quarreled with Vater. But it would be foolish to revert to old patterns now, dishonoring almost to Vater and Max.

"You ought to ask him that." She kept her tone measured. "I should wash and dress before breakfast. I have a busy day ahead." Reins still in hand, she led Sternenlicht in the direction of the stables.

Mutter's questions about Pastor Bonhoeffer were pointless. They would have no cause to meet for the foreseeable future. Right now, she must fix her mind on work and strive, with everything in her, to move forward in a way that would make the two men lost to her proud.

November 9, 1942
Berlin

"Why?" The whispered word shattered the stillness in the Bonhoeffer parlor.

Dietrich glanced at his mutter, grooves of pain evident in her face. It was not a question asked in naiveté, but from the disbelief of seeing horror played out before their very eyes.

"Can we do anything to stop it?" Vater stepped heavily away from the window and sank into a chair. Mutter joined him in the seat nearest.

"You know we can't bring suspicion upon ourselves now." Dietrich still stood at the window, peering through the curtain at the scene playing out two houses down, across the street.

Herr and Frau Gerstein, marched from their home just as twilight touched the sky. Two expressionless Gestapo prodded them with rifle butts, as the elderly couple struggled down the steps, each clutching a single suitcase. Dietrich tensed as Frau Gerstein tripped on the sidewalk, the petite woman in her late seventies fragile as a brittle twig. Herr Gerstein rushed to help his wife, but the guards shoved him away. Shoved away that immaculate gentleman who always had a tip of the hat to passersby, a courtly smile for the ladies.

The guards hustled them into the back seat of a car, first Frau Gerstein, then her husband. For an instant, the man stared across the street, directly at the Bonhoeffer house, eyes blank with terror. Was it Dietrich's imagination, or was the elderly man's hollow expression a plea? A cry? Moments later, he disappeared inside the car, the door slammed behind them.

Dietrich let the curtain fall.

"Why didn't we consider them for Operation 7?" Mutter asked, thin fingers twisting and untwisting the folds of her apron.

"Because we couldn't smuggle out more than fourteen. Even that was pushing it." Dietrich rubbed a hand over his jaw, a weight pressing against his chest. The Gersteins weren't even practicing Jews. Dietrich didn't know what religion they ascribed to. He hadn't really known the couple at all, since they'd moved to Charlottenburg when he'd been in America. But then his brother-in-law Gerhard and friend Franz Hildebrandt weren't practicing Jews either, and had they not escaped, the same fate would doubtless have awaited them.

It was blood. Blood and race. That was what the Nazis fed upon. The superior were permitted to live, the inferior, eliminated.

Vater nodded. Logically, they understood. It was human emotions they struggled with.

The day when the world ceased knowing that kind of feeling would be a tragic one.

"I'm going upstairs."

His parents sat motionless, as if weighted down by what they had seen. Dietrich left the room and climbed the steps.

There were a handful in Berlin—both Confessing Church members, and others who weren't religious, but acted out of conscience or to save friends and loved ones—who sheltered Jews, risking everything to do so. He'd gladly have opened their home to do the same.

But already, the Bonhoeffers were watched more carefully than most. Hans suspected he was being tailed. With their steep participation in the conspiracy, they couldn't risk the lives of Jewish families when and if the Gestapo discovered their plot and made arrests.

Again, logical.

But the faces of the Gersteins haunted. Even more so, since he knew their eventual destination. Their future fate.

Dietrich sat at his desk and picked up a fresh sheet of paper, staring down at the blank whiteness, turning over recent events. Hans and he had begun work on a set of falsified documents to have at the ready in case the worst happened. The Gestapo loved nothing more than to follow a paper trail, so Hans and he would give them one.

And then there was the war. The Allies had landed in North Africa, forcing the German army to retreat. Retreat was not a word Germans liked to hear, and the people began to complain about privations that had previously seemed their contribution to a grand and glorious cause. No definitive news from the soldiers in Stalingrad, save endless lists of casualties, line after line marked with names and black crosses, signaling the fallen. Max von Wedemeyer appeared on one such list, finality spelled out in black type on white newsprint.

So much death. A few days ago, Hugo Distler—one of Dietrich's favorite composers and church musicians—had locked himself inside his home. Bible and crucifix in hand, he had gassed himself to death out of despair after a heavy round of Jewish deportations. No one seemed much to care, the papers only briefly reporting his death, front-page space given, of course, to the usual propaganda kitsch.

Why did so few raise their heads and look about them? Why did those who took a stand remain in the minority? Why, at the beginning of all this, had the Reich Church been permitted to get away with bullying the Confessing Church, bending the wills of weaker men to suit their own agendas? Why, why, why?

Dietrich threw down his pen, concentration eluding him. He couldn't write about ethics today.

He could well picture Distler's agony—a man whose music reverberated with godly truth—and the desperation of his soul that brought him to end his life. If only more people who felt that pulsing desperation would cry out and take a stand, perhaps Adolf Hitler and his machinations could be ended for good. The Confessing Church, well, a few still tried, but many had been deported, sent away to camps. A majority of the rest had bowed to the Reich Church's demands, allowing Germany's gospel to outweigh Christ's.

"Silent witnesses of evil deeds," he whispered the words into the stillness of his room, Herr Gerstein's face raw and fresh before him. "That's what we've been."

He flipped over the piece of paper and jotted the phrase down.

"Telephone, Dietrich." Lotte called up the stairs. "It's that lady from Pomerania, wanting to speak with you."

Ruth? At least the call wouldn't bring more depressing news. Or would it? These days, one never could tell.

Leaving his desk in a state of disaster he'd never have permitted from one of his Finkenwalde seminarians, Dietrich descended the stairs.

Reaching the study, he picked up the phone. "*Guten Abend*, Ruth."

"Hello, Dietrich."

"How are you feeling now that you're home again?"

"A good deal better. Physically, at least." Ruth's tone bespoke weariness. "How are you?"

"Pretty well. You've heard about Herr Distler?"

"*Ja.*" Ruth sighed. "I always felt so at peace whenever I heard his music. A great man."

The phone against his ear, Dietrich nodded.

"I called to invite you to Max's memorial service. It's on the fifteenth. Could you manage to make the journey?"

It was a seven-hour train trip from Berlin to the Wedemeyers' home in Pomerania. But he wasn't doing anyone any good sitting around in Berlin. And the chance to become acquainted with the von Wedemeyers, see Maria . . .

"I think Maria would be very grateful to have you there." Ruth must have read his mind. "Max always thought so highly of you. It would comfort her if you could talk to her about her brother. The two of them were always so very close. She needs a man's guidance and support more than ever now. But she has no one."

Dietrich envisioned Ruth's earnest expression at the moment. She'd be pleading, yet determined, so like his own departed grossmutter, Julie Bonhoeffer. He couldn't bring himself to refuse her this request. Hans would surely allow him a leave of absence for a day or two.

"I'll be there."

"Excellent!" Ruth smiled—he could tell by her voice. "I'll call my daughter and see to it they have a room prepared for you."

"I'll see you then."

"Safe travels."

They hung up. Dietrich planted both hands on the edges of the desk, staring blankly out the window. He hadn't expected an invitation to the memorial service. After all, he hadn't seen any of the Wedemeyers except Maria for years. Ruth had given him an opportunity to become reacquainted. The chance to be there for Maria in her grief would be more than worth the journey. Ruth had spoken of her need for support. He could image her loneliness, the ache of loss.

He'd make the most of the time they had together, even if it was just as a pastoral friend. Even if, as the days waned, his longing increased for whatever it was between the two of them to become something more. Daily, he told himself that more was impossible, but still the feelings held him captive.

For right now, he'd return upstairs and see if he couldn't add to the phrase about "silent witnesses of evil deeds."

Someday, there would come a time when the fog would lift and the world would want to know whether or not all citizens of Germany had a hand in the atrocities of their country. Some might always refuse to believe in the existence of good Germans. But there would also be those who would seek answers, delve deeper into the why of it all.

And for them, Dietrich would write the truth.

Chapter Fourteen

November 11, 1942
Berlin

R ibbons of steam curled into the air, wafting from a basin of blue-patterned china. Looking into the cup, one could almost imagine the beverage was *kaffee*—that decadent, pungent drink of peacetime. The ersatz substitute really wasn't all that bad—the contents made of chicory or barley—just different. Dietrich took a sip.

All right, it was awful. But at least they still had it.

In fact, when he looked across the family breakfast table, he felt only gratitude. They still had plenty of bread, an occasional egg, porridge sweetened with the tiniest pinch of sugar, some milk. So much wealth, when others—Martin Niemöller imprisoned in Dachau—had so little.

The time might come when Dietrich would be among those reduced to starvation rations, and as his gaze traveled the table, the faces of his parents, he committed it all to memory, storing up each scene like an art collector locking away his beloved masterpieces. The clean white tablecloth. The silvery sheen of the cutlery glinting in the slants of morning sunshine. Vater at the head of the table in a neat gray business suit, sipping from a large cup and reading the paper. Mutter on his left, graying hair in her usual tidy knot, smiling at Renate, who'd come from next door to join the family for breakfast.

Lotte entered with the mail, her maid's cap atilt atop her curly brown hair. Dietrich set down his fork, awaiting his pile of correspondence. He always had the largest stack, a fact which his young nieces and nephews forever liked to tease him about.

Renate stood with sudden haste. My, but his niece was growing up fast. She'd recently passed her final high school exams and had already taken over many of her mutter's responsibilities around the house.

"I'm going to run home and see if there are any letters for me. Danke for the breakfast, Grossmutter." She went around the table and gave her gross-mutter's shoulders a quick squeeze, then did the same to her grossvater, before hurrying from the room with a haste that seemed out of place with her new grown-up clothes and hairstyle.

"Who's she so eager to get a letter from?" Dietrich asked after the front door closed behind her.

"How should I know?" His mutter shrugged, lifting her hands palm up. "You know young people and their romances." She stood to refill her husband's cup.

Not really. It had been years since he'd been as young as Renate, and he'd been occupied with serious theological study at that age. He'd had friends, a few at least, but only Elisabeth had ever crossed his thoughts in youth. And he wasn't proud of the way that had ended.

Directing his attention to the letters Lotte placed beside his plate, Dietrich flipped through them. A reply to the birthday letter he'd sent his friend and comrade in the ecumenical movement, Max Diestel. Poor man had recently been interrogated by the Gestapo, an experience that left him shaken. A letter from Rudy Detwiler, a former Finkenwalde student who'd been conscripted into the army several months ago. Dietrich would be sure to answer that today. What those soldiers suffered, the young men who had once been his students, the lifeblood of his illegal seminary . . .

What was this? Dietrich picked up the bottom envelope. He pushed up his glasses.

From Frau von Wedemeyer, Maria's mutter. Why would she have reason to write to him? Unless she knew he was attending the memorial service and wanted him to bring her something from Berlin. Since he'd officially been forbidden to preach, she couldn't be asking for services in that regard.

Though he usually waited until alone in his room to peruse correspondence, he opened the envelope and pulled out the single page.

> *Dear Pastor Bonhoeffer,*
> *I am sure you're wondering why I would be writing to you. So I shall allay your curiosity by coming straight to the point. My mutter mentioned to me that she'd invited you to Max's memorial service on Maria's behalf. Needless to say, when I heard this, I was astonished. That my daughter and you should have formed such a close relationship, one that my mutter hinted was serious enough that the question of marriage has come up, is seriously distressing to myself. My daughter is simply too young and in no*

*emotional state to be even considering such a possibility. So it is with that
in mind that I'm afraid I must withdraw the invitation made without my
knowledge and consent.*

*I hope you'll forgive me for the abruptness of this letter, but it had to be
said. I know you will understand.*

Dietrich set the letter on the table with shaking hands. Whether they
shook from indignation, shock, or a mixture of both, he couldn't tell. Frau
von Wedemeyer's words ran through his mind, each bringing a new wave of
astonishment. How had things come to this? Frau von Wedemeyer couldn't
actually believe he'd declared intentions to marry her daughter. That would
be madness.

"Something the matter, Dietrich?"

He looked up. Mutter studied him with furrowed brow.

He took a deep breath. If he told his parents the story, he'd likely say
things he would regret. Things not entirely complimentary where Ruth von
Kleist was concerned. Eberhard always remonstrated with him about his
temper, and the man was right. Dietrich did have a temper, and this letter
had certainly lit a fuse.

"Everything's quite all right." Or would be after he had a talk with Ruth
von Kleist. He pushed back his chair and collected his letters. "Danke for
the breakfast." He smiled at his parents. "I'm going in to make a phone
call."

His mutter hardly looked convinced.

Inside the study, he dialed Ruth's number. Forcing a deep breath, he tried
for a measure of calm. His heart raced anyway. To think, Ruth had actually
told her daughter something so outrageous . . .

"Hello, Ruth."

"Dietrich!" Her voice sounded almost cheerful. "How are you?"

Keep calm. This can be sorted out just so long as I keep calm.

"Not very well." He cleared his throat. "I just received a letter from your
daughter that came as a complete shock. What do you mean by telling her
you invited me to the memorial service on Maria's behalf? I thought Frau
von Wedemeyer had approved my coming before you decided to ask me."
He kept his words measured, forcing himself not to raise his voice.

"I think it quite proper and right that you attend." Ruth sounded pee-
vish. No doubt she'd already had a heated talk with her daughter. "Why
shouldn't you come to be there for Maria?"

"Everything would have been perfectly acceptable, if you hadn't made
it out like Maria and I . . . Maria and I were anything more than good

friends." He swallowed. It was incomprehensible for him to even be having this conversation. Nothing between him and Maria had gone beyond the bounds of propriety. Nothing. Only in his thoughts had he cherished the dream of anything more, at a later date. And now Frau von Wedemeyer, his hoped-for future in-law, had good reason to be seriously displeased with him.

"It wasn't my intention to cause trouble." Ruth's voice lifted an octave. From the window, Dietrich glimpsed Lotte, shopping baskets in hand, heading to market. "I merely told her that the two of you seemed well-suited, and it would be a very good thing if you considered a future with Maria sooner rather than later."

"But that's . . . that's . . ." He flailed for words.

"Nonsense? Out of the question?" Ruth spoke quietly. "Is it really, Dietrich?"

And how ought he to answer that?

He heaved a weighty sigh. A headache drummed at his temples. "I'm sorry if I spoke too harshly, Ruth. We'll talk soon, *ja*?"

"Of course." A wounded edge infused Ruth's tone, as if she were a schoolgirl wrongly accused by the headmaster. He'd been a bit harsh, perhaps. But wrongly accused, she was not. "Auf Wiedersehen, Dietrich."

"Auf Wiedersehen, Ruth."

He took off his spectacles and rubbed a hand across his eyes. The whole situation reminded him of the time when he and Sabine had been playing stickball, and he'd hit the ball into the window of the neighbor he'd hoped to beg a puppy from. Guilty. Ashamed. Then he'd wanted only to crawl into his old tree fort and never emerge. He'd never gotten that puppy, never had the courage to ask, though his parents had paid for the damaged glass. All because of a simple accident.

Like the accident his words to Ruth had been that day in the hospital. He must've given something away, some indication of his feelings. Or had Maria? At any rate, the damage was done. Frau von Wedemeyer was angry, almost to an unwarranted extreme. So there'd been some gossip. Was it really enough to ban him from attending the memorial service of one of his confirmands? Apparently. Did Maria know about any of this? No doubt she'd be equally astonished. She, who no doubt thought of him as nothing more than a family friend. What must she think of him now? He blew out a sigh.

He could do nothing about what had happened except try to seek Frau von Wedemeyer's pardon.

Perhaps, someday, the time would be right to ask for more.

November 11, 1942
Pätzig, Pomerania

The moment the line clicked, Maria threw down the receiver. A meager fire did little to warm Vater's library, but she scarcely noticed the cold. Nein, the fire in her cheeks could warm a dozen rooms this size.

"Your mutter has written to inform Pastor Bonhoeffer he is not welcome at Max's memorial service." Grossmutter had sounded shocked and more than a little irritated. Maria splayed a hand against her chest, fighting for calm.

Mutter must have discerned something from their conversation on the avenue, and questioned Grossmutter about it. Exactly what had Grossmutter inferred? Crazy, out of proportion things regarding Maria's stay in Berlin and the time she'd spent with Pastor Bonhoeffer.

Things along the lines of the two of them being thought of as . . . a couple.

Maria rounded the desk and curled up in the chair Vater sat in to write correspondence and conduct estate business. The worn leather still bore his indentation, the faintest whiff of his favorite cigars. She kicked off her shoes and drew her knees up to her chest. Mutter was in the village, taking a basket to a sick family. It was almost a relief she wasn't home. Had she been, the words Maria would've said . . .

Ja, she needed to collect her thoughts before facing Mutter.

How had Grossmutter gathered this information? Had Dietrich told her something? What? What must he think of her, of them? Or had this been his intent?

Unbelievable. That he'd actually consider her as a future wife.

Impossible. It had to be impossible.

She pressed her face into the leather, breathing deeply. If only Vater occupied this chair. Then she could go to him with this confusing situation. He always understood her, intrinsically, in a way Mutter never had.

In his absence and Max's, she was left adrift. Alone in a little rowboat amid this ocean of confusion. Ruth-Alice might know what to do, but her sister was so busy these days. And she tended to take Mutter's side over Maria's.

A letter. She could write to Pastor Bonhoeffer. Together, they could gain some clarity.

Retrieving paper and a pen from the meticulously organized desk drawer,

Maria focused on organizing her thoughts. This letter had to set just the right tone, not as if she too were as angry as Grossmutter implied Mutter was.

It took several attempts and a shameful amount of wasted paper for her to finish. Stretching her aching fingers, she gave the letter a final read through. It would have to suffice. Would he respond? She'd received his kind note of condolence about Max. It now rested within the pages of her diary and she'd taken to reading it after making her daily entry. Every word sounded so like him, as if his very voice lay within each page and line. And he'd written to her, despite how busy he must be.

Max always said that every trial has a golden side. It wasn't always easy for her to find one, but in this mess of gossip and confusion, she could.

She'd gain another letter from him.

Chapter Fifteen

November 12, 1942
Berlin

The evening was what one might expect from old friends gathering together to celebrate the birthday of one of their circle. *Kuchen* and ersatz *kaffee* had been served on the family china by Frau Zimmermann. There'd been laughter, a few presents. Dietrich had brought his former Finkenwalde student a book by Kierkegaard as a birthday remembrance.

But as Frau Zimmermann left to make more *kaffee*, the party smiles fell from the faces of the men around the dining-room table, amid a haze of smoke and half-empty cups. Dietrich studied them in turn. Wolf-Dieter, a few years younger than himself, square of jaw and dressed in a well-mended suit, his lack of financial resources compliments of his work as a Confessing Church pastor. Eberhard, with an elbow on the table, savoring one of Wolf's birthday cigars.

And Werner von Haeften. Younger in appearance than his thirty-four years and a staff lieutenant of the Army High Command since being wounded. Blond, slim, and usually smiling, tonight Werner said little, his furrowed brow suggesting he thought much.

Frau Zimmermann returned, closing the dining-room door softly behind her. She carried a pot in one hand, leaning over the men's shoulders to pour. Wolf turned and smiled at his auburn-haired young wife.

"You really shouldn't have gone to all this trouble for us, Frau Zimmermann," Eberhard said.

"It was for Wolf's birthday. And it was a pleasure." Frau Zimmermann poured steaming liquid into Eberhard's cup. "It's been too long since we've all met together like this."

"*Ja, ja.*" Wolf wrapped both hands around his cup. The heavy blackout paper covering the dining-room window gave the cramped room the feel of being underground, a lamp in the center of the table offering scant light.

Dietrich turned to Werner, seated on his right. The man stared hard into his full cup, as if attempting to discern the future within its murky depths. Frau Zimmermann seated herself beside her husband with a sigh.

The talk turned to Hugo Distler's recent death, Eberhard and Wolf discussing the why behind his suicide, the misery Distler must have experienced to resort to such means. Dietrich didn't interject. He studied Werner. Ought he speak to him, ask the reason for his silence? As Eberhard and Wolf continued, Werner's expression grew more and more troubled. Outside, a car motored past.

Frau Zimmermann lifted her cup, bringing it to her lips.

Werner looked up. Something sharp, almost visceral, flashed in his blue eyes. "Shall I shoot?"

Frau Zimmermann gasped, liquid sloshing from her cup and onto the table.

His face was lightning unleashed, as the words poured out. "I can get inside the Führer's headquarters with my revolver. I know where and when the conferences take place. I can get access. I can *do something*!" He stopped, chest heaving in and out, as if the effort of releasing feelings long held back had exhausted him.

Wolf, Eberhard, and Frau Zimmermann exchanged stunned glances. First to each other, and then to Dietrich. The words, speaking of action so plainly, so boldly, hit them all with the force of an explosive.

Dietrich drew in a slow breath. Werner looked to him. The man's gaze begged for answers. These weren't just impetuous words thrown out in the moment, but the product of a long struggle with himself.

God, You are an authority on all situations. Even one such as this. Grant me wisdom.

Recalling the many discussions with Hans, Dietrich forged ahead, thankful the Zimmermanns' house was on the outskirts of Berlin, and as unassuming a residence as could be imagined. Those in this room could be trusted.

"What you speak, we've all thought. And you, with your day-in, day-out exposure to those in power, have experienced this temptation more than most." The others had abandoned their *kaffee* and cigars and riveted their gazes upon him, as his was fixed on Werner. "Even I have asked myself the question. Would I be willing to assassinate the madman at the helm of our country? It's one thing to talk and think and hold secret meetings. It's another to act. And to kill. That takes an entirely deeper kind of decision."

Werner gazed steadily back. "I'm not afraid of death. And I'm one of the few privileged to have access. It would be all too easy to do the deed quickly. One shot . . . and it would all be at an end."

All at an end? It wasn't that simple. Nearly ten years of Hitler's rule over Germany could not be undone by a single bullet. But Werner couldn't be blamed for his line of thinking. Not when he'd had a front-row seat in the amphitheater of both current and planned atrocities.

Dietrich chose his words carefully. "But what would be gained? The Führer would be dead. That is all. If there is to be an assassination, something must be gained by it. A new government. A change of circumstances. Hitler's liquidation would be by itself of no use. Others would take his place before the end of the day. Things might become worse. That's one of the difficulties of the resistance—the planning of the thereafter."

Werner slammed a hand against the table, rattling the china. "To the deuce with theoretical rhetoric! How can I stand by and *not* take this chance, while millions are daily being sent to their deaths? When men like Distler are ending their lives out of sheer despair? Tell me how, Pastor Bonhoeffer. Tell me how I can do that and remain guiltless."

Dietrich caught Eberhard's gaze. His friend nodded, awaiting his answer as much as the others.

But what *was* the answer? Were they, all of them, standing by and contenting themselves with simply planning, while daily, new links were added to the chains of depravity? Did that make them guilty, as surely as if theirs were the hands that drafted deportation orders and executed the innocent?

"I only ask you to be discreet, to plan clearly. A plan not thought through is no plan at all. In a matter such as this, nothing can be left to chance." Dietrich leaned forward.

"If only you knew how much this torments me." Werner pressed a hand into his forehead, voice muffled. "Niemöller, the man who confirmed me in the faith, has been rotting in Sachsenhausen and Dachau for five years! The pastor who was as much a vater to me as my own, locked up by the Führer's command. And every day I put on a uniform and serve in an army for a cause I despise. There's blood on my hands." Werner stared down at them, fingers clenched on the table. "Because I've done nothing."

"But you *will* do something, my friend," Wolf interjected. "When the time is right, your willingness to act will stand fast, and you will be used for good."

Dietrich nodded. "It's not up to me to decide this for you." He scanned the faces around the table, solemn and ringed in lamplight. "For any of you. The risk is yours, Werner, and yours alone. In the situation you are in,

it's impossible to emerge without guilt. But"—Dietrich cleared his throat—
"your guilt is one borne in suffering." The words hung in the air, lingering.

"Danke, Pastor Bonhoeffer. I will bear that in mind," Werner said, voice
hushed and achingly sincere.

These men, how deeply they craved guidance. Not just in how to reorganize a government or whether Hitler's end should come through a pistol or
explosive, but solid, spiritual direction.

Now, more than ever, all of them needed to cling to Christ beyond the
benign niceties of religion.

"Above all, these concerns must be taken to God. His is the only authority to which we can rightfully answer. Seek Him," Dietrich said quietly.
"He will not fail you."

Werner's eyes found his. Confusion still clamored in their depths, but it
had lessened. "What of you? If you were called upon to act, if the opportunity presented itself, would you, a man of God, take the life of another for
the cause of a greater good?"

Eberhard snuffed the remnants of his cigar into the ashtray. Frau Zimmermann folded her hands on the table. Dietrich's shoulders tightened.

It was not a question asked simply for the sake of an answer. If there was
one thing life in the Bonhoeffer family had taught him, it was to stand by
one's statements. If something was said, it must be followed up with action.
No patience could be given to those who merely rambled in a stream of
verbosity.

Few questions had ever presented themselves in such vivid color. Few
actions would hold such finality.

"I don't believe in allowing another to do what I cannot, simply to
absolve myself of guilt. You asked if I would be willing to take up arms
and assassinate Adolf Hitler?" Dietrich swallowed, throat suddenly dry. "I
know I would have to resign from any position I held in the church. But *ja*,
I would. Guilt must not be left to others, but taken upon ourselves."

Werner seemed to be absorbing the words, drawing something from
them. On the opposite wall, a clock marked time in rhythmic strokes.
Dietrich fixed his gaze upon the unchanging movement, while the others
spoke quietly amongst themselves.

His words to Werner had not been spoken lightly. Although, considering
his knowledge of firearms was rudimentary at best, it was doubtful such
action would ever fall to him. It was more about the willingness to act, the
bearing of responsibility.

Above all, the acceptance of consequences.

Whenever and however they came.

November 13, 1942
Berlin

Fundamentally, you and I have nothing whatsoever to do with this.

Every other word of her letter vanished from his mind, except three: *You and I.*

What had she meant by it? Sitting at his desk, Dietrich stared at the single leaf of stationery in his hand, wishing it was Maria's face he looked upon instead. Words—such blank things at times. If he could but see her, he would know in an instant if the phrase had been merely a turn of speech, or if something beyond it was meant.

He stared out his bedroom window, eyes gritty from lack of sleep after the late night at the Zimmermanns'. Snowflakes floated down like powdered sugar, dusting the panes. Dim light from the desk lamp illuminated the built-in bookcases, the neatly arranged volumes.

Why? Why, now of all times, was he drawn to this woman in this way? Ten years ago, even five, it would have been safer, more acceptable, to have . . .

Fallen in love.

Had he? His breath halted, as if snatched by the wind. Had he truly fallen in love with Maria von Wedemeyer? He, a balding bachelor of thirty-six, in love with a beautiful eighteen-year-old who could take her pick among any aristocratic young man she fancied. What could he offer her? He didn't have a regular income, lived with his parents in Berlin and his aunt when in Munich. He'd written a few books, preached lots of sermons, and now worked daily in a conspiracy that could just as easily get him killed as not.

Yet . . . *Ja.* His heart, so long guarded and consumed with work, had somehow, during that summer's eve in June and then in October, become no longer entirely his own. She possessed a part of it now, a part growing more encompassing with each bygone day.

He'd prayed about it, thought about it, all without any change. Years ago, there'd been another woman in his life, a fellow theology student at Berlin University. He'd been twenty-one, she, twenty. For eight years, they'd danced around their feelings for each other, until, one day, Elisabeth's brother came right out and asked the two of them how long they intended to keep playing games. Dietrich heaved a sigh, Elisabeth's face swimming before him, her expressive eyes always sparkling with some new idea, the lilt of her voice. After that, it had been too late for both of them. They'd evaded and misunderstood each other for too long, and Elisabeth had moved on to marry another. The wound caused by their parting had since scabbed over, leaving him older. Wiser.

And not about to repeat past mistakes.

He needed to answer Maria's letter. She'd obviously been perturbed when she'd sent it. Perhaps his answer could offer her clarity, even hint at a way forward.

Had this not been wartime, he might have waited, sought a longer delay or a more opportune time. But war raged all around them—evidenced by the recent German occupation of southern France, a blow to the already oppressed French, a seizure of power by the German army in light of their recent failure in North Africa. *Wait* could easily mean *never*.

And *never* was something he could not endure.

This letter would define things for the both of them. It couldn't fail to.

He cleared a space, pushing aside books on theology to make room for a fresh sheet of writing paper, its surface pristine against the worn wood of his desk.

The words spilled from his pen, thanks for her attempt to clarify things, apologies for her grossmutter's behavior, an explanation for it, however feeble.

Then . . .

> *But only from a peaceful, free, healed heart can anything good and right take place; I have experienced that repeatedly in life, and I pray (forgive me for speaking thus) that God may give us this, soon and very soon, and that God may bring us back together with such hearts, soon and very soon.*
>
> *Can you understand all this? Might you experience it just as I do? I hope so, in fact I cannot conceive of anything else. But how difficult this is for you too! I think I know and understand this completely; for otherwise when one is inwardly anxious it is so difficult to be still and wait on God, and yet that is the only healing. You must often feel very lonely these days; if I may, I would like to write you from time to time. And if you could let me know how your grossmutter is doing (I mean emotionally), I will be very grateful to you.*
>
> *Please forgive me this letter, which says so clumsily what I am feeling. I realize that words intended to say personal things come only with tremendous difficulty to me; this is a great burden for those around me.*

He added a few more paragraphs about his plans to write her grossmutter and ended with a request that after she had time to think about what he had written, she might write him again.

He scanned the pages. Again, it was a poor reflection of the depth of his emotions. But he couldn't delay in sending it. Who knew when he'd have time to write again? Already, he was late in leaving for his appointment with Hans and General Oster at Oster's house. Hans had promised to pick him up in his car.

Snow sprinkled his overcoat and hat, wind driving it like needles into his face as he stepped out the front door. How quickly the gentle embrace of summer had been replaced by the bony arms of winter. Already it was shaping up to be a bitter one, rife with food shortages, gaunter faces.

Everyone had suffered enough in this war, yet Germany still forged ahead—the Führer and his minions bulldozing, the people trudging along obediently, or rebelliously, after him.

Dietrich looked both ways before making his way to Hans's utilitarian black motorcar parked in front of the Bonhoeffer house. These days, he had an uneasy, nagging sensation he was being followed. Watched. By whom, he couldn't say. He glimpsed no one and ducked into the waiting car. His brother-in-law sat in the driver's seat, smoking tersely. He said little by way of greeting, and the car turned in the direction of Oster's residence.

Half an hour later, the two men sat in Oster's thickly paneled library— decorated thus for secrecy purposes, rather than ornamental ones. A fire burned in the marble hearth, and Oster sat at his desk, one hand propped against the side of his balding head. Despite the stress of recent weeks, Oster cut as fashionable a figure as ever in a velvet-collared smoking jacket, a departure from his usual uniform. A large, well-groomed German shepherd lay on a rug near his feet, tail twitching as he slept.

Dietrich stood with his back to the crackling fire, letting the welcome heat chase away the bitter chill. The scents of wood smoke and cigars pervaded the room.

"I called you both to discuss the necessity of continuing preparations for Dietrich's trips abroad." Oster drummed his fingers upon a nearby stack of papers. A silver ring on his left hand glinted in the meager light. "It's best if we make it out like he's involved in highly essential work. The more essential to the Fatherland, the better. We mustn't seem like we're at all ruffled by Schmidhuber's arrest."

"Bluster our way along, you mean," Dietrich interjected.

"Precisely." Oster looked to Hans, as if giving him permission to take over.

"We need to start planning for if the worst happens. By all appearances, it must be clearly documented that you'd been with the Abwehr before the call-ups for your age group began. A letter should take care of that. We'll do it out on paper that's no longer in use today, so everything will match up. And the family, those of us in the know, need to come up with a system of codes. But we won't go into that now."

Dietrich never ceased to be grateful for these men who'd breathed the dust of military politics far longer than he had. But the words still sent a lump of lead to the pit of his stomach. The worst. Imprisonment if they were discovered. Interrogation. Execution. It was not only possible, but probable.

Unless Hitler's government could be overthrown first. It was a mad race against time. With each day, the tide could turn.

God, help us all.

"That sounds wise," Dietrich said. Oster's dog awoke and trotted to his master, pressing his nose into Oster's palm.

"Have you heard about Helmuth?" Oster ran his fingers through his dog's thick fur. "Tomorrow, he's meeting with the Armed Forces High Command to talk about vetoing further Jewish deportations. I highly doubt he'll be successful, but he's determined to try."

A member of the Abwehr and the resistance, Helmuth von Moltke had started a group called the Kreisau Circle, whose members championed non-violent resistance and focused on making plans for a government after the war. A member of nobility and a committed Christian, Moltke believed that if Hitler were killed, Germany would only consign him to martyrdom and continue further down the road of degeneration. Once, Dietrich would have sided more strongly with the man's beliefs then he did now.

Hitler was a madman. He needed to be stopped, no matter the means.

"Count von Moltke believes, at least more than we do, that these people can still be talked to sensibly." Dietrich moved to the window, covered with impenetrable blackout shades. "I only wish he could be proved right."

"Wishing isn't acquiring, Herr Pastor Bonhoeffer." Oster's tone was not meant to be condescending, but it still reminded Dietrich that the only reason he was part of the resistance was because Oster trusted Hans, and Hans trusted Dietrich.

A quarter of an hour later, Hans and Dietrich motored back to the Bonhoeffer home. Dietrich chafed his hands together to stave off the cold. Hans kept his gaze straight ahead, with frequent glances in the rearview mirror. His hands tightened around the steering wheel, skin taut against his knuckles. Dietrich followed his brother-in-law's gaze.

A solitary car, its body black against the winter white, drove a distance behind them. It turned down the same streets they took, a dark shadow.

They were being followed.

"Whatever you do, don't look behind you," Hans muttered through gritted teeth. His forehead creased, tension evident upon his features. "They can follow us all they like."

"Aren't you going to try to shake them?" While in New York, Dietrich had seen a few suspense films featuring thrilling car chases. Though this wasn't quite the same thing, it still brought back the feeling of sitting in a darkened theater, watching a criminal in hot pursuit of the hero. Only worse. This wasn't the cinema. This was an actual car and actual proof they were indeed being watched.

Hans shook his head, the movement slight. "I'm not. Because we're not going to the Abwehr office. We're going to the dullest restaurant to talk about the dullest topics. They can follow us all they like." He turned, meeting Dietrich's gaze. His eyes sparked with a flash of anger. "Those devils can try to beat us, but we won't let them win. Not that easily."

November 15, 1942
Berlin

A circle of lamplight shone onto the polished wood of the dining-room table, the only illumination they allowed themselves for this late-night meeting. The darkness suited the mood of the discussion.

Though one could never be sure what lurked in shadows.

Hans sat at the head of the table, the commander of their group. Dark rings bruised the space below his eyes, telling evidence of one too many long nights. He nursed a cup of ersatz, and every so often placed his hand atop Christel's, who sat beside him, Dietrich on the opposite side. The rest of the group—Rüdiger and Ursula, Renate, Klaus and Emmi, Mutter and Vater—clustered around the table, their faces solemn in the meager glow. They'd put cushions over the telephone, though it was in another room, and periodically, Renate stole out to check for eavesdroppers.

Tonight's topic was crucial. If any of them were imprisoned, they had to have a way to keep their stories corroborated during the interrogations. It could prove life or death to those on the outside if new developments in the case failed to reach the appropriate channels.

"Jam jars would be allowed inside the prison." Hans pulled an empty one from his half-open briefcase and held it up to the light. "You see this double lid." He unscrewed the top of the jar and pulled out a small, circular piece of cardboard. "You can fit a decent-sized message on one of these, and the guards will be none the wiser. They can be quickly read, and easily shredded. But we need something else. They'd get suspicious with too many jam jars."

"No one has much sugar to make jam," Christel remarked.

Dietrich stood, grabbing empty cups, and stretched his legs as he walked to the kitchen. How else could one smuggle a message? Invisible ink? Some kind of signal?

He deposited the cups on the counter and left the clean and solitary kitchen. Passing the front hall, he spied the coats and winter wrappings awaiting their wearers' return. On the end table near the door sat a pair of books next to Renate's handbag. What was his niece reading these days, now that she'd finished her formal schooling?

He picked it up and glanced at the spine. Rilke? He'd need to have a talk with her about good literature. There were far better poets she could spend her time perusing.

The book fell open to a page. He scanned the words printed in small, black type, the lines so close together he almost needed to resort to squinting.

Words. Lines.

An idea took shape. He dashed back to the dining room. Seven pairs of eyes lifted in his direction. He held up the book.

"What are you doing with my Rilke?" Renate gave him a curious look.

"I have a thought on how we can get messages past the guards." Dietrich resumed his seat, opening the book and tilting it toward Hans.

Hans pressed his lips together, a skeptical slant to his brows. Hans trusted him, of course. But a clergyman couldn't possibly be expected to know more about conspiracy than a legal genius. Still, his idea might work.

"We have plenty of message material right here." Dietrich tapped his finger against the page. "What if we put a small dot below one of the letters on this page, then on the next page did the same, and so on. We could spell out the message and, if the dots were small enough, no one would be able to guess it was anything more than a slight irregularity in the printing."

Hans cocked his head, gaze on the page in front of them.

"It might work." Christel rested her hands atop the table.

"We'd have to be more precise than random dots." Hans spoke as if talking to himself. "And not on every page. They'd be too easily discovered. Every five . . . nein, ten pages, we could put a dot, starting from the back and working to the front. They'd have to be made with pencil and as minuscule as we can manage."

"How should we know to look for the dots?" Klaus had listened thoughtfully to the entire exchange.

Hans rubbed a finger along the open page. "In the front, on the flyleaf, we'll write the person's name who's to receive the book, and underline it. If it's not underlined, the recipient will know not to look for a message."

Nods and murmurs of approval filtered around the table.

"Decoding the messages must be done with the utmost secrecy." Hans closed the book with a clap. "All of you know the fire we'll be playing with, if one of us ever has to make use of these techniques. The Gestapo flatter themselves that nothing escapes their notice." He pulled out a cigarette, lighting it.

"But we can prove them wrong." Dietrich met his mutter's eyes with a look of reassurance. She smiled, nodded, as if this were the most natural conversation in the world. Only it wasn't.

They were discussing how to confront the true danger they faced, no denying it.

"*Ja.*" A thin column of smoke wafted from between Hans's fingers. "We can prove them wrong."

November 15, 1942
Pätzig, Pomerania

Low-hanging clouds scoured the sky in shades of impenetrable gray, as those gathered for Max's memorial service made their solemn way back to the manor house from the chapel.

Maria followed her mutter and siblings, wind seeping through her black skirt and jacket. Max wouldn't have liked the service. Maria pressed her lips together, forcing her face into a mask of calm. Max liked bright colors and laughter, not black clothes and sad faces. The hymns chosen were not his favorites. He always preferred those that spoke of God on earth, instead of heaven. Before he went away, they'd never discussed . . . never expected a need for a memorial service program. Never dreamt . . .

The Führer promised to lead them toward victory. He said nothing about leading them to the deaths of boys not yet twenty-two.

She wrapped her arms around herself, fighting the chill. Dry, frostbitten grass crunched beneath her heels. Friends and relatives, those who were able, had made the journey. Ruth-Alice held Grossmutter's arm, helping her along the path, Grossmutter's shoulders stooped with age and illness. Aunts and cousins who'd become accustomed to attending similar services for their own loved ones walked beside Mutter, offering what support they could.

The presence of two of the guests particularly surprised Maria. Henning von Tresckow and Fabian von Schlabrendorff, along with their wives, Erika and Lutigarde. In the days before Vater left for the front, these two men had been frequent guests at Pätzig. Late at night, when the servants had all gone to bed, they met in Vater's library, talking in whispered voices about their plans to overthrow Hitler's regime. Once, Maria had crept downstairs in search of a book, and she'd crouched outside the door, listening. They spoke boldly—even then. How much bolder they'd become since, she didn't know. Were there plans for drastic action, an overthrow?

Fiercely, she hoped so. How could she not wish dead a man who'd orchestrated this horrible war, causing the death of Vater, Max, and so many others? The unspeakable atrocities he ordered inflicted on Jews, Poles, and other "undesirables" were rarely spoken of, but hinted at nonetheless.

Uncle Henning and Cousin Fabian did right. As did Pastor Bonhoeffer, whatever his role in the resistance.

If only she could do something for the cause herself. But how could she? What they needed were men in high places, generals and suchlike. People able to gain access to Hitler . . .

They reached Pätzig. Maria stole a glance at Henning and Fabian. They looked grave, even for a memorial service, their dark suits and even darker expressions giving them a forbidding air. Their wives spoke quietly together, but the men didn't interject. They just walked, posture military-straight, eyes fixed ahead.

As if marching toward something even they themselves feared.

Feet aching, Maria ascended the stairs, still in her too-short black dress— some relative's castoff—the fabric tight against her shoulder blades. The last guest had only just departed, train-bound to Berlin. Thank goodness they'd gone. Why was it that everyone felt compelled to share their remembrances of the deceased person after a memorial service? Someday, she'd be ready to talk openly about Max, but the pain was still too fresh. Like unbandaging a wound only recently dressed. She needed to keep the bandage on a while longer, cradle the memories of Max tucked away inside her heart.

Responding to Pastor Bonhoeffer's letter would be a reprieve. She wouldn't give details about the service. No doubt he still regretted that he'd been commanded not to come. He asked about her work, and she'd tell him that tomorrow she traveled back to the Vogel home to resume her national service. The work would be good for her, keep her from thinking overmuch.

She could scarcely discern the enigmatic emotions behind the words he'd penned.

"Only from a peaceful, free, healed heart can anything good and right take place."

A beautiful sentence. She wanted to own it for herself, to be peaceful, free, and healed when everything around her was at war, constrained, and broken. He hinted at a desire to see her again. In her reply, she'd echo it.

A finger of light shone beneath her bedroom door. Maria started. Who was in her room? The younger children had gone to their rooms an hour ago.

She turned the knob and stepped inside. Her desk lamp emitted the light, Mutter sat at the desk. She'd changed from her severe ebony dress into a dressing gown, graying hair still confined by pins and comb.

What was that in her hand? Maria stepped closer, heels noiseless against the rug. Why was Mutter in this room, at her desk? Light slanted across the paper in Mutter's hand, revealing the writer's script.

The letter from Pastor Bonhoeffer.

Maria bit her lip. She had no wish to hide anything, but to have Mutter in her room, reading a letter not addressed to her, felt like a bald invasion of privacy.

Mutter set the letter down. Not an ounce of guilt filled her eyes.

For the space of a moment, they regarded each other in the lamplight. Maria didn't bother to keep her emotions from her face. As a grown woman, she had every right to her own private correspondence.

"I take it this isn't the first letter you two have exchanged." Mutter spoke quietly, slowly, as if measuring out each word for impact.

Maria shook her head. Mutter's words made a correspondence with a pastor friend of the family seem like something disreputable.

Mutter's chest lifted with a sigh, the sound amplified in the stillness. "Let me speak plainly, Daughter. I know how you are feeling and thinking. His letters, the time you spent together, comfort you. And there's no harm in that. You are not to be condemned." She reached out and grasped Maria's hand. Maria didn't pull away. Nor did she close her fingers around her mutter's larger, bony ones.

"Then why are you condemning me? Grossmutter has no objections. She encouraged us to spend time together in Berlin." Her words came out sounding childishly defensive. She winced.

A dry smile curved Mutter's thin lips. "I'm sure she did. She always was one to *encourage* things, however subtly. But this isn't the time for this, any of it. You are still so young to be thinking of any sort of relationship. And so soon after your vater's and Max's—"

Death. The word hung in the air, its malodorous odor stark, yet unvoiced.

"I don't know why you and Grossmutter are intent on making so much out of so little." Maria pulled her hand from Mutter's grasp, paced to the curtained window, wishing she could pull back the fabric and let fresh air dispel the room's oppression. "It's not as if I'm writing love letters to some dashing soldier. He's a Confessing Church pastor, for heaven's sake. And he's old enough to be—" Her vater. Well, probably. But nothing about his letters or their time in Berlin seemed fatherly. Kind, *ja*. Pastoral, *ja*. But not in a parent to child sort of way.

"*Ja*, he is. Which is one of the many reasons why I'm going to ask him to refrain from further communication with you for the foreseeable future."

Maria spun, hands fisted at her sides. She opened her mouth.

Everything in her wanted to protest. Already, the two people she loved most in life had been ripped from her grasp. Was now the correspondence that offered some relief from it all to be taken from her? Could she not be allowed some small shred of happiness?

Try to keep the peace between you and your mutter. It would grieve me beyond anything to think the two of you are at odds.

Vater's words, whispered in her ear the morning before he left. She'd promised him, tried hard to keep her word even though she hadn't always succeeded. But in something this large, that upset Mutter to this degree, Vater would want her to cede to Mutter's request.

Though Vater wasn't here to reinforce them, she'd still obey his wishes.

"If that is what you wish, I will obey you." She forced her mouth to form the words.

Mutter stood and placed a hand on Maria's cheek, with a weary smile. "It's for the best, *Liebling*." She gently kissed Maria on the cheek, then slipped quietly from the room.

Maria moved to the desk, brushed her fingers across the paper lying there. Imagined Pastor Bonhoeffer in Berlin, sitting at his desk, writing each word to her. He'd cared enough to care for her.

But no longer. Once Mutter told him he must stop all communication, it might distress him, but only at first. Soon, his mind would turn to other things. War left no room for useless pining. He'd quickly forget about her.

Her fingers trailed the paper's edge, lamplight illuminating each boldly penned word.

If only she could find it in herself to do the same.

Chapter Sixteen

"*Guten Tag*, Dr. Sauerbruch." Dietrich greeted his vater's old colleague, who stood in the front hall, donning hat and gloves. "I didn't know you'd dropped by."

"I was just leaving." The elderly physician wrapped a scarf around his neck. "Your vater was kind enough to provide me some refreshment, but I have a meeting to attend and must be on my way. *Guten Tag*, Herr Bonhoeffer." The man nodded politely, his overlarge spectacles tilting over his prominent nose. He opened the door and stepped outside, letting in a gust of bitterly cold air. Chills prickled down Dietrich's shirtsleeve-clad arms.

He made his way into the living room. His parents sat on the sofa, Mutter's mending on the seat beside her, Vater speaking quietly, but with animation in his eyes.

Mutter turned, breaking off mid-sentence. "Dietrich, where have you been all morning?"

"With Hans." Dietrich lowered himself into an armchair by the window. "I got home half an hour ago and was upstairs trying to write a letter." To Ruth von Kleist, attempting to tell her, in the kindest way possible, to refrain from interfering in affairs that didn't concern her. He hadn't succeeded in composing anything suitable. The meeting with his brother-in-law pressed into his brain like the worst headache.

Vater blew out a breath. He wore a white clinical coat over his suit, as if he'd passed the morning in his consulting chamber. "My former colleague, Dr. Sauerbruch, was just here."

"*Ja*, I saw him as he was leaving. What did he have to say?"

Vater leaned forward on the sofa, elbows on his knees, fingers steepled beneath his chin. "Sauerbruch is convinced Hitler is out of his mind. He was called in to see him the other day. Said he looked positively ill, aged beyond his years, muttering all sorts of phrases like 'for every German killed, ten of the enemy must die.' He blames everyone else for everything, all the generals. When Hitler spoke of them in the most lurid language, Sauerbruch feared the man would start frothing at the mouth."

And this is who is in charge of our country? Some might call it just punishment for Germany's sins during the Great War, but I don't believe that.

"Why did he tell you about this, Karl?" Mutter resumed her darning, as if this were a cozy, familial chat by the fire, instead of a discussion that could be lethal if overheard. Anything either written or verbal against the Führer stank of sedition to the Reich and was dealt with accordingly.

"The man wanted my opinion, as a professional. I told him I agreed, had known for some time that Hitler displayed characteristics of a number of mental disorders. Sauerbruch seemed genuinely upset about the experience, almost as if he wanted to do something. I wouldn't trust him to join the resistance though."

Cold seeped through the windowpanes at Dietrich's back. What he wouldn't give to return to Spain again, that blazing heat, the brilliant rays.

"How did things go with Hans? He was supposed to meet with some military prosecutor about the Wilhelm Schmidhuber's case, wasn't he? What was the man's name? Ritter?" Mutter bent over the sock.

"Manfred Roeder." Hans hadn't liked the man. Nor had he gotten any satisfactory information out of him regarding Schmidhuber's fate. Very civil, Roeder had been, Hans said. But like a veneer slicked across rotting wood, his civility barely permeated the surface. "I told Hans to go home and rest, which he refused to do. He's working at a fever pitch, communicating with Tresckow and Schlabrendorff, while Canaris is doing his best to placate everyone and cast doubt on the credibility of anything Schmidhuber might have said while under interrogation. He's got the ear of higher-ups more than the rest. Before Heydrich's assassination, Canaris used to ride with him through the Tiergarten almost every morning."

Mutter lowered her work. "What an appalling prospect."

"What else does Hans say?" Vater rubbed a finger across his mustache.

"The Gestapo are almost gleeful about the whole thing, thinking they've found some fault in their Abwehr rivals. They've always in-fought with each other, you know." Dietrich stood and crossed to the curio case. One of the figurines he'd brought Mutter back from Spain sat crooked. He straightened it until it aligned with the ceramic vase Hans's daughter had painted for her grandparents last Christmas.

If only the disorder outside these walls could be rearranged so easily.

The telephone rang.

"I'll get it." Dietrich crossed to the table in the hall just outside the living room, where they kept their second telephone. "Hello, Bonhoeffer residence."

"May I speak to Pastor Bonhoeffer? This is Ruth von Wedemeyer." Her voice came through loud and clear on the other end. She sounded like who she was—the wife of a Prussian officer and mistress of an estate.

"Speaking. How are you, Frau von Wedemeyer?" What did the woman want with him? Had she called to straighten things out? Or to make them worse?

"Well. And you?"

"Quite well, danke."

Dietrich glanced behind him. Mutter stood inside the door, arms folded, concern drawing creases in her brow. Once, the telephone had been a means of sharing pleasant conversation. Today, its ringing rarely heralded glad tidings.

"I spoke with Maria last night. Both of us desire that you put an end to the correspondence between the two of you. It's causing more harm than good."

Maria actually said that? His heart plummeted. If so, why hadn't she told him herself? It wasn't like her. Above anything, she wasn't afraid to speak her mind. Frau von Wedemeyer must be the one behind this.

"I see," Dietrich said quietly.

Perhaps Frau von Wedemeyer was justified. After all, it had been years since she'd met him face-to-face. After her husband's death, it was only natural for her parental instincts to heighten. But this was too great a matter, both to him and to Maria, for things to end this way.

Maybe if they met in person. The telephone was such a poor means of communication. Surely some sort of compromise could be come to.

"I will, of course, abide by your request. But my relationship with Maria is a matter of deep importance. I'd welcome the opportunity for an interview with you to discuss the matter in person. I know I cannot ask you to travel to Berlin, but would you be willing to receive me if I came to Pätzig?"

Silence pulsed on the other end. Dietrich tapped his foot against the floor.

Then, finally, Frau von Wedemeyer's voice.

"Come on the twenty-fourth. You can stay the night."

"Danke. I'll look forward to it."

Dietrich hung up and turned to face his mutter. She leaned against the doorframe, studying him with her piercing blue eyes as if waiting for an explanation.

He volunteered none. What was he to say, after all? That Maria and he were at an impasse in a relationship he hadn't known existed until her grossmutter brought it into the light.

"It's about the Wedemeyer girl." It wasn't a question.

"Nein, Mutter." Dietrich shook his head, the truth full and heavy in his heart. "She's much more to me than that."

———————————

November 24, 1942
Pätzig

Maria's childhood home.

Ja, Dietrich could well understand her love for it. One's favorite place was said to reveal a great deal about a person, and the rolling hills and dense forests, the quaint manor house nestled within their embrace, exuded freedom and light. As Maria did.

The carriage—they still made use of carriages here, apparently—that had met him at the station rolled to a halt in front of the palatial stone house. It looked like something out of an English novel, neat, symmetrical gardens and a circular, snow-frosted drive, the house tall and stately. He'd visited Pätzig before, but the details had blurred in his memory. Those same details he now drank in.

Dietrich climbed out, suitcase in hand. How he remembered, so often longed for, fresh country air. He drew his lungs full of it, inhaling the scent of air not tarnished by city odors. It smelled of his days as an instructor at Finkenwalde, that rambling clutter of a house where, in between theology lessons, his students and he went for hikes and played ball games. And of that evening in Klein-Krössin—*ja*, this fragrance had been there too— when he had walked beneath a twilight sky and given away a piece of his heart to a girl with Danube-blue eyes.

He approached the door, his palm going damp around the suitcase handle. What would these von Wedemeyers be like? People didn't daunt him much. His parents had raised him to be unafraid to speak his mind if he had something vital to say, and he'd never had a problem doing so.

Why, then, did walking up to the home of the family von Wedemeyer fill him with the type of trepidation he imagined a raw youth of eighteen must feel approaching the parents of the girl next door, asking if he might take her to a dance?

He knew why. He'd come here to ask a question—one far more life-altering than going to a dance. To be honest with the von Wedemeyers about his intentions toward Maria. If he were a parent, he would expect no less of anyone wishing to pursue an understanding with his daughter.

Dietrich rapped on the door.

He knew the von Wedemeyers championed the Berneuchen movement, a Christian group that worked to bring spiritual vitality into staid Lutheran churches. He'd never much cared for the movement. The participants tended to take an overly religious tone about things. Would he find it to be so here?

The door opened, bringing him face-to-face with Frau von Wedemeyer herself, dressed in trim dove gray.

"Welcome, Pastor Bonhoeffer." Her lips turned up in a quiet smile. But her eyes spoke of weary days and sleepless nights.

"Danke, Frau von Wedemeyer. I'm truly grateful for your permission to come."

She held the door and motioned him in. The grandeur of the interior matched that of the outside. Walls accentuated with fine paintings. A polished hall table. Gleaming floors and carpeted stairs that swept upward to the second level like the train of a fashionable evening dress.

He half expected Maria to come dashing down those stairs to greet him with a smiling invitation to tour the grounds. But she was back with her national service family. Nor would Hans von Wedemeyer welcome him with a hearty handshake, as he'd done when Dietrich had met to discuss Max's confirmation.

Only the lady of the house, with her statuesque frame and erect posture, was left to represent both.

"The house is very fine." He smiled, hoping to put them both at ease. "When I was here last, I don't remember being so struck with its artistry."

"Much has changed since those days, Herr Pastor." Frau von Wedemeyer stood with hands clasped in front of her, completely controlled and serene. From the gist of their phone call, he'd half expected a chillier reception. "If you'd care to come this way, I can show you to your room."

He hesitated, swallowing back the tension in his throat. "If you don't mind, I'd rather speak with you now. I'll have to leave very early in the morning, and it's already close to evening mealtime." With food shortages rife, guilt nudged him. He'd not only invited himself here, but he would also stay for dinner and then breakfast. If Frau von Wedemeyer or her children ever traveled to Berlin, as Maria had, he'd see to it their expenses were covered.

"Very well. We can go into my sitting room. You may leave your case here along with your hat and coat. One of the maids will take your things to your room." Without waiting to see if he followed, she led the way, heels clicking against the floor.

He paid little attention to where they went. His heart pounded too much for that. The words he meant to say jumbled together in his mind in a mass of letters and syllables that suddenly made no sense.

They entered a sitting room. He waited until Frau von Wedemeyer seated herself in an easy chair beside the hearth. A crackling blaze burned within. He took the chair on the opposite side.

Did Maria sit here of an evening, reading or confiding in her mutter?

Somehow, the notion calmed him, almost as if her presence, instead of a whisper of memory, sat beside him.

Spine straight, hands on both armrests, Frau von Wedemeyer regarded him.

"What are your reasons for corresponding with my daughter? What do you hope will come of it?" She spoke as one accustomed to being heard and obeyed.

Dietrich took a deep breath. All he needed to do was open his mouth and say the words. It was an easy enough task when one viewed it in that sense. It was the nature of those words and the effect Frau von Wedemeyer's response to them would have on his future that accounted for the tightness in his stomach.

"Though I've only known her a short time, I care very deeply for Maria. I wish to court her and, at the appropriate time, seek her hand in marriage." He uttered the words with firm clarity. The sheer relief of having got them out in the open lessened the tightness. Marginally.

Frau von Wedemeyer's soft inhale filled the silence. A wall clock marked time in rhythmic strokes above the mantle. One minute. Two. Her fingers clenched the armrests, drawing attention to the tasteful rings adorning her pale fingers.

She swallowed, as if gathering inner resources. "I'm grateful for your candor, Herr Pastor. And please take what I say not as an insult to yourself, but a reflection of my maternal instincts. I don't dislike you. In fact, someday the time may be right for a renewal of your suit. But it is not now. Maria is deeply grieved over the death of her vater and brother. She needs time to find some peace. The world in which you live is certainly not peaceful."

"Are any of our worlds?"

"I did not mean that." Her gaze turned toward the fire, then back to him. She lowered her voice. "My mutter has told me a little about your . . . work of a dangerous nature."

"I see," was all he could think to say. Outside, a dog barked, each sound high-pitched and incessant.

Without relaxing her posture, she leaned forward. "I commend you for what you do. My husband endured a great deal of inward struggle as he debated whether or not to join those who work as you do. Our relatives Henning von Tresckow and Fabian von Schlabrendorff had many long discussions with him on the topic. He was always firm in his hatred of the Nazis, so much so that they tried multiple times to stain his good name and take away his rights to the estate. He refused to hang a swastika anywhere on his property and got drawn into a beastly legal battle in the early thirties as a result. But in the end, Hans felt bound to fight for his country, regardless of the leader over it. Now that he's gone, I can't help but wonder if our choices shouldn't have been different . . ." Desolation lined her features.

"I've spoken to Maria, to some degree, about my participation in the resistance." He kept his gaze on the worn carpet. Now wasn't the time to debate whose decision had been right, Hans von Wedemeyer's or his own. It was only normal that Frau von Wedemeyer should question his doings, the potential risks. He opened his mouth to reassure her, but she cut him off.

"As I said before, there are many reasons. She may be mature, but she's still only eighteen. Now is not the time for such an enormous decision to be forced upon her. It is with all of this in mind that I must reiterate my wish that you and Maria have no contact with each other, either by letters or in person, for a year."

A year.

A full 365 days and nights, each stretching forward until they seemed to encompass eternity. Only the Lord knew where they all would be at their conclusion. He'd hoped to have her beside him, sharing with each other the burdens and struggles faced by them both. Shock pounded over him.

"If I might venture to speak thus, a year seems extreme. In the times in which we live, a year could easily turn into five or ten. Forgive me, Frau von Wedemeyer, but the thought of that long of a delay—"

"A year. No more, and no less." There was no debating with such a tone, calm, yet utterly in control. Had this conversation been with Hans von Wedemeyer, Dietrich would have said more, pressing his case with reasonable argument. But he wouldn't subject this woman to that. She might appear strong, but defenselessness lay beneath her surface. He wouldn't trample over that. To do so would be a cold exploitation of her weakness. He'd have to accept.

Even though he didn't agree.

"I understand. Out of respect for you as Maria's parent, I will abide by your decision." The syllables sounded hollow, like his heart. Two words chanted through his mind, over and over.

A year.

Was this truly God's will for him? To endure separation from Maria when they could have found hope and strength together?

"I thank you for that. And I'm sorry if you now feel your journey has been wasted." Frau von Wedemeyer rose. "Shall I show you to your room?"

He nodded. Once upstairs, he'd attempt to work out his feelings in a letter to Eberhard. Eberhard, who strangely enough found himself in much the same situation. He'd proposed to Renate, but the Schleichers expressed hesitation due to Renate's youth. But they knew Eberhard's character and would doubtless soon come around. Eberhard would be granted his wish, Renate would become his fiancée.

Dietrich had never felt jealous of his closest friend. But he did now. Blazingly, shamefully so.

They climbed the steps leading to the second floor, their footsteps echoing. Neither of them seemed inclined to speak.

A noise drew him up short. Weeping. Frau von Wedemeyer must have noticed it too, as she called out softly down the hall.

"Marta? Is that you?"

A young woman dressed in a maid's uniform appeared from behind a door. Tears splotched her oval face, her eyes puffy and red-rimmed. Sobs continued to shake her narrow shoulders.

"Whatever is the matter?" Frau von Wedemeyer approached the girl. Dietrich stood back, hands at his sides, as Frau von Wedemeyer placed a gentle hand on the young woman's shoulder.

"It's . . . Wolfgang." Marta held out a crumpled slip of paper, fingers shaking. "Word just came. The army is surrounded by Russian troops at Stalingrad."

The word shuddered through Dietrich.

Stalingrad.

Chapter Seventeen

November 27, 1942
Pomerania

Sunset painted the sky in swirls of pink and umber. A gust of wind swept in from the east, fluttering Maria's unbuttoned coat like the tails of a sky-bound kite.

She'd put the Vogel children to bed early, longing for solitude. Since her phone call with Mutter earlier that day, she'd kept her thoughts at bay, ignoring how they nipped at her heels, demanding attention.

She leaned against a tree, the solitude of the snow-frosted trail through the forest near the house seeping into her. The rough bark scraped against the wool of her coat, and she shoved her fast-chilling fingers deep into her pockets.

Dietrich had been to Pätzig. The thought of his presence at the place she loved best made warmth spread through her. He'd been to Pätzig, spent the night, spoken with Mutter.

"He wants to marry me," she whispered the words, her voice lost amid another howl of wind. "He asked Mutter for permission to marry me."

In an instant, his face flooded her senses, almost as real and vital as if he stood before her now. The smile meant for her alone, the strength of his presence. The way he'd taken her arm as they walked across Berlin, gentle yet protective. The ridiculous wish that rose inside of her whenever she reread his letters—to see him again and press her face against his strong chest, wrap her arms around him.

His brilliant mind. The many books he'd composed. Their shared opinions on so many things.

Oh, he was too good for her. How could he be otherwise? She was . . . well, little *Miesenmaus*. Always confounding people with outrageous comments, running helter-skelter through the forests. Good at mathematics perhaps and looking after children, but dreadful at the arts of a good *hausfrau*—cooking and sewing. What a wife she would make such a man. What would his theologian friends think when they heard Pastor Bonhoeffer's bride preferred dancing to American music than discussing Barth's latest essay, riding like mad across muddy fields than debating the merits of Greek and Hebrew translation?

Still, she couldn't deny the longing in her chest. To be loved by him in a way deeper than Vater and Max had ever loved her. To love him in return.

She wound her way deeper into the woods, her sturdy shoes crunching over disintegrating leaves and frozen twigs.

But not now. Not for a year. That was Mutter's edict. They weren't to meet, to write, to talk over the telephone for a year. In a year's time, she'd be nearly twenty. Better able to make a wise decision. In a way it was a relief, a lessening of a burden to avoid a concrete choice, to postpone all her musings, deliberations, and worries till later.

What changes would a year work in them both? What changes would a year bring to the war, to the world?

The days stretched before her like trees, 365 of them, each waiting to be felled. Long, wearisome days. Each she must face alone, wandering through her world, while he wandered his, until the days expired and they could find each other again.

Overhead, a bird swooped in circles, hunting its prey. A shiver crept up her spine. All she could do was determine to lay aside her longings and let the days pass. Like all of them, she had a duty to fulfill, and right now that meant obeying Mutter.

She had another duty as well. To Boris. Though she sensed his life, like that of so many others, was nearing its final days. He'd grown worse since she'd come back from Max's memorial service.

Pulling a kerchief from her pocket, she knotted it beneath her chin, concealing her hair. With quick steps, she moved in the direction of their meeting place, the woods noiseless as a whisper around her. Would he have the strength to come? Each time, he risked being caught and killed without questions asked. She'd tried to care for him as best as she was able, but he was sick. In need of medical care and attention not given to prisoners of war such as he. All of them were worked to the limits of their strength. What did it matter to the German guards whether one, twenty, a thousand prisoners lived or died?

The Russians are not like us, after all. Frau Vogel's voice drilled through Maria's mind. *They're Untermenschen.* Subhumans.

They aren't, Maria had wanted to shout back. They were flesh and blood, with hearts that loved and arms that longed to embrace children, wives, parents. As human and worthy of a future as the others murdered by the regime—Poles, Jews, the mentally handicapped.

She couldn't save them all. But she could do her best for Boris.

She reached the tree, hands tucked in her pockets, pacing and waiting. Finally, a twig crunched, and she turned to see him appear. His ragged clothes hung on his scarecrow-thin frame, his eyes like beads in their sunken sockets. But they were still the same shade of blue as Max's, and the feeble smile he gave her held a spark of life.

Wordlessly, she pulled the small brown bottle of vitamin drops from her pocket, along with a paper-wrapped piece of bread and pork fat. He took them, his dirt-encrusted hands closing around hers in silent thanks. His thin shirt revealed gaunt ribs and a chest that heaved painfully with each breath. His body had been beaten down to a fragile and aged shell, but . . . how young he was.

"Danke, Fräulein von Wedemeyer." He transferred the items to his trouser pockets with the care one would bestow upon an ancient relic.

"It isn't much. Frau Vogel has eyes like a hawk. She notices when anything goes missing."

"It's something." He drew in a wheezing breath. "Which is more than anyone else does. But you must not meet me here anymore. I'm too weak to slip away and return without being caught. You've been kind to me, very kind, and I offer you my gratitude. Your brother would be proud of you."

Maria swallowed. She wanted to plead with him to continue their appointments, but it would be of no use. Boris was waning fast. Even she could see it. Soon he'd be too feeble to work altogether. Would be left to rot like a vegetable past all use.

"I'll pray for you," she whispered. What else could she say? Truth was a difficult thing to reason with, and Boris spoke it when he said he was too weak.

"God and the saints will receive me when it's my time. I'll see your brother, yes." He smiled sadly through cracked lips. "Tell him what a fine sister he has."

She nodded, tears stinging her eyes, but she smiled through them. "Auf Wiedersehen, Boris."

"Auf Wiedersehen, Fräulein von Wedemeyer." He turned, disappearing into the dense woods moments later. Maria took the opposite path leading toward the Vogel home.

Her food and medicine had not been enough to sustain Boris. Just as her love had not been enough to keep Vater and Max alive.

Would anything she did ever be enough?

Max's face flitted before her like a candle flame almost spent. What would he say if he knew the pastor who'd confirmed him sought to marry his sister? She smiled slightly. First off, he'd probably have a good laugh at the notion of someone wanting to make a wife out of his untamed riding companion. But then he'd grow serious and tell her how glad he was for the both of them, that he hoped she'd still occasionally find time for a gallop across the fields.

After all, I don't know if we can trust your intended to stay on a horse, he'd say with a grin. And she'd give him a playful shove and be happy.

Happy. She lifted her gaze to the sky, as the sun died beneath its horizon, replaced with a cloak of darkness. Happiness existed in memory. As something once experienced, instead of a thing vital and ever present. How they'd all once taken it for granted.

If their separation was truly to last a year, she must do her best to remain content. At the end of the year, perhaps she would realize it had been for the best, that she was a more worthy person because of it.

The future stretched ahead, beckoning her to enter. Whether with kind intentions or to make her stumble, she didn't know. A road not yet mapped. A journey untraveled.

December 18, 1942
Klein-Krössin

Maria placed the china plates on the tea table. A small piece of strudel rested on each. Unlike prewar strudel, thick and liberally sprinkled with sugar, these pieces were thin and sweetened with a touch of honey. But it was still a treat, one she'd actually baked herself.

"These look wonderful, Maria." A blanket on her knees, Grossmutter sat in front of the snapping fire in the living room. "I'm quite surprised."

"What? That I didn't burn them? No more surprised than I." Maria kicked off her shoes and tucked her feet beneath her on the sofa. She cradled one of the plates in one hand, relishing the sight of a favorite treat. Along with the strudel, two cups held precious tea, albeit weak. Steam threaded upward from the brew.

Grossmutter took a bite. Maria watched as she chewed, waiting for a response. She'd been known to scorch and over-salt most of her previous attempts. Only Vater ever dared eat them.

"Very good." Grossmutter dabbed her mouth with a napkin. "As good as any I've ever made, if I do say so myself."

Maria sampled her own piece. It actually wasn't half bad. Considering the time she'd spent following every instruction in the recipe, it would've been a sorry thing if it'd turned out to be a flop.

They savored the pastry and tea, the low notes of instrumental Christmas songs crackling in from the radio. Snow drifted down, wreathing the windowpanes in icy swirls.

"Are you happy to be going home?" Grossmutter held her teacup with both gnarled hands. Age's infirmities showed themselves more and more each day in the tremble of her limbs and restless nights of insomnia.

"*Ja.*" Maria savored warm tea as it slid down her throat. "I am." The last weeks at the Vogels had been long and empty. Days spent corralling children into submission while inwardly she missed her own siblings. Subjected to Frau Vogel's constant discussion of her husband and the wonderful ways he served the Führer. She'd heard, in passing, that several already ill prisoners of war had succumbed to their diseases with the winter temperatures and had known instinctively that one of them was Boris. There'd been no grave to put flowers upon, no relatives to send letters of condolence to. But she'd whispered a prayer for the family of Boris, a young Russian whom no other soul in Germany would mourn.

Visiting Grossmutter was a welcome reprieve from the Vogels, particularly Gottfried. Tomorrow, she'd travel to Pätzig for Christmas with her family.

Their first Christmas without Vater and Max. Yet Maria had determined to make it as joyful as possible. Max and Vater wouldn't want otherwise. No one was celebrating as they used to anyway. A school friend who lived in Berlin had written that this year, instead of fine window displays, all the shops bore signs saying: "Think first of victory. And afterward of presents."

Victory for Germany was a lie.

"Have you given any more thought to the way things stand between you and Pastor Bonhoeffer?" Grossmutter eyed Maria over her teacup.

The bite of strudel in her mouth turned the consistency of brown paper. She forced a swallow. She'd wanted to avoid this conversation, though Grossmutter had seemed bent upon having it since the moment Maria arrived on Klein-Krössin's snow-covered doorstep.

"A bit." A vast understatement. She took another sip of tea.

"And? Don't you think it's time to challenge your mutter? A year is much too great a delay. I've done my best to convince her of this, but she remains unmovable. I think you need to be the one to talk to her."

Maria said nothing. Anything she attempted to voice would do no good.

Despite Grossmutter's exaggerated wishes and ideas, the innermost reality still held true. Had held fast during the past weeks when, instead of her own deliberations and worries quieting, they only clamored louder.

Despite all the superficial arguments against it—and oh there were many: their difference in age, his bent for academia and hers for fast-paced activity, the war, his involvement in illegal activities—one thing remained constant. Though she didn't yet love him in the way of a woman on her wedding day, she knew beyond anything that she would.

And she intended to talk with Mutter over the holidays.

"I will make whatever decision I make when I feel it to be right." She kept her tone calm. "I'm a grown woman. And if I am destined to be the wife of Dietrich Bonhoeffer, I must learn to form my own opinions and make my own choices."

At this, Grossmutter looked positively aghast. "Of course you won't. He'll tell you what your opinions are and what decisions to make."

Maria stood, shaking crumbs from the folds of her skirt, attempting to shake her frustration out with them. Grossmutter and her old-fashioned ideas. For a woman so strong-willed herself, she expected a great deal of submission from others.

"I'll put these things in the kitchen." She picked up the plates and stepped from the living room. She placed the plates in the sink and ran warm water over them, staring out at the gently falling snow. Somewhere out there, men and boys continued to fight the Russians. War did not stop, not even for Christmas. Many of their troops fought bitterly to rescue those stranded in Stalingrad, while earlier this month others had engaged in heavy battle as they were pushed farther and farther into the corner of North Africa.

Like the warmth of an embrace that lingers long after the giver has pulled away, the memories of Christmases past touched her mind and heart. Decorating the tree with Vater and Max. The long dining-room table piled high with Christmas treats and laden to bursting. The service in the little church awash with the soft light of candles.

Since the beginning of the war, these events hadn't ceased. But they weren't the same. Never could be again, with missing places at the family table, the departed ones present, but only in memory.

"Maria!" Grossmutter's voice. Unusually loud and almost frightened.

Maria dashed from the room, her stocking feet slipping on the hardwood. Clapping a hand to her chest, she stopped short in the doorway, expecting to see Grossmutter lying prone on the carpet. But she hadn't moved, didn't appear injured. A familiar melody lilted from the radio.

"You scared me half out of my mind! Why did you shout?"

Grossmutter put a finger to her lips. She turned back to the radio. Maria leaned against the door, the familiar notes of "Stille Nacht" filling the air.

Silent night! Holy night!
All is calm, and all is bright
Only the Chancellor steadfast in fight
Watches o'er Germany by day and by night
Always caring for us.
Always caring for us.

Silent night! Holy night!
All is calm, and all is bright
Adolf Hitler is Germany's wealth
Brings us greatness, favor and health
Oh give us Germans all power!

The last notes died away. Maria stood motionless. Grossmutter turned, her pale face illuminated by tendrils of firelight. The two women exchanged glances. No words were needed between them.

It was only a song.

But much, much more than that.

Chapter Eighteen

W hat better way to spend the last days of the waning year than in looking to the promise of the future? Eberhard and Renate embodied
that future, as they stood beside the refreshment table in the Bonhoeffers'
dining room. The center of everyone's attention, Renate looked radiant in a
made-over dress of deep mauve. Eberhard, his hand brushing the small of
her back, grinned ear to ear.

Dietrich smiled, half listening to Bärbel's story about the crafts the children were making for Christmas.

Tonight, his best friend became engaged to his niece.

Leaving Dietrich more alone than ever before. Not that things would
change. Much. They'd still have their theological discussions, their shared
ideas and thoughts. But Eberhard was no longer free to simply go off on a
weekend skiing trip whenever the fancy struck them. He had Renate now,
would have children with her someday.

Dietrich curled his fingers into a ball.

He missed Maria. Devastatingly, he missed her. If she'd been beside him,
tonight would be better able to be borne. He'd have rejoiced completely in
Eberhard's good fortune, instead of being . . . well, more than a little jealous that Eberhard had attained what Dietrich lacked.

The woman he loved.

*God, forgive me. It's so easy to preach that "anything we do not thank
You for, we reproach You for." How often I fail at putting it into practice.
I know You guide every aspect of my life. Help me to trust You completely,
even in this separation, which seems so hard to take.*

"It sounds like you'll be spoiling your parents with gifts this year."
Dietrich focused on Bärbel, trying to make up for the fact that he'd been

oblivious to her chatter for the past five minutes. "Are you hoping for any-thing special yourself?"

Bärbel shook her head, ribbon-tied braids swinging around her face. "Mutti says we aren't to expect much from Father Christmas this time. Wartime keeps him from bringing as many presents as he used to." She gave a resigned sigh.

"Now, I don't know about that." Dietrich tweaked one of her braids, coaxing a smile from the twelve-year-old. "Father Christmas has lots of surprises in store, I'm sure." At least as long as her Uncle Dietrich was around. He did his best to buy presents for the younger ones, even in war-time. In his bedroom closet, a brightly wrapped package containing a book of children's poems had Bärbel's name on it.

"You really think so?" A spark of excitement entered her too-serious eyes.

He stood. "I really do."

Crossing the room crowded with family and friends, he reached the happy couple, whose eyes fixated solely on each other.

"Ahem." Dietrich cleared his throat.

They both started, dropping their clasped hands as if caught in some illegal activity. "Uncle Dietrich." Renate hugged him. "Where have you been hiding?"

In the corner with Bärbel and his own discontented thoughts. But Dietrich only shrugged.

Eberhard gripped his hand, feeling in his gaze. "You, of all people, should be sharing in our happiness tonight. After all, if it weren't for our friendship, Renate and I would never have found each other." The warmth in his eyes as he looked at his betrothed said it all.

"I can't claim to take any credit for it." Dietrich smiled. "But I can say that the two of you have such a good foundation and true mutuality in your love you surely have many happy days ahead of you."

Eberhard slipped his hand around Renate's waist, pulling her close. "I only wish this same happiness upon you, my friend."

"*Ja*, well, we both know where that stands." Stopped, more like. At least for eleven more months.

"I think it's very hard of Frau von Wedemeyer to impose such a restric-tion upon you and her daughter." Renate's expression turned indignant. Eberhard must have told her. Not that he expected the affianced couple to keep anything from each other, but wasn't that sharing a bit much? "Per-haps for a little while, but to be separated for an entire year seems too harsh by half. Particularly these days."

"I'm sure Frau von Wedemeyer is doing what she thinks best," Dietrich said quietly. "But enough of that. Tonight is for the two of you. I must say I'm looking forward to the wedding. I haven't been best man before. I hope I can do the office justice."

"Justice or not, I wouldn't have anyone else." Eberhard's smile grew. "By the way, Dietrich, I've been thinking about that passage from *Ethics* you shared with me. And I've come up with a few minor suggestions."

"And this is my cue to go find Mutter in the kitchen." Renate slipped from her fiancé's side with a grin. "I know when I'm not needed." She tripped away, stopping to chat with Eberhard's parents, who'd made the journey from their farm in Saxony to attend the party.

Eberhard was expounding upon his suggestions, when someone tapped Dietrich on the shoulder. He turned.

Flakes of white melted on the collar of Hans's overcoat, his face ruddy with cold. "Can I see you for a minute? You too, Eberhard."

They left the room and entered Vater's study, the party atmosphere dissipating as speedily as the snow dusting Hans's coat. Dietrich flicked on the desk lamp. The feeble light didn't do much to banish the darkness. Eberhard gathered cushions stashed for just this purpose and placed them over the telephone.

Hans dropped into a chair next to the desk, stretching out his legs. Eberhard and Dietrich stood in front of the bookshelves.

"To put it bluntly, Himmler is working overtime, trying to get approval for our arrests. He's ordered the Gestapo to proceed with comprehensive investigations into the Abwehr. Of course, they're thrilled to comply. As is that bloodhound Roeder."

Dietrich stared into the swirl of dust motes spinning in the lamplight. This wasn't the time to dwell upon the implications of the word *arrest*. "Then our best hope is for a successful coup before investigations conclude."

Hans nodded. "Tresckow is coming up with a plan. Operation Flash. The main trouble is finding a way to get past the Führer's massive security. Do you know he's got a steel helmet that weighs as much as a cannonball? The man might strut about like a powerful peacock, but he's frightfully afraid of people wanting the end of him."

"Tresckow will find a way if anyone can." Eberhard spoke up. "If they can get him into the Führer's headquarters in Smolensk, there's a greater chance of penetrating security."

Hans steepled his fingers. "That's what his thoughts are. I'm advising them the best I can. But Dietrich, after the holidays I want you to travel to

Munich and secure the required visas. We absolutely cannot act as if we're under suspicion. That would just be an admission of guilt."

Dietrich nodded. "At least if the worst happens, we have all the papers in place." He'd spent hours composing a false diary to leave on his desk in case of a Gestapo search, making every entry out to be the thoughts of a dull-minded clergyman, clueless about the finer points of politics. Along with that, he'd typed a letter dated 1940, in which Dietrich requested Hans to find him a place in the Abwehr. That way, the authorities wouldn't think Dietrich had become a civilian for Military Intelligence just to avoid conscription. Suspicion hung like fog over anyone not actively serving in the Wehrmacht, whether their papers marked them essential in other ways or not.

"*Ja*. The documents." Hans stared at the bookshelves as if hoping to see the future laid out amongst the rows of thick volumes.

Dietrich checked his watch. Approaching nine. The party would be breaking up, everyone returning to their own homes in time for the air-raid warnings.

He turned back to Hans. "We're prepared for the worst. But there's also a chance of success." With enough reasonable men in high places behind their endeavors, surely there was still hope for the coup.

Hans stood. "So Christel tells me. And I believe her. My wife is a wise woman." The three men returned the pillows to their places and extinguished the lamp. They exited the darkness and reentered the living room, where the partygoers were making their way out. Hans went to Christel's side, Eberhard to Renate's. Dietrich stood on the fringes, the conversation with Hans fresh as newly typed ink across the pages of his mind.

There was hope, and then there was reality. Hope that Tresckow's plans would succeed and the government that had caused so many to suffer would be overthrown. But the reality remained that the year 1943 could bring many things, including their arrests. With that in mind, every day spent in freedom became even more precious against the knowledge that it could be one of the last.

Carpe diem—seize the day—became not simply a motto but a way of life. Evidenced by tonight's engagement party, a stand for claiming the future for family and loved ones.

Hans helped Christel on with her coat. Klaus and Emmi rounded up their children, Klaus calling for them in his booming voice. Eberhard and Renate held hands, looking into each other's eyes. Dietrich's vater laughed, making some joke about the engaged couple, which his mutter promptly countered.

You're in my thoughts far more than your family would approve of, Maria von Wedemeyer. I still remember the look in your eyes when I arrived at your Grossmutter's hospital room. I wish I could see that look again, even for a moment.

God alone knew what 1943 would bring.

Dietrich only prayed that somehow, some way, Maria had a place in it for him.

December 24, 1942
Berlin

It no longer mattered that the tree was but a scrawny one, the candles and decorations few. In fact, Dietrich looked upon it with greater wonder, his gratitude all the more fervent. They were together, this Bonhoeffer family of his, faces wreathed in a soft glow by the candlelight's flame. His parents, side by side in chairs pulled close to the piano. Hans and Christel; Klaus and Emmi; Ursula and Rüdiger; Eberhard, his brother in all but blood, and Renate. The children clustered near, their faces a mirror of innocence. With them all, the memory of faces departed—either to other places, like Sabine and Gerhard in England, or to heaven above, like Walter. Missed, but still present in every heart.

Together, they kept Christmas Eve, doing as they'd always done.

Dietrich's fingers brushed the ivory keys, each note clear and true. The chorus of "Stille Nacht" rose from every throat, the words laden with feeling.

"Stille Nacht! Heilige Nacht . . ."

Christ had been born to a world in need, one much like theirs. Full of chaos, sorrow, and depravity. A world in need of a Savior and a people in want of grace. Not the false kind, peddled to the masses like cheapjack's wares, but costly grace, real and abiding. This year, though the traditional parts of Christmas—masses of gifts, lavish celebrations, and plates of food—might be lacking, their very lack perhaps added a truer quality to their humble celebration.

The last note died away. Dietrich stood from his seat at the piano. The room smelled of evergreen. Outside, snow fell in giant flakes, though the blackout curtains concealed the view. Eberhard slipped his arm around Renate's waist, Hans and Christel stood side by side, perfected in their love by life's tempests.

"Go ahead, Dietrich," Hans urged. Even he seemed at peace tonight—for his family's sake, perhaps, more than his own. Even the holidays hadn't stopped the Gestapo from beheading members of the Red Orchestra resistance group just two days ago, Roeder again in charge. The Red Orchestra had been made up of Communists vehemently opposed to the Führer. Young women were among those executed, gender affording one no privileges when it came to Reich justice.

Christmas and death. A combination all too familiar during the Great War and again these past years. But wasn't death a part of Christmas as much as life? For if one followed Christ, the passing from this life was simply the final point on a journey straight to God, the Savior who came to earth as God made flesh, beginning in the unlikeliest of places—a tiny manger.

"You're sure?" Dietrich picked up the small pile of papers. As a Christmas gift to Hans, Eberhard, and Oster, but also as a way to work things through himself, he'd penned an essay. Entitled "After Ten Years," he'd done his best to write a moral reckoning of all they'd learned and experienced since Hitler's ascension to power. It had been difficult, but essential. Perhaps less to them now than to those who might read it once the smoke cleared and people outside Germany sought answers.

Hans and Eberhard nodded their assent.

Dietrich cleared his throat. It had been an unlikely thing to write at Christmastime, this place and day an even less likely setting for its reading, surrounded as they were by candles and a Christmas tree and the group in Sunday best. Or was it?

He read aloud page after page, all of those gathered, even the children, listening quietly.

As he read, the enormity of what he'd written filled him anew. The rest seemed to feel it too, their gazes intent, weighty with all they'd experienced. They'd lived it too, faced choices, grappled with conviction. Struggled for truth in a world where black and white had ceased to be. And it wasn't over. Choices still befell them, the days grew darker yet.

He reached the last paragraph.

> We have been silent witnesses of evil deeds; we have been drenched by many storms; we have learnt the arts of equivocation and pretense; experience has made us suspicious of others and kept us from being truthful and open; intolerable conflicts have worn us down and even made us cynical. Are we still of any use? What we shall need is not geniuses, or cynics, or misanthropes, or clever tacticians, but plain, honest, straightforward men. . . .

There remains for us an experience of incomparable value. We have for once learnt to see the great events of world history from below, from the perspective of the outcast, the suspects, the mal-treated, the powerless, the oppressed, the reviled—in short, from the perspective of those who suffer.

He concluded the last paragraphs. When he finished, everyone sat. Silent.

Finally Hans stood and crossed the room. He faced Dietrich, so much in his eyes. What a burden this man had borne. How willingly yet regretfully he'd shouldered it.

"Danke, Dietrich. For writing that." His throat jerked, yet a faint smile lined his face. "And if I may say so to all of you"—he turned and faced the group—"my family, 1943 is upon us, but not yet. The future awaits, but tonight, let us have together, a happy Christmas."

Chapter Nineteen

January 13, 1943
Pätzig

Steeling herself to stand her ground, Maria knocked on her mutter's door. Her fingers shook as she lowered her hand. From anticipation? Or fear? Or a combination of the two? She'd put off this conversation, letting Christmas and New Year's pass in peace. But she couldn't delay it another day. If Vater's and Max's deaths had taught her anything, it was to hold nothing back. Now was the time to make the most of every moment. Not six months, nor a year, but this instant.

And for her, *now* intrinsically included Dietrich Bonhoeffer, as surely as if they were already joined together by vows said before God.

"Enter." Mutter's voice emerged.

Maria stepped inside. Her mutter sat at her tidy desk in the light by the window, her posture straight as a measuring rod, all except her head, which she inclined slightly over her paper, as her pen moved fast across the page.

"What is it, Maria?" Mutter's pen continued its race.

Maria's resolve weakened. She was an interruption. With all her cares and responsibilities, Mutter didn't have time for this. Better that Maria go and return later. But would later be any better? Nein, Mutter would still be occupied. Only the task interrupted would differ.

Maria lifted her chin. Mutter must make time. Not to speak or dictate, but to listen. And Maria wasn't leaving until it took place.

"May I speak with you for a moment?"

Mutter lifted her head, still grasping her pen. "*Ja*, Maria. What is it?"

Maria took a breath, as if she could draw courage along with air into her lungs.

This is right. This is right.

She sensed it, knew it, more than anything she'd ever sensed or known before.

"It's about Pastor Bonhoeffer."

"I thought that topic was no longer to be brought under discussion." Some people showed emotion in the lowering and raising of their voice. Mutter had never been one of those, her tone always calm and controlled. She made her point in the substance of her words.

"I wish to speak of it again." A strand of hair bumped her ear. She shoved it back again. "I've been giving it a lot of thought, and have decided . . . decided . . ." Nein, no hesitation. In her heart, she felt none. Her words must match. "My decision is irrevocable. I'm going to marry him, Mutter."

Five words. Those words. In them embodied a future. Not Mutter's or Grossmutter's but her own. And no one was going to change her mind. She could still scarcely believe he wanted to marry her, but if he still did, she would be his without hesitation. Committing herself to him was at once the easiest and the bravest thing she'd ever done.

Mutter's complexion paled. For long seconds, she regarded her daughter, as if taking her measure. Maria straightened her shoulders.

"Be sensible, Maria. You can't possibly be deciding to marry a man you know so little of." She spoke as if trying to rationalize with a child.

Maria took a step closer. "But that's not true. I don't believe in time dictating depth. For some, it might take years to grow toward togetherness. For others, a space of hours need be enough. There's something in me . . . whenever I think of him. I cannot turn my back on this. I won't." Unexpected tears welled in her eyes.

"You love him then?" Mutter's keen eyes probed her defenses.

Maria swallowed back the dryness in her throat. If she said what she did not feel, Mutter would see through the subterfuge. Only truth would suffice now. "I know that I will love him. And that matters more to me than some silly, infatuated emotion others name love. I don't want to be separated. At the very least, I want to be able to write to him."

Outside a low, cold wind howled. The fire snapped in the hearth. Mutter stared into the orange flames.

Maria held her breath. Happy moments were like hummingbird wings, flying by. Crucial ones trudged on as if weighted with lead.

How strange it was that this was how it would go down for her. For Ruth-Alice, her intended had requested an interview with Vater in his library. It hadn't taken long: everyone was pleased, and they'd had an impromptu celebration afterward. This time it was her, the woman, asking permission. Someday, they would laugh about this, Dietrich and she. As their children scampered around them, they'd smile and recall the uncommon way they'd begun their engagement. She'd probably laugh at herself, mature lady she'd be then.

If only time could speed itself forward to that day.

"Very well." Mutter sighed. "Though I can't pretend I believe your decision will hold good, you're not a child. You may write to him, but that is all. The postponement on further meetings still holds. Does that satisfy you?"

Joy swirled in her chest. Bittersweet, but there regardless. When she'd first found out about Max's death, she'd doubted she'd ever experience it again. Yet here it was. Present within her.

In a few months, Mutter would relent about the separation. After she grew to know Dietrich better, she couldn't possibly expect them to wait a year for a reunion. And for now, writing to him would be more than enough.

"Danke," Maria whispered, putting her arms around her mutter.

Mutter drew back after a moment. "There now." She smiled slightly, wearily. "Go on and write your letter. Doubtless he'll be glad to receive it."

She needed no further invitation. Half running from the room until she gained her own, she reached the door and closed it behind her. Leaning against the frame, she tried to still the frantic pounding of her heart. Now that she'd received permission to write, what would she say? What would he think if she answered a question he'd never even asked her?

Still, answer it she would.

Another thing to add to their "someday we'll laugh about it" list.

She crossed the room. Sunlight broke through the gray sky, casting its rays upon the polished surface of her desk. Sunlight. Beauty. Even amid a colorless world.

She pulled a piece of paper from her drawer and uncapped her fountain pen. Propping her chin in her hand, she stared down at the blank page, imagining it covered with her handwriting, him holding it in his hands. Those same hands, someday, holding her.

"Today," she whispered into the silence. "Today, Dietrich Bonhoeffer, I can now say yes to you."

January 17, 1943
Berlin

The New Year dawned and the conspirators waited, not always sure what they waited for. As a precaution, Dietrich updated his will. No one knew what would come next. It was all a matter of wait, and behave with normalcy. Easier said than done.

Discouragement reared its black head, much as Dietrich tried to lock it away. These days, Eberhard walked around with a perpetual smile, talking about Renate in the rose-tinted manner a man speaks of the woman he loves. Dietrich listened and did his best to share in the joy. Much as he tried, much as he wanted to, maddening jealousy stalked him. Eberhard had everything. And all Dietrich had wanted, he'd been denied.

He threw himself into writing and doing all he could to assist Hans, anything to avoid thinking. Thinking only led to discontent, and discontent to misery. Enough of that was going around.

But a hollow emptiness in his heart, like the crumbling walls of a shelled-out building, lingered. Aching. Ever present.

Snow slicked beneath his shoes as he walked, head bent low, to his parents' home. A cup of weak ersatz was just the thing he needed to warm his frigid fingers. That and maybe a piece of rye bread.

Stomping snow from his shoes, he opened the door. A gust of wind blew it shut behind him, and he shucked off his gloves, coat, and scarf, hanging them on the coat tree. Grabbing a towel, he wiped up the traces of mud his shoes had left behind and stepped to the hall table. A stack of mail lay upon it. Fingers still wooden with cold, he flipped through it clumsily. Two letters for Vater. A holiday postcard, likely delayed, for Mutter.

An envelope lay at the bottom of the stack. Plain white, postmarked Pomerania. Addressed in flowing script to *Dietrich Bonhoeffer, Marienburger Allee 43, Charlottenburg.*

From Maria.

His heart sped. Gently, as if it might crumble, he picked up the letter, staring down at it in his hand. Was it a figment of his overworked imagination, a flight of fancy that would vanish in an instant?

Nein. He ran his fingertips across the smooth edges of the envelope. Not fancy. Reality.

A reality he'd scarcely dared hope for.

He took the stairs two at a time with the speed of a schoolboy. Once inside his room, he gazed at the envelope again, his breathing short and fast. What words could be within?

He almost dropped the envelope, his fingers shook so.

There. The top was slit. He pulled out two pages, unfolding them. For a long moment, he stared at his name penned in her hand at the top of the page: "Dear Pastor Bonhoeffer."

What? Was he half afraid to read more? Where was his logical, calm mind now?

Banished with one glance at her script.

> *I've known, ever since arriving home, that I must write to you, and I've looked forward to doing so.*
>
> *I recently spoke with my mutter. I'm now able to write to you, and to ask you to answer this letter.*
>
> *I find it hard to have to tell you in writing what can scarcely be uttered in person. I would rather disown every word that demands to be said on the subject, because it makes things that were better conveyed quietly sound so crude and clumsy. But, knowing from experience how well you understand me, I'm now emboldened to write to you even though I've really no right whatsoever to answer a question which you have never asked me.*
>
> *With all my happy heart, I can now say yes.*

Over and over, he ran his gaze across those words.

Maria had given him her yes. She'd agreed to become his wife. What should have been done with him on his knee and the asking of an age-old question had been sealed with one letter from her. Unbelievable. Wonderful.

"Oh, my dearest," he whispered.

What right had he to this *yes*? How could he be worthy of this gift? Of this woman?

But worthy he would be. For her.

The remainder of the letter explained her mutter's continued reluctance to waive the delay, but that they could exchange letters from time to time. And shyly, she wrote that she wondered if she were truly worthy of him, and she pleaded with him to tell her if he no longer thought her good enough.

What a question. She was too good for him by half.

He must write her directly. The letter had already taken four days in arriving, no doubt she daily waited for his answer. He sat at his desk, paper in front of him, pen at its side, and a ridiculous smile on his face.

In these past weeks, he had never expected God would grant him this gift. He was to be content with what he had already been given and not ask for more, work out his inward struggle with the help of God and vanquish it. Much as he had longed for her, that longing must be put away and forgotten. It was only natural that in the midst of a life lived from hour to hour, one desired to build a future. Such a prospect had seemed too wonderfully fantastic to be his after all these years. He had almost reconciled himself to putting it behind him. For he knew beyond a doubt he could never feel for another what he cherished for Maria von Wedemeyer.

This letter changed everything. These words from this precious young woman. His future wife.

> *Dear Maria,*

An explanation of the four-day delay, to avoid confusion on her part. Then:

> *May I simply tell you what is in my heart? I feel, and am overwhelmed by the realization, that I have been granted a gift beyond compare. I had given up hope of it, after all the turmoil of recent weeks, and now the inconceivably great and happy moment has come, just like that, and my heart is opening wide and brimming over with gratitude and confusion and still can't take it in—the "yes" that is to determine the entire future course of our lives. If we could speak together now, there would be so infinitely much to say—though all that would really amount to is a repetition of one and the same thing! Will we be able to see each other soon, without having once more to fear what other people say? Or is it still impossible for some reason? I think it has to be possible now.*
>
> *And I can't speak otherwise than I've so often spoken in my heart in recent weeks—I want to call you what a man calls the girl with whom it is his desire and privilege to go through life, and who has given him her consent. Dear Maria, thank you for what you said, for all you have endured on my account, and for all you are to me and wish to be.*

He stopped, overcome by the sudden burn of moisture in his eyes. Bonhoeffer men did not show such emotion.

But he couldn't help these tears. This gift, this promise for the future overwhelmed him like nothing had ever done before. Rightly so. To each other, they would occupy a place no other soul on earth could hold. Friends, lovers. Husband and wife.

"For all you are to me," he whispered, brushing his fingers across the pages of her letter as if it were her hand he clasped. "And for all we will be together."

January 20, 1943
Pätzig

Don't say anything about the "false picture" I may have of you. I don't want a "picture," I want you; just as I beg you with all my heart to want me. . . .

Could this truly be real? That Dietrich would write such things to her befuddled Maria's mind in the most stunning of ways.

She slipped the letter within the pages of her diary and closed the cloth-bound cover. Propping her chin in her hand, she stared out at the sky, rose-gray with twilight. She'd spent the day with Lala and Peter, drilling them in their lessons while snow fell in great tufts. After the studies, they'd donned hats and mittens and raced outside to build snow forts and pummel each other with snowballs. What would Dietrich think of her if he could see her thus, hair disheveled and nose beet red with cold? Would he wish to join them? Or would that be improper for a theologian? If he did join in their games, she'd mercilessly pelt him with snowballs, just to see the look on his face. Perhaps one would knock him off-balance, and he'd fall into the deep drifts, pulling her with him. They'd lie, nose to nose, surrounded by the children's laughter and sparkling white. She'd look into his eyes, and . . . and . . .

A glance in the mirror above the desk revealed that her face had turned the earlier shade of her nose.

The sooner she was enrolled in the student nursing program at the Clementinenhaus Hospital in Hanover, the better. The work would be hard, but the struggle would clear her mind—make her better, worthier, when the time of separation expired. Better hospital work than the Arbeitsdienst—the Reich Labor Service—another looming possibility. She'd already endured enough Reich ideology during her stint at the Vogels. Since ending her term of service there, she'd no desire for a repeat.

A knock sounded. Maria turned, a strand of still-damp hair slipping from behind her ear.

"Come in." She shoved the hair behind her ear and the diary in her desk drawer.

The door opened. Mutter stepped in, still wearing her coat, a blue wool scarf knotted at her throat.

"I haven't seen you since breakfast," Maria said.

Weary lines fanned themselves through her face, in the corners of her eyes. "I was in the village." She sank onto the edge of the bed.

"With whom?" Mutter had always taken her duties as leading lady of the area seriously, but it wasn't like her to be absent this long.

"Fraülein Kurtz." Mutter's chest lifted in a heavy sigh. Maria went to her side and knelt beside her. Gently, she unwound the scarf. Mutter's hands sat limp in her lap.

"Can I fetch you anything? Supper? Some tea?"

Mutter shook her head, brownish-graying hair frizzed around her face as if she'd just taken off her hat. Maria laid the scarf on the carpet, beside her feet.

"Nein. I came upstairs directly, to tell you about Fraülein Kurtz. I'll get something later."

"What about her?" Maria remembered the woman from church and village events. Mutter's concern for the inhabitants near Pätzig was legendary, and she'd continued the practice since Vater's death. But though she'd dealt with all manner of misery, particularly since the war, little of it wreaked havoc on her soldier-like control.

Mutter swallowed, pressing her cold-chapped lips together. "Fraülein Kurtz is well. Physically, there is nothing I can do for her."

"Then what?"

"Fraülein Kurtz is a spinster. For all her life, she's relied upon the support of her brother."

Mutter spoke too slowly. What was she not telling?

Maria broke in. "*Ja*, I know. He writes her weekly from Munich, and she reads his letters to practically anyone who will listen. Every time he takes a holiday, he comes to visit her."

Mutter nodded. "He repairs radios in Munich. Has for more than twenty-five years. But two days ago, the Gestapo came to his shop. They arrested him for suspicious activity regarding the distribution of his radios. He's in prison somewhere now. Fraülein Kurtz doesn't know where. The woman is terrified." Mutter's voice rose. "She's frightened they're coming for her next. I tried to calm her, to assure her that, despite her association, she was safe. While I spoke, inwardly, I began to hate myself. My assurances, my calm were all lies. I could promise her nothing. By her association with Jan Kurtz, Hilde is in danger."

Maria placed her hands over her mutter's shaking ones. "Surely they wouldn't arrest Fraülein Kurtz just because she has a brother all the way in Munich. That's absurd."

"Is it?" Mutter stared out the window, as if she spoke only to herself.

"Once, perhaps. Not anymore. I'm going to help Hilde locate her brother's whereabouts. But that's not why I came to speak with you. Dietrich Bonhoeffer, whatever his role in any conspiracy, is in danger. You, by your connection with him, are also at risk, if . . . the worst happened."

She squeezed Maria's hands, her bony fingers gripping Maria's, as if through her touch she could anchor them both in safety. "You must know, my daughter, I don't disapprove of your feelings for him, nor his for you. In fact, he made a great impression upon me when he came to visit. But . . . I fear for you. If something were to happen to him, and they discovered his connection with you . . ." Tears slid down Mutter's cheeks, tracks of moisture against the chalky pallor of her skin. "After your vater and Max . . . I cannot bear to lose any more of my family in this wretched war."

Maria sat back on her heels, helpless in the face of her mutter's pain. Her earlier arguments about their difference in age could be refuted. This, however, could not. How could she live with herself if she caused Mutter this pain?

How could she live with herself if she went back on her promise to Dietrich?

Both meant so much to her. But Dietrich had a family of his own, friends. Mutter had lost her oldest son and beloved husband. Whom should she put first?

Vater's eyes filled her mind, solemnly telling her what to do, memories of him guiding her as surely as he once had. She had her answer.

Swallowing back the ache in her throat, she pulled a handkerchief from the pocket of her skirt and pressed it into her mutter's palm. "I'll request he not write to me for six months. If the way he spoke when I was in Berlin is true, this madness will soon be over. After that, we can begin again. No one outside of his close family and mine knows of our engagement."

Mutter dried her eyes. "That would be best." She stood, curling the handkerchief into her fist. "You must tell him you need some time to be alone. Mention nothing about your real reasons."

Maria nodded, the movement suddenly leaden.

"I should go see to the children. Get something to eat. Fraülein Kurtz offered me tea, but her larder is already so sparse. If word gets out in the village about her brother, things will only become worse for her."

Maria said nothing as Mutter crossed the distance to the door, closed it behind her with a soft click. Maria stared after her. Only moments ago, she had been actually giddy at the thought of writing to Dietrich again. Now, realizing what she must say, the task filled her with nothing but dread.

How would she endure the ache of separation, when he'd so eloquently pleaded with her otherwise? She, who had already lost the two men foremost in her life.

Separation. Loss. The lack of something one valued most.

A tear slid down her cheek. She forced herself to swallow, brush it away, and pick up her pen.

The middle of a war was no time for emotional outbursts. She must be brave and strong.

"Brave and strong," she whispered. "Brave and strong."

January 24, 1943
Berlin

Dietrich stared at the letter on his desk, unwilling to believe what he'd just read. Maria, who'd so boldly given him her yes, now requested distance. Time to be alone, she'd said, the words written so formally. She'd ended with a reaffirmation of her wish to someday become his wife, as if trying to soften the blow.

If he could, he'd travel to Pomerania and see this thing set straight. Surely if they met in person, everything could be brought to light. Made clear and simple and straightforward again.

But he expected to depart for Switzerland any day now, and he couldn't leave Hans and the others. Not now. He had meetings to keep, including an upcoming one next month with a member of the resistance in Munich—a young university student named Hans Scholl.

Germany was well and truly losing the war, with Stalingrad almost completely lost, though Hitler still demanded the beleaguered General Paulus fight to the last bullet. Weekly, officers came to Hans, or to Oster and Canaris, expressing their disgust for Hitler and his methods. Occasionally, another member was added to their circle of conspiracy. A circle about to meet its climax at a date yet undetermined.

He gazed at the letter again, wishing he could see the face of the woman who wrote it. Wishing he could discern her intentions as easily as he read the loops and letters of her script. He wanted to know her, really know her. Her thoughts and wishes, likes and dislikes. They needed time together to learn these things. Time to fall in love, well and truly. And now even their correspondence must be put aside.

An almost palpable ache engulfed his heart.

Attempting to push her toward a different decision would be wrong. If she desired space, he'd give her what she needed, much as it pained him.

It wasn't permanent. At least she'd reaffirmed that.

The bedroom door opened. Eberhard stuck his head inside.

"Do I disturb?"

"When has that ever stopped you?" Dietrich turned, not bothering to cover up any of the papers cluttering his desk. Ever since the days at Finkenwalde, he'd never kept any secrets from his friend. Eberhard was a worthy confidant. Never pried. Never insisted on being told anything. Just listened when Dietrich had something to say. A mutual sharing of ideas and impressions, questions and answers. The perfect friendship.

"Never, I guess." Eberhard smiled. "I just came to tell you the good news. Hans has officially made me a member of the Abwehr."

"Renate will be pleased." As a member of military intelligence, Eberhard would now be deemed essential to the war effort without having to serve as a soldier. Though with the type of work the Abwehr did, Dietrich almost wished his friend had allowed himself to be conscripted instead. No telling which was safer. That he even entertained this thought gave testament to the times. Once he'd been a strong pacifist. Still was. But every choice had become more circumstantial rather than concrete. Concrete only bound one to a code of conduct that wasn't always the right course.

"I hope so." Eberhard pulled up a chair and sat backward on it, leaning his arms on the top rail. "I'm glad to officially be one of you. To finally have a capacity of sorts."

"You've always worked in a pastoral capacity. Been able to continue preaching, whereas I haven't been able to do that legally since the Gestapo restricted me."

"I know. But I'm glad to be able to start being put to some official use. At any rate . . . What were you looking at so intently when I came in?"

Dietrich reached for the letter and handed it to Eberhard. Sat back in his chair, following Eberhard's expressions as he read.

Finally, he lowered the letter, brow tightening.

"Well?"

"I don't know what to make of it. Why would she suggest a cessation in your correspondence after it's only been so recently resumed? And what does she mean about time alone? It's not as if you're knocking on her door day and night."

"I know. It seems unnatural. To be engaged, and not even able to write my fiancée a letter on her birthday." Which was April 23, still within the six-month period.

Eberhard stood and put the letter on the cluttered desk, leaning one hand on the edge. "My guess is there's something more at play here. Probably her family requested this for some reason or other. From what I saw of her at Hans-Walter's party, she didn't seem the type to vacillate between one extreme and another. But I guess you never can tell. I still don't understand Renate all the time."

"Renate, at least, has the full support of her parents for her engagement, a fact which I'm quite pleased about." Dietrich smiled. "It's high time you were an official member of this family."

Eberhard grinned. "You know how much I desire it."

For several moments, silence lingered. Dietrich took in the variety of correspondence on his desk, his gaze landing on one letter in particular. He turned to Eberhard. "I keep thinking of the soldiers fighting at Stalingrad. I heard from Hubert Illing yesterday. I don't think you knew him very well when he was at Finkenwalde. He was barely able to pen the letter, his hands were so frostbitten. He said he used to take his little finger for granted, but now, he's lost it." Whatever the future held for Hubert, his music-making days were over. How many evenings had they worked out melodies on the piano and guitar? Too many to count. Hubert had been determined to learn to play the African spirituals they were all so fond of.

He hadn't gotten past "Steal Away" before his notice of conscription came.

"Hitler can't keep them fighting at Stalingrad much longer."

"Hans says Hitler refuses to allow surrender, though the generals are all begging for it. Fight to the last bullet, he tells them. It won't take much longer for that to be literally true." Tilting his head, Dietrich glanced up at the rafters. He had hidden his copy of "After Ten Years" beneath one of the beams. Hopefully, at least one of the copies would survive the bombings.

"And Tresckow? How are his plans progressing?" Though there was nothing in Dietrich's sparse room that could be used for surveillance, Eberhard still lowered his voice.

Dietrich leaned forward. The aroma of baking bread and vegetables wafted up the stairs. "With some success. He's trying to get Hitler's adjutant to convince the Führer that a visit to the Army Group Centre in Smolensk is just what everyone needs to boost morale. Subtly, of course. I feel sure he'll succeed. Tresckow has a way of talking people 'round. He's Maria's uncle, you know."

Eberhard crossed to Dietrich's bookshelves, running a hand along a row of volumes. "The real key is knowing how to proceed after they've carried out the plans. And that's where you and Hans have done so much. You'll be able to make good use of your ecumenical contacts when the time comes. We'll need men like you more than ever."

"I wouldn't do it without you. You've always been the one with all the charm."

They both laughed. Dietrich turned to make some order of the papers on his desk, while Eberhard flipped through a book.

Moments of calm amid approaching storms.

———————

Nine days later, defeat drenched the spirits of Berlin as surely as snow pelted the sidewalks and bombs fell from the sky, when the news came.

Stalingrad had fallen.

Chapter Twenty

Silverware clinked. The children chattered over their breakfast. Maria wiped a strand of hair from her cheek, hands still sticky from cleaning up Peter's spilled milk. Thankfully, she'd learned to fill his glass only halfway.

"There. Now drink that quickly before you knock it over again." Maria handed Peter a fresh glass.

Peter obediently gulped it down. When he set down the glass, a film of milk dotted his upper lip.

Lala laughed. "You have a mustache, Peter. You look like the old gamekeeper."

Maria resumed her seat, picking up the letter from Grossmutter she'd been reading, her breakfast cooling on her plate. These days, her main duties involved looking after her siblings and assisting them with their studies. The course of her future was tenuous, at best. Mutter was attempting to pull strings and get her a temporary exemption from the labor service so Maria could take up nursing. But such things took time to arrange. The prospect of entering the National Labor Service, with its Reich allegiance and grueling factory work . . .

Forcing the thoughts away, she returned her attention to the letter:

> *When do you leave to begin nursing? I think you will find the duties*
> *suit you very well. It's hard work, but you've never been afraid of that.*
> *It will do much better than the labor service. I truly hope you are spared*
> *that. Is there any news?*
> *I was made so happy by Dietrich's letter on his birthday, sharing*
> *the news of your engagement. I know I've already written you on the*
> *subject, but it is one so near and dear to me, I could not fail to take the*

opportunity to do so again. I hear your mutter is still insistent upon the period of separation. For my part, I cannot see how that can be a good thing; particularly since the danger surrounding Dietrich is great. One never knows what might happen, and would it not be best for you to face whatever comes together? Already, his trips have been canceled due to warnings from those in high places. Who knows what will come next.

The children's high-pitched chatter faded into the background, the ink-penned lines conjuring images that wound her stomach into a knot of fear and uncertainty.

Dietrich in danger? How great? The letter, still unfinished, dropped from her hand onto the table. She stared into her half-empty cup, renegade tears pricking her eyes. Words became images . . . late night meetings, Gestapo ears listening on telephone lines . . .

She ached to contact him, hear his voice, even for a few moments. Get reassurance that Grossmutter was mistaken or learn how bad things truly were. What was happening? She knew so little. The lack of facts spoken by him overwhelmed her with powerlessness. She could endure the truth, even if it was hard. But silence, maddening silence that drove at her with ambiguity . . .

Oh, to pick up the phone and dial Berlin. It would take only moments.

But she'd promised Mutter. Mutter, who had enough worries with running the estate, managing their funds, coping with the shortages. Mutter, who looked wearier by the day. How could she burden her with this on top of everything else? She couldn't. Without Vater and Max, and with Ruth-Alice married, she was the eldest, the strongest support Mutter had. She couldn't willfully cause Mutter pain. Not even for Dietrich.

Her eyes slid shut, as she pressed her hand over her mouth.

God, protect him. For I cannot.

February 23, 1943
Berlin

The events of the past two days blurred together, blood mixing with blood. First, Goebbels's speech.

Total war is the demand of the hour. . . . The danger facing us is enormous. The efforts we take to meet it must be just as enormous. The time has come to remove the kid gloves and use our fists. . . .

Do you believe with the Führer and us in the final total victory
of the German people? . . .

Do you want total war? If necessary, do you want a war more
total and radical than anything that we can even imagine today?

Then Hans and Sophie Scholl. University students, barely out of their
teens. Bravely distributing leaflets. Proclaiming truth in a written cry for
action. Flitting through the University of Munich, pamphlets in hand,
while the propaganda leader bellowed his rhetoric and garnered earsplit-
ting cheers. Arrested while Goebbels filled the Sports Palace with thunder-
ous applause. Five days later, in the courtroom of the infamous People's
Court, their vater, Robert, broke through the crowd of uniformed Nazis
and shouted for all to hear. "One day there will be another kind of justice!
One day they will go down in history!"

Dietrich pulled his glasses from his face, staring at the Reich newspaper.
A word-for-word rendition of Goebbels's speech had made the front page.
He'd been scheduled to meet secretly with Hans Scholl on February 25.
He'd looked forward to the introduction to this bright young man who
fought so bravely at only twenty-four years of age. Now—his body slaugh-
tered by the Nazis, tossed in a grave—there would be no meeting.

Dietrich stared down at Goebbels's words, evil encapsulated in newsprint. "That is the duty of the hour. Let the slogan be: Now, people rise up
and let the storm break loose!"

Hans and Sophie Scholl had faced their accusers with bravery during
their trial at the so-called People's Court. Dared to speak out, even in the
courtroom, the girl, Sophie, only twenty-one years old, saying with quiet
conviction that after all, somebody had to make a start. They'd met death
with calm courage. Bright young lives, snuffed out by order of Roland
Freisler and Führer-ordained justice.

Christel had come to the house and told the family. Christel, usually so
in control, had tears running down her cheeks.

Tears for those Germany deemed traitors.

Could there be any worthier benediction?

Robert Scholl's words filled Dietrich's brain. Another kind of justice.
Justice that Tresckow and the other Abwehr members plotted. Dietrich
included.

"They that take the sword shall perish with the sword."

God's word. Truth. Dietrich had long reconciled himself to it. One day,
it was Hans and Sophie Scholl upon the guillotine's blade. The next . . .

The guilt of their actions they must be willing to accept. Otherwise they couldn't move forward with plotting and bomb procuring and secret midnight meetings with the telephones covered.

Goebbels had brought Berlin to its knees with patriotism. Stalingrad was merely a loss on the road to total victory. The Scholl siblings, turncoats. And on it went.

Dietrich sucked in a breath, pressing his forehead into his palm.

You, O Lord, know the future. Grant us Your peace.

March 9, 1943
Pätzig

Maria shook out the folds of a blue summer dress before refolding it and placing it in the suitcase where several garments already lay. Soon, Pätzig would be exchanged for Hanover, these clothes for a nurse's uniform. Still, she'd need things to wear on her days off.

She stepped across her bedroom and pulled another frock from her wardrobe. Her lavender dress. The one she'd worn at Grossmutter's the night Dietrich Bonhoeffer entered her life. She held the garment against herself, the airy fabric floating against her skin. It wouldn't fit as well if she tried it on today. She'd lost weight since then.

Lost so many things about herself.

She pressed her lips together. Returned the dress to the back of her wardrobe. No sense packing what she couldn't wear.

She carried two pairs of shoes to the case—one serviceable, the other dressier pumps. Her foot hooked the edge of the rug. She lost her balance, dropping the shoes. They splayed themselves in all directions. With a sigh, she bent to gather them. One had rolled beneath her bed. Down on her hands and knees, she lowered herself onto her stomach and reached beneath the frilly bed skirt. She twisted this way and that, trying to reach the shoe.

Her fingers bumped something hard, like the edge of a wooden box. Using both hands, she pulled and tugged, bringing the box into the light.

Oh . . .

No matter that it had been months since they'd received them from the front, a fist still closed around her throat at the sight of her brother's personal effects. She kept it here, with her mutter's permission, but only once had she looked into their contents.

Smoothing a hand across the top, she brushed off the accumulated dust.

The lid came off easily, and she laid it aside. Max's dress uniform, the one everyone had teased him about looking "snappy" in, lay close to the top. She pulled it out, hugging the fabric to herself. Fingers of sunlight spilled across the rug, pooling around her—a young woman clutching her dead brother's uniform, as if it were him she held.

"Oh, Max," she whispered, her nose pressed against the wool as if she could drink in his scent, piney wood and a whiff of cigar, instead of the musty fragrance of packed-away fabric. Such an inanimate object compared to the body of her strong, handsome brother. Somehow, though, holding it calmed the tumult inside her.

Something fluttered from within the fabric's folds. The uniform resting in her lap, she picked up the piece of paper. This, she hadn't seen before.

Gently, she unfolded the page.

Dear Max,
    Know that my thoughts and prayers are with you during these days of loss. . . .

Tears pressed against her eyes. Dietrich's letter to Max. Dietrich had told her of it in Berlin. She hadn't imagined Max keeping it, though it was so like him to do so. Gazing upon the familiar writing only reopened the crater of loss inside her—both that of Max and that of her relationship with Dietrich.

Since hearing from Grossmutter, she'd striven to keep her fears at bay.

Dietrich. Her future husband. And though she knew of his danger, she'd done nothing. Her diary entry from yesterday, one of the many she'd written as if talking to him, begged him to tell her what was happening.

Only silence. A silence imposed by her out of fear for others.

If she abandoned Dietrich and the worst happened, she'd not be sent a box of his belongings. She'd not be entitled to them, the shadowy half-engaged girl who'd cut herself out of his life. There'd be no coat to clutch in her arms, no final letters to read over and over again.

What they had shared would simply . . . vanish. Like the mist, beautiful but fleeting.

Head bent, Maria clutched her brother's coat, pressing her lips against the scratchy fabric, rocking back and forth.

Fear had imprisoned her. And she wanted nothing more than to rip off the chains. She'd taught the children, tended to the house, all the while waging an inner battle that left her spent.

She would do everything in her power to keep Mutter and the children safe. But she wouldn't withhold herself from contacting her fiancé any longer. If danger came to her, so be it. She was ready for it. They all faced danger daily. Wasn't it right and good to meet it with those who mattered most?

She was through with waiting. This time, she wouldn't turn back. As she returned his uniform to the box, she could almost imagine Max smiling approval at his determined sister.

Her feet fairly flew down the stairs, through the sunlit hall, and into the library. She shut the door firmly behind her. The telephone waited for her on Vater's desk. Only the shelves of dusty books and heavy curtains and Vater's stalwart desk would witness their reunion.

Heart pounding, she picked up the receiver and requested the number.

Crackling on the other end. A distant ringing. Her ears strained for sound.

"Hello, Bonhoeffer residence." His voice. So quiet yet assured all at the same time. Just hearing it sent relief all the way through her body.

"Dietrich. I . . . I . . ." Tears rolled down her cheeks. Stupid her. Why was she crying?

"Maria?" He sounded as surprised as she to hear from her. And she couldn't answer. Only stood there, clinging to the phone, to this connection with him, sobbing.

"Hey." Gentleness filled his voice. "What's the matter?"

She wiped her hand across her cheeks. "I had to call you. I've wanted to for weeks now, ever since I heard from Grossmutter. Are you all right? I've been so afraid."

"Why?"

"Grossmutter told me you were in danger." She gulped away the lump in her throat.

He chuckled softly. "I'm fine. You shouldn't worry about me."

"Are you sure?"

"I'm sure. For now, at least. It upsets me to think of what she wrote to you. She shouldn't have done that. She's interfered far too much in this whole affair. But I'm all right. Set your mind at rest."

She sat on the edge of the desk, basking in the measure of relief that accompanied his words.

"I've missed you." She wouldn't embarrass herself by telling him how much and how fiercely. She'd already shamed herself enough by her tears.

"I've missed you too." He sounded as if he were smiling. If she closed her eyes, she could almost imagine that slight smile, the way it curved his lips. His face. Those riveting eyes on her.

"I'm sorry. About everything. I feel as if I've behaved badly. I'm not usually like this." She had to ask him. "I wouldn't blame you if you decided you were well and truly tired of me."

"I could never be tired of you, my dearest." The endearment sent a thrill of sweetness through her. "Thoughts of you have been my constant companion."

She nodded, about to say the same of him, but he continued. "What have you been doing? Are you going to start working as a nurse?"

"That's all up in the air. I hope so. I've been packing a little today. But there's still the possibility that it will be the labor service instead." She leaned one hand against the desk, cradling the phone beneath her chin. Inhaling this moment, cool water to the dry soil inside her.

"I don't like that at all. Do you want me to help you arrange things?"

"Nein. Mutter is working on it. You have enough to do."

"Like thinking of my sweet fiancée and wishing I could be at her side?"

She laughed. He sounded so charming, almost schoolboyish. To think, as a child she'd thought him boring. And considered him a good choice to officiate her wedding.

What a pity that was now impossible!

"I might be leaving on another trip. I don't know when. But if you write to me, the letters will be forwarded. You will write me? It would make me so happy to hear from you . . . though I will of course continue to abide by whatever wishes you and your family have."

"I'll write you. Mutter will still insist on our not seeing each other, but we must be together in some way." If she wanted to share life with this man as his wife, she must be willing to accept whatever came as his fiancée. Including the dangers.

Especially those.

"Danke." Gratitude resonated through his voice, over the wires connecting them. Too much gratitude. How fully he seemed to care for her, though they knew each other so painfully little.

"You don't need to thank me, Dietrich."

Voices sounded in the background, his talking to someone else. A few beats passed before he returned on the line.

"I have to go."

"All right." Hopefully, her reluctance to end their conversation didn't show in her voice.

"I . . . *Ja*, Hans. I'll be right there." He cleared his throat. Then it came, whisper quiet and just as fleeting. *"Ich liebe dich."*

Before she could reply, the line clicked.

She lowered the phone, heart pounding.

"Ich liebe dich."

"I love you."

She drew in a quick breath, fingers tightening around the phone as she stared at the wall opposite her. Words she'd dreamed about hearing her entire life, from the time she'd been old enough to read about princesses and knights in silver armor. And he'd uttered them in the space of an instant. Words that should be lingered over had come quickly. A declaration that wanted to be followed by something more. A kiss.

But worst of all?

She hadn't been able to say it back to him. Though she wasn't sure of the texture of her emotions toward him, each day they grew. Becoming something beyond what they had once been.

"Ich liebe dich," she whispered into the emptiness, heart full and aching.

March 11, 1943
Berlin

It looked like a pencil case, the kind boys put in a rucksack and take to school.

Strange that something so small, almost ordinary looking, could be used to obliterate tyranny.

Dietrich stared at the bomb on his vater's desk, the study door closed and locked. Hans stood next to him.

"The British call it a clam. It's of English make and doesn't have any ticking or fuse." Hans fingered the plastic edge, a suitcase lying beside it ready to take to the station.

Dietrich couldn't tear his gaze away. "How does it detonate?"

"When Schlabrendorff is ready, he'll press this button here." Hans pointed. "A vial of corrosive chemicals will shatter. As the chemical eats away at the wire, the spring will activate and strike the detonator cap." Hans said all this in the calm tone of a university lecturer, looking the part in a pressed gray suit and tie. Beneath his right eye, a muscle pulsed. An uncontrollable reaction revealing deeper anxieties.

"When does he intend to do it?"

"During the meeting, if he can safely. If not, he'll try to smuggle it aboard the plane right before takeoff." Hans carefully placed the items into the well-padded suitcase. Dietrich closed the lid. The latch snapped and clicked.

It was impossible not to imagine the situation. Hitler and his generals, sitting around, perhaps having lunch. Tresckow and Schlabrendorff, outwardly congenial, inwardly tense. There'd be final salutes, quick farewells. Hitler would board the plane. Feverishly, they'd work to smuggle the bomb aboard, disguised as an incongruous case of brandy. The doors would shut. As the propeller blades whirred, Tresckow and Schlabrendorff would watch the ascent, catching the last glimpse of Adolf Hitler before he combusted into a million pieces midair.

"We'll need to get going if I'm to take you to the station." Dietrich checked his watch. Almost time for the night train. They'd have to drive fast to get Hans there on schedule.

"You're not coming." Hans hefted the suitcase, spearing Dietrich with an unyielding look. "We shouldn't be seen together in case someone's tailing us."

"It's Vater's car, but you can't expect him to drive it." It was already risky enough, using Karl Bonhoeffer's official physician's Mercedes on such an errand, though it would provide a good cover if they were stopped. But putting Vater behind the wheel when the vehicle carried an illegal explosive meant to assassinate the Führer was out of the question.

"Whom do you suggest?" Hans lifted a brow.

"Eberhard, perhaps? He hasn't been in the Abwehr long enough to arouse suspicion."

"Fine. I'll go to the Schleichers' and see if he's available." Hans started for the door.

"Wait."

Hans swung around.

"Are you going to tell him what's in it?"

"Of course not." Hans shifted the suitcase, testing its weight. "He knows little enough, and it's best to keep it that way. In case we're stopped."

It went without saying that if Hans and Eberhard were stopped and searched, found to be transporting a British-made explosive, the consequences would be extreme.

As if on impulse, Hans crossed back to Dietrich, his brother-in-law's features steadfast in the lamplight. To Hans, action meant everything. He'd see the operation carried out to the best of his abilities.

"Auf Wiedersehen, then." The two men gripped hands.

"Auf Wiedersehen, Hans."

At the door, Hans paused, glancing over his shoulder, a shadow falling across his face. Everything the conspirators worked for and hoped lived in his brother-in-law's eyes in that moment. So much lay at stake in the success or failure of the delivery of a bomb to the train station, and that bomb to Hitler's proximity. So many lives—millions. The fate of the Jews who still remained alive. The future of Germany.

Their own destiny. Least among all the other concerns but ever present on the list.

"Pray for us, Dietrich," Hans whispered.

Dietrich nodded. How God would answer his petition, he knew not. But pray he would.

Pray he must.

March 13, 1943
Berlin

Everything was set. Hans returned from Smolensk, confirming the bomb's safe delivery and Hitler's arrival on Saturday—today. Key members of the conspiracy had been notified, along with political contacts in Cologne, Munich, and Vienna. Hans and Tresckow had arranged code words, so immediately upon receiving word of the plane's—and the Führer's—demise, government reorganization could begin straight away in Berlin.

Seconds, minutes, ticked by. Operation Flash could be taking place at any moment.

After leaning his bicycle against the side of the house, Dietrich rang the doorbell at the Dohnanyis'. Better to be here with Christel and the children than waiting at his parents'. Spring sunshine broke through the low-hanging clouds above Berlin, the rays feeble but radiant.

Children, two boys and a girl, in Hitler Youth and BDM uniforms, played across the street, the boys goose-stepping in unison, while the girl, long blond braids bouncing, pushed a miniature baby pram.

Children bred by Third Reich dictates.

The world would change drastically for them, for all of them, when the announcement of the Führer's death exploded throughout Germany.

Christel cracked open the door. His older sister's eyes begged for news.

Dietrich shook his head, as she motioned him inside. She shut the door. Sunlight streamed through the dormer window, illuminating polished wood floors and a swirl of dust motes floating lazily in the air.

Dietrich hung his hat on the empty stand and wiped his shoes on the braided rug in front of the door.

Christel hugged her arms across her sweater-clad chest, releasing a long exhale.

"It was good of you to come. I thought I'd manage to be calm today, but I can't sit still for more than a few minutes. I keep going to the radio, turning it on, and off, and back on again." She rubbed a hand over her eyes. "The children will think I've gone mad. I've been trying to distract them all day, though I don't know why. They don't know anything."

"How about I make you some tea?" Placing his hand on his sister's arm, Dietrich guided her down the narrow hall and into the dining room. The windowless room was long and rectangular, occupied by a polished table, beige wallpaper, three paintings, and a carved oaken clock.

"That would be lovely, but at the moment, we're out." Christel sank into one of the straight-backed chairs.

Dietrich pulled a packet of tea from his pocket. "Then I can supply the deficiency. Want anything else to go with it?"

Christel shook her head with a small smile, leaning her elbow on the table, one hand against her cheek. "Though I'd rather eat your cooking then Hans's any day. What you fix actually tastes edible."

"Hey now. I'd go a step above that and say I'm pretty good." Dietrich made his way into the adjoining kitchen, the room smelling of dishwashing powder, spotlessly clean, like everything in the Dohnanyi house. He filled a kettle, put it on the stove, and set to grabbing cups. Christoph and Bärbel's voices drifted in.

Bärbel wandered into the kitchen. "Hello, Uncle Dietrich."

"Hello to you too. What have you been doing all day?"

"Painting pictures with Christoph's watercolor set." She held out her hands to show the smudges of red and blue adorning her fingers. "Mutter says I need to wash up." She stepped to the sink and turned on the water, lathering her hands with a minuscule amount of soap, meticulously careful not to use too much of the rationed substance.

"What have *you* been doing all day?" Bärbel rubbed her fingers together.

Dietrich paused in his tea preparations.

Waiting for the months of inactivity to give way to action? For the world to change?

"Writing a few letters this morning. Then coming over here to see you."

"Your hand must get *really* tired writing all those letters." Bärbel hung the towel up to dry and left the kitchen.

Several minutes later, Dietrich carried in a tray of tea things. Christel's chair stood vacant. He found her in the living room, peering through a gap in the curtains.

"Tea's ready."

She spun like a startled animal, hand splayed against her chest. "Danke schön, Dietrich."

He laid a hand on her shoulder. "You need to stop worrying."

She nodded, a strand of dark hair falling against her cheek. Though a university graduate, the mother of three, and older than him by three years, Christel suddenly looked like a frightened child, pale and wide eyed.

"It's just . . . if the worst happens, and they take Hans . . ."

"If the worst happens and they take Hans, you won't be alone, Christel. God will give us the strength we need at the time we require it. Not a minute before." He met Christel's gaze.

If they took Hans, they'd soon come after him. The conspiracy would fall like dominoes, one member leading to the next, despite their hours of planning and determination not to give names.

Then he'd need that strength he spoke of more than ever.

"I know. If that is what I must bear, then I know I can. It's the waiting that's the worst part." She straightened her slim shoulders, strength returning to her gaze.

"Come." He motioned her from the room. "You don't want that tea to get cold now, do you?"

They sat for two hours.

It felt like two years.

Every so often, Christel got up and turned the radio on. Only the usual broadcasts and patriotic music crackled onto the air. Dietrich and Christel worked on teaching Christoph chess. Christel smiled, but it looked forced, more so, as the hours wore on. Christoph, perhaps sensing the grown-ups weren't fully engaged, got tired of the game and headed upstairs with Bärbel to read.

They sat in silence for another quarter of an hour.

From its place on the wall, the clock seemed to tick louder and louder.

Christel tapped her nails against the edge of her cup.

Dietrich clenched and unclenched his fingers atop his pant legs.

A noise, like the rattle of a doorknob, came from the foyer. Christel jumped to her feet.

Hans entered the dining room, still wearing his overcoat and boots. Heart thudding, Dietrich searched his brother-in-law's face. Christel looked to be holding her breath.

Wordlessly, Hans dropped into an empty chair. Failure—a mantle that could not be hidden.

Christel knelt beside him, pressing her hands around his.

"What happened?"

Hans met her gaze, but it was as if he didn't really see her. "I don't know. We waited and waited. Midmorning, Schlabrendorff called and said everything was going well. At two o'clock, he called again, said the flash was set in motion. Around four, the last call came. It failed." He rubbed a hand over his eyes, features haggard. "Of course, he couldn't tell me why."

The little pencil case called a clam had somehow failed to explode. How was that even possible? It had sounded so sure when Hans explained it in Vater's study. The button would click, the vial break, chemicals dissolve the wire.

The *why* wasn't important right now. Determining their course of action came next. And figuring out if this attempt would lead to consequences for any of them. Had the package containing the bomb been discovered?

Dominoes. How many would fall as a result of this failure?

"Do you know anything else?" Dietrich asked.

For once, Hans didn't jump to give an answer. He grabbed Dietrich's cup of cold, half-drunk tea and downed it like two shots of alcohol. He set the cup down, porcelain rattling against wood.

"Wait until we hear from Schlabrendorff. Find out the details. If he disguised the bomb as a bottle of brandy, as he figured he would do, and gave it to someone boarding the plane, the most imperative thing is to get the bomb back. If I know Schlabrendorff, he's on his way to wherever it ended up this very second. He's got a cool head. If he can get it back undetected, he will."

Dietrich nodded. "And we'll try again." It wasn't a question. Uncertainty had become a luxury they couldn't afford.

"As soon as possible. I don't know how or when, but we will." Hans rubbed a finger around the rim of the cup, as if just now realizing he'd drunk out of it. "Oh, more bad news. You've been ordered by the Munich recruiting station to report in one week with all of your papers. Ordered, being the operative word." Hans passed Dietrich an envelope. "I stopped by your parents' house, and they gave me the summons. Since Stalingrad, the state offices are combing their files, trolling for any able-bodied male not already at the front."

Dietrich inhaled sharply. Being labeled by the Abwehr as essential to the war effort had withheld the call-up thus far. Now it had come. Official papers ordering him into uniform. Would it truly come to that? He must prepare himself. He'd have to report. But as for actually putting on a uniform and picking up a gun, going into battle . . . Hans would tell him to report, the last thing they needed was to draw attention. Dietrich would have to follow orders.

Anyone who didn't, who refused to serve, was lined up against a wall and shot.

"I'm going to try to have Oster get it reneged. He knows as well as I do that if our next coup is successful, we'll need you right away for negotiations with the Allies. We must get you to Switzerland and Rome as soon as possible, make it look like you're doing terribly important work. We'll meet with him tomorrow." Hans's tone was brisk, snapped out of his earlier stupor. He looked now to Christel, squeezing her fingers. As if oblivious to Dietrich's presence, he ran a hand along her cheek, their gazes mingling.

"I'm sorry, *mein Liebling*. I was so sure that by tonight Germany would be ruled by a tyrant no longer."

Christel smiled, leaning into her husband's touch. "We'll try again, Husband. But for tonight, you absolutely must rest."

Dietrich moved toward the door. "I'll show myself out."

"Danke, Dietrich." Christel turned her soft smile on him. What a sister he had.

"No thanks needed. I'll see you tomorrow, Hans." He headed into the foyer, grabbed his hat from the stand.

The wind picked up as he wheeled his bicycle onto the street.

Try again. All they could do was try again.

But with each passing day, time, that precious commodity, seemed to be moving faster, like a sprinter bent on a win.

How long before it ran out on them altogether?

Chapter Twenty-One

March 19, 1943
Berlin

Whatever he was showing up for, it wasn't a music rehearsal. Hans's short phone call that morning, filled with forced cheer: "Come over. We'll run through some of the music for Vater's birthday."

Dietrich knew his brother-in-law—and the phone tapping situation—too well to believe the ruse for a moment. Why then? What did Hans want him to do today? He'd soon find out.

Spring was slow in coming to Berlin, and trees marked by desolation lined the street where the Dohnanyis lived. Barren branches, frozen by winter's chilling breath, lifting arthritic arms at intervals toward the sky. As if nature also wearied of living and wished to join its Creator in heaven above.

Passing few as he bicycled, it didn't take Dietrich long to reach the house and deposit his bicycle. Striding up the front walk, he fumbled in his pocket for his key—Hans had recently given him one, though Dietrich had forgotten it on his last visit—and unlocked the door. Silence echoed through the foyer, with its glossy floors and tidy hall table. Today, no sunlight shone through the dormer window, giving the house a dark, lifeless appearance.

Dietrich walked through the empty living room, the squeak of his shoes the only sound. Another hall led to Hans's study, the mahogany door closed, the passageway dim.

He knocked. Once, short, followed by two quick raps.

The handle on the other side rattled. Hans opened the door and stepped to the side for Dietrich to pass. The room was almost as dark as the hallway, curtains drawn. A desk lamp cast muted shadows of light.

A man he'd never seen before sat in a wing chair next to the desk. About his own age, Dietrich guessed, though much better looking. Military bearing, though he wore civilian garb—a black suit. Dark hair, a thatch of it curling over his aristocratic forehead.

The man stood, both hands behind his back. There was something in his expression. A sheen across his brow. A tension to his erect posture that went beyond military protocol. A strange light in his pupils.

Dietrich glanced at Hans, then back to the man.

"Dietrich, this is Colonel Rudolf von Gersdorff. Rudolf, my brother-in-law, Pastor Dietrich Bonhoeffer."

Dietrich approached and held out his hand. Colonel von Gersdorff shook it politely. When Dietrich withdrew, a clammy stickiness from the other man's hand slicked his own palm.

For a long minute, the three said nothing. Who was this von Gersdorff? What purpose did this secret meeting have?

"Please, sit, both of you." Hans motioned to the two wing chairs that sat a foot or so apart.

Colonel von Gersdorff sat. Dietrich followed suit. Hans stood, facing both of them.

"I know you're wondering why I called you here today, Dietrich."

Dietrich shrugged.

"I did so because Colonel von Gersdorff—"

"Rudolf, please," interjected the colonel.

"Because Rudolf requested it," Hans continued. "Operation Flash failed, due to faulty explosives. Schlabrendorff was able to retrieve the bomb without suspicion. As it happens, we have an opportunity to try again in just two days. Hitler is to be in Berlin, accompanied by Himmler and Göring. They're scheduled to attend Heroes' Memorial Day at the Zeughaus Museum. After the ceremony, they're to go through an exhibit of captured Soviet weaponry. Rudolf will be their tour guide."

Deep in the pit of his stomach, Dietrich sensed something more was coming. Rudolf seemed calmer now that Hans was speaking, sitting stiff in his chair.

"In his pockets will be two explosives, one on each side. When the time is right, Rudolf will ignite the explosives and begin his tour with Hitler and the others."

What? He must've misheard. Hans couldn't be saying . . . "I don't understand. He's going to carry them in his pockets! But that's—"

Rudolf turned slightly in his chair. Dietrich met the man's gaze. Earnest blue eyes looked back at him. A beat passed. "My life will be ended along with his. It's a sacrifice I'm willing to make. Better I than someone else, though others have volunteered. But . . ." Rudolf looked down at his hands, clenched atop his pant legs. Against the dark fabric, the man's knuckles stood out pale, the skin stretched taut. A jagged sigh fell from his lips. "I would like . . . that is, it will comfort me to know . . . will God have mercy upon my soul?"

Dietrich drew in a breath.

Dear God, what am I to say?

In the eyes of God, suicide was unquestionably sin. That was the black and white of it. And for some, the end of the matter.

Sin boldly, yet accept grace more boldly still. The essence of Luther's quote. Christ did not condone sin but forgave the repentant. And God omnipotent saw their world in all its blood-red atrocities. Those who had died at the hands of persecutors and those willing to give their lives for the persecuted.

If what I'm about to do is wrong, forgive me too, Lord.

Dietrich scooted his chair closer. Hans came around to stand behind it, as if waiting to hear what Dietrich would say.

Dietrich cleared his throat and fixed his gaze on Rudolf. The man's answering stare pleaded for hope.

Slowly, he spoke. "Christ tells us that He is the Resurrection and the Life. And that whoever believeth in Him, though he die, yet shall he live. If you've put your trust in God, Rudolf, I have no doubt you will dwell with Him in Paradise." He shifted, unsure how to go on. "Christ gave His life so that we might live. Perhaps ours is not an age for black-and-white morality, but simply a time to ask what He would do."

Rudolf nodded. "Might you"—he cleared his throat—"pray with me?"

"Of course." Dietrich reached across and placed his hand on the man's shoulder. Rudolf bowed his head. On that day, those final hours, there would be no pastor or priest. Rudolf would meet his end alone. The words spoken over him now he would carry with him during his last moments on earth.

Slowly, Dietrich began to speak. "Almighty God, You are the Discerner of hearts, and the Giver of all. Guide Rudolf in all his ways and decisions. You know him, and You love him. When the time comes for him to take his last breath on earth, receive him to Yourself. We are Yours, Lord. Yours to command. Yours to protect, even in these dark days, in whatever way You will. Amen."

"Amen," Rudolf breathed.

Dietrich lifted his head. A single tear shone on Rudolf's cheek.

"Danke, Herr Pastor," he whispered, a catch in his voice. "I'm at peace now. I wasn't before, but now I'm sure of what I'm to do, and what my end will be. I doubt we'll meet again on this earth, but I'll look for you in the next, eh?" A crooked smile.

Was this then what it was to resign oneself to death? Not reluctantly, but fully, willingly.

As he rode home, through the swastika-scarred streets of Berlin, one thought repeated itself. Was this what Rudolf von Gersdorff had been born for? To give his life for the sake of others? Embracing death, so that others might live. A sacrifice, in the greatest sense of the word. If all went as planned, his earthly existence would end in mere days.

Dietrich stared up at the sky—that endless expanse of washed-out blue.

For Rudolf, it would be an end.

But more than that . . . a beginning.

March 20, 1943
Pätzig

Early morning sunlight rained its warmth upon winter's drab last days, the air carrying spring's new scent. The handle of the heavy basket dug into Maria's palm. Breathless from her brisk pace, she stopped a short distance away from Fraülein Kurtz's cottage. Her hastily tied-on headscarf had slid halfway down her shoulders, and she tugged it up, boots squishing in the damp ground.

She was to travel to Hanover to begin nursing within the week. This would be her last opportunity to visit Hilde Kurtz and bring her the provisions she desperately needed.

Weeds sprouted in tufts around the perimeter of Fraülein Kurtz's cottage. Grime coated the windows and the roof sagged. The house looked tired, as if its care was a burden on the owner, rather than a pleasure.

Since hearing of her brother's arrest, Hilde's eyes had lost all spark of life, a hacking cough settling deep into her chest and confining her to bed. She no longer had the strength to walk to the grocer's for her part-time job, no longer received her weekly allotment of pay.

Maria gave a soft rap against the wooden door, shifting the basket that contained a loaf of bread and some canned vegetables.

Hilde opened the door a crack, wan face framed by her braided graying hair.

"Ah, it's you, Maria." A faint smile touched her pale lips. "Won't you come in?"

Maria shook her head. "I'm sorry, but I can't this time. I just came to bring you some things." She held out the basket. "I'll be leaving to start nursing soon, and I wanted to say goodbye."

Hilde's frail hands reached for the basket, gratitude evidenced by the tears welling in her eyes. "Danke, my dear. How can I ever repay you?"

"Mutter will be by to visit you soon." Maria smiled gently. As a little girl of five or six, she remembered Fraülein Kurtz—so stylish she'd been then, her hair in an effortless bob, always smiling and smelling of lilacs. Though she'd never married, she'd danced at every party, golden and girlish.

War had ended her dancing days as surely as it had ended much else, sapping the joy from Hilde's eyes and leaving behind hollow emptiness.

A cough cut off Hilde's reply, her shoulders heaving. "I'll go put these things away, so you can have your basket." Still coughing, she disappeared inside.

Maria turned, glancing at the row of humble dwellings lining the small village street, mist bathing their aged stone exteriors. The occupants of the cottages were stirring, breaking the morning quiet, children off to school, women beating rugs and feeding chickens. Common, everyday sights.

Save for the man. He leaned against an opposite cottage, riding boots planted on the muddy ground, smoking a cigarette.

And watching her.

"Here you are." Hilde's soft voice made Maria spin back around.

Maria took the empty basket. "If you're in need of anything, anything at all, please let us know. Your brother would want us to help you."

Hilde nodded, throat jerking. "God be with you, Maria." The woman clasped Maria's hands, her touch like faded tissue paper.

"And you, Fraülein Kurtz."

The woman closed the cottage door, and Maria turned her steps toward Pätzig. She sensed the gaze of the man upon her and, looking in his direction, found that it was so.

Who was he? Strangers in the village were a rarity, an occasion for unease.

She tore her gaze away and walked faster, Max's riding coat loose around her shoulders, headscarf slipping free again, cold piercing the tip of her nose.

"*Guten Morgen*, Fraülein," he called out.

She halted. The command in his tone would've made it impossible to do less. He approached. He was older than he'd appeared at a distance, closer to her vater's age than her own, gray sprinkling his temples. He wore a tan hunting coat flung over a white shirt, unbuttoned at the collar, pristine riding boots, despite the mud.

"Are you speaking to me?" Her tone emerged sharp; better that than fearful. So far the authorities had left Hilde alone, but every day brought no guarantees.

A smile curved his mustached lip. "I am." He dropped the cigarette, scuffing it into the mud. His gaze was sharp, as if it had been trained to miss nothing. "What were you doing at that cottage just now?"

Her heart skittered. "Visiting a friend who is ill. Why do you ask?"

He shrugged. "Passing interest."

She nodded briefly, and tugged her coat tighter around herself. "I must be going."

"Don't walk away. Please." His tone softened, something unexpected from a man with such wide shoulders and imposing height. "I only wanted to say hello. To introduce myself. Oskar von Scheffler, at your service." He made a slight bow.

She sifted through her mental catalog of names, saying nothing in response to his introduction. It wasn't a name she recognized. Obviously, he was a person of consequence considering the sheen of his boots—she couldn't remember the last time she'd seen someone in new-looking shoes. And the poise of his speech.

"You're probably wondering why I'm here. I'm certainly wondering about you." His gaze perused her, as if she were an unopened book he wanted to read. "I'm on leave. I've been ill. My physician ordered rest, and I've only been out of bed this past week. Pneumonia is a nasty business."

"I'm sorry," she said, without being sure why. Pneumonia was nothing compared to what millions of others had suffered. And his illness didn't look to have dampened his physical vigor much.

"Don't be." The corners of his forest-green eyes crinkled. "My work in Berlin is . . . strenuous. I needed a vacation. And I couldn't think of a prettier place, or one I love better."

"I agree." A breeze stirred the damp air with the sweet scent of springtime. "Pätzig is very dear to me."

"You live at Pätzig?" An incredulous smile broke across his face. "Then you are one of the von Wedemeyers?"

"Maria," she replied.

"Maria," he repeated. "A very pretty name. I'm surprised I don't remember you. Years ago, I used to rent a cottage nearby during the summer holidays. I knew your vater. How is he these days?"

She pressed her lips together, brushing a stubborn strand of hair behind her ear. "He's . . . He fell at Stalingrad."

Herr von Scheffler's eyes softened. With sorrow first, then compassion.

Two things foreign in a world when everyone was supposed to consider death for the Fatherland the highest honor imaginable.

"My condolences. He was a genuinely good man, your vater."

"He was." She nodded.

Herr von Scheffler rubbed a forefinger across his mustache, looking at the ground. "Ghastly business, Stalingrad. My brother . . . He was younger than I, by ten years, but we were inseparable as children. He fell on the Russian front six months ago." He looked up. Met her eyes. "There's nothing quite like loss, is there, Fraülein von Wedemeyer?"

She shook her head. "Nein. There isn't."

"But let's not talk of sad things. We've only just met. I could walk with you to wherever you're going. We could speak of your vater. That is . . . if you like to." A smile void of anything but hopefulness replaced the shadows lining his face moments ago.

Perhaps it was compassion, a shared sadness and experience. Or perhaps it was simply the renewed longing to enjoy the outdoors with a companion, as she'd done with Vater and Max. Whenever it was, it made her nod and tilt her head in the direction she'd just come.

"I'm on my way back to Pätzig."

His smile deepened, revealing a cleft in his chin. He motioned her to precede him. "Shall we then?"

Chapter Twenty-Two

March 21, 1943
Berlin

They performed on two fronts. As musicians, they rehearsed for Vater's birthday recital.

But for Dietrich, Hans, Rüdiger, and their wives, today was anything but a simple preparation for the family patriarch's seventy-fifth birthday celebration.

"And from the top, again." Eberhard had been put in charge of directing the cantata. A wise choice. He didn't know all that lay at stake today.

As if by rote, Dietrich began his part on the piano, Rüdiger on the violin, and Hans with his choir music. The rest of the family all had parts in the choir, and Klaus played the cello. The living room was crowded with Bonhoeffers and music stands.

Never had such tension taken a seat at their musical performances. Bärbel, in the choir, seemed confused as to why her vater kept forgetting his place, repeatedly glancing up at him, forehead wrinkled.

The music drew to an unmelodious halt mid-piece.

"You must not have been practicing very hard, Vater." Bärbel looked up at Hans.

He patted her on the head with an absent smile. "I guess not. You'll have to help me out then, won't you?"

"Shall we try once more?" Eberhard flipped through his stack of music atop the stand.

"*Ja, ja*, we'll try it again," Hans said. But he wasn't looking at Eberhard or the music. Instead, his gaze fixed on the window to where his car sat, waiting near the front door to carry him to government meetings, as soon as the news broke.

Dietrich stared at the spaces between the ivory keys, wishing he could see into the events taking place at the Zeughaus as easily. The clock showed the ceremony had probably concluded. Had Rudolf von Gersdorff begun his explanation of weaponry to the Führer? Had the bombs detonated?

Rudolf, talking calmly with Adolf Hitler about weaponry, knowing his own end would take place within minutes. How could his heart not beat hard and fast beneath his uniform coat? His voice fail to falter? Would he sense the urge to check his watch? But Rudolf knew he must show no such emotion in front of the Führer and his generals, who'd listen, interject a question. He'd play a part, right up to the end.

How many minutes are left?

Rudolf's days might be at an end, but Hans, Tresckow, and the others would see him remembered as a hero for years to come. A life ended on earth, not in memory.

Dietrich's fingers moved methodically across the keys, forcing concentration. The voices of his family members rose behind him, filling the room with the melodious chorus of Helmut Walcha's cantata "Lobe den Herren" ("Praise the Lord").

"It must go off at any moment," Christel, just behind him, whispered to Ursula, her voice drowned by the others singing.

"Keep calm," Ursula murmured. "The end will come soon."

The end. What words. How did one even begin to comprehend all they entailed? The nightmare encompassing the Third Reich would cease to exist. Freedom would come to the Jews and the others imprisoned, the many Confessing Church pastors, those awaiting trial for crimes against the people. A new, better government would attempt to make peace with the Allies.

Germany could begin repentance for its many sins. Dietrich intended to begin preaching on this as soon as possible. No longer would he be forbidden from taking the pulpit.

Once again, truth's light could shine.

Everyone tried admirably not to make mistakes. They were Bonhoeffers, after all. Everything must be just right for Vater's birthday. All attempts had been made to keep this performance a complete surprise.

Many of them had become much better at keeping secrets than they'd ever expected.

Praise to the Lord, the Almighty, the King of Creation!
O my soul, praise Him, for He is thy health and salvation!
All ye who hear . . .

Fitting, that this hymn would be sung, now of all times. When Germany most needed to remember that the Almighty was, contrary to popular belief, not Adolf Hitler but Jesus Christ. What a task it would be to alter the thinking of an entire generation. It could be done, though. With the help of God, and fellow members of the faithful Confessing Church—there were so pitifully few who'd stood fast.

Movement caught the corner of his eye. Without missing a note, Dietrich turned his head slightly. The Schleichers' maid, Gisela, slipped to Hans's side. Hans turned, as the maid whispered something inaudible to all but the hearer.

> . . . Now to His temple draw near;
> Join me in glad adoration.

Eberhard continued to conduct. Christel's hands, holding her sheet of music, trembled, her color heightened as Hans strode from the room.

Dietrich's heart thudded in his ears. His fingers tripped, landing on the wrong keys. A discordant note sounded from the piano.

Time playing music usually flew by in a whirlwind of oneness with melody.

It dragged today. The hairs on the back of his neck prickled.

Hans had undoubtedly received *the* phone call. Any minute now, he'd rush in, the music at a halt.

The Führer is dead.

Rest in peace, Rudolf von Gersdorff.

Footsteps sounded, their cadence louder, it seemed, than the music.

Dietrich turned. Hans tapped Eberhard on the shoulder. A few soft words passed.

"Let's be done for today." Eberhard ran a hand down his tie. "You've all performed very well."

Dietrich stood from the piano bench. Where was the announcement? Why had Hans not spoken up?

He caught his brother-in-law's unreadable gaze. Hans jerked his head toward the study.

The children chattered. Ursula attempted to corral them with the promise of crackers in the kitchen.

Christel followed her husband out of the room. The three entered the study. Hans, then Christel, then Dietrich. Shadows skated across the rug. Outside, a car rumbled by.

Hans drew in a sigh weighted with disbelief.

"Nothing happened." His fingers curled into a fist. He spun toward Rüdiger's cases of books, turning his back on them.

A word Dietrich had never thought to hear his brother-in-law utter sizzled in the air.

Christel pressed her lips together. She moved to her husband's side, slipped an arm around his slumped frame, her cheek against his suitcoat.

A moment later, Hans turned around, Christel still at his side.

"I'm sorry," he said quietly. "I just . . . well . . . I don't know what happened, except that there was no explosion. I'll have to go and find out tomorrow. Too risky today. When Schlabrendorff rang, he used the code for *failure*."

Failure. Two times, in less than ten days. It was as if an impenetrable wall surrounded Hitler that no one could break through, despite how loudly and with what bludgeoning rods they beat against it.

Hans and Christel spoke quietly, speculating what had gone wrong.

Dietrich pulled off his spectacles, rubbed a hand across his eyes.

Rudolf von Gersdorff would live another day.

As would the monster at the wheel of their country.

Driving Germany faster and faster toward the gates of hell themselves.

———————

March 26, 1943
Hanover, Germany

Isolation gulped her in as surely as if she'd fallen into the deep end of Wartenberger Lake and been swallowed by the murky waters.

Maria trudged down the street, bone weary after her long shift at the Clementinenhaus Hospital. A city under blackout was a cave one could get lost in. She focused on squinting at street signs, pulling out the directions to her apartment from a mind jumbled with medical terms and Sister Mueller's chiding voice. The starched blue uniform skirt swung around her legs, feet clad in painfully tight shoes. Her arches seemed to scream with each step.

Hanover had once been a city of ancient churches, blue skies, and the gentle lapping of the Leine River. Now factories for metal works, rubber, and other wartime industries occupied much of the city's space and energy.

Tonight Maria could make out little of either the prewar Hanover or the current one, as she put one weary foot in front of the other. The apartment she rented with Ermengarde Dolff, another student nurse, beckoned, along with a warm cup of ersatz.

She missed Dietrich. He'd written on the twenty-fourth, telling her he'd heard Grossmutter had been booked into the hospital in Stettin and had suffered a decline in health and spirits. Maria had already planned to visit her on her first weekend off. Dietrich seemed to think that Grossmutter had upset herself overmuch over the events of the past winter and would welcome a message from her.

She'd be glad for a break from Hanover. It wasn't the work she minded; that she enjoyed. Caring for the sick was an absolute pleasure, despite the dragon of a ward sister and the gossipy young nurses who couldn't put together two rational thoughts if their lives depended upon it. But she didn't belong here; she sensed that much. The work had a purpose of sorts, but somehow it wasn't enough.

In the face of the war and the dangers surrounding the Bonhoeffer family, her own tasks seemed almost shallow by comparison. She ached to go to Berlin, to see Dietrich and be together as an engaged couple should. But Mutter was no closer to lifting the ban on future meetings, and she saw no sign this position would change.

Reaching the apartment building, Maria pulled the key from her handbag, unlocked the door, and slipped inside. A single, flickering light bulb provided the only illumination against the blackout. She climbed the cement stairs, the air smelling of mildew and stale cheese. At the top, she unlocked the third door down and stepped inside the dark room, bracing herself for another sleepless night spent listening to Ermengarde's snoring.

Of course, Ermengarde wasn't within. She never was at this hour. Which officer was it tonight? Maria couldn't fathom how the girl managed the energy to put in a full day's work, and then go dancing all evening.

Maria turned on the desk lamp. Even so, the apartment was cold. And silent. And empty.

She hung up her coat, slipped off her shoes and the standard-issue apron and dress, and exchanged them for her worn dressing gown and slippers. She headed toward the kitchen—if a room approximately the size of a shoebox could be called that—and winced at the pile of dirty dishes stacked upon the counter. Ermengarde hadn't yet discovered the meaning of a division of labor.

Suddenly too drained for the effort it would take to prepare a pot of tea, she made her way into the bedroom and curled up atop her faded coverlet, trying to get warm. Slowly, she began to take the pins from her hair, letting the strands fall around her face.

A knock sounded.

"There's a telephone call for you, Fraülein von Wedemeyer."

Maria's pulse kicked. Could it be Mutter? She'd phoned Pätzig the night of her arrival. She didn't, wouldn't, dare hope it was Dietrich. He didn't even have her number.

Tugging the tie of her dressing gown tighter, she crossed the room and opened the door. The landlady stood aside to let her pass, doughy face partially shrouded in the darkness, the end of her cigarette glowing orange.

"Danke for letting me know," Maria said.

She reached the communal telephone in the middle of the hall. The paint was dingy and peeling, and everything seemed to be coated with a fine layer of grime. The landlady's steps plodded in the direction of her own rooms. Maria lifted the receiver.

"Hello."

"Hello, Fräulein von Wedemeyer." An unfamiliar male voice sounded over the crackling wires.

"*Ja*, I'm here. Who is this?" Her forehead wrinkled.

"Oskar von Scheffler. How are you?"

A jolt went through her. They'd enjoyed a pleasant enough walk back to Pätzig. She'd shown him some of the farm animals—he'd been particularly interested in the pigs. But why was he calling her now, of all times? And how had he known her number?

"I'm fine." She kept her voice flat.

"I'm sure you're wondering how I discovered your whereabouts." He sounded as if he were leaning back in an easy chair in a fire-lit room, slippered feet propped up on a footrest, a glass of brandy at his side. And smiling.

Ought the mental picture calm or disconcert her?

"I was, actually," she said at last.

His laugh rumbled low. "I happened to meet your sister Christine on my last day in the country. I asked her where you had gone, where you were staying. She told me. You don't mind, do you?"

She said nothing. Why had her sister willingly given such information to a stranger? Of course, Herr von Scheffler had a charm about him. He'd probably told Christine his connection to Vater.

"You do mind. I'm sorry. I didn't mean to frighten you. I only wanted to hear a friendly voice. It's been a ghastly day. Those worthless—well, never mind. I thought talking to you might bring back memories of the clean air of Pätzig."

She found herself softening, much as she had that day in the village. Between Ermengarde's snide comments and the sharp-tongued ward sisters, she'd heard few friendly voices herself.

"It's all right. You needn't apologize." She shifted her grip on the telephone.

He chuckled. "You sound like your vater. I remember we went fishing one afternoon. There was a particular kind he was trying to catch. Wooing it, you might say. Well, I got a bite on my line and began to reel it in. Only I lost my grip halfway and dropped the pole. I expected him to be angry, but your vater only said, 'It's all right. Better luck next time.'"

She laughed then. "That sounds like him. He was always more concerned about the feelings of others than his own wishes."

"It's done me good to hear your voice. And that laugh. May I call you again? And send a letter, from time to time? I'm trying to decorate my new apartment and not doing a very good job. I could use some feminine advice."

He certainly was persistent. What should she make of him? She couldn't tell him she was engaged and to leave her alone. No one outside the family was to know about her and Dietrich. Nor did she want to push him away. He sounded lonely, perhaps as lonely as she. They could be friends, acquaintances, at the very least.

"I suppose you can." She turned at the sound of footsteps. Ermengarde, coat slung over her shoulders, red-lipped and dressed in fashionable marigold organdy, clipped down the hall in her best pair of heels. "I have to go now."

She said goodbye and hung up, returning to her apartment. Ermengarde stood in the center of the room, undressing, scattering her hat, heels, and coat in a trail after her. Maria pressed her lips together.

"I thought you'd be asleep." Ermengarde arched one sculpted brow.

Maria shook her head. "I just got in half an hour ago."

"Party was a frightful bore. No one of any interest showed up. Just a lot of puffed-up young striplings talking of victory. I'm dead tired and going to bed. Are you going to be up much longer?" Ermengarde flopped onto her bed, lighting a cigarette and winding her hair into pin curls. The picture of everything Maria didn't want to be.

Maria turned down the coverlet and climbed into bed. She closed her eyes, as Ermengarde continued to put up her hair.

Drowsily, she replayed her conversation with Herr von Scheffler. He'd begun to say something, after he'd told her his day was ghastly. Something about someone being worthless, in a tone veering toward disgust. She shivered involuntarily.

Who did Herr von Scheffler mean?

And what exactly did he do?

Chapter Twenty-Three

March 31, 1943
Berlin

"All right everyone. Focus on the camera please. That's right. Look this way." The photographer's head disappeared beneath the black cloth.

Dietrich reached up to straighten his tie. Only Sabine and her husband were absent today, by necessity rather than choice. The rest of the Bonhoeffers—those nearest and dearest to Vater—gathered in celebration of a birthday milestone.

Before he could lower his hand, the flashbulb shattered.

Sealing the moment, the group of them, in all their smiling, looking at the camera, not looking at the camera, glory. Standing in front of the family home, even the weather honoring the day by sending sunlight shining down upon them.

Everyone seemed to talk all at once, the children climbing down from older ones' laps, smiles wider, perhaps due to the *kuchen* they'd eaten less than an hour ago. It had been a fine *kuchen* too, a treat for them all.

"Everyone, into the house for the birthday toast." Klaus elevated his voice to be heard above the crowd. The photographer packed up his things. Rüdiger and the two Dohnanyi boys gathered up the chairs that some of the older adults had sat on during the picture.

As they made their way inside, Dietrich fell in step beside Hans.

"Did you get the money moved?" He leaned toward his brother-in-law, who, despite carrying the heaviest load of tension, had admirably managed to maintain a studied gaiety throughout the party, joining in the cantata performance with gusto.

Hans nodded, weariness in his gaze, the party smile leaving his lips. A large number of Reichsmarks belonging to the Confessing Church had been relocated from Hans's safe at the Abwehr office to a more secure location.

Precautionary measures. The attempt at the Zeughaus Museum had them on edge. It was still difficult to believe that Rudolf von Gersdorff's efforts had come to naught—all because Hitler decided to leave the museum in the middle of the tour, minutes before the explosives were set to go off. Minutes. They'd failed by only minutes.

"I've been over my office with a fine-tooth comb. You should go through your desk too, in case something happens while you're in Switzerland and Rome."

Dietrich nodded. "The middle of April still set for departure?"

"All the paperwork should be in place by then. I've got the file in my office to give to you. Remind me if I forget." They continued to the front door, the yard still overflowing with family members. The Dohnanyi boys eyed the large oak tree with a greedy look, as if imagining themselves high upon its branches.

The day would come when Hans would have time to teach his sons to climb trees, instead of working himself to the point of exhaustion plotting a government takeover.

Christoph's excited voice carried on the wind. "I think I'd like to know what it's like up there. Wouldn't you?"

Now surely held more import than someday.

"You never forget anything." Dietrich gestured to the boys. "Why don't you go play with them? Klaus won't care if you're there for the speech, and . . . they need you more."

Hans watched his sons, as if seeing them for the first time in many months. He nodded, clapped a hand on Dietrich's shoulder, then crossed the yard, calling to his sons.

Dietrich smiled after them and followed the rest inside. Lotte and Ursula, along with Renate, distributed glasses. Everyone had chipped in something to purchase the wine. Yet another way they pulled together during these hard times.

Dietrich moved to stand next to his parents, who sat in pride of place on the sofa. He smiled at Vater.

"Having a happy birthday?"

A smile creased his vater's lined cheeks. He placed his hand around his wife's. "I'm a fortunate man, Dietrich. Very fortunate."

Renate hurried over, handing Dietrich a glass, then raced to stand beside Eberhard before Dietrich could get out a hasty danke. Dietrich smiled at the sight of them together, willing away the ache that spread through his own chest.

He had received a letter from Maria two days ago. If it hadn't been for

Frau von Wedemeyer's edict, they could have been the other engaged couple at the party. At least they were permitted to correspond. She'd sent him a picture with the last one. Taken last summer before her vater's death, it showed her, face turned slightly away from the camera, hair pinned up. When he had seen her in Berlin, she'd looked older, with her curled hair and dark red suit. But her smile remained unchanged. Small, serene, yet with traces of the mischievous girl who teased him about running in the rain.

He missed her.

Love. What pleasure and torment it could bring to a man.

Klaus stood in the center of the room, the rest of them forming a very crowded circle around him. He held up his glass.

"I'll try to keep this brief, Vater."

Everyone chuckled. Dietrich knew his vater wasn't much for this sort of thing but would go along with it and be gratified anyway.

"Growing up with you to lead and guide our family is a privilege I'm sure all of us children realize the magnitude of. You led us, not so much with words, but by example. Which, as the old saying says, speaks far louder. You raised us to value truth and intelligence and encouraged us to pursue our talents for the good of mankind. You have done the same for each of your grandchildren, and it is with our hearts full of love and gratitude that I wish you, on behalf of everyone present, a very happy birthday." Klaus spread his hands, a gesture encompassing them all. "Everyone, a toast. To Karl Bonhoeffer. Husband, Vater, Grossvater, physician, and friend."

Everyone lifted their glasses. "To Karl Bonhoeffer."

"To Grossvater!" Bärbel called out, half a beat later than the rest.

Laughter rippled through the crowd. Glasses clinked.

Hans entered the room, the boys two steps ahead. Instead of looking relaxed, as Dietrich had hoped, a too-studied calm and control owned his brother-in-law's features.

Directly behind them, another figure followed. One wearing an official uniform and a severe expression on his smooth Aryan face.

Dietrich tensed.

Not today. Not today. Not on Vater's birthday.

The official brushed through the crowd, pushing past the youngest children as if they were little more than troublesome ants. "Karl Bonhoeffer?"

Vater? They were here for Vater? He hadn't done anything . . .

"*Ja*, that is me." Vater stiffened on the sofa, still holding his wine glass.

Hans placed a hand on each boy's shoulders. Christel stood against one wall, face pale in contrast with her bright red party dress. Eberhard slid a protective arm around Renate.

"I'm here with greetings from our Führer." The man pulled out a document from a leather binder, holding it out with a flourish. "And to present you with the Goethe medal as a token of gratitude to your lifetime of service to Germany."

Dietrich exhaled a breath he hadn't realized he was holding. They weren't going to be arrested. The Goethe medal was a great honor, and one Vater certainly deserved. Although if the benefactor of the medal knew how often its recipient had called him insane, Dietrich doubted the privilege would have been extended.

"I . . . I am honored." Vater seemed about to say more, but the official began to read.

"In the name of the German people, I bestow on Professor Emeritus Dr. Karl Bonhoeffer the Goethe medal for art and science, instituted by the late Reich President Hindenburg. Signed the Führer, Adolf Hitler." Stiffly, the man procured a box from under his arm and took out the medal. With a click of his heels, he crossed to Vater and pinned the coin-sized medal to his coat lapel.

"Danke." Vater looked down at the medal, touching it with his fingers.

"I will intrude upon your party no longer. Heil Hitler!" The official saluted, clicked his heels again, and retreated to the door.

The grandchildren eagerly crowded around for a peek at the medal.

Dietrich made his way through the crowd to Hans, who sagged against the wall.

"You all right?" If they weren't in the middle of a conspiracy, looking at his brother-in-law would have made Dietrich recommend a strong sleeping draught and bedrest for a fortnight.

"I don't know what came over me," Hans whispered. "When I saw that official car pull up, I panicked. I led the man inside, without even looking to see who he was. All the time, I was thinking, 'I don't know why they've come for Vater. He hasn't done anything.' I should never have lost my composure."

"You didn't. I was the only one who noticed it." Dietrich stepped aside as Lotte carried empty glasses toward the kitchen. "We're all on edge. It's understandable. But look, nothing happened today." He tried for a reassuring smile.

"Nein." Hans sighed. "Not today."

April 5, 1943
Berlin

Rolling the kinks from his neck, Dietrich picked up the phone. His stomach growled. Was it already lunchtime? He'd spent the morning in his room, working on a few pages of *Ethics*. He'd made more progress than in a long while. A good thing, too, since he wouldn't have time to write once his travels began.

He'd call Hans and ask him if tomorrow was all right to meet and go over final preparations, then see if he couldn't get Lotte to fix him a sandwich. Calling the Dohnanyis at lunchtime might not be the most polite thing to do, but at least he knew he'd find Hans at home.

He gave the operator the number. Waited.

Seconds ticked by.

Nothing. Why no answer?

Then, a click, someone picking up the phone.

"Dohnanyi residence." A gruff voice. Terse. Not Hans.

Dietrich slammed the phone down.

Blood rushed in his ears, the realization jabbing every nerve with needles of dread. Of reality. Of something much talked over, long expected, finally happening.

The Gestapo were searching Hans's house. Arresting him.

Next, they'd come here.

His eyes slid shut. His soul sent up a silent prayer. Then he took a breath and opened his eyes.

He didn't have much time. Every moment must be used rationally. No feeling, only logic.

Upstairs, his parents napped, their afternoon custom. He wouldn't rouse them.

Like a spectator in a nightmare, he made it up to his room, unsure how his legs had worked enough to carry him. In a glance, he assessed the four walls, his neatly made bed. The rows of books. The desk. His desk. Where the Gestapo would soon search. His footfalls echoed louder than usual on the hardwood floor.

He'd left his writing materials scattered. He straightened them, pens in their drawer, two pieces of scrap paper into the wastebasket. Everyday tasks. Empty tasks. Perform them he must.

He opened the desk drawer where everything lay in readiness for this moment. The fictitious diary entries he'd written while in Switzerland last year, he placed on top. Hans had looked them over, declaring them the perfect mix of ponderous clergyman and bright intellectual. How long ago that day seemed. Next, the letter he'd typed out on specially procured paper, the one dated 1940, typed for the benefit of making the Gestapo think he'd joined the Abwehr from the very beginning, instead of, as they'd surmise, to avoid a military call-up.

There. What should be there was in place. Now to get rid of what shouldn't.

Methodically, he turned over each piece of paper, no matter how insignificant. Some reinforced his status as a good Lutheran. He left those in his desk. Others, he added to a pile. He couldn't miss a single one. A slip, two pages stuck together, leaving anything unchecked, could spell the end for him and Hans.

He lifted his gaze to the rafters, where he'd secreted his copy of "After Ten Years." Would it be safe? Should he burn it, along with the rest? The Gestapo were nothing if not thorough.

It would be fine. He'd hidden it well.

Back down the stairs, outside, into the garden. Sunshine. Birds. Springtime. They welcomed him, almost sympathetically, as he crouched in a corner near the shrubbery, lit a match, fed each paper into the flames. The heat seared his face. Like their cook, at their childhood vacation house in Friedrichsbrunn, rotund face red with heat from the stove, frying doughnuts.

What a time to have such a memory.

The papers destroyed and the ashes concealed beneath a bush, he dusted off his hands and strode down the street. Ursula would be making a hot lunch as she always did. He needed more than the meager sustenance of a sandwich. Though his stomach had stopped protesting, hunger would come eventually.

Who knew when he'd have the opportunity to eat again.

He opened the gate and hurried up the small path to the door. Save the fact that he wasn't one to drop in around mealtime without bearing an addition to the table, this could have been any other afternoon. Walking over to see Eberhard, who could be found next door more often than not, to talk over something he'd read. Bringing a portion of his butter ration for the children, though Ursula generally refused the offer.

Any other afternoon.

Only it wasn't.

He knocked. How calm he was. His hands didn't even shake.

Ursula opened the door, wiping her fingers on her apron.

"Ah, Dietrich." She smiled, her expression surprised, pleased. "We're just about to sit down for lunch."

At least he'd timed things right. "May I join you?"

She raised a brow.

He took a deep breath. Reached across and placed his hand over hers. "Ursula." He kept his voice low, calm. "The Gestapo are at Hans and Christel's. They'll be here next. Can you give me something to eat before I go?"

Ursula's eyes widened, her face blanching stark and white. Wordlessly, she nodded. She'd known, just as the rest of them had, that today was a real possibility. They were all informed of the facts.

Knowing was one thing. Facing the actual experience, another.

"Is Eberhard here?" Oh, he hoped this wasn't the day the engaged couple had decided to hunt for potential apartments.

When Ursula nodded, warm relief filled every part of him.

They went into the house and entered the dining room, set in true Schleicher fashion, neat and fine as if it were a Sunday. Eberhard and Renate were the only occupants around the spacious, cloth-covered table. The scents of potato pancakes, steamed cabbage, and bread wafted up from serving dishes. Ursula disappeared in the direction of the kitchen.

Breaking off their conversation, Eberhard and Renate stared at him, half-empty plates set before them.

"Hello." He sat down, picked up a clean plate. Doggedly, he filled it, aware of the questioning looks in his direction. There wasn't time to waste.

Ursula appeared in the doorway, face a mask of studied calm, still pale. In her hands, she held a plate of *apfelstrudel*.

"What's going on?" Renate broke the silence. "Uncle Dietrich?"

Dietrich set down the serving spoon. He locked eyes with Eberhard.

"The Gestapo are searching the Dohnanyis'. They'll be coming for me next. I've put everything to rights upstairs."

Thank goodness Eberhard didn't turn pale, or look shocked, like Ursula and Renate. He simply nodded.

"Then you'd better have that last potato pancake." He scooped it from the dish and added it to Dietrich's plate.

Dietrich lowered his head.

Thank You for this meal and for those who prepared it . . .

That was it. That was all he could pray. He raised his head, picked up his fork. The hunger pangs had long since vanished, replaced by . . . Well, he didn't quite know what, but he needed to eat. A favorite method of interrogators was starvation. They figured lack of sustenance weakened one's mental reserves.

He'd be interrogated. No doubt about that.

Ursula sank into her chair beside Renate.

"How long before . . ."

He swallowed, wiped his mouth with a napkin. "I don't know. Could be an hour, could be less." Another bite.

"Rüdiger's study?" Ursula breathed, wide-eyed.

"We'll go through it once I've finished. Get rid of anything suspicious." Chewing and swallowing had never seemed like such a task. Everything tasted like cardboard.

"You could get out, you know. You have travel permits." Eberhard's gaze swung to the window, then back to Dietrich.

Dietrich shook his head, shoulders lifting with a weighted sigh. They'd get him at the border for sure. And if they arrived and discovered him gone, they'd take his parents into custody. Rüdiger and Ursula. Even Eberhard. He wouldn't do that to any of them.

"It's too late for that, my friend."

Eberhard nodded, reluctance in his eyes. But his friend wouldn't press him.

"It's better this way." Dietrich rubbed his finger across the tablecloth. So white and pristine. Like fresh clothes and clean sheets. Like things prisoners weren't granted.

Only those who cry out for the Jews have a right to sing Gregorian chants . . .

He'd written that. Said it. Meant it. Still did.

Now, more than ever.

"Hans and I have it all planned out," he continued. "He'll take all the responsibility. I'll play the dimwitted pastor. And Canaris will back us up. It'll be fine. I'm sure none of us will be gone for long." He tried for a smile.

Ursula and Renate looked mildly reassured. Eberhard did not. Dietrich had learned to read his friend well, the pattern of thoughts that went on in his mind. Right now, they went something like: *What if they torture you, Dietrich? What will you do then?*

I don't know, Eberhard.

They have methods pulled from hell itself. How will you bear up?

God will give me strength.

Torture, Dietrich. Torture! Everyone thinks they'll stay brave and not talk, but few do. Those who do rarely live to tell about it.

Stop. Just stop, Eberhard.

Once he'd finished his plate, Ursula slid the dish of strudel in front of him. Golden brown around the edges, fruit oozing from the slits, it smelled like the days when one didn't worry about dictators or arrests. Like freedom.

Treats like that came dear.

"Where did you get that . . . ? I'm not going to eat it, Ursula. The children should."

His older sister reached across the table, his hands around one side of the plate, hers around the other. Her fingers brushed his, the hands of a strong, capable woman. She pierced him with a look made of steel, edged with softness.

"From Frau Linz across the street. And you're going to eat it, and that's an order, Dietrich Bonhoeffer." She gripped his hands.

He wasn't going to ask what she'd paid for it. Wordlessly, he took his knife and sliced the strudel into four pieces. Passed one to each of them on a napkin, locking eyes with each.

When would they sit around a table, share a meal again?

They ate the strudel in hallowed silence.

Then the four of them made their way into Rüdiger's office. It was doubtful they'd find anything, since Rüdiger possessed few incriminating papers. Dietrich moved to the desk, piled things on the table. Ursula, Eberhard, and Renate combed through each paper, every file. Most were related to his legal work, only a handful made mention of anything hinting at conspiratorial activities. These, Eberhard and Renate took into the garden and burned.

The four of them returned to the dining room and sat. No one spoke much. The coding systems had all been arranged. There was no way of finding out what had happened to Hans or to any of the rest. There was only waiting.

Dietrich traced a pattern on the tablecloth, a figure eight.

He cleared his throat. "Have you and Renate looked at any good apartments?"

Eberhard nodded. "A few. We saw one yesterday you particularly liked, didn't you, Renate?"

"It was nice. Small, but nice." Over Renate's head, the wall clock, the wedding present Dietrich had given to Ursula and Rüdiger, marked the passage of time in placid strokes. Almost four.

"You want to be sure to be clear with the landlord about expectations straight up. Don't be fooled into terms after the fact." Dietrich's gaze went to the window overlooking the pathway between the two houses.

Vater walked that pathway now.

Dietrich's stomach tightened.

They'd come for him.

He stood, urgency tamping down anxiety. "It's time. I need to go over there."

The three others stood, chairs scraping the floor. He faced them, drinking in the sight. Ursula, in her green housedress, dark hair smooth and shining in its knot at the back of her head, her strong half smile. Eberhard, whose expressions and ideas he knew as well as his own, his forehead a mass of concerned furrows. Young Renate, eyes brave and fearful, arms hugged over her chest, a grown-up and a little girl all at once.

He hugged Ursula. "It'll be a few weeks, nothing more. And when I come back, I'm going to repay you for the meal. We'll go out somewhere nice."

Ursula nodded, the lines in her face revealing the firm rein she kept upon her self-command. "I'll let you foot the bill." She smiled.

Next, he pulled Renate into his arms. She hugged him tight, a faint tremble shaking her.

"When I come back, I want to hear all the wedding plans. Take notes on everything you do. I'll be thinking of a good text for the sermon."

Renate stepped back, moisture in her eyes. "We'll wait on you to decide."

He reached Eberhard, just as Vater's knock came. He gripped his friend's hand tightly.

"Pray for me," he whispered, holding his gaze.

Eberhard nodded. "Already am."

Dietrich strode to the door. His legs didn't shake. His breath didn't falter. He opened the door.

Worried eyes beneath a knitted brow met his. "They're here." A myriad of questions spun through his vater's face, a face that had aged ten years in the space of minutes, the skin beneath his eyes pale and waxen.

Dietrich smiled slightly. "I know. Come."

Out the door, down the steps, into warm sunlight and spring breezes. Soft blue sky, feathered clouds. It was picnic weather . . . when had he last gone on one of those? Gravel crunched beneath his shoes, the sound like little pieces of shattered bone rubbing against each other.

His mutter met them at the door and led them into the house. Creases from her pillowslip marked her cheek, her hair frizzing around her face, a sweater tight around her shoulders.

"They're upstairs." Fear poured from her eyes. "In your room."

"It's all right. I'll be all right." He embraced her, his tall frame dwarfing hers. How strong she'd always been, yet how fragile. Full of faith, and strength of will, but with broken places, human ones, too. He hated to subject his parents to this. In their old age, they should be living in comfort, not witnessing their son led away in disgrace.

He held her close as long as he could. As a child, whenever he'd scraped his knee or been hit in the eye with a soccer ball, she'd always been strong for him. As his arms surrounded her, he drank in that strength again, let it embolden him.

"I'll be down in a minute." He moved toward the stairs. Each step seemed loud and echoing. Who awaited him at the top? Shadows hovered at the head of the stairs, as if he walked into choking fog.

He sucked in a breath, ran a hand down the front of his tie. Hans's instructions replayed through his mind.

You're an innocent pastor. You're calm, a trifle confused, the typical Lutheran.

All the world really was a stage, like that British playwright Shakespeare had written.

But few roles played out against the backdrop of life and death.

He couldn't just pretend innocence. He had to *be* innocent. Anything less and that would be it.

God, help me.

He entered the room, stride even, studied. Both men looked up. The one in Gestapo uniform stood next to the desk, papers strewn all over the place. The other sat in the desk chair as if lounging at the seaside, long legs stretched out, a cigarette dangling from two elongated fingers. Ashes scattered the floor.

"You are Dietrich Bonhoeffer?"

Dietrich nodded, once and short. The man's gray gaze reminded him of a fox, smooth and crafty.

"Judge Advocate Manfred Roeder." He took a leisurely puff. "Over there is Criminal Commissar Oskar von Scheffler. Care to have a seat while we finish our search?"

Dietrich stood motionless. Scheffler pawed through the pile of papers, movements sharp and meticulous. Almost scientific. Had he found the diary entries and letter?

"Very well. Stand then. Makes no difference to me." Roeder's tone dripped with suave smoothness, a veneer of congeniality.

Hans . . . Hans had spoken of this man.

I don't like him, Dietrich.

Roeder tossed the cigarette on the floor, grinding it with the heel of his polished black shoe. He wore a suit the color of coal and the aura of a panther about to pounce.

"I suppose you know why we're here."

Scheffler sauntered from the desk and to the bookcase. As he passed, he gave Dietrich a look of bland disgust. Older than Roeder, taller, his brawn seemed built to captain the Nazi war machine.

"You don't say much, do you, Pastor Bonhoeffer?" Slowly, almost lazily, Roeder unfolded himself from the chair. "It's a wonder you're able to string together enough words to fill a sermon."

Time to build his case. Dietrich spread his hands. "I am not sure what I should say. To be frank, I'm in shock. I was at my sister's house, having lunch. My poor vater was visibly shaken when he came over to tell me. And now to find you here, in my room, going through my things . . ." He hoped his expression held a suitable look of bewilderment.

"Standard procedure, I assure you," Roeder said. "As an agent for the Abwehr, you should know that."

"But these are my private quarters." It was easy to add a touch of annoyance to his tone. He couldn't let himself be hauled away too easily. That alone would invite suspicion. They couldn't guess he already knew the fate of the Dohnanyis.

"Are you acquainted with Wilhelm Schmidhuber?" Roeder asked in a bland monotone.

Scheffler paused and leveled an unblinking stare at Dietrich.

Dietrich kept his jaw tight, not wanting the men to see the relief draining through him. They thought him an accomplice in Schmidhuber's currency smuggling. For now, at least, they knew nothing about the wider conspiracy.

"He's a colleague of mine."

"Is?" Scheffler barked a laugh. "*Was* you mean? The man's been arrested."

"I knew that." Dietrich kept his tone equally bland.

"Then do you also know he's told us all about your *interesting* activities?" Roeder spoke like one who'd produced a trump card.

An image came to Dietrich's mind. Vater, arguing with a medical colleague in his consulting room. Only Vater hadn't answered. He'd stood there, arms crossed, studiedly indifferent. Even half smiling.

Dietrich adopted the same pose. "Has he? How interesting. He knows little about them. I work for the Abwehr, gentlemen. Confidential matters, you understand."

Roeder crossed to the desk, picked up one of the papers. He held it to the window, scanning the sheet, light filtering through paper. Dietrich's shoulders tensed. What was he looking at? Had he neglected to burn something?

A dribble of sweat slid down his back. Scheffler skimmed books, throwing the searched ones onto the floor with staccato claps.

Thud.

Roeder threw down the paper. "If you're hiding something, Herr Pastor, be assured, we will find it. We always find what we look for." A lethal shrewdness glimmered beneath his indolent expression. It chilled Dietrich to his core.

Roeder was a foe to be reckoned with.

And the man knew it.

"You missed one, Commissar." Roeder picked up a volume from the bookshelf and riffled through it. "I'd better help you."

They left nothing untouched. Every item of clothing, every pocket in every pair of his pants. Scheffler stood on a chair and tapped the rafters, neck extended, as if listening for some hiding place. Even Dietrich's socks were unrolled, searched, and thrown onto the floor. The lack of care for another's belongings wasn't just about speed. It was a tactic to exert superiority. An invasion.

His heart banged against his rib cage. He'd hidden the essay on the other side of the room. They'd find it.

His mouth went dry. There wasn't anything criminal written in the pages, not outwardly. But Roeder would find some way to use it against him.

Moments passed in slow motion. The room stank of Roeder's cigarette smoke and Scheffler's overpowering cologne. If there was any other odor that could be said to permeate the room, it was fear. His own, much as he tried to tamp it down. He forced himself to appear uninterested in the proceedings, staring instead at the mass of books littering his floor, recalling titles, where each volume had originated from.

Scheffler climbed down from the chair. Roeder threw a book onto the floor. It skated across the hard wood.

"Enough."

Dietrich fought to keep his expression free of triumph.

They hadn't found the essay.

Whistling a popular marching song, Scheffler pulled a pair of handcuffs from a briefcase, dangling them from one hand. Dietrich's eyes widened as the man approached. He took a step back.

Hans had never said anything about handcuffs.

Manacles of the condemned.

Calm. He couldn't lose control. Control was everything.

"If you gentlemen will pardon me." He stepped to the table beside his bed. His Bible lay on top. He'd placed the picture of Maria within its pages a few days ago.

Taking the Book in his hand, he leveled the men with an even stare. If he was going, then this was going with him.

"Wrists." Ice diffused more warmth than Scheffler's voice.

His Bible secure under one arm, Dietrich held out his hands.

The handcuffs snapped, unyielding metal noosing his wrists. Dietrich focused his gaze on the blank wall.

A prisoner. He was now a prisoner.

Even through this, You are with me, O Lord.

"Out we go." Scheffler jabbed him in the back. Dietrich stumbled. He ground his jaw, and righted himself.

If he could spare his parents the sight of their son being led away, he'd have given all the Reichsmarks he possessed.

Scheffler dogged his steps, as if expecting him to bolt. Roeder followed behind. The cuffs dug into his wrists as Dietrich struggled to keep his balance. He tripped on the third stair. His Bible slipped from beneath his arm, and fell two steps down, face-up, pages splayed. Maria's picture poked out from one corner.

"Clumsy, aren't we?" Scheffler made a *tsk*ing sound and bent to pick up the Book. He lifted Maria's picture, held it aloft. Maria's face stared out innocently in black and white. Scheffler studied the picture. A slow smirk spread across his face.

"Can I have that back, please?" Dietrich fixed the man with a cool, hard stare. Inwardly, he wanted to scream.

"Pretty little thing, isn't she?" Scheffler returned the picture to the Bible and gave it back to Dietrich. Using one hand, he repositioned it under his arm and kept his head low the rest of the way down the stairs, focusing on each tread.

His parents waited at the bottom. Vater's expression revealed little emotion. Even at a time like this, Karl Bonhoeffer wouldn't lose control. But Mutter's lower lip trembled.

"I won't be gone long. Take care of yourselves now." Dietrich managed a smile.

Heedless of the two guards flanking him, Mutter hugged him again. "I love you, Dietrich."

Roeder tapped his foot against the floor. Scheffler looked away.

"Come, Frau Bonhoeffer. We haven't all day." Boredom laced Roeder's tone.

His mutter pulled away. Her eyes remained dry. Brave, brave woman.

Dietrich kept his head low as they led him from the house. He didn't care to witness the shocked expressions of the neighbors, if any happened to be watching. In the tree Hans and his sons had climbed only five days ago, a bird trilled a high-pitched chorus. His gaze followed the bird, that winged creature able to fly to freedom.

He'd be back soon. He had to keep telling himself that.

A black Mercedes waited at the curb. Scheffler shoved him into it. He sprawled against the seat, hitting his head. Sparks of pain burst in the back of his skull. Roeder sneered.

Both men got into the front, Roeder taking the wheel.

The engine whirred to life.

Dietrich fixed his gaze on the smudged car window. His parents stood in front of their home, their forms small and blurred. Vater had an arm around Mutter. They watched him, motionless.

He smiled, doubtful they could see it.

As they disappeared from view, an almost physical pain tore through him.

Down the street they drove. Dietrich tried to push himself into a comfortable position using only his legs. Finally, he gave up and slumped against the seat, focusing on the direction they headed.

Where were they taking him? Where had they taken Hans?

Roeder braked just in time to avoid hitting an older woman carrying a shopping basket. Her alarmed face flashed through the window for an instant. Roeder swore. They passed her by.

Gray skies replaced the sunshine of earlier. Fitting.

Familiar streets caught his gaze, laying themselves out in a mental street map. They passed the Charlottenburg Palace, heading in the direction of the northwest part of the city. At least they hadn't turned in the direction of the deadly Prinz-Albrecht-Strasse Prison.

Perhaps they were taking him somewhere worse.

Roeder drove like one accustomed to people making way for him. Dietrich jolted forward as they braked again to avoid hitting a cart-bearing adolescent.

They passed the expansive Borsig Iron Works Factory. Ah, so that was to be their destination. Ought he to be worried or relieved? Right now, he was sick of sorting through his emotions and giving them names. They jumbled around inside, like one of Christoph's one-hundred-piece puzzles.

The sky had surrendered to twilight by the time they drove through gates that few entered willingly. A massive wall of red brick surrounded two large buildings. At their tops, like a crown of thorns, gnarled barbed wire prevented any daring attempts at escape. Windows, spaced at even intervals, stretched low and high. High windows. Barred windows.

Dietrich squared his shoulders. It could've been worse.

The car halted in another jarring motion. Uniformed officers snapped to attention like toy soldiers, each knowing their place in formation. Only these officers wore grim expressions and carried pistols.

The car door opened. One of them grabbed his arm. Pain shot through Dietrich's shoulder. He stared up at the buildings, those expressionless eye-like windows.

They'd arrived at Tegel Prison.

Chapter Twenty-Four

April 5, 1943
Hanover

Maria jolted awake, a scream on her lips. Clammy sweat dampened her blouse. Semidarkness cloaked the cramped room.

Only a dream. Nothing more.

She collapsed against the pillow, spent, heart pounding.

Figments of sleep-coated memory pieced themselves together. Tightness rose in her throat. Dietrich's face surrounded by utter blackness. She'd run and run, trying to reach his side, but by the time she'd arrived, the darkness had closed utterly around him. Despite how far she reached out her hand or how loudly she screamed his name, it hadn't been enough to vanquish the darkness and bring him into the light again.

She pressed her damp face into the pillow, willing the horrible images to recede. Throughout her work at the hospital that day, a sense of foreboding had gnawed at her. She'd dropped a tray of dirty dishes, broken plates and bits of food splayed across the floor. The ward sister had shouted—oh, how awful that had been—told her she was a clumsy oaf, and ordered her not to show her face for the rest of the day. Maria had returned to the apartment, collapsed onto the thin mattress, and fallen asleep.

She reached across to the lamp on her bedside table and flipped it on. The glow warmed the room. But it didn't reach inside her.

Grabbing her diary in an attempt to calm herself, she opened its pages. The few letters Dietrich had sent her lay within the front cover, the pages creased from the many times she'd read them. She unfolded one, ran shaking fingers across the lines of his handwriting. If only she could see him. Be with him and know that he was well.

Was this what it was to be in love? Wrenching and beautiful all at the same time? Did she love Dietrich Bonhoeffer? How could she? She knew him so little. Was it the image she'd conjured of him that she loved or the man himself?

She folded the letter gently and turned the diary to a blank leaf. Someday when they were safely married, she'd let him read all the letters she'd filled the pages with. By then, these cares and anxieties would be forgotten, and she could laugh at her silliness.

Pencil in hand, she scribbled the words, each scratch of the tip renewing the skitter of unease within.

> *Dearest Dietrich,*
>   *Has something bad happened? I'm afraid it's something very bad.*

April 5, 1943
Tegel Prison

The cell door slammed shut.

Darkness. Though a faint shaft of light fell from the high, barred window, it did little to penetrate.

Rubbing his wrist, Dietrich stood in the center of the room. They'd strip-searched him, then gave him back his clothes. At least they'd removed his handcuffs. Small consolations. They'd also confiscated his Bible on the pretense of searching for hidden, sharp objects. And just before pushing him through the door, the guard jerked off Dietrich's tie. So he wouldn't use it to hang himself.

They obviously wanted to keep him alive. But for what purpose?

He drew in a breath of rank-smelling air. In one corner, a blanket lay tossed atop the narrow, rusty cot. He crossed to it, the stench doubling. He picked up the blanket and nearly gagged.

The clean white sheets Lotte changed weekly never seemed so far away.

A petty thought to have, considering he still stood here in one piece. But he wasn't using that blanket. He balled it up and tossed it in the corner. The cell reminded him of an underground hole, its size roughly nine feet by six, if that. A rusty bucket crouched in one corner, the reason for the foul odor coming from that side of the room.

His gaze landed on the opposite wall. Crude letters scrawled across the squares of cement. Desperate etchings of the forsaken.

In a hundred years, it'll all be over.

A shudder crawled up his spine. What fate had met the man who penned those words? Did he walk free? Or had he met his end through interrogation and torture, a noose around his neck, a single shot to the back of his skull?

A ragged breath lifted Dietrich's chest, compressing his lungs like a heavy hand. Thoughts like those would get him nowhere.

He sat on the cot, hands between his knees. Utter solitude pressed in on him. It couldn't be past eight o'clock. He had nothing to do but go to sleep. Though how one could sleep after a day like this . . .

His thoughts drifted to his parents. No doubt their mental suffering was worse than his. He'd done his best to prepare himself for this. They knew only vaguely the extent of his conspiratorial activities and were neither of them young. But Ursula and Rüdiger would care for them, and Eberhard, almost like their own son, would see to anything they needed.

What of Oster and Canaris? Were they, too, behind bars? What would happen to the resistance without its leaders? Perhaps they'd escaped this fate and still walked free.

But Hans . . . where was he? In a cell much like this? Had they interrogated him?

Tortured him?

He couldn't ask. It would give too much away to reinforce their connection.

Lack of solid knowledge about loved ones was far worse than the darkness, the stinking blanket, the chafing on his wrists. Like a festering burn, it cried out for tending. For answers.

Maria. Amid the tension of the day, he'd not thought of her until now. Why hadn't he asked Eberhard to telephone her? Or his mutter? His parents, Ruth von Kleist, Eberhard, and Renate were the only ones he'd told of the engagement, out of respect for Frau von Wedemeyer's wish for secrecy. How long would it take for the news to reach her?

Oh, Maria. To think you've promised yourself to such a man.

He closed his eyes, leaning back against the wall. Tried to remember happy memories of that silly American song he'd played while she looked on with awestruck eyes. Of sitting beside her in the hospital corridor, the way her silky hair brushed her cheekbone. Her hand in his, warm. Her scent, feminine and soft. Blissful.

Low, anguished weeping broke through his reverie.

Dietrich sat up with a start. It had come from the cell next to his.

Again, a wail of utter misery. Pleading as a child and wounded as a trapped animal. Such a sound coming from the throat of a human man . . .

What was his story? There were many reasons to bring a person to tears in this place. It was impossible to tell which part of the prison they'd put him in. All that had registered were long, white hallways interspersed with gray, closed doors. Like pens for holding cattle.

The sobbing continued. Minutes passed. Dietrich wanted nothing more than to cover his ears and block out the terrible sound. Why did no one shut him up?

"Just stop, will you," he muttered, immediately regretting the words. What a hypocrite, to become so base after only an hour in this place of darkness.

He wouldn't. He might be forced to stay at Tegel, but it wouldn't own him. He wouldn't become dark.

Forgive me, Lord.

He stood and crossed to the wall. Pressing his ear against it, he called.

"Hallo there. Can you hear me?"

Muffled sobs.

"Please, answer me. I'm in the cell next to you. I know I can do little, but I'd like to bring you comfort."

"You can't. No one can," came the low reply.

"Perhaps I can't do more than speak to you, but there is comfort to be had. God is with all of us, even when we are alone. Would you like to hear something?"

No answer, though he sensed the man still listened.

This wasn't a church. But the need of this prisoner surpassed many who warmed formal pews week after week. No airs. No starched Sunday best. Only raw pain and bald honesty.

He cleared his throat, recalling passages from memory. One hand braced against the wall, clammy cement chilling his fingers, the cell air dank and desperate, he recited Psalms to a faceless, nameless stranger.

By the time he finished, the man no longer wept.

Chapter Twenty-Five

April 6, 1943
Tegel Prison

B anging on the door jarred him awake.

Rubbing his eyes, Dietrich sat up, vision bleary. His neck and back ached from sleeping on the hard cot, and a gritty dryness coated the inside of his mouth. Why wasn't he in bed, cocooned beneath a warm comforter, the scents of breakfast wafting up the stairs? Who was making that racket? Where was he?

More banging. "Are you deaf, you filthy swine? Bring your bucket to the door!"

The realization fell over him like a crushing hand. He wasn't at his parents' home on Marienburger Allee.

This was Tegel Prison. Only a few kilometers from home, but worlds away from the life he'd lived.

He stood stiffly and shuffled across the floor, grabbing the necessary bucket.

Outside, the guard continued to spew foul language.

"Here," Dietrich called, setting the bucket just inside the door.

"It's about time, you blackguard. Next time you move faster, or mark my words, you'll not get anything." The door opened, just a crack, revealing a burly man in a gray uniform and cap. One hand snaked in, grabbed the bucket, and set it outside. He shoved a tin cup half full of murky brew into Dietrich's hands, then tossed something onto the floor, where it landed like a rolled-up pair of socks.

The door slammed shut again.

Dietrich inspected the item on the floor. A piece of bread—if the brownish square could be called that. Gingerly, he picked it up.

And surprised himself by devouring it in a few bites. He gulped down the lukewarm contents of the cup, the liquid calming the irritation in his throat.

He sat back on the cot, staring at his empty hands. He hadn't even said grace.

With a sigh, he rubbed the back of his neck, fingers finding something small and round. He held it up to the light.

A bed bug.

He squashed it instantly. How many more lived within this cell? Wiping the remains of the offending insect from his fingers, he decided it best not to contemplate that concern.

What should he contemplate then? Thinking upon his current state would only lead to misery. Thinking on his family would only swamp him with sorrow.

Memories of Finkenwalde rushed over him. At his insistence, they'd always begun the day with total silence—something the young men initially chafed at, considering they slept six to eight in one room on beds that belched dust whenever one sat down on them. After a forty-five minute service, the seminarians retired to their rooms to meditate on a passage of Scripture for half an hour. That way the first thoughts, the first words spoken would belong to God.

There was no preventing total silence at Tegel. He'd no one to break it with.

Leaning back on the bed, he closed his eyes, running over the second Psalm.

What does this passage mean for me today?

He could hear his own voice, instructing his boys. How often he'd posed that question to them. Now he put it to himself.

As he mulled over the words, framing them, peace descended.

Time passed, he wasn't sure how much. Forty-five minutes maybe?

Someone banged on his cell again.

The door opened. A different guard stood outside. Younger than the last. Broad-faced, light brown hair.

"Come now. Outside we go." A firm tone, but not an unkind one.

Dietrich followed the man through the halls, taking note of his surroundings. Several stories rose upward, each framed by an open passageway, so that on the first floor, one could look up to the top story and view the whole. Rows of barred doors at intervals, each sealed off from the others. The place was too dirty to be called sterile—though sterile it seemed—too cold to be called warm. But no matter his environment, it was a fine sensation to walk along a hall, even escorted by a guard. And he'd only been inside a cell for one night.

"Who are you, anyway?" The guard turned to him. The ugly military gray uniform decorated with insignias and rank hung loose on his frame, as if he'd recently lost weight.

Dietrich studied the man's expression. Not calculating, but curious. Still, he must choose his words carefully.

"A pastor."

The young man actually grinned. An honest grin, or a mocking one?

"You're the first of that kind we've had here." The keys jangling at the guard's waist clinked together as he kept a brisk pace.

Since he'd volunteered some information, perhaps he could ask a question of his own. "Do you know if I can have my Bible back?" *And whether my fiancée's picture will still be inside?*

"Maybe." The guard shrugged. "Maybe not. Depends on if you've smuggled anything in it. They'll be consequences if you have, you know." His tone was conversational. Almost normal.

They stopped before going out into the prison yard. Sunshine streamed upon a group of ragged men standing in rough formation on the gravel, watched by two bored-looking guards.

"I haven't. It's just a Bible. Could you try to get it back?" Dietrich asked quietly. "I've nothing else of my own with me. It would be a great comfort if I could have that."

The young guard looked at him. Dietrich held his breath, trying to read the other man's expression. Would he respond with anger? Punishment? Perhaps withhold it from him just because he knew Dietrich found it of value? Here they condoned treatment some would deem inhumane if tried on an animal.

Here men were given jurisdiction to trample over their fellow creatures.

Finally, a short nod. "I'll see what I can do." As if to reestablish his authority, he gave Dietrich a shove toward the courtyard, Dietrich's answering *danke* muffled by the clomp of boots against the unyielding floor.

———

April 12, 1943
Tegel Prison

He'd gotten his Bible back.

And spent the last six days in solitary confinement in a different cell. The new cell at least had the distinction of a decent blanket, and from what he could tell, no bed bugs. But after nearly a week, endless hours broken only by the bringing in of food and the taking away of the bucket, he'd begun to wonder. Was this what it was to go mad?

Separation.

He'd scrawled the word on the only scrap piece of paper he had one hellishly long night.

Prison was a shadowland existence. Living neither in the past nor the future. He had no work to claim his hours nor the solace of knowing what had become of his family. He didn't even know if his fiancée had been informed of his arrest. And God . . . even God seemed distant.

Each new item on the list chanted through his brain. Laughing at him, a man in a wrinkled suit, sitting on a cot in the dark.

Nothing had been said about interrogation, or the reason for his arrest. He didn't want to appear eager and ask questions of the guards who carried in food. The man who'd given him back his Bible, Corporal Knobloch, was the friendliest of the lot. Apparently, the man had once known Martin Niemöller.

Dietrich stared at the gray wall, Bible on his lap, another day looming in front of him.

He needed a routine. Something beyond waking up, eating the bread, washing in the small amount of water provided. Occasionally, one of the guards brought a razor and stood glowering while Dietrich shaved. Then long hours, then another meal, more long hours, another meal, then bed. Sleep became a merciful angel.

When he slept, he no longer saw the ugly walls of the cell, heard the abuse of the guards as they berated prisoners for nameless offenses, calling them all sorts of vile epithets. Listening to these made anger boil inside at the treatment endured by those confined nearby.

When he slept, he could live inside his dreams.

A knock on the door. Dietrich's pulse sped. They'd already gone through the food-and-bucket ritual. And he'd been permitted to shave yesterday.

The door opened with a metallic whine. A guard whose name he hadn't learned stood outside.

"*Schnell.*" He jerked his hand toward the door.

"Where are we going?" Dietrich asked the question instinctually, though he probably wouldn't get an answer. Prisoners were moved like cattle, as if they were brainless beasts oblivious to where they were taken.

"Interrogation."

A surge of ice shot through his veins. The moment of reckoning. He glanced down at his attire with a wince. He was to meet whatever awaited him in a rumpled, dirty suit.

The guard held out a pair of handcuffs. Snapped them around Dietrich's wrists.

He ignored the sensation of being trapped. Right now, his very life and the lives of those involved in the conspiracy depended upon his skillful handling of the questioning.

They marched him outside and into the back seat of a car, another guard climbing into the passenger seat. Dietrich stared out the window as they turned down the street, hungrily taking in the sights they passed. Trees. How wonderful it was to be so close to trees.

Sunlight warmed his face. He placed one manacled hand upon the window, letting warmth seep through his fingers. Warmth.

He closed his eyes in sheer pleasure.

Finally, the car stopped in front of an edifice of gray stone. The War Court. Uniformed officials marched across the courtyard, intent on errands. The vibrant colors of the swastika hanging in front of the building billowed in the breeze.

Red. For years, though really only days, it seemed his world had been cement walls and gray uniforms.

He almost laughed at himself. To think, he'd just admired the Nazi flag.

Maybe he actually was going crazy.

The car door opened, and the guards led him across the cobblestone courtyard. He purposely slowed his steps to feel the fresh air on his face a few seconds longer. One of the guards gave him a shove toward the door, and they marched inside into an anteroom.

Windows let in sunlight. But sunlight was the only thing inviting about this place. Guards and men in suits paraded the halls. A life-size portrait of the Führer hung on one wall flanked by two swastikas. At the front desk, a cold-faced clerk directed the guards. They marched down the hall.

"They brought Daniel, and cast him into the den of lions."

What was worse? Facing real lions, or human ones?

"Now the king spake and said unto Daniel, Thy God whom thou servest continually, he will deliver thee."

The verse emboldened him as they entered the interrogation room. He'd never been inside an interrogation room and had tried to keep his imagination from conjuring all sorts of horrors. The reality looked like a place one would hold a meeting. Bright lights. Oak-paneled walls. A long, polished table. A narrow-faced man at a stenographer's desk in the corner, pen and paper in front of him, a typewriter next to that. He didn't look up as they entered.

No truncheons, whips, or anything else resembling torture devices. The room smelled of paper and ink, not metal and blood. Dietrich drew in a breath of relief.

The guard came around and undid his handcuffs. Dietrich rubbed his wrists.

The door at the opposite end of the room flung open. Roeder sauntered in, followed by Scheffler.

Gestapo, both.

Hans had always feared they'd fight to get jurisdiction in the case, if ever members of the Abwehr were arrested. Their chance to be the victorious party.

Dietrich linked his hands in front of him.

"Ah, Herr Bonhoeffer. Delighted to see you again." Roeder smiled, as if this were a country estate and he the squire welcoming his guest. Only no welcome emanated from the man's cool, gray gaze. More like the look of one relishing the sensation of power.

A feline pouncing upon a cornered *maus*.

"How have you found your accommodations? Tegel isn't Charlotten-berg, I know, but we do try." The smile became a smirk.

"Herr Prosecutor, would you please explain why I am here?" Dietrich met the man's gaze head-on. "To be frank, my accommodations are worse than what I'd offer a dog, and the sooner we get down to business, the sooner this nonsense can be cleared up."

Roeder seated himself at the other end of the table, steepling his slim fingers atop the rectangular expanse of gleaming wood. Scheffler availed himself of the seat to Roeder's left, spreading out an array of files. A uniform encased Scheffler's wide shoulders, whereas Roeder wore a sharply tailored black suit and pinstripe tie.

"Very well then. Let us 'get down to business.' I must begin by informing you that we've arrested von Dohnanyi . . . and his wife. Keep in mind all you say will affect our treatment of them."

Christel imprisoned. If the way Dietrich had been handled was any indication of how they treated the men, what did they inflict on women? Her poor children must be terrified, without their vater and mutter. Christel, alone . . . Christel . . .

His face must have paled, as Roeder's self-satisfied expression grew, completely overtaking his hawkish face. "You didn't know they'd taken your little sister too? Of course not. How could you have? Rest assured, she's getting fabulous . . . treatment. So where were we? Ah, *ja*, you wanted to get down to business."

Dietrich's heart pounded. He straightened his shoulders and tried to stand taller. Scheffler coughed. The secretary's pen scratched. Sunlight fingered a path across the table. Roeder began by asking him his name, birthdate, and residence for the benefit of the transcripts. Dietrich answered each question. They started out this way to lull him into a false sense of security, as much as for record keeping. But Dietrich wouldn't let himself relax. And then . . .

"What do you know of treasonous activities in the Abwehr?"

"Nothing," Dietrich answered automatically. "There are no treasonous activities in the Abwehr. Even if there were, I would know nothing about them. I'm a pastor." He forced a sheepish smile. "Treason is completely beyond my comprehension."

Better a lover of truth to tell a lie . . .

"Aha!" Roeder's eyes gleamed. "So you admit, then, to there being a possibility for treasonous activity? Write that down, Herr Secretary. Be sure you wrote that down!"

"I admit nothing." Dietrich kept his voice even, his gaze direct. "I spoke hypothetically. If there were to be any hint of anything taking place that dishonored our great Führer, I'd know nothing about it."

"But you do." Roeder spoke patiently, as if he explained to a child how to count to three. "Herr von Dohnanyi himself said you knew all about it."

Than for a liar to tell the truth . . .

Sweat trailed between his shoulder blades. Roeder had to be lying. Hans wouldn't have said anything like that. Would he?

"That can't be true. My brother-in-law wouldn't say anything of the kind."

"Are you calling me an idiot?" The feline, unable to capture the *maus* as quickly as expected, grew livid. Roeder's face reddened, his eyes bulging.

"Never, Herr Prosecutor. I'm merely explaining the truth."

"Feast your eyes on this then." Roeder handed a paper to Scheffler, who stood and handed it to Dietrich.

Dietrich scanned the typed page. It contained, in veiled verbiage, the points for Dietrich to use in Rome. In ecumenical terms, it outlined the German Protestant Church's so-called desire to bring about a lasting peace with the Vatican, and their awareness of the aims of brother churches to do the same.

Below the typed letters, General Beck had scrawled the letter O, his code initial approving the document.

Dietrich laid the paper onto the table. He didn't like holding it. "I don't understand what the problem is."

"Of course," Scheffler said dryly. "Simple pastors don't understand treason. But you won't trick us by playing that game. Herr von Dohnanyi has already confessed to writing the thing with your help and General Oster's support."

Oster? Why had they come to that conclusion?

The O. They'd mistaken Beck's code initial for Oster's signature. Had Hans played along? Or not?

Dietrich's feet ached to sit down, but he didn't dare. Roeder would think him weak.

What should he say? What if what he said didn't line up with what Hans had already implied?

He wiped damp hands against the sides of his pant legs.

"My planned trip to Rome was to further intelligence aims. The memo was written for that purpose. Our hope was if the Vatican read it, they'd be more eager to give out the information we were seeking. Information that would further our efforts to thwart the Allies."

Dietrich studied Roeder's expression. Did his statements match Hans's? If not, what would Roeder do about it?

"Interesting." Roeder drummed his fingers on the table. "More interesting still, because when my men entered Dohnanyi's office, General Oster himself was there and seemed particularly anxious to destroy that particular piece of paper. I wonder why, since you say it's so innocent?"

Dietrich kept silent. Scheffler seemed to be mentally picking apart each statement. He scrawled something on a piece of paper, one finger pressed against his mustache.

Roeder scoffed. "What? No quick rejoinder?" Again, that masterful smile. "I should think you'd have plenty to say on the subject, seeing as you were the one making the trip to Rome."

"I honestly don't. In all my dealings with the Abwehr, I merely followed the instructions of those wiser than I." Over and over, Hans had made Dietrich rehearse statements like these.

This wasn't a rehearsal. It was real, and these men were deadly. Each word he spoke would be torn apart and twisted. He'd thought he'd come prepared for this. But he hadn't. Not really.

"So you've no names to give me? When we had our little chat with Schmidhuber, he mentioned a 'clique of generals.' I'm anxious to know who they are. Herr von Dohnanyi wasn't willing to tell me. Won't you be more obliging?"

"I don't know what I must say to convince you of my ignorance." How much longer would this last? The sunlight, so welcoming at first, now glared through the window and hurt his eyes. He blinked, seeing spots.

"I only entered the Abwehr because my brother-in-law, who knows much about these things, thought it would be a beneficial way for me to serve Germany. Along with my duties there, I've also been employed in matters befitting my education. Writing letters of encouragement to friends at the front and so forth. I've not had the time nor the desire to embroil myself in a hotbed of intrigue." He tried a conciliatory smile.

"Don't you want your sister to be released?" Scheffler cocked his head, tone liquid. "She's sick, you know. Prison has been hard on her. If you tell us what we want, we could have her out within the day. She could go home to those parentless little children of hers. Come now, Herr Bonhoeffer."

Dietrich tightened his jaw. He wouldn't put it past these men to fabricate the extent of her illness in order to break him. But if what they said was true and she genuinely was sick. Oh, Christel, Christel . . .

Roeder swore and slammed his fist against the table. "Don't you know you're dealing with the highest authorities in the country? We could make your current accommodations look like a room at the Hotel Adlon if, in future, you don't prove yourself a more apt conversationalist. Keep *that* in mind while you're sitting in the dark." His voice echoed off the high ceiling.

Dietrich didn't flinch.

Drawing in a breath, Roeder wiped a hand across his forehead. "You're a canny liar, Herr Bonhoeffer. Rest assured, I've dealt with canny liars before. Dealt, being the operative word. Enough." He flicked his fingers toward Scheffler, who stood.

"Wait." Dietrich wanted to return to the prison and slump onto his cot from mental exhaustion but instead kept his tone calm, authoritative. Who knew when he'd get this chance again? "I'd like to be allowed to write letters. My elderly parents are, no doubt, anxious about me and would be comforted by a word of assurance regarding my welfare. You understand, I'm sure."

Roeder and Scheffler put their heads together, whispering. Interminable seconds passed. Roeder chuckled. "I find it ironic that you, who will not cooperate with me, expect me to cater to you."

Again, Dietrich chose silence.

Roeder sighed. "Very well. You may write to your parents, once every ten days. The letters will be read and censored by me. If you receive letters in return, those will also be read by me, then handed over to you."

A letter every ten days. And censored by Roeder himself. Letters that would have to be written as an act, a facade for the benefit of the Gestapo. But at least he'd be able to reassure Mutter that he was well.

Could he try for another favor?

"I'd also like to request permission to correspond with one other person. My young fiancée is no doubt equally concerned. She's an officer's daughter, you know. Both her vater and brother served the Fatherland faithfully, until their deaths on the Russian front."

"A letter to your parents is latitude enough."

"I should think it's regulation." Dietrich shot the words back without thinking.

Roeder's hands curled into fists. "Take the prisoner away," he bellowed to the guards who'd appeared in the doorway. Then as if collecting himself, he smoothed one hand down the front of his pressed suit. "This won't be our last meeting, Herr Bonhoeffer. Nor, I assure you, our most productive."

April 18, 1943
Pätzig

Maria tucked the letter into her skirt pocket. Now wasn't the time to dwell upon why Herr von Scheffler continued to write to her, this letter a polite congratulations on her brother's confirmation. She wanted word from Dietrich. Not this man. Something about him, buried just beneath the surface, sent chills down her spine.

Today, she had more important things to think about.

Across the lawn, her brother-in-law Klaus sat unoccupied beneath a tree. Just as she'd instructed him in the note she'd passed him before the confirmation service.

Pätzig wore springtime like a schoolgirl wore ribbons. Bright and beautifully. Here in the garden, children playing lawn games, tables set for tea—it was as if they existed in an idyll.

But the outside world entertained no such fantasies.

Serving work finished, she left the group of guests who milled about the lawn dressed in made-over finery and hurried to where Klaus sat.

"Danke for meeting me." She gave him a smile. When Ruth-Alice had announced her decision to marry the von Bismarck's son, Maria hadn't been keen on the first break in the family unit. She'd since grown in real affection for the husband her sister had chosen. He now served in the Wehrmacht, a reluctant duty-fulfiller.

"The pleasure's all mine." He smiled his easy, handsome smile, making room for her on the bench. "I'm only curious what's behind your cryptic message."

She smoothed her hand across the rough wood of the seat. Overhead, wind rifled the spreading branches of the ancient tree. "I need your help." She faced Klaus.

"What? You want me to rescue you from those dragons at the hospital?" He grinned, his tanned, lined face accustomed to wearing such an expression.

"This is serious." Her damp palms found purchase on the pale green fabric of her spring dress. "You know all the problems that have arisen before and since my engagement." She'd never spoken directly to her brother-in-law on the subject, but surely Ruth-Alice had told him.

Klaus nodded, grin fading. "I know Mutter has enforced a year of separation between the two of you, if that is what you mean."

Maria nodded. "That's exactly what I mean. I want you to help me speak to her about revoking that year. You're a man. She'll listen to you."

Klaus shook his head. "Nein . . . Maria, I—"

"I know you and Ruth-Alice share Mutter's concerns." Leaning forward, she allowed desperation to infuse her words. She was going to fight for this. "I'm engaged to a man who's almost twenty years my senior and likely under surveillance by the Gestapo. I don't know him as well as is customary, but these are not normal times. And I'm not going into this blindly. I know there is no one else I want to spend the rest of my life with. Think, Klaus. If you and Ruth-Alice had been separated from each other for so long, when your hearts yearned to be united, to be together, wouldn't you have fought valiantly to change that?" She sat back, letting her words sink in.

Slowly, Klaus nodded. "I would've tried. You know how deeply I love your sister."

"Then will you help me speak to Mutter?" Her words tumbled over each other. "Today, before I must return to Hanover? Please, Klaus?" She gave him her most persuasive smile.

He stared down at his hands for several seconds. Maria fixed her gaze on where her mutter sat, Ruth-Alice at her side.

He sighed and chuckled at the same time. "All right, all right. We'll talk to her. But I can't make any promises."

She looped her arm through his, pulling him to his feet. "Then you'll be on my side?"

He grinned, obviously exasperated. "I'll be on your side."

Together, they crossed the lawn. Ruth-Alice and Mutter looked up from their teacups.

"Whatever have the two of you been up to?" Ruth-Alice smiled at her husband.

Klaus looked to Maria. "We've been talking." He pulled out two white iron chairs and sat beside his wife, Maria on the other side.

"What about?" Throughout the day, Mutter had seemed in better spirits than in months. Hopefully, this was a good time to bring up the subject.

"I want to see Dietrich." Maria met her mutter's gaze. "I'm not asking for an official engagement. I just want to go to Berlin once he returns from his travels, and visit him and his family. Klaus agrees with me."

In unison, Mutter and Ruth-Alice looked to Klaus.

Klaus coughed. "I don't see how it would do any harm." Klaus placed both hands on the chair rests. "It *is* rather a long time for the two of them to be apart. And surely today, a day of beginnings, proves that all of us can move forward with the future." He leaned forward in his seat. "I believe your husband would agree, Mutter von Wedemeyer. During this time of grief, he'd want your daughter to have every support, and if Pastor Bonhoeffer brings her this, why should they be denied each other?" He finished with one of his flashing smiles.

Maria tracked her mutter's expression.

Please, let there be no more impediments.

Finally, her mutter nodded, with a little smile. Maria jumped up and threw her arms around her neck. She had Mutter's blessing. Dietrich would be so pleased, their reunion so joyful.

Could it be true that her horizons held happiness? After the deaths of Vater and Max, could she truly begin to move freely beyond loss and into life and love?

"Oh, danke! You must come to Berlin too, of course. I know once we're there with Dietrich, you'll realize how right this is."

Mutter returned the embrace, patting Maria's back. "We shall see. Ah, Hans Jürgen."

Maria turned. Her uncle, bags in hand, suit dusty, stood on the lawn, watching them with a bewildered expression.

"Uncle Hans." Maria hastily returned to her seat, forcing herself to cross her ankles when all she really wanted was to twirl and laugh and phone Berlin. "Why weren't you at the confirmation?"

He took the chair Klaus quickly vacated and sighed. "I was delayed in Berlin. The train was late. Where is Hans-Werner?"

"With the other children." Ruth-Alice prepared a plate of sandwiches, handing it to their uncle.

"I'll be sure to make my apologies to him. I truly didn't want to miss the confirmation. So what was going on when I came up? You all seemed excited about something." Her uncle smiled, the weary edges of his face softening.

"It's rather wonderful news." Maria couldn't contain her giddiness. "Mutter has finally agreed to allow me to see Pastor Bonhoeffer, for the first time since we've become engaged."

Her heart sang. She'd telephone the Bonhoeffers as soon as the party ended. She hadn't heard from Dietrich in so long, perhaps he was still out of the country. Never mind, though. She could find out from Frau Bonhoeffer when he was expected to return and plan a visit for the week after. He'd introduce her to his parents as his bride-to-be . . .

Her uncle's expression shifted. Tightened. He set down the plate Ruth-Alice had given him. China clinked against the glass-topped table. He leaned forward.

"There is no way to say this gently, I'm afraid. I saw the Bonhoeffer family while in Berlin. Dietrich has been arrested."

Her surroundings spun. Maria closed her eyes, willing the words to recede, to not have been spoken at all.

Arrested. The word bespoke visions of high-walled prisons. Guards and seclusion.

It couldn't be true. Why? Why would they have arrested Dietrich?

His work for the conspiracy. It had to have something to do with that.

She fought for breath, but a band tightened around her lungs, as if she'd run a kilometer in the biting cold.

Voices. Mutter and Uncle Hans. The echoing laughter of the children. She needed to focus. To plan . . . to . . .

But all she could hear was that one, horrible word.

Arrested.

"When? Why?" She met her uncle's gaze, her voice a strangled whisper.

"On April 5. He's being held at Tegel Military Prison. His parents are hopeful his release will come soon, but one can never tell in these cases." Her uncle spoke quietly, as if he wanted to spare her the worst of the details. But she couldn't be spared.

She belonged to Dietrich Bonhoeffer too much for that.

The date seared itself in her mind. April 5. The day of her nightmare. The memory of what she'd written in her diary scrolled itself across her mind.

Something bad had indeed happened on that day.

Something worse than she could have ever imagined.

Chapter Twenty-Six

April 18, 1943
Tegel Prison

Dietrich opened the front cover of his Bible. Down the hall, one of the guards, whose voice he'd come to know by its especially cruel verbiage, began his nightly barrage against two prisoners several doors down.

"You stinking vermin! What do you need this time? Oh, sick again? Swine!"

At first, the sound had made Dietrich want to cover his ears. Now he ached to demand the prisoners be shown some mercy.

But as one of them, he could make no such demands.

He brushed his fingers across the picture in his hand, silhouetted in the dim light. Maria's clear, innocent gaze stared back at him. Gently, as if it were her he touched, he brushed a finger across her cheek, her hair.

Empty paper, not flesh and blood, met his hand.

"How are you tonight, dearest?" he whispered. "By now, you surely know what's become of me. I wonder if my parents have passed their letter on to you." Four days ago, he'd been allowed to send his first letter home. He'd kept it light, glossing over the horrors of prison life, focusing instead on how well he was doing, knowing the whole thing would be read by that snake Roeder. He'd spoken of Maria, hoping the message would be passed on, his words about how difficult this must be for her to bear, the best apology he could offer. But the sentences had sounded trite when he read them again.

"Truthfully, Maria, I want more than a few words with you. I want hours, just you and me . . . you and me . . ."

The "paper Maria" watched him, that same half-smiling expression on her face.

A knock on the door. Lighter, almost polite. Knobloch hurried in, casting a quick glance behind him, as if checking to make sure he wasn't followed. Dietrich placed the picture back inside the front cover.

"*Guten Abend.*" Dietrich smiled.

Knobloch's broad face flushed. He shifted from foot to foot.

Dietrich watched the young man from his seat on the cot. Most guards wielded their authority like poison-dipped swords. This one seemed different. This one seemed decent.

"There's been a discovery."

Discovery. A loaded word. Discovery could mean a beaten-down prisoner confessing everything during torture. A telling paper found during a search. Discovery could spell the end for the conspiracy.

Every muscle in his body stood at attention. "Go on."

"It's been going around, who you are." A tiny grin crept across Knobloch's boyish face. "It's kind of funny actually, to hear the others carry on."

"What do you mean 'who I am'?"

"General von Hase's nephew! None of us knew we had a relative of the great military commandant of Berlin in our midst. You can imagine if we did . . . well, you wouldn't have been treated as you've been. Arrangements are already being made to move you to a different cell. And you'll receive bigger rations. The boss, Maetz, is coming here to tell you all this." Knobloch laughed. "I think he wants to apologize. Wants to make sure you're not going to make a fuss to the 'great General von Hase' and get him demoted." Knobloch swept his hands wide with a flourish, in a perfect imitation of Maetz's pedantic mannerisms.

So they'd somehow discovered he was related to Uncle Paul. Of course few prisoners could boast the impeccable Bonhoeffer family lineage. Would that give him influence here? Perhaps enough to do some good for the poor souls abused within these walls?

"I don't want the bigger rations," Dietrich said quietly.

Knobloch's jaw dropped. "Are you crazy? You really should take them up on it—"

"I don't want the bigger rations. If I get more, others will get less. We all already receive so little. I have family on the outside who will send me as many food parcels as I'm allowed to receive. Perhaps this new information will make the guards all the more lenient when it comes to permitting me them. And keeping their contents intact." He'd already received one. His parents had sent him a letter, along with an extra blanket and bread, both smelling of home so strongly it made his throat ache. In the letter, they'd mentioned other food, but by the time Dietrich received the parcel, it had come up missing.

It wasn't difficult to guess what had become of it.

Knobloch swallowed, his Adam's apple jerking. "You really are something, Pastor. Can I call you that?" A tentative expression crossed the young man's face.

"Of course." Dietrich smiled. It had been a long while since he'd been called by that title in a tone not derogatory. Alone for hours on end, it had been easy to forget his chosen vocation. He was an "enemy of the state," contemplating how he might best evade Roeder's probing questions, trying to figure out how to exist in a world of guards and cement walls and encroaching despair.

"And . . . I know I'm probably bothering you, but might you mention my parents? In your prayers? My mutter is sick, and my vater's at the front. They're both in a pretty bad way."

Simple things like preaching a sermon no longer seemed applicable to him in a place like Tegel. But here was Knobloch, calling him Pastor and asking him to pray for him. It warmed him, this harkening to who he'd once been. Who he was still.

Pastor Bonhoeffer.

"Gladly," Dietrich answered. This young man reminded him of one of his Finkenwalde students. So many of them now served on the front, choosing military duty over death as a conscientious objector. Perhaps Knobloch, like them, did not wish to do what he did.

"Danke, Pastor Bonhoeffer." Knobloch smiled shyly.

"Can you tell me why the guards are so vile toward the prisoners?"

Knobloch shrugged. "Because they can be. Why do any of us choose to use our power over others?"

Dietrich nodded.

Less than twenty-four hours later, they moved him to a different cell. As Knobloch predicted, many of the guards came crawling with profuse apologies, saying they hadn't known who his uncle was. Dietrich wanted to retort that it didn't matter who one's relations were and merely having influential family didn't entitle one to better treatment than those equally miserable. When he had an opportunity, he fully intended to mention the abuse to Captain Maetz, the head of the prison.

The next day, they came for him again and drove him to the War Court. This time, he'd an hour advance warning and dressed in the spare suit sent by his parents. He stood straighter, wearing the pressed dark suit, despite his lack of a tie.

Roeder greeted him with a sarcastic smile.

"I hear they've discovered you're related to the city commandant. What jolly luck for you."

Dietrich said nothing as the guard undid his handcuffs.

"Too bad. I take it you would've remained more malleable had you been kept in your present situation. But no matter. I have means to get what I want."

"You really do delude yourself." Dietrich met Roeder's gaze evenly. He'd breakfasted on some of the bread sent by his parents, and the extra energy had already improved his state of mind. "The truth will come out. And as soon as it does, I'll be released."

Roeder seated himself at his place at the end of the table, Scheffler at his side. "At least we agree on one thing, Herr Bonhoeffer. The truth will come out. In view of our charming oneness of mind, let us begin." He leafed through papers with slim, almost effeminate fingers. "Accusation of high treason and treason against the state is no joking matter, let me tell you."

"To my knowledge, I haven't been accused of such a thing."

"For now. Once you are, we'll make short work of you and your brother-in-law. Perhaps you'd care to tell me something about your work for the Abwehr. It's quite interesting; we've searched their files and can't seem to find your name listed on the payroll." Roeder leaned back in the leather-upholstered chair.

He answered promptly. "That's because I never was on the payroll. I didn't think it right to take money for something I considered my duty to perform for the Fatherland."

Rain drummed against the windows, each droplet of water blurring together.

Roeder gave a short laugh. "Your duty, hmm? And was it your duty also to avoid signing the customary oath of secrecy upon joining the Abwehr?"

Dietrich spread his hands. "No one informed me it was required."

"I doubt that. So tell me, when did you first become a member of Intelligence?"

Why were they asking him this? Surely the letter he'd left on his desk would have afforded that information. Did they think to slip him up?

Good breakfast or not, his head began to ache, little pickaxes drumming into his skull. "In the fall of 1940. My brother-in-law's encouragement proved the catalyst for my becoming involved. He thought I could use my contacts in the—"

"*Ja, ja,* I know all that." Roeder steepled his fingers atop the table. "What I want to know, and I daresay the Gestapo does too, is why this letter"—he jabbed a finger against a piece of paper in front of him—"is here and not with Intelligence."

Don't falter. Answer quickly. Hans's voice. Sharp. Drilling him.

"As you can see, it's a draft. They have the original in their files."

"Then why can't we find it?" Roeder shouted, the sound echoing off the walls, overriding the cadence of the rain. He blew out a breath. "I may not be a great theologian, Pastor Bonhoeffer, but I do know something about the basic principles of religion. And from what I can remember, thou shalt not lie is still on the list of commandments. Do you agree with me, at least, about that?"

Dietrich swallowed back the dryness in his throat. "Of course I do."

"Then why do you insist upon breaking that commandment with me?"

He didn't answer. It went on for another hour, the questions rapid-fire and endless. Several times, Roeder asked the same question twice, as if trying to get a different answer.

Finally, Roeder stood, chair legs scraping the floor. He stalked across the room, until he stood nose to nose with Dietrich. Dietrich didn't budge. Malice streamed from the man's gaze.

"If you care anything for Dohnanyi and your sister, you will answer my questions." His breath stank of sauerkraut.

Dietrich's throat tightened. If only he could hear news of Christel. Was his sister also given privileges due to her relationship with their uncle?

He could reveal nothing. Not even under threat. The entire fabric of the conspiracy depended upon each playing their part and remaining steadfast under interrogation. Not all of them had been arrested. There were still those working to overthrow Hitler. Once they succeeded, all of them would go free.

Dietrich continued to stare steadily back at Roeder, lips pressed tight.

"Fine." Roeder stomped back around the table. "Take him away!"

April 20, 1943
Pätzig

She could stifle tears beneath her pillow, but she couldn't erase their existence. Blackness enshrouded her bedroom. Tears trailed down Maria's cheeks and landed on the pillowslip. Her throat ached.

Her heart ached more.

She was Dietrich's fiancée, yet her uncle—her *uncle*, for goodness' sake—had known about Dietrich's arrest before she had. If their engagement had been official, his parents or friends would have notified her instantly. Instead, she'd waited for two weeks, full of anxieties but unable to comprehend the reason behind them.

She stared up at the ceiling through a blur of tears. Somewhere in far-off Berlin, a tiny cell in Tegel Prison held the man she'd promised herself to. How was he faring? Was he hungry, cold, alone? Surely, all three.

On what charge had they arrested him? The Reich dealt with offenders swiftly and with an iron fist. Just look at what had happened to the Scholl siblings. For distributing pamphlets—measly pieces of paper, paper!— they'd both been executed within days of being discovered.

Since first hearing the news, she'd kept a brave face, determined that Hans-Werner's day shouldn't be spoiled.

Now alone with the agony of her thoughts, she let herself weep.

Her door groaned on its hinges. She turned onto her side, squinting into the slant of light emerging from the door as a figure entered her room.

"Mutter?" She swiped a hand across her cheeks.

Her mutter, dressing gown untied, her hair in a long braid down her back, crossed the floor with noiseless steps. She sat on Maria's bed, the springs creaking. Light from the half-open door fell upon her features.

"*Mein Liebling.*" She placed a hand upon Maria's shoulder.

It was all the invitation Maria needed to go into her arms, let the warm embrace enfold her. Her shoulders shook with gulping sobs.

"There now, my dear, dear daughter. Shh." Mutter rubbed circles across Maria's back, as she were a little girl of three crying over a scraped knee, instead of a woman of nearly nineteen with her heart in tatters.

"I . . . didn't . . . know. . . No one . . . told me." Maria choked out the words. "I'm his future wife, and . . . no one told me." She pulled away and met her mutter's eyes.

"I'm sorry," Mutter whispered, pain radiating from her features, visible even in the darkness. "It's because of me and my determination to keep you apart, because of my misplaced belief that what the two of you shared wouldn't last and my fear that his activities would come back to haunt our family. I regret my actions and now have only to ask forgiveness. From you both."

Maria looked down at her hands, twisted around her sheet. It was true. Mutter had kept them apart, and her actions would remain a regret she must carry. But she hadn't done so out of any desire but for their good.

And Dietrich would not reproach her, knowing her actions provided enough reproach.

"Don't upset yourself." Maria placed her hand over her mutter's. "We cannot undo the past. You thought what you did was for the best."

Mutter nodded, the moisture on her cheeks shining in the semidarkness. "I want you to make your engagement public. You must become acquainted with the Bonhoeffer family. They have as much a claim on you now as we do. You must be known to everyone as his fiancée, otherwise you won't be able to obtain visiting rights, and so forth. I trust he won't be imprisoned long, but however lengthy the duration, the two of you must be as united as possible."

A rush of gratitude swelled within her heart. "I'll write to Frau Bonhoeffer straightway. Dietrich has told his parents about us, I think. Will you go with me to visit them in Berlin?"

"Of course." Mutter nodded, smiling slowly, almost wistfully. "Your vater, he said the most outrageous things. When we became engaged, it was the middle of the Great War, and when he proposed, he told me, 'Well, Ruth, if we're going to hang, it might as well be from the same tree.'" She laughed, gaze soft and far away. "What a man he was."

Maria smiled. "I want Dietrich and me to have as good a marriage as the two of you had."

Dear Vater. If only they had more of him than memories. His absence would forever be a presence in her life, one more prominent at moments like these. She missed him, the cadence of his voice, the way his arms wrapped around her in a solid hug. She tried to remember these things.

But forgetfulness was a symptom of time's passage. Unavoidable.

Mutter reached out and cupped Maria's cheek with her soft, warm hand. "Then you must stand together now, through the hard times as well as the good."

Maria nodded. "We will." She closed her eyes, recalling his face, wishing she had more of him to call her own than the short time they'd spent together. "Whatever comes, I want to face it by his side."

May 15, 1943
Tegel Prison

He was to have been best man today.

Dietrich stared out the window of his cell. Only a few, short kilometers away, his closest friend prepared to wed the love of his life.

Sunlight trickled through the window, illuminating a swirl of dust motes in the air. At least they had a fine day for it.

How happy they all must be. Eberhard and Renate on the brink of a future together, the rest of the family joyous in that expectation. In the succession of letters he'd written, he'd urged them to be happy and not let his absence cause any sad thoughts, that even here he would be joining in their happiness.

But he hated that this confinement had cruelly stolen today from him, the moments of anticipation before the ceremony. He wouldn't be there to help Eberhard straighten his tie—assure him that nein, it wasn't actually crooked. His usually levelheaded friend would be wearing a hole in the carpet. And Dietrich wasn't there for any of it.

Since his parents had sent him a substantial amount of stationery, he'd written Eberhard and Renate a special sermon to be read at the ceremony. He'd enjoyed the process of putting down on paper his hopes and wishes for their future, but it had been painful, knowing he'd not be there to read it himself. His parents had described all the preparations in their letters and continued to send packages. Food, clothes, and books. How innocuous those volumes of *Church History* and Gotthelf seemed to the guards who searched the parcels before he received them.

Coded messages, dots, every ten pages. Words meant to guide him in the *katze-und-maus* game against Roeder.

So far, according to the messages, Dietrich had managed to keep his answers during interrogation in line with the stories of others. Roeder began to let up, as if falling for the ploy that Hans was the brilliant lawyer, and Dietrich, the brainless clergyman. Still, the man continued to summon him, each time with a barrage of more questions.

At least Christel had been released late last month. During one of the interrogations, Roeder signaled the guards and brought Christel and Hans into the room. A mean trick to try to shock them into revealing evidence.

Dietrich shuddered. Even now, he could see his sister's ashen face, the exhaustion in her eyes. Hans had looked sick and beaten-down, but when Roeder turned his back, Hans smiled, a silent reassurance of well-being. Both of his physical state and that of the conspiracy.

Soon, Roeder would realize he had no solid evidence against either of them. Hans had covered their tracks well. So far, their stories had held up.

Their release would come. Dietrich only hoped it came soon. For all their sakes.

On the wobbly table serving as his desk lay the letter he was writing to his parents. He did his best to keep from sharing the stress he was under, partly because Roeder pored over each and every letter, and partly to keep from alarming his family.

With each note from various family members, more and more people mentioned his engagement. His parents wrote that they'd received a message from Maria, and she soon planned to visit them. If only he could make the introductions—walk into the living room at Marienburger Allee with her on his arm and proudly introduce her as his fiancée. Witness for himself the way his family took to her—they couldn't fail to. There'd be a party and smiles and he'd put his arm around her waist.

Only he wouldn't.

Because he was in Tegel.

A knock sounded on the door. Knobloch came in. A small grin—he was one of the only guards familiar with such an expression—accentuated the young man's face.

"I've got good news for both of us, Pastor."

"Wonderful." Dietrich returned the smile. "And what particularly does the news concern?" He wouldn't allow himself to get his hopes up about the trial. A mere prison guard wouldn't know anything about that. But simply seeing a smiling face improved the landscape of his day.

"I visited Mutter yesterday, since it was my day off, and she's much better. Your prayers must've worked, eh, Pastor?"

"That's great news." Dietrich stood, rubbing the back of his neck. In an hour, it would be time for his allotted walk around the prison yard. That and mail time encompassed the highlights of his day, since the food wasn't much to speak of. He couldn't remember the last time he had tasted meat.

"And this is for you." Knobloch thrust out his hand. "I filched it from where they were sorting the mail. I thought you'd want it right away." The boyish expression on his face was at stark odds to the severe uniform he wore.

Dietrich took the letter, holding it in both hands, the paper smooth and flat beneath his fingers.

The writing on the envelope—it belonged to her.

The sight stole the breath from him as surely as if she herself had entered his cell.

"It's from her, isn't it? The girl whose picture you keep in your Bible? I should guess you spend more time studying *it* then you do all those verses."

"I do not," Dietrich said, his gaze still on the letter. She wrote like she lived, a flourish to each letter. As effervescent and free as the thrush that sang outside his window.

He looked up at Knobloch. "Danke." Once upon a time, he'd been the one to do for others. Now others—this young guard who'd been an utter stranger but weeks ago—did for him. It brought one a whole new perspective on gratitude.

"I'll leave you to read it then." Knobloch grinned as if he understood what it was to receive a letter from the girl you loved. Dietrich didn't heed the sound of the cell door being bolted again. He sank down on his cot, drinking in the incredible realization that he held words penned by her. A letter had once been an ordinary thing. Special, perhaps, but still ordinary. Now they were his link between those nearest and dearest. The only connection he had here—this otherworldly universe of darkness and despair.

Almost reverently, he undid the envelope, slid out the pages.

Dear, beloved Dietrich,

He smiled, picturing how she'd looked as she'd written it. Her hair would fall over her cheek. She'd push it behind her ear. Smile, her full lips tipping upward in an infectious expression. Whisper the words as she wrote them. The image was all at once vivid and blank. He only imagined these nuances. He hadn't seen her enough times to conjure the picture for himself. He didn't know her the way Hans knew Christel.

But this letter was a start.

Your mutter has given me some photos of you—eight little photos. They're in front of me as I write. I look at them, and everything seems close enough to touch you and your ideas, the days we spent together, and the days when we'll be together again.

With what confidence she proclaimed those words. If only he could answer this letter, put into it everything he felt without any threat of censors or prying eyes. Tell her how completely she belonged to him in his heart, even here. How he had long conversations, staring at her picture. How their end always left him empty, the lack of her presence sharper than before.

Don't be sad when you think of me, Dietrich. I'm determined to be very brave, believe me. I sometimes think I couldn't ever be sad, because your thoughts, which are with me, simply don't permit it, and because what you give me by thinking of me means so infinitely much more.

Knobloch couldn't have brought him a better gift other than Maria herself. She wrote about her time as a nurse—apparently she told her young patients lots of stories about him. He envied those children able to be with her, see her face, feel her hand.

I hold your picture in my hand every night, and tell you lots of things—lots of "do you remembers," and "later ons"—so many of them that I finally can't help believing that they're only a small step away from the present. And then I tell you all the things that can't be put into writing—certainly not if other people have to read my letters—but things you already know without my writing them down.

He pressed the letter against his heart. With it close to him, he was with her. Every sentence bound them together.

Someday when it was her he held instead of her picture, he'd do his best to be worthy of her and all she'd bestowed upon him.

Chapter Twenty-Seven

May 23, 1943
Berlin

The last time she'd stood on this street, the man she'd never dreamt would come to mean so much to her had been at her side.

Clutching a bouquet of roses from the gardens at Pätzig, Maria opened the gate with her free hand, her heels tapping the path. Mutter followed behind.

Then she'd only glimpsed the Bonhoeffer house from next door at the Schleichers. She'd thought it a fine, upper-middle-class residence, the siding done in tones of warm tan and brown, shuttered windows adding a homey, countryish touch.

Now, she thought of it as *his*. His home.

She'd written to Paula Bonhoeffer, but never met the woman or her esteemed husband.

At the front door, Maria hesitated. She smoothed a hand down the front of her cranberry-colored suit, brushed a wisp come loose from the bobby pins pulling the front of her hair back on each side. She'd drawn a line down the back of her calves to imitate stockings. Her last pair she'd worn in Hanover until they had fallen apart in her hands. She rued their lack, but there was nothing to do about it.

Perhaps they wouldn't like her, disapprove of their son's choice . . .

The door opened.

A dainty woman gowned in a lavender dress, graying hair pinned in a wispy bun, beamed when she saw them.

"Dear Maria, you've arrived at last. And Frau von Wedemeyer. Come in, come in, both of you!" Frau Bonhoeffer eagerly motioned them inside before they could return her greeting. She closed the door. They stood inside a spacious front hall smelling of linseed oil and baking bread. Just looking at it gave one the impression that this was a home in the best sense of the word.

"Now, let me have a look at you."

A flush filled Maria's face.

"You're just as Dietrich described you." Frau Bonhoeffer's smile deepened on her faintly lined cheeks.

Dietrich had described her to them. What had he said? Her heart tripped at the thought.

"These flowers are from the gardens at Pätzig." Maria held out the bouquet. "A small way to thank you for your generosity."

Frau Bonhoeffer took them and inhaled their fragrance with closed eyes. "They smell wonderful. How thoughtful of you. Both of you."

"We're so grateful for your kindness in inviting us," Mutter said.

"Think nothing of it! You're both family, welcome any time. Now come into the living room so I can introduce you to Karl." Frau Bonhoeffer led them through the hall and into the parlor. Patterned wallpaper and a few tasteful pictures decorated the room. One on the mantle caught Maria's eye.

She hurried to it. It was of a younger Dietrich, leaning, arms folded, against the back seat of a motorcar. He looked ready to set off on an adventure, an almost jaunty smile on his lips. An answering smile unfurled on her own mouth as if put there by a force beyond her control.

"I like that one too. He looks particularly handsome, don't you think?"

Maria turned. Frau Bonhoeffer watched her with a twinkle in her eye.

Her cheeks burned. "I do apologize, Frau Bonhoeffer. I didn't mean to be so forward, gaping at your family pictures."

Frau Bonhoeffer's laugh rang out like a chime. "No apology necessary."

"Who's apologizing for what?" came a voice from the doorway.

The tall gentleman with neatly combed white hair and a pressed gray suit could be no one but Dietrich's vater. His smile confirmed it. It matched Dietrich's exactly.

"There you are, Karl. Maria and her mutter have arrived at last."

"Ah good!" Dr. Bonhoeffer crossed the room. He greeted Mutter first, then came to his wife's side, with a stride exceptionally spritely for one having passed his seventy-fifth birthday.

"You're very welcome here, Maria. Please think of our home as yours." Sincerity in his eyes, he took her hand in his.

"Danke, Dr. Bonhoeffer. You're very kind," Maria murmured.

"And we have good news, don't we, Paula?" He turned to his wife.

"*Ja*, we do. We received a letter, not half an hour before you arrived.

After frequent applications to the War Court, we've finally been granted a visiting permit. We make our first visit to Dietrich on Tuesday."

"Why, that's wonderful!" Maria smiled, ashamed by the stab of jealousy that needled her. Of course, his parents should be the ones to get the letters and visits. They had far more of a claim upon him than she. They should be the ones to go and sit beside him, hear his voice and look upon his face. But . . . selfishly, fiercely, she wished it could be her.

"Indeed it is." Mutter came to stand next to the group. "I'm sure it will relieve your anxieties a good deal, Frau Bonhoeffer, to see your son again."

"Oh," Maria said, remembering the shoulder bag on her arm. She reached into it and pulled out a small tin of real *kaffee* beans and a week's ration of butter. The Bonhoeffers watched her with curious expressions. "I know you're allowed to send food parcels to the prison. Here is my contribution." She handed both items to Frau Bonhoeffer.

"Danke, my dear," Frau Bonhoeffer said softly. "We'll see to it he gets these."

"But you really shouldn't go doing that, Maria. You need those things yourself." Dr. Bonhoeffer moved to one of the couches and sat down.

"I'm truly happy to. Knowing he'll get them gives me far greater pleasure than having them myself. I only wish I could do more."

Frau Bonhoeffer placed the items on an end table. "We've some time before lunch. The Schleichers will be joining us. Shall I take you upstairs and show you around?"

Maria nodded, perhaps a bit too eagerly.

"Karl, I think Frau von Wedemeyer would enjoy a tour of the gardens."

"Of course." Dr. Bonhoeffer stood and offered his arm. "Shall we, Frau von Wedemeyer?" Mutter smiled her assent and the two made their way out.

Frau Bonhoeffer leading the way, they reentered the hallway and climbed the narrow steps. Maria ran her hand along the railing. Day after day, Dietrich's fingers had touched this very spot as he came up and down the stairs. She smiled.

Several doors led off in various directions. Frau Bonhoeffer stopped beside one.

A swirl of anticipation started in Maria's chest.

"This is Dietrich's room." Frau Bonhoeffer opened the door. With a laugh, she added, "I did tidy it up a bit in advance, though not too much, mind you. You ought to know what you're in for later on."

Maria drank in the sight. His presence was everywhere. In the armchair next to the bookcases. At the desk, the desk where he'd written his letters to her. A pair of slippers lay next to the neatly made bed, and she had to stop herself from running to pick them up and clutch them to her chest.

Was it possible for someone to be absent yet still there?

This room seemed to embody his essence, his love for reading, for art. Carefully, breathlessly, she walked to his desk. Frau Bonhoeffer remained in the doorway.

She smoothed her fingertips across his desk pad. A few inkblots dotted its top. A volume lay on one edge. She picked it up, the cover falling open to the flyleaf.

"To my dear parents. Thank you for everything."

She turned the volume to look at the spine. One of his books Grossmutter admired: *Creation and Fall.* Maria had never read it. Admittedly, her favorite thing to read by him remained his letters to her.

"I'm going downstairs to check on lunch. Stay up here as long as you like." With a smile and a wave, Frau Bonhoeffer disappeared from sight.

"Danke, Frau Bonhoeffer," Maria called, but the lady's footsteps already echoed down the stairs.

She set the book aside and moved to the bookcases. They'd been built into the wall and simply designed. The row after row of tomes, each in an orderly fashion, seemed to matter far more than the construction of the shelves. She glanced at the array. He'd probably read them all. How shameful her own lack of literary knowledge seemed compared to this.

Once they were married, they'd have plenty of studying to do together.

She approached the closet, feeling a bit like a child snooping where she shouldn't be. Someday, each of these items, the books, pictures, even the slippers by the bed, would find their way to the little home the two of them would make together.

The closet door creaked when she opened it.

Several suits hung on wire hangers. Maria reached out and trailed a hand down the sleeve of one. His scent lingered in the fabric. Sudden tears rose to her eyes.

Is there a limit to how much one heart can miss another? If so, Dietrich Bonhoeffer, I haven't found it.

May 24, 1943
Berlin

"You're proving yourself quite useful to have around."

Maria looked up at Frau Bonhoeffer's words. They sat in the Bonhoeffer living room, a basket of socks at their feet. Darning was a task that made one's shoulders ache and one's eyes blur, but Maria had enjoyed the past hour alone with Dietrich's mutter. They'd mended and chatted, the basket of worn-in socks fast emptying.

She smiled, warmed by the woman's praise, and bent to her task again. Noises sounded in the hall, a commotion like someone arriving. Tongue between her teeth, Maria snipped a stray thread and held the sock up to the light for inspection. Some of the socks were for the men in prison—Hans von Dohnanyi and Dietrich. The intimacy of the task had not been lost upon her, and more than once, her thoughts had drifted to the man whose clothing she mended. In the day she'd spent with the Bonhoeffers, reminders of him had greeted her around every corner. His very self so close, she could have reached out and touched him.

If only he'd not been so achingly far away.

The door opened. Christel von Dohnanyi stepped inside. Maria remembered the woman from Hans-Walter's send-off. Tall and dark of hair and eyes, she possessed the regal bearing shared by all the Bonhoeffers.

"Hello, Mutter." Christel crossed the room and gave Frau Bonhoeffer a brief hug. "It's good to see you." She turned, meeting Maria's eyes.

"Fraülein von Wedemeyer. How long have you been in Berlin?" The Christel before her now seemed a different woman than the one from the night of the party. Her fine cheekbones were more pronounced, her skin paler, the brown dress and blue sweater hanging limp on her frame.

"Since yesterday. My mutter is at the home of my aunt, Spes Stahlberg."

Christel nodded. She seemed to linger upon Maria, as if taking her measure. Maria straightened her shoulders at the assessing gaze.

"Vater is asking for you." She turned to Frau Bonhoeffer. "He's in his study. I'll help Maria with the socks."

Frau Bonhoeffer left the room, and Christel took her place on the sofa. She pulled a sock from the basket and began to darn it. Maria followed suit. She watched Christel out of the corner of her eye. The woman had been taken the same day as Dietrich and her husband. She knew what Maria didn't—what it was like in those prison cells, what one was subjected to at the hands of the Gestapo. Christel's experiences had altered her, aged her.

For long minutes, they bent to their task in silence. Maria bit her lip, forehead scrunched as she focused on the heel of the black woolen sock.

"Do you know what you're in for?"

Maria looked up, the muscles in her neck cramping in protest. "Pardon me?"

Christel's eyes were twin orbs of steel. Sock discarded in her lap, she repeated, "Do you know what you're in for?"

"I . . . I don't understand."

"Then allow me to explain. You're how old? Nineteen?"

Maria nodded. The expression on Christel's face rooted her to the spot. Somehow she sensed she must prove herself to this woman, though she didn't fully understand why.

"You're little more than a girl. Engaged to my brother. I don't hold it against you. In ordinary times, you would have my warmest congratulations. You seem intelligent, and Dietrich obviously cares a great deal for you. But these are no ordinary times." She leaned forward, hands clenched around the darning egg. "What do you know about the reasons for Dietrich's imprisonment?"

Maria swallowed. Was Christel putting her through some kind of test? "I know that he's involved in something dangerous. That he avoided joining the Wehrmacht by serving Military Intelligence. That whatever it is, it entails an end to the government as it is now. He's under suspicion by the Gestapo for something."

"You know more than I thought," Christel murmured, as if to herself.

"Henning von Tresckow is my uncle, and Fabian von Schlabrendorff my cousin." She lifted her chin. "They're involved too. I know this because they used to come to Pätzig to try to convince my father to join them. He would've been one of them, had he been able to reconcile it with his conscience. He hated the Nazis and refused to fly a swastika on his property. They became angry with him and tried to take away his license to manage his own estate."

Christel nodded, sock motionless in her lap. "By openly declaring yourself my brother's fiancée, that entitles you to certain privileges. Visiting rights and so forth. You'll be allowed to apply for permits. I cannot say whether they'll be granted, but you can try. It's a game of chance when it comes to leeway with that nest of hornets." Her jaw tightened, the bitterness in her gaze speaking of her own experiences. "All we can do is wear them down with persistence."

"I will. I don't care how bad it is in there. I just want to see him. To help him however I can." She spoke the words as if she meant them more than anything else she'd ever said.

Christel smiled slightly. "How innocent you still are. During a visit like that, you say everything you don't want to, and leave unsaid everything you do. You'll be watched. Some of the guards may be kind, others . . ." She looked down at her clasped hands. A simple wedding band glinted on her finger. She twisted it, lips pressed together. Looked up again. "There are things . . . ways we're smuggling information into the prison."

"I want to help." The words rushed from her lips before she could fully contemplate them. "Just tell me what to do."

Christel's gaze sharpened. "It's not child's play. It's dangerous. For the men and for us."

It would be foolish to deny the dangers. Christel was right. This wasn't a game. It was real. It was war. Germany fought to reign supreme over the world. The Bonhoeffers fought for their men.

Maria could do no less. She drew in a breath. "I'll accept the dangers."

"All right then." Christel met her gaze. The woman studied her not with respect but with acceptance. Maria sensed that from Christel, even acceptance was something hard-won. "Let me know if you receive a visitor's permit. Call my home and ask if there are any books to deliver to Dietrich. If I say yes, you can come and collect them."

"Books? I don't understand. How do you pass messages through a book without being discovered?"

"Don't ask questions." Christel picked up the sock and resumed her darning in a businesslike fashion as if they'd just finished a conversation about *kaffee* substitutes, something ordinary. "Before anything else, you'll need to learn to be content without answers."

June 10, 1943
Tegel Prison

"Dear Senior Military Prosecutor Roeder."

Rereading the letter, Dietrich scratched out the words Operation 7 and replaced them with Fraülein Friedenthal, the name of the middle-aged Jewish woman who'd been transferred to Switzerland and whose participation Roeder had called into question.

He'd gotten the idea to put his thoughts down in a letter to Roeder, instead of relying solely on the interrogation questioning to make his point. He'd always been able to write better than articulate. Hopefully, reading the lengthy exposition would put Roeder to sleep.

Dietrich pulled off his glasses and rubbed his eyes. Today's meeting with Roeder had been particularly taxing. If ever a man was gifted with the ability to twist words to suit his own benefit, it was this one.

How much longer could it all go on? Days turned into weeks, weeks to months. Roeder grilled him on his special exemption status as an Abwehr agent, on the currency issues that came into play with Operation 7, on the military exemptions he'd tried to secure for pastors of the Confessing Church.

Every day, he told himself soon he'd never have to look into Roeder's feline visage again.

And every day came and went with no outward results.

Your will always supersedes mine, dear Lord. You know that I trust You.

He stood and began the ritual he performed several times a day. Pacing from one end of the cell to another. In all honesty, he'd gotten more exercise during his months at Tegel than in the years where he'd been engaged in the church struggle and in teaching the Finkenwalde seminarians combined. Then there'd been so many different demands upon his time. Here, his tasks were limited.

Though of recent days another had been added to that list. One he was particularly grateful for.

As if on cue, Knobloch knocked on his door and opened it.

"Ready to visit the sick bay?"

Dietrich grabbed his coat from the cot and shrugged it over his shoulders.

"How was your last leave?" he asked as they made their way through the echoing prison corridors, passing endless rows of locked doors.

"Mutter isn't as well as she once was." Knobloch's expression tightened. "But I saw Fraülein Slagle again." He lowered his voice as they passed a duo of guards. Knobloch straightened his shoulders and looked straight ahead, as if he were a surly guard overseeing a truculent prisoner.

It wasn't looked favorably upon to be seen as friendly toward the prisoners. Only his secret friendship with Knobloch defied that rule.

When they'd passed the guards, Knobloch continued. "Did you know she's friends with Frau Niemöller?"

"Has she heard anything of Martin?" Truly, Dietrich's situation was luxurious, compared to Pastor Niemöller's confinement in Dachau.

Knobloch shook his head. "Things are much the same, I guess." They reached the swinging doors of the sick bay.

"*Guten Abend*, everyone." Dietrich greeted the room at large.

The half dozen prisoners currently filling the hospital beds chorused greetings. The room smelled like sickness and unwashed bodies. Dietrich had gotten so used to such smells that they hardly fazed him. He concentrated instead on faces—a few eager smiles, some more hesitant, others emotionless. Knobloch said he'd never seen so many men eager to be "sick," whenever they heard Dietrich planned to visit.

"I'm going to sit down." Knobloch ambled to the radio and fiddled with the dials, turning it to some light music.

Knobloch, bless him, always timed Dietrich's visits to the infirmary for when the least amount of staff was present, leaving him free to converse with the prisoners without prying eyes.

"How are you today?" Dietrich stopped beside one of the first beds. A young man barely out of his teens smiled weakly. He'd been caught attempting to desert from his unit last winter in Russia. During the frigid winter, he'd lost all of the fingers on his left hand from frostbite. Currently, he occupied the infirmary due to a lingering case of pneumonia.

"Better, I think." Peter adjusted the skimpy pillow with his one useful hand. Dietrich reached behind and helped situate it.

"I brought you something." From his pants pocket, Dietrich pulled out a half a piece of white bread wrapped in paper.

"You remembered!" Peter took the package eagerly.

"It came from my parents yesterday." Dietrich sat on the edge of the bed. They'd better blankets here than in the cells, but they were still thin.

"Danke." Peter's tone echoed with feeling. "So what else do you have for me today?"

"Another Paul Gerhardt hymn." Dietrich took a scrap of paper from the same pocket. Carefully, using the smallest handwriting, he'd penned the verses. "Shall I read it?"

Peter nodded, leaning his head against the pillow, face pale.

Dietrich read the few verses loud enough for those in the neighboring beds to hear, letting the comforting words wash over them all. He handed the paper to Peter. "That's all I could fit on this piece." He smiled. "My handwriting has never been the greatest."

Peter squinted at the letters. "You're not kidding about that. How does your family manage to make out your letters?"

"Time and practice, my friend." Dietrich stood. "Enjoy the bread." He moved on to another bed.

As a young theology student, he'd welcomed the prestige of being top of his class, the darling of all the professors. He'd wanted to make something of himself. The years, even these last months at Tegel, had convinced him of the falsity of such a desire.

Even here, one could live in freedom, knowing by whose hand the future was led.

Chapter Twenty-Eight

Her swollen and aching feet had proved a useful excuse for her departure from Hanover and transfer to Berlin. A visit to a physician friend of the Bonhoeffers, a letter putting her on medical leave, and all had been arranged. Her feet weren't all that bad. But she'd jumped at the chance to be in Berlin again. For Dietrich's sake. If she ever received a positive answer to her requests for a visiting permit, she wanted to be close by.

Not wanting to impose upon the Bonhoeffers, she'd asked Tante Spes to put her up, and Maria did her best to keep busy helping around the house and visiting Dietrich's parents as often as she could.

And today entertaining Oskar von Scheffler.

She'd mentioned her trip to Berlin in one of the two letters she'd sent him. The first day she'd arrived at her aunt's, he'd phoned with a request to visit.

Sitting in the parlor, awaiting his arrival, Maria smoothed her skirt across her knees.

Why did he wish to call upon her? For that matter, why did he keep sending her letters? Did he so lack for company?

It was easy to believe. Though vast and populated, Berlin was an easy city for one to feel lonely in. These days, bombs turned streets formerly vibrant into desolate graveyards of what once had been. If only she'd had a chance to see the city when it had been beautiful. The scars of war had altered the landscape almost beyond recognition.

Germany's crowning glory, they'd once called it.

Neither their city nor their glory seemed likely to survive.

The cadence of footsteps sounded in the corridor. Maria gave a glance at the table to make sure all was in readiness. She'd managed to finagle some *kuchen*, ersatz *kaffee*, and Tante Spes's good linen napkins. Per the doctor's orders, she sat on the sofa, elevating her feet with a throw pillow.

The door opened with a creak, the girl Tante Spes employed to cook and clean stepping aside for Herr von Scheffler to pass. He handed her his hat. She curtseyed and hurried away.

"*Guten Tag*, Fraülein von Wedemeyer." The months in Berlin had altered him. Today, a three-piece suit, rather than riding clothes, made broad shoulders appear even broader. Wind no longer licked his dark brown hair, new touches of gray appearing in the slicked-back strands. A trimmed mustache shadowed his upper lip.

He looked powerful. Like the type of man the Führer would put in charge of half the army.

"*Guten Tag* . . . I'm sorry, I don't know your rank," she faltered, flushing. In his letters to her, he'd simply put his surname and street as the return address.

He smiled, a glimpse of the man who'd regaled her in his letters with stories of his pet Saint Bernard. "Oskar is fine. Surely there's no need to stand upon formalities."

"Won't you sit down?" She gestured to a chair placed near the table heaped with tea things.

"Danke." Herr von Scheffler sat. He surveyed the table, an appreciative lift to his brows. "Quite the spread. I hope you didn't go to a lot of trouble."

"It's all right." Maria smiled. "The least I could do was offer some refreshments. *Kaffee?*"

"Real *kaffee?*"

She shook her head. "Unfortunately not."

"That's all right. I never could stand the substitute stuff, though don't tell. They might accuse me of demoralization." He winked. "But the *kuchen* looks excellent. Did you make it yourself?"

She cut a piece of the dry *kuchen* dotted with raisins and plated it. "I did. Though don't look excited. I've never been much of a cook."

He tasted the *kuchen*. "You're far too modest." He swallowed a few more bites without taking his eyes from her face. Maria watched him, her cup of lukewarm ersatz cupped in both hands. She wore a gray skirt and pale blue blouse. Suddenly, she wished her skirt covered more of her legs.

"So what brings you to Berlin? I know you said over the telephone you've been unwell. Are you any better?"

She shrugged. "It's all rather stupid, this matter with my feet. I have to sit for hours a day. But the orthopedist assures me that if I keep to this regimen, I'll soon be recovered."

"All good soldiers need a pair of strong legs." He laughed, finishing the *kuchen* and setting the plate on his knee. Silence lapsed. She sensed his gaze on her, the intentness of his piercing eyes somehow discomfiting. She pushed back a strand of hair.

"I'm sure you're wondering why I wished to visit you. Other than to taste your very fine *kuchen*, of course. I've made a discovery, I think." He set the plate on the table, leaning forward. A shaft of sunlight fell upon his greased-back hair.

"A discovery?" She fiddled with the tea things, placing her cup on the tray. A lorry rattled by.

"I haven't told you exactly what I do in Berlin, have I?"

She shook her head. "I don't believe so."

"I work for the Gestapo."

The words forced the breath out of her lungs. Why had he withheld this information from her before? Foolishly, she realized, she'd guessed him employed at some desk job, serving the Fatherland, but . . . Gestapo. The same company of men who'd arrested Dietrich and orchestrated so much violence and death. And here she'd been feeding him *kuchen*, replying to his letters about puppies and interior decorating.

Serving as an officer in the Wehrmacht, like Vater and Max, was one thing. But the Gestapo reigned over Germany with a scepter of terror.

Oskar von Scheffler was not who he'd presented himself to be.

She curled her fingers into fists atop her skirt.

"You look unwell. Have I distressed you?" A slight edge hovered in his tone.

She shook her head. "Nein . . . I'm just a bit surprised." What she didn't say was that that word conjured visions of grim men marching Dietrich away in a black car. Jail cells and interrogations.

Gestapo.

"Perhaps I shouldn't go on. I have more to say."

Her hands trembled. She wanted to tell him to go. She'd been stupid to let him write to her, thinking he was lonely, bonding with him over a similar loss. By omission, he'd deceived her.

Christel's words shook her to her senses. No longer was she an innocent bystander in this thing some called conspiracy, others resistance. By linking herself with Dietrich, she'd become entangled. Involved.

She drew in a breath of composure. "Nein. Please, continue."

"I only speak because I thought this would be of interest to you, seeing as you're engaged to Dietrich Bonhoeffer. He is your fiancé, is he not?"

For the second time in as many sentences, he'd rattled her. How did he know so much? She'd never mentioned her engagement, seeing as it wasn't widely known outside the family circle.

She met his gaze and nodded. "*Ja.* Why?" Her heart stammered against her rib cage.

"I can't reveal a great deal, but part of my duties entails my coming into contact with prisoners being brought to the War Court for interrogation."

She jumped to her feet, hand splayed against her chest. "You've seen Dietrich! Do you know what's going on? I've been so desperate for news. They won't let me visit—"

He held up a hand, smiling faintly. "Please, Maria, sit back down."

A hot rush of resentment hit her at his almost mocking smile. He didn't know the torment she'd endured over Dietrich's welfare. How she hungered for every word the Bonhoeffers passed on regarding his case. How she saved her butter ration, loaves of bread, anything she could manage, for the Bonhoeffers to include in their weekly parcels. How night after night, unbidden tears wet her pillow. He knew none of this, this man who was one of them.

Left with no other choice, she sat, feet planted on the floor, facing him, hands clenched in her lap. He sat, arms folded across his wide chest, muscles straining beneath his fitted suit coat.

"I've seen him. He's well."

She forced her mind to steady. To become calm and logical as Christel would be. She'd already laid her emotions bare. She must stop. He must witness only what she chose for him to see. That was all.

Herr von Scheffler had influence. She needed to do whatever it took for him to use that influence for Dietrich's benefit. "Can anything be done for him?" Her shaking hands would serve her well. Herr von Scheffler would see her as a fragile young woman, frightened for her fiancé. She dipped her gaze and looked down at her hands through lowered lashes.

"Very little, at the present moment. The case must be played out. Rest assured, Maria." He reached across and placed his hand on her knee, briefly, then drew away. "If I could do anything, it would be done without hesitation. You'll be interested to know that it is because of my influence Herr Bonhoeffer has received as good of treatment as he has. I've spoken with Judge Advocate Roeder, the person most directly involved with his affairs, and pleaded eloquently for his welfare. The moment I learned he was your fiancé, I couldn't fail to do otherwise."

She wouldn't trust him. He wanted something. No man of his ilk would perform an act of kindness without expecting something in return. But she would use him. And hope Dietrich's release came quickly so she never had to lay eyes upon Herr von Scheffler again.

"Danke," she whispered. "You're very kind."

"No thanks necessary." He pulled a silver case from his breast pocket and lit a cigarette. Tante Spes would have a fit when she smelled smoke in her parlor. But one didn't tell the Gestapo what they could and could not do.

She waited while he took a leisurely puff, choosing her next words with care. "Might I visit him? I'd very much like to."

Smoke created a haze around him. "I'll see what I can do. I imagine, with the right words spoken at the appropriate time, I can convince Roeder. In confidence, he's not the easiest man to work with. But I have ways."

"If there's anything you can do, I'd be so grateful."

"Of course." He held the cigarette between two fingers without putting it to his lips. Smoke wisped from the cylinder, the end glowing red. "If I might ask, could you refrain from mentioning this development to anyone? I wouldn't want information to fall into the wrong hands, you understand."

She nodded.

"I'd like to meet with you from time to time. That way I can share the latest developments, inform you of how he's doing. I'm sure I can arrange for you to see him yourself before long, but if I have something to share, I'd rather not do it over the telephone. And notwithstanding your fiancé, may I dare to hope that you'd welcome my visits?"

She forced a smile. "Of course. Come whenever you wish. I would have to make sure my aunt and cousins are out, but they are most days, so there should be no difficulty."

He leaned forward, running his thumb across her cheek. "There's a tear there. There shouldn't be tears when you're smiling. Not on a face as beautiful as yours."

She started at the familiarity of his hand against her skin. Dietrich should be the one touching her.

But Dietrich wasn't here.

And right now, it was in all of their best interests that she not push Herr von Scheffler away.

June 24, 1943
The War Court, Berlin

In a childhood storybook, Dietrich had once read a cautionary tale about a little boy who'd lived in the jungle and disobeyed his parents by wandering off after they'd bid him not to. The lad had larked about for a while before

266   My Dearest Dietrich

coming face-to-face with a python that subsequently strangled the disobedient boy to death.

In the eyes of the Reich, Dietrich was the little boy, the Führer the parents. And Roeder made an apt python.

Only Dietrich wasn't about to allow the python to grasp hold. So far he'd
escaped no matter how deviously Roeder twisted.

"You're not saying much today, Herr Bonhoeffer." Roeder drummed his
fingers on the table, the surface polished to such a high gloss that it reflected
like a mirror. "Perhaps you need a little something to cheer you up."

Dietrich tensed. In Gestapo terms, *cheer* usually went the route of pulling out one's fingernails, or simply drawing a revolver.

"*Ja*, now that I look at you, you do need cheering up. Fortunately, I've
got just the thing." Roeder smiled, an expression he wore surprisingly often
considering he never wore it well. His smiles always looked unnatural, like
a clown's smile. Painted on.

Overhead, a ceiling fan tried vainly to obliterate the heat.

Dietrich looked up at the spokes, turning around and around. Soon
Roeder would send him back to his cell where he could finish the letter he'd
begun to his parents. Though it was even hotter there, at least there were
no pythons.

Roeder strode to the door. Where was he going? To fetch a cool glass of
lemonade? The temperature certainly warranted one. A memory of sitting
in the garden with Sabine and her children drinking cool, frosty glasses
filled to the brim with half-sweet, half-sour liquid—

Roeder returned.

Breath fled Dietrich's lungs. The room spun, then righted itself again.

Maria. Beside Roeder, his hand on her arm.

"Surprise!" Roeder chuckled. "This is great, eh, Herr Pastor? To see
your lady love again? Go on, both of you may sit on that sofa."

Dietrich could do nothing but stare. Why was she here? Had Roeder
summoned her? This place, she didn't belong in it. She belonged in his family's parlor, her Pätzig estate.

Not the interrogation room of Manfred Roeder, a place where many a
lesser man had fallen prey to ruthlessness personified.

Another one of his tricks. That's what this was. Roeder wanted to startle
him into revealing some pertinent detail.

Dietrich clenched his jaw. He wouldn't fall for it.

Maria walked to the sofa and sat on one end. Her gaze hadn't left him.

"Go on now." Roeder seated himself in his chair, turning it so it faced
the sofa.

Dietrich forced himself to walk to the sofa and sit on the other end. He stared at her, half of his mind struggling to comprehend that she was really here, while the other half screamed that she'd been brought here for Roeder's benefit, not for the two of them.

He couldn't deny what the sight of her stirred in him. All the emotions he'd bottled rushed to the surface, Roeder or no.

"Hello, Dietrich." She smiled, a soft, beautiful smile, and it made him ache just looking at it. How many dreams had he dreamt of this moment— dreams both waking and sleeping? Hours he'd stared at the ceiling, imagining her face, and now it was before him. The curve of her throat, the wisp of hair curling against her ear. Her eyes, such a deep and fathomless blue, framed by dark lashes. Her full lips gently parted.

She distracted him, just as the interrogator hoped she would. He forced himself to remain impassive. Silent.

He glanced at Roeder, who sat, legs crossed, head tilted to one side, the way a cinemagoer might sit while viewing the newest film.

Dietrich turned back to Maria. He had to do something.

"How are you?" His voice sounded hollow.

"I'm well," she said softly. "And you?"

"Very well."

She smiled again. Nothing in her outward expression suggested she was frightened of this place, of Roeder looking on. Her focus was all on him. "Your parents told me you were, but I'm happy to see so for myself. I'm staying in Berlin now. I wrote you a letter about it, but perhaps you didn't receive it yet?"

He shook his head.

"I've been able to visit your parents several times. They've been ever so kind to me. Your mutter especially. She's always showing me new things of yours, and I can sit in your room whenever I want. Which I do, a great deal." Her smile deepened. "I hope you don't mind. But it's so inexpressibly wonderful just to be near your things. I've even looked through some of your books, though to be honest, I've not heard of most of them. You'll have to tell me about them sometime. I do so want to know your favorites."

Listening to her voice calmed the maelstrom inside him. He reached across the expanse of sofa between them and took her hand. Instantly her fingers twined within his. He gripped hers, savoring this tangible link between them. His larger hand within hers, the softness of her skin. A lifeline of mingled pain and pleasure.

"I'm not sure all of them would interest you." His voice came out calm, at strange variance to the flood of feeling inside him. "Some would, I think."

"I spent yesterday afternoon with the Schleichers. Ursula was over at Renate's, so they put me in charge of presiding over dinner. They're such kind people."

"Is . . . Renate well?" He knew better than to ask after Eberhard. With Roeder in the room, bringing up the name of his friend would only arouse suspicion. Exactly the type of information Roeder hoped to get out of this visit.

"Very well." Maria gave a little nod, as if she sensed why he withheld mentioning his niece's husband. "She misses you, as we all do. But she's been keeping busy. Newly married people always seem occupied. But they're both happy and say you're not to worry about them."

Dietrich nodded.

"We've already begun to discuss our wedding. Mutter is in quite a state about how everything should be. As for my part, I don't care about any of the superficial details, though I have been thinking about where I can find some material for my dress." She leaned closer, enfolding him in the scent of her hair. "I just want to be together with you."

Roeder coughed.

And I, you, Maria. What these moments with you would look like if we were alone . . .

He squeezed her fingers, the most he could offer her with Roeder's gaze upon them.

Though she still kept smiling, a trace of something like sadness passed through her eyes. How painful this must be for her. And he'd given her little but cold civility. With his parents, it had been different. They'd been guarded by an underling, not Roeder. There'd been greater freedom to talk, to be themselves.

"Grossmutter sends greetings. She's in better health than she was over the winter. Her eyesight is improving too."

"That's good. I can't help but be grateful to her for those hours in the Franciscan Hospital. I think about them often." He moved closer to her. Afraid to look away, afraid she would vanish into nothingness if he did. Foolish thoughts for a rational man.

But what was rational about love? And what was normal about any of this?

"Me too." She seemed about to say more when Roeder's voice broke in.

"Enough. Time for you to go." He crossed the room, standing over them.

Maria stood. The other guard came and gestured for Dietrich to follow him.

In the opposite direction. Toward opposite doors.

Into opposite worlds.

Everything he'd wanted to say but hadn't rushed to his mind, begging release. Building inside him as the guard marched him to the door. He turned. Maria and Roeder neared the other exit. Fervently, he tried to drag out the seconds, to memorize her profile, every feature, before she left him.

Only seconds. What were seconds of air to a man gasping for breath? They wouldn't sustain.

Suddenly, Maria wrested herself from Roeder's grasp. Dietrich's heart pounded as she rushed across the room. He glimpsed Roeder's gape-mouthed stare, before everything vanished except her arms around him.

He crushed her against him, bliss mingled with agony. Willing his touch to transmit the love that filled him with every beat of his heart. She was softness and strength all at once, softness as she leaned against his chest, strength as she clung to him with all her might.

He pulled away, just long enough to look into her eyes. In them he read everything a man could wish to see in the gaze of his beloved and more. Had this been another place, a different time, he'd have lingered. But they didn't have the luxury of delay. It was carpe diem, or not at all.

So he kissed her. In the joining of their lips, he was no longer Dietrich Bonhoeffer, conspirator and theologian, but simply a mortal man, held captive by her touch. In this moment, it didn't matter where or who they were. Only that he loved her, and no prison bars could destroy the fact that they belonged like this.

When he forced himself to draw away, they were both breathless. Shaken. Yet more whole than either of them had been upon entering this room of Reich interrogation.

There weren't words enough for him to express what had just happened, so he watched her walk toward Roeder without a word. In the past moment, he'd told her all he could, what couldn't be voiced in a letter written to his parents and read by a censor's piercing gaze.

She left, head held high. Only one glance back. The look in her eyes, such joy and wonderment, made him smile slightly as the guard led him outside.

Their first kiss.

A moment of beauty in a place marked by death.

Maria pressed her fingers to the window as the car drove away. Her expression stared back at her, a faint reflection in the glass.

Her eyes shone.

She leaned her head against the seat, each moment they'd spent together playing out across her mind. He'd been visibly shaken when Roeder brought her in. Obviously, the military prosecutor thought to use her as some sort of a tool, a human leech to suck out information he'd been unable to obtain. She'd kept smiling, caught between elation at seeing him and bitter wonderment over why he remained distant.

Finally, he'd gripped her hand as if she were the link between him and a fathomless abyss. Slowly, he became himself. But what could either of them say that truly mattered with Roeder—what a vile man—looking on? Painfully little. She'd done her best not to be deterred by the man's presence and focused on the sweetness of being, at long last, together with Dietrich. But the moment had passed all too quickly. And when Roeder clamped his fingers round her arm and escorted her to the door, she'd been seized by madness.

If the kiss they shared was madness, sanity was vastly overrated.

She'd dreamed about how it would be to be kissed, even pestered Ruth-Alice for some inkling of what it was like, after her engagement to Klaus.

Fantasy did not prepare one for reality. Nor for the mix of emotions afterward.

She pressed a hand to her lips, touching the place his had been.

Call her terribly selfish, but she wanted this to be over. Surely they'd soon release him. To freedom and to future kisses, where they could truly be alone.

Ja, she was selfish. War engulfed the world, a war their country was fast losing. Her petty trouble of a fiancé in prison seemed small compared with those women who sacrificed their men on the battlefield, those losing homes in the bombing raids now battering Berlin, the horrors only whispered of all that had gone on in Poland, the railcars stuffed with humanity shipped away never to return. It was an inferno.

One none of them could escape.

Only endure.

Chapter Twenty-Nine

July 6, 1943
Tegel Prison

In the suffocating heat, the cell became an oven.

I guess that makes me a goose being roasted alive. Dietrich smiled wryly. He sat at his desk, sweat making his spectacles slide down his nose, squinting over each page in the book his parents had brought him. The underline beneath his name in the front cover meant a message, and he was determined to make it out before evening's end.

He tugged at his collar, loosening some of the buttons. Having started off the day in a suit, he'd since discarded everything but the short-sleeve shirt and a pair of trousers.

Pushing up his glasses, he bent over the thick volume, running his gaze beneath each line.

A knock sounded on the cell door.

Dietrich turned. Who could that be? It was too late for the evening meal. "Come in." He kept his tone measured. Perhaps it was Knobloch to chat or bring some news. The young guard passed much that went on within the walls of Tegel Prison on to Dietrich—"The prisoner in Cell 41 will be taken away for execution tomorrow. A message from you would bring him comfort. There's a new arrival in Cell 89. They've got their claws in him, that's for sure . . ."

The door opened. It was Knobloch, but he didn't enter. Instead, he stepped aside, and another man ducked inside the crowded cell. Middle-aged, brown hair combed back from a high forehead, dressed in a simple dark suit.

Knobloch bolted the door.

"Guten Tag." Dietrich grabbed his suit coat from the cot, and shrugged it on.

The man nodded, posture seeming to relax. "I'm Harald Poelchau. Corporal Knobloch said you'd be glad to see me."

"Why, of course." Dietrich stood and shook the prison pastor's hand with a smile. He'd heard of Chaplain Poelchau, but they'd never met before. "Heartily glad to meet you. Sit down, please. Pardon the mess. I wasn't expecting company." He gathered his tie, which he was now permitted to wear, and a couple of books from the cot and smoothed a hand across the gray wool blanket.

Poelchau sat on the edge. Dietrich resumed his seat, turning the chair to face him. The man glanced down, twisting his hands in the blanket. As if organizing his thoughts. Or fighting something inside of himself.

Dietrich watched him, biding his time. He could have filled the silence with polite pleasantries, but he didn't. Poelchau had come to him for a reason. He'd speak when he was ready. So Dietrich waited and wondered. And sent up a prayer for this fellow brother in Christ.

Poelchau raised his eyes. The look they held made Dietrich catch his breath. It spoke of bitter anguish, torment long tamped down.

"Knobloch says that even here you're a source of strength. He said you know how to listen."

Dietrich nodded. Poelchau looked out of the high, narrow window, slatted with bars. Angry clouds slurred the sky.

"A storm is coming," he whispered. He met Dietrich's gaze again. "I've tried." The words emerged raw. "When I'm with them to the last, I'm strong. When I break the news to their families, I'm calm. But the burden presses on me. I must . . . I must speak to someone." He worked the blanket again, as if the motion could loose whatever burned inside him.

"Tell me," Dietrich said quietly. "I'm listening."

"Do you know what I've done since the war began? Before that, even?" Dietrich shook his head.

"I'm the last one they see." He pressed his forehead into his palm, shaking his head back and forth. "Not their parents, or their sweetheart. Me. Sometimes they want to talk. Others say nothing at all. I pray with them. Hold their hand. Speak to them of God, a future beyond this earth. Because"—his voice broke—"when I see them, there's no hope for them in the present. They have only minutes. I'm the last kind face they see. I go with them as far as the door. Do you know what kind of a walk that is? From the prison to the room where it all ends? It takes only a minute. Maybe two. Their whole lives pass by them in that minute." He stood and paced. "I know they do, because I see it. Some are weeping. Others have faces of stone. They all know where they are being taken." He faced Dietrich, features wracked with suffering.

Dietrich said nothing. He doubted Poelchau would have even heard him if he had.

"I've done this 786 times—786. You'd think it'd get easier, wouldn't you? Today"—his jaw trembled, beads of sweat streaming down his forehead—"there was a girl. Number 786. She was just sixteen. Could have been my daughter." His gaze drifted far away. "She had . . . the most beautiful blue eyes. Like sapphires, they were. Not even prison, not even her death, could take their shine away. She was sentenced for giving a piece of bread to a Jewish mother and her baby. That was all. That was her crime."

Dietrich's chest constricted.

"I sat across from her at the table in the cell. She wore a yellow dress. It shone like the sun in that cold room. We prayed together, recited some verses. Then she looked at me . . . and do you know, she actually smiled. 'They're coming for me, aren't they?' she said, smiling while she spoke. I nodded, and then she said, 'It's all right, Pastor. It'll be all right. Life is a beautiful thing. But the end can be beautiful too. I don't regret for a minute what I've done. I'll go out there, and I'll face them, and I'll let them see their cowardice.' And she did. She made that walk like a queen." A smile spread over his face, a glimpse of the strong man the prisoners must see. "Triumphed over them in death more than she ever could in life. It was an honor to escort her on those final steps." He drew in a long breath. "And it's for her, for each of them, that I'll do it again. If I don't, someone else might not show them kindness. Everyone deserves kindness in that hour." Poelchau seemed to steady, hands loose in his lap. But his words had opened to Dietrich in vivid color the cruel fate of those who dared to resist.

"What was her name?" It seemed a fitting question. Perhaps at this moment, the best that could be offered. The war would no doubt require many more such hours of Harald Poelchau. Lives would be taken by the Reich. Who knew when each of them might be required to surrender theirs. But spirits would live on, and someday, someday their stories would not be silent.

"Ina," Poelchau whispered reverently. "Her name was Ina."

July 30, 1943
The War Court

Maria clutched the coveted piece of paper in both hands, gaze straying to the gray stone edifice in front of her. The powers that be had chosen an impressive building to conduct business in—legal or otherwise. Swastikas hung at intervals, ugly splashes against the fine exterior. The pedestrians who passed moved quickly, clutching bags or children close, casting nervous glances, as if the structure emitted a foul vapor, warning: *Keep away, or you'll end up here.*

Drawing in a breath of a city smothered in summer heat, Maria crossed the street and climbed the stone steps, her worn heels making brisk, clipping sounds on the pavement. A statuesque guard in greenish-gray opened the door, and she gave a nod of thanks before entering the echoing, tiled vestibule. A few uniformed guards strolled past, giving her a leisurely once-over. Or perhaps they just wondered what she was doing here—a nineteen-year-old girl in a gray skirt and lilac summer blouse in a building where men wore either uniforms or handcuffs.

She smiled at the severe man behind the desk. Almost tentatively, he started to smile back, then stopped, as if the picture of the Führer behind him possessed mortal eyes and would rebuke him for behaving like a human, not a machine.

"State your business." He peered down at her behind glasses perched upon an exceptionally long nose.

She passed him the visiting permit. He made a show of over-scrutinizing it. She waited, tucking a strand of hair behind her ear. Marching footfalls sounded on the upper level.

He stamped the pass, handing it back to her with heightened efficiency. A man in a black suit descended the stairs, one hand trailing the sleek railing. Little about this place actually frightened her.

Manfred Roeder did.

"Ah, Fräulein von Wedemeyer!" He greeted her in the elevated tone of an experienced actor, as if he knew his voice would reverberate through the room, and he relished the sound of it.

"*Guten Tag.*" She nodded. "Danke for allowing me to visit."

"No trouble at all." Like a man accustomed to treating humans like biddable animals, he took her arm and led her down the hall. She shivered at the grip of his bony fingers on her elbow. "You made such a delightful impression on your last visit, I couldn't refuse you permission again." Condescension weighted his smile. He wasn't very adept at hiding his emotions—she could read everything he thought about her in his gaze. To him, she was a stupid girl who ought to be overcome by the great favor he granted her in allowing her to see her fiancé. She looked steadily back at him, emboldened by her assessment. What one could assess, one could handle.

"Bothering the lady, are we, Roeder?" A familiar voice, though it held a superior cadence.

Roeder removed his hand, turning sharply. She spun, facing Oskar von Scheffler garbed in uniform, a briefcase under one arm.

Perhaps the shorter man feared Herr von Scheffler, with his height and bulk. Or perhaps he simply didn't want a quarrel. At any rate, Roeder gave a curt nod and brushed past them into the interrogation room.

"Danke," Maria whispered, when he'd vanished.

"No thanks necessary." He smiled down at her. "I hope he wasn't a nuisance."

She lifted a gloved hand to adjust her pillbox hat. "I'm fine. And you? Are you well?"

"Well enough. Lacking sleep, of course, due to these blasted air raids. But quite refreshed upon seeing you. There's a definite lack of anything resembling loveliness here. I miss the countryside."

"I imagine." She fixed her gaze on his face. "Any news?"

"As a matter of fact, there is." He lowered his voice. The scent of cologne and cigarette smoke overwhelmed her senses. "The interrogations are at an end for now, and the charge of high treason has been dropped."

"That's wonderful." Surely that had to mean Dietrich would soon be released. They couldn't keep him imprisoned without good reason.

There was little to smile about in this austere monument to power, but Maria's lips turned up in one.

"Shall I take you to dinner tonight to celebrate? I found a place that actually gives the amount specified on a ration card. It took a bit of scouting about, believe me."

She bit her lip. "I'd planned to visit Dietrich's family . . ."

He stiffened, drawing himself taller, a hardness entering his gaze. "Some other time perhaps."

"*Ja*. That would be lovely." She added a slight smile to her words.

"Shall we go in?"

She nodded. He opened the door and stood aside to let her pass. He crossed the room with the familiarity of one who knew it like his own parlor. Roeder already sat within, turning over some papers. He looked up briefly, putting a cigarette to his lips.

"Wait there." Herr von Scheffler gestured to the burgundy plush sofa against one wall. "He hasn't arrived yet."

Maria situated herself on the edge of the sofa, gaze toward the door. Herr von Scheffler joined Roeder at the long table. They did not speak, and she didn't look at them. Silence hung over the room, cloying and clammy.

Minutes passed. She pulled off her gloves and clasped and unclasped her hands. All month she'd lived like a starving woman sustained by one meal.

Their last visit. Each day, she looked at the calendar, awaiting the time when she could apply for another permit.

Now she'd returned to the War Court. For one hour. Another meal to last her another month.

The door opened. Her heart sped up. She brushed a less-than-steady hand across her hair.

An unsmiling guard led Dietrich in.

Last time, he'd appeared unkempt, worn out. Today, he seemed almost like a stranger, dressed in a well-fitting dark suit. He greeted Roeder with a formal nod.

Roeder directed him to sit down.

Dietrich crossed the room, as if seeing her for the first time. She smiled. He smiled back.

Out of the corner of her eye, she glimpsed Herr von Scheffler. He sat, hands folded on the table, tracking their every move.

She swallowed. She had to act natural. To forget their audience and focus solely on Dietrich. It was him she'd come to see. Him she *would* see.

"You look well," she said. How was one to begin to say in an hour the thoughts and dreams of a month? Especially with these two men watching. Newly engaged couples were supposed to be together for hours on end. She had one. And already had used up a minute of it speaking to him as if they were indifferent acquaintances.

"So do you." He sat on the other end of the sofa.

She cursed the regulation distance. Christel was right. Everything that truly begged to be said must be silenced. *How are they treating you? Have you been receiving the coded messages? When can we be together in freedom?*

"Judge Advocate Roeder has informed me that my letter-writing privileges have been extended. I'm to be permitted one letter every four days. I'll alternate between you and my parents."

"You'll write letters to me?" She could scarcely dare believe it. Since April, she'd written him as often as she could, receiving a response only through messages contained in letters to his parents. The thought of letters written only for her seemed at once too much to ask for and too little. She needed more than letters and hour-long visits to quell the ache of loneliness. But it was all they had.

He smiled. "I'll write letters to you."

They both laughed, some of the tension dissolving. Maria looked over her shoulder. Roeder occupied himself with his papers, but Herr von Scheffler continued to watch them, gaze unblinking. Her stomach tightened.

She turned back to Dietrich. A bad play, that's what this was. A terrible, tasteless theatrical. Still, act on she must. For Dietrich's sake, more than anyone's. She smiled and spoke as brightly as she could. "I'm to see your parents this evening. They'll set upon me the moment I enter the room and demand any and all news about you."

A touch of sadness entered his eyes. "Tell them I'm well. And that I'm very grateful for everything they send me. They've gone to so much trouble to bring the books I ask for, and I know it's a sacrifice of their time, especially with conditions outside the way they are."

It was a risk, but Christel had bid her to ask.

She lowered her voice. "The books . . . they've been satisfactory?"

The barest of nods indicated he understood. A beat passed, weighted with silent communication. Maria didn't dare look in Roeder's direction.

"Now tell me everything. About your family, what you've been doing." Dietrich's gaze urged her to continue speaking of normal topics.

And at least her life was a safe subject for discussion. "It's not very interesting. I've been staying with my aunt in Seefield while I'm still on sick leave. She runs a rather large model farm, so I do secretarial work for her while I rest my feet. And she's got this thing going called a school of breathing."

"A what?" He raised a brow.

She laughed, forgetting Herr von Scheffler for a moment. "A school of breathing. It's a cure for those with respiratory illnesses."

This was probably the most inane conversation they could have. The things they talked of at such times were so lifeless yet so *alive* simply because they were words shared. "I know it sounds ridiculous. They teach all sorts of things like how to walk, sit, and *ja*, breathe properly."

"So you're taking lessons?" he asked, straight-faced.

She shook her head. "I tried a couple of classes and got kicked out. Apparently I'm a hopeless case. But enough about that. Tell me about you."

She'd left out so much in her lighthearted depiction of the pattern of her days. The news of another cousin, killed at the front. Grossmutter's ailing health. Her own loneliness and lack of purpose.

He shrugged, spreading his palms. "I have a routine of sorts. Writing, reading, that sort of thing. I've been able to get to know some of the prisoners. And I think about the family." He reached for her hand. "You." He lowered his voice. "From dawn to dusk and in the night, when I wake."

The words circled through her, leaving her undone and unsure how to reply. Had they been alone, she'd have flung her arms around him and whispered how longingly and how often she thought of him.

She glanced at Herr von Scheffler, the bald way he watched them confirming their privacy worthless, and Roeder, his probing eyes. She wanted this visit, this time with Dietrich more than anything.

Herr von Scheffler cleared his throat.

She must say something . . . "I baked you some *kuchen*. It's at your parents' house. They'll give it to you in the next parcel. I hope it's all right. To my dismay, I'm not a very good cook. Are you?"

"I used to be." He traced circles across her palm. His touch soothed the tension inside her, as if to say: *It's all right. They can't steal what we have.* "I could teach you someday."

A smile tugged at her lips. "Only if you let me teach you how to do something too. Otherwise I'll feel unutterably stupid."

"What shall it be then?"

She tilted her head, thinking. "Do you know how to dance?"

He shook his head. His hand on hers was doing beautifully crazy things to her heart.

"What? They didn't teach you that at seminary?" Despite the limitations, it felt good simply to be with him. To see his smile, trace it in her mind. "Well, your education won't be complete until I give you lessons."

"Cooking and dancing lessons. After the wedding."

The wedding. The day that would turn her into someone still herself yet different all at once.

Frau Maria Bonhoeffer.

Who gave dancing lessons and let her husband teach her how to cook.

"Time's up." Roeder stood. Surely an hour hadn't passed already. But she wasn't about to debate it, not if she wanted another visit.

She turned to him, the urgency of knowing they had only seconds left together filling her anew. "I'll be counting the days until I can see you again. Not here, but outside. We'll visit Pätzig straight off. Your parents can come too."

"It won't be much longer, I'm sure." This time, it was him, not her, who pulled her into his arms. She closed her eyes, imprinting this moment in her mind as his lips brushed hers in a gentle kiss.

How little she knew this man. How deeply she longed to know him more. So much separated them, barriers beyond the physical.

"Did you enjoy your visit?"

Maria turned. Herr von Scheffler had escorted her out of the War Court.

They stood on the wide stone steps overlooking the street below, while one of Herr von Scheffler's lackeys went to hail a taxicab. They were alone, save for two guards flanking the front door. It had grown hotter since she'd entered the building, and the back of her blouse clung unpleasantly to her skin.

"Your visit?" he repeated. "Did you enjoy it?"

She forced a smile and the expected words. "*Ja*. Danke, Herr von Scheffler, I did."

He leaned against one of the pillars, arms folded across the front of his uniform jacket. "Oskar, remember." He took a step closer. The wind carried the scent of his cologne and the odor of perspiration. "You're to call me Oskar."

She inhaled sharply but said nothing. In his company, she was nothing so much as a trapped animal, unable to pull her foot from iron-toothed claws.

He took another step, until his boots almost touched the tops of her shoes. He reached out. She lifted her chin, stilling.

He captured a stray curl that brushed against her cheek. Slowly, he tucked it behind her ear.

She swallowed. Her heart thudded in her chest.

"Oskar," he whispered roughly. "Say it, Maria."

An invisible noose wrapped her throat. "Of course I will call you that, if it's what you wish."

Footsteps sounded behind them. A young man in uniform puffed with exertion. "The taxi is waiting for Fraülein von Wedemeyer, Herr Commissar."

Herr von Scheffler dismissed him with a flick of a finger. "Very well." He glanced back at her, gaze cold. "Go then, Fraülein von Wedemeyer."

Relief coursed through her. "*Guten Tag*, Herr von Scheffler." She barely looked at him as she hurried past him and descended the steps.

Just before entering the black taxicab, she turned. Herr von Scheffler leaned against the pillar, a cigarette between his fingers.

He blew out a column of smoke, watching her.

August 26, 1943
Tegel Prison

I will not falter.

Over and over, the words ran through Maria's mind as she approached the gate of Tegel Prison. Both times before, she'd visited Dietrich at the War Court. Today, she'd see for herself the place where her fiancé was held.

She approached the sentry at the gate.

"State your business." The guard at the gate was young, but he spoke the words like an automaton. No deference would be given her here. She was at their mercy, and they could refuse her whatever they wanted.

She tried for a tentative smile. "I have things to deliver to one of the prisoners. And I have a visitor's permit." She had the paper ready in her hand and held it out to him. He took it, running his gaze along the words. She watched him, scarcely daring to breathe.

He grunted, handed her back the paper along with another sheet, then waved her through. The black iron gate opened with a groan. Clutching her precious package beneath her arm, she walked up the graveled courtyard.

Before her loomed the prison. A massive building of red brick with barred windows at intervals. Scraggly exercise yards enclosed by fences. It was unashamedly ugly, cloaked in an ominous aura that not even the warm August sunlight could dissipate. How small she seemed before this place, a girl in a blue suit and black beret, face flushed from the walk, eyes gritty from lack of sleep. She'd been up all night en route from Pätzig to Berlin, with only a brief stop at Christel von Dohnanyi's house to collect the books. Her feet ached and weariness pressed over her, but she pushed aside both.

What mattered was making her delivery and seeing Dietrich.

Two more guards stood at opposite posts in front of the door. One flicked his gaze in her direction. How young these men were, yet their austere uniforms and barely veiled disdain made them all seem older and angry.

Papers again. A brusque nod. The door opened into a long dingy passageway. Maria followed the sign marked Package Reception Area, her low heels clicking with each step. Her stomach roiled. The air stank of must and sweat.

She entered the waiting room. Windowless, mustier still, and smelling of stale cigarettes. Three people—two women and one man—sat stiffly on a backless wooden bench close to the wall. Each cradled a small case or package in their laps. The gentleness with which they held these items was their only visible expression. They stared straight ahead. The youngest woman's face paled, stringy strands of dark hair falling over her eyes, her rounded middle bulging beneath a worn brown overcoat. Her gaze darted toward the uniformed official, who looked over an array of items spread on the counter, a man and a woman waiting on the other side. How frightened she looked. How hard she tried not to show it.

Maria took a seat on an empty bench. She swallowed, her throat dry. She stared down at the books. Sweat slicked her palms. She wiped them on her skirt. Did she look as nervous as the pregnant woman? She mustn't. If she aroused even the slightest suspicion, the guard would look more closely. Might see the tiny dots beneath letters on the pages, the ones Christel had told her of in a whisper that left no doubt of the fire they flirted with.

The couple walked away, carrying a satchel filled with what looked like dirty laundry.

Maria waited, staring straight ahead at the peeling whitewash on the wall opposite. The dank air closed in around her. She didn't dare let her eyes fall shut, to rest for a moment while those first in line were checked over.

To think, Christel and the Bonhoeffers did this weekly. No wonder Christel's face had been so drawn, circles ringing the delicate skin beneath her eyes. She'd handed the books to Maria warily, as if she scarcely dared to trust her with their delivery.

She must prove herself to Christel. She'd walk up there, wouldn't falter, wouldn't let them know a fearful thought existed in—

"Next."

Her turn. Maria stood. She walked up to the counter with straight shoulders and the impeccable posture of a Prussian officer's daughter.

"Prisoner name." The tic beneath the man's bulbous right eye was the only sign he was flesh and blood, and not a well-tuned machine.

"Dietrich Bonhoeffer," she said smoothly.

"Put everything on the counter. Spread it out."

My hands will not shake. My hands will not shake.

She did as instructed. Three books. Christel had told her only one contained any sort of code. The others were simply volumes of theology Dietrich had requested. How innocuous they seemed. A small bar of soap. Socks. A paper-wrapped package of cheese and bread.

"That's all." She folded her hands in front of her.

The man unfolded the socks, inserting his hand into each and feeling down to the toe. Undid the wrapping around the soap, and held it up to the flickering bulb. The same for the cheese and bread.

The first book. Her breath came out jagged. He flipped through each page. Checked the spine for hidden objects.

An ache speared her ankles. She didn't dare shift position.

He set aside the second book. Picked up the third. Again, the same inspection. Skimming through the pages. She began to relax.

Suddenly, he stopped. Her heart pounded against her ribs as he focused on a page, thumb running along a line. Could he hear it? Had he found the dots?

Time hung suspended.

A gruff laugh escaped his lips. She almost jumped at the sound. He flipped through the rest of the book and tossed it on the counter. His eyes met hers for the first time since the beginning of the procedure. She swallowed.

"The items will be delivered to the prisoner. You may go."

"Danke." She turned and forced herself to take slow steps out of the package reception area.

Only when she stood alone in the corridor did she realize how badly her legs shook. But she'd done it. Dietrich would receive the books and the messages within. She'd gotten them through.

"Thank God," she whispered. Next time, she'd do better.

It was useless to try to pretend there wouldn't be a next time.

November 27, 1943
Tegel Prison

The building shook. Lying on the floor of his cell, Dietrich made up his mind that after the war he would have no desire to view a display of fireworks. He'd already seen enough, as Allied bombs turned Berlin to rubble.

A shout came from somewhere in the building, animal-like and echoing.

Another explosion. Dietrich squeezed his eyes shut.

"The Lord is my rock, and my fortress, and my deliverer; my God, my strength, in whom I will trust; my buckler, and the horn of my salvation, and my high tower."

It couldn't go on much longer. Soon the guards would sound the all clear.

Were his parents safe? They had an air-raid shelter, but Dietrich hadn't been inside to know the quality of its construction.

The shout turned into a cacophony of screams as another bomb, nearer than the others, rattled the building as if it were no more than a handful of dice.

"Then the earth shook and trembled; the foundations also of the hills moved and were shaken, because he was wroth."

God, You alone hold our future in Your sovereign hands. Calm and comfort my fellow prisoners with Thy presence.

Sirens whined. Planes whirred overhead. Colors—a blaze of white, deadly light; the orange of flames leaping from nearby buildings; the red and green "Christmas tree" flares that the leading aircraft dropped almost directly over the prison roof . . .

Ja, from this vantage point he had a front-row seat to a spectacle as deadly as it was visually brilliant.

In the next cell, its occupant swore terribly. The building shuddered.

Dietrich reached with one hand and grabbed the mattress off his cot, covering himself as best he could. Calm slid through his body. He wasn't afraid for himself. God already knew his future. That alone was enough to trust in.

"We've been hit!" the cry echoed through the halls. Somewhere in the building, glass splintered. Shattered.

Thou alone are the master of our days, O Lord. Thou alone.

Last night had been even worse than this. The planes had set as their target the Borsig munitions factory. Hans's cell in the nearby Wehrmacht Prison had been hit by an incendiary bomb. He'd been dangerously wounded and taken to a nearby hospital for treatment.

Lord, thank You for Corporal Knobloch, and all he's done to keep me informed.

More than informed. Knobloch had begun to smuggle mail correspondence between Dietrich and Eberhard. Dietrich suggested the possibility once he learned Eberhard was in Berlin before joining his military unit in Italy—working for the Abwehr no longer guaranteed protection from orders of conscription. Knobloch had agreed to help without hesitation.

Sweat clung to his skin, despite the cold. He let his thoughts wander, turn to yesterday. How fine it had been. Due to the devastating air raids, the visitor permit policies had relaxed, and his parents, Maria, and Eberhard had come to Tegel for a visit. What an hour it had been. Seeing Eberhard again, talking of so many things—books, theology, Renate's expected baby . . . How he'd once taken for granted the pleasure of communing with those nearest and dearest.

Even now as the bombing died down, he could see the faces of the four of them—his parents glad to see him, weariness around their eyes from the sleepless nights brought on by the raids; Maria, who'd brought him an Advent garland to decorate his cell and whose kiss he'd stolen just before they'd departed was sustenance sweeter than any other; and Eberhard looking more nervous than the other three but cheerful once he saw Dietrich had changed but little, eager to share news and ideas in the way of old, bringing a bounty of hard-boiled eggs and a bar of chocolate.

The all-clear siren sounded. Dietrich stood, feeling his way gingerly through the blackness. He opened the door of his cell—Knobloch left it unlocked during the raids, now that Dietrich had taken the post of assistant medical orderly. The air smelled charred, like smoke. Screams reverberated through the prison. From the mouths of those genuinely wounded, or from men frantic with hysteria?

In the hall, he made out the murky figure of one of the orderlies.

"Bonhoeffer? That you?"

"*Ja*, Reetz. What do you want me to do?"

"Go to the sick bay. See if you can be of any help there. It's a wreck." Reetz handed him a medical kit.

Sidestepping what glass he could see, Dietrich raced down the hall. Some of the windows had been shattered either in this raid or the previous night's. A draft of cold air soaked through his thin shirt. Several of the cell doors had already been opened by the orderlies. He checked them, darting down the corridor, weaving around the piles of glass and debris.

"Is anyone hurt?" he called down the rows. "Answer if you can hear me!" Only a handful of the prisoners were permitted unlocked doors. The ones undergoing interrogation remained trapped, even during the heaviest bombings. A horrific practice. He needed to do something about it, use his position to try to get a report written.

In the shadowy blackness, Dietrich made out a figure crumpled against the wall in one of the cells nearest the end. He squatted down, mindful of the glass splayed across the floor, and gently turned the man's body over.

Peter's bloodied face stared up at him. He blinked as if in recognition.

"Hey, Pastor." His voice sounded hazy, a gurgle in his lungs with each breath.

"Hello, Peter." Dietrich opened the medical supply kit. The lacerations on Peter's face looked nasty, but not too severe. He checked for other injuries.

As he probed Peter's chest, his fingers came away warm and wet. Bloody. He ripped the front of Peter's shirt. Two daggers of glass had impaled themselves into his chest.

Dietrich swallowed back fear's sour taste. His pulse sped.

He'd learned through the medic handbook how to bandage basic wounds, staunch bleeding, calm hysteria. Of internal injuries, he knew nothing.

Reetz. He needed to find Reetz. Surely the medic would know what to do.

He started to stand. Peter grabbed his hand with surprising strength.

"Don't leave me, Pastor," he rasped, bony fingers clutching, begging. "Stay with me, *bitte*."

Reetz couldn't save him. Dietrich nodded.

He rested his hand on Peter's forehead, silently praying. Voices came, calls for help, footsteps pounding through the prison. High in the cell, a beam of light shone through the broken window, falling upon Peter's face.

Peter's breaths came further and further apart. "I'm not scared. Why should I be? There'll be freedom then. Here, there's none. In this whole place, you're the only person who's been kind to me. If this hadn't done me in, I'd have died for lack of kindness before long. Talk to me, Pastor. Tell me . . . about death . . ."

Slowly Dietrich began to speak. Peter had only moments. The weight of those moments pressed upon the room, heavy as the smoke, the metallic scent of fast-ebbing life.

"Death is not the end. Never the end. It's freedom and light and promise. It's grace, Peter. Ours to accept with our own free will. Without Christ, it is cold and dark and empty, but with Him . . ." Dietrich smiled, throat tightening. "With Him, death is beautiful. He transforms it."

Peter smiled, gaze unfocused, as if he saw not Dietrich, but the land to which he went.

"Pray for me," he whispered. "It's coming. I can see it coming."

Dietrich lowered his head and began to pray for peace to dwell in Peter, for his pain to be eased. For the young man's loved ones, who might never learn that their son had not been alone in the moments before his last breath.

And as he prayed, Peter, a man whose last name Dietrich did not know, made the final passage on the journey to freedom.

Chapter Thirty

December 22, 1943
Tegel Prison

Snow fell like soothing whispers upon the bomb-scarred streets of Berlin. The flakes dusted Maria's hair, coat, and the branches of the Christmas tree hauled by the barrow-toting lad behind her.

"We're taking this tree to prison?" His freckled face scrunched in amazement, coat sack-like on his scrawny limbs.

Maria nodded. "*Ja*, we are. You shouldn't have a problem with it, since I'm paying you in sugar cubes." She forged ahead through the courtyard.

The prison building, like the citizens of Berlin, had taken a beating over the past months. Missing windows, rubble piled up at intervals. Surely, the war must end soon. Nightly, the British unloaded ton upon ton of bombs, hundreds of planes filling the sky. The city had become something out of a ghost story—once proud structures reduced to decimated ruins of brick, the sky sickly yellow the morning after an attack.

In spite of this, daily life went on—*hausfrau*s picking their way through the streets with their marketing baskets, investigative little boys poking around the piles of wreckage. When the warning sirens whirred, alerting everyone to take cover, many simply hauled their blankets and pillows with them and fell back to sleep on the shelter floor. She'd experienced bombed-out Berlin only at intervals when she visited Dietrich's family. Dietrich's vater always smiled and said *brave girl*, when he saw her carrying her blanket into the air-raid shelter and curling up on the floor.

Look at the Reich now, she always thought, lying beside a pile of boxes, staring up at the shelter ceiling. *Look at how glorious we've become. We're losing, and it's only a matter of time before surrender comes.*

Dietrich had written her that, despite it all, it was going to be a good Christmas. Truly, she didn't know how he found the strength to write like

287

that. Every day brought with it more news of friends killed in action, families losing all they possessed due to the bombings, including Eberhard and
Renate who'd received a direct hit last month to their newlywed apartment. Poor Renate, heavily pregnant, and living with her parents while she
waited—for her baby and for Eberhard's return from fighting in Italy.

In the face of everything, pre-Christmas activities seemed forced and
hollow. Yet the desire for holy tranquility and universal peace kindled
afresh in the hearts of them all.

And if Dietrich had the strength to declare this a good Christmas, she'd
stand by his side and give him the best one she could.

Thankfully, the friendly guard stood near the main door, chatting with
the sentry on duty. Corporal Knobloch. Cheeks rivaling dried cranberries
from the nippy cold, his eyes widened.

"A Christmas tree?"

Maria nodded, turning to the boy. She handed him the paper sack of
sugar cubes. He grinned, unloaded the tree, and took off with his wheel-
barrow through the snow.

Knobloch shook his head with an awed grin. "You're on record as being
the first person ever to try to smuggle one of those inside. I hope Pastor
Bonhoeffer realizes what he has in you."

"I think he does." Maria smiled. "Come on now. Help me get it inside. I
want to put it in Dietrich's cell."

He laughed. "I doubt it'll fit, but we'll try. He'll get the surprise of his
life." Knobloch summoned another guard, and they hauled the tree inside
without complaint. Only at Christmas could one find such laxity from the
guards of a Berlin military prison. Up the three flights of stairs, down the
echoing hall, they went. It was scarcely warmer in here than out of doors,
bomb damage still in the midst of repair.

The stench of the prison no longer bothered her, nor the sight of the
severe-faced guards. Today, she noticed none of it, as they moved along the
hall, passing rows of numbered cells. They stopped before the closed door
of Cell 92.

Knobloch turned and gave her a wink, before dropping his end of the
tree and knocking on the door. Maria scarcely resisted bouncing on her
toes with anticipation.

"Delivery." Knobloch unlocked and opened the door.

Dietrich sat at a makeshift desk, a book in hand. Grinning, Maria
watched his face transform from open-mouthed astonishment to a grin that
matched hers.

"What's all this?" He stood. The room was more closet than cell. A narrow cot covered with a gray blanket, the desk, and a chair. That was it. Not that the room could have fit much else.

"We've orders from the lady to try to fit this inside." Knobloch and the other guard hauled the tree inside with a rustle of branches. Maria watched from the doorway as they maneuvered it this way and that, Dietrich pressed against one wall, chuckling at their efforts.

"I don't think it's going to fit." One of the limbs had left a scattering of needles on Knobloch's brown hair.

Dietrich lent a hand to the maneuverers. "Well, if I moved the cot out, and stood up against the wall, then maybe . . ."

Laughing, Knobloch threw up his hands. "Nothing doing. We'll put it in the guards' break room. You can enjoy it in there." They hauled the tree out, its trunk scraping the floor. "They'll be back to get you for your visit." He relocked the cell. As the bolt slid, Maria heard Dietrich's voice calling, "You know, Maria, I feel slighted. You didn't bring me an Easter bunny over Easter."

Maria and the guards laughed. "Well, I tried, but he squirmed all over the place and needed too many carrots," she called back.

What a turn her life had taken. She'd grown up sheltered, protected from all polluting influences, yet here she was standing on the third floor of a military prison, laughing with guards. Everything had changed. Grown harder, perhaps. But today, she wanted only to dwell upon the good.

She oversaw the positioning of the tree before Knobloch escorted her to the visitor's cell. Visitation at Tegel was far more relaxed than at the War Court. The guards usually stood against one wall and tactfully ignored them, courtesy of Dietrich's relation to the Berlin city commandant.

Dietrich arrived a few minutes later. He'd donned his suit jacket and straightened his tie. He'd grown thinner during his months in prison, but the food shortages had done that to them all. Each month, upon seeing him, she always exhaled a breath of relief that he looked well.

She went into his arms without hesitation. How well she fit there. Some couples might take an embrace for granted.

To them, it had become something longed for, dreamed about. Treasured.

"Merry Christmas, my love," he whispered, holding her close. She pressed her cheek against his chest, savoring the warmth and strength of him, knowing this moment would have to last her for weeks before it could be repeated. Hating the waiting, yet surrendering herself to the sweetness of being held by him.

"Merry Christmas." She lifted her face to his. He brushed a strand of hair away from her cheek, his fingers cupping her chin. His lips met hers.

Each kiss between them was a physical action but also something beyond. A union of hearts. A promise for both the present and the future.

"I was only teasing about the tree. It was a very special thing for you to do." He smiled as they went to sit on the bench. The visitor's cell was as sparse as they came—bare walls, a high window, and the bench. Opposite them, the guard on duty lit a cigarette and put it to his mouth.

But in these moments, the small room transformed itself into the home of their future. The bench became the blue sofa Grossmutter had promised them, where after supper he'd take a break from his work and sit beside her. Then, as now, they'd talk and laugh.

Though now, even when they were laughing, it all seemed a bit sad.

"I wanted you to have a tree like the one we'll have at Pätzig. I brought you other things, that I sent over yesterday with the weekly delivery. A book with nativity pictures and some candles. I knitted you a pair of gloves, but promise me not to laugh when you see them." The guard was too absorbed in his cigarette to care whether they sat the regulation distance apart, so Maria scooted closer, leaning her head on his shoulder. "I sat for a photo and had it framed."

"I'll like that best of all." He twisted his finger around a strand of her hair.

"Since you haven't taught me yet, I let our cook make the gingerbread. I had a piece yesterday, so I know it's good. And"—she looked up at him—"I brought one thing with me, to give you myself. Do you mind?" She addressed the guard, who studiously smoked and looked out the window. "It's nothing he shouldn't be allowed to have."

The guard shrugged. "I guess it's all right."

Maria rewarded him with a smile. Before leaving, she'd slip him one of the fine cigars she'd brought in her pocket to give to Knobloch as a gift for his kindness to Dietrich.

She took the package from her pocket and passed it into his hands. The paper crinkled as he unwrapped it. She watched, as full of anticipation as if she'd been a little girl opening her own presents.

The paper fell open, revealing the silver wristwatch. She'd done her best to polish away the tarnish, shining the glass face to a gloss.

She owned little of value. This was the best she had, and to him she gave it gladly.

"It belonged to Vater. He was wearing it when he died, and I've kept it with me since it was returned in his belongings. I wanted you to have it."

Emotion shone in his eyes. "Maria, I couldn't possibly . . ."

"Of course you can." She took the watch and fastened it on his wrist.

"There." She smiled, an ache in her throat. "That's where it belongs. Before I met you, it was owned by the man I loved best. It's only right you should have it now."

"Then I'll consider it an honor to wear it." He ran a hand along the face of the watch, then looked into her eyes and kissed her again, his hands tangled in her hair.

Soon she'd return to Pätzig for the Christmas festivities with her family. But this, this hour with him, was her true Christmas.

He drew away with a shake of his head. "I feel dreadful."

"Why?" She laughed. "Was our kiss that terrible?"

"Nein," he said quickly. "It's just . . . I've nothing to give you. Here you've brought so much." He looked down at his empty hands. "I wanted to get you a ring, but it couldn't be managed with things like that so hard to come by. While I've been able to purchase gifts for others through my parents, I can't bear the thought of someone else picking out what I should rightly choose for you myself. But I feel wretched about it."

"Please don't." She clasped her hands around his, delving into his gaze. "You, Dietrich Bonhoeffer, you are my gift. And I need no other."

December 25, 1943
Tegel Prison

There'd always been something about Christmas. A power, of sorts, stemming from Christ, the reason for the celebration. The power permeated even at Tegel, making the most hardened of guards slightly soften their expressions. Dietrich had requested and was granted permission to visit the prisoners in the sick bay and managed to distribute part of the contents of his food parcel to some of the inmates, his offering the only Christmas present most would receive.

After that, he'd been invited to sit in the guards' break room. Maria's tree sat in one corner, decorated with a few handmade ornaments. The guards passed around saved-up bottles of *bier*, the radio dial turned to a station playing instrumental Christmas music. Male laughter, a bit raucous after the *bier*, made harmony with the music, reminding Dietrich of the Christmases spent at the illegal seminaries with Eberhard and so many other friends, many now fallen.

Dietrich had shared some of his gingerbread with Knobloch, who sat beside him at one of the round tables near the tree, savoring every crumb.

"I hope you're planning on marrying the girl who made this." Knobloch finished the last bite, eyes half closed in satisfaction.

Dietrich gave a smile. "My fiancée's family cook? I don't think so. All the same, I'm glad you like it."

"Best I've had since the beginning of the war. When I was a kid, my mutter made plates full of it. Even though we never had a lot of money, she always saved up so we'd have a good Christmas." Knobloch's eyes took on the faraway look many wore today. In the face of all they'd endured this past year, one couldn't help but think back on the carefree joy of Christmases long gone. Like remembering summer when one was locked deep into the heart of winter.

Summer would come again.

Even if for some it was found in the life beyond this earth, the life eternal.

"What is your mutter doing today?"

Knobloch shrugged. His uniform coat was halfway unbuttoned and gingerbread crumbs dotted his upper lip. "She'll be with friends."

"I'm sorry you're not with her." On the opposite side of the room, one of the guards loudly recounted a story, causing a wave of uproarious hilarity among the listeners.

Another shrug. Knobloch traced circles on the table. "Who today is with those they truly want to be with? You're certainly not. Besides, I get leave over New Year's." He continued tracing a pattern with one stubby finger. Looked up, meeting Dietrich's eyes. "What do you think life will be like? After the war, I mean? We can't go back to the way things were before, that's for sure."

Knobloch had already shared his disgust for the Nazi regime, so Dietrich felt safe to answer honestly. "Of course not." His thoughts turned to last Christmas and the essay he'd written, still hidden under the beams of his room. "We've been drenched by too many storms, witnessed too many things not easily forgotten. The only hope for any of us, for Germany, is a true turning back from sin, and an honest desire for repentance in Christ. Without people willing to openly preach those things and live them out in daily life, nothing in this world will ever really change. I suppose that's why I returned to Germany instead of staying in America."

One of the guards began to dance a solo jig, accompanied by much whistling and hand clapping by the spectators. The noise provided a cover for their quiet conversation.

Knobloch's eyes widened. "You came back? Why?"

Dietrich took a sip from the cup of already-cool *kaffee* at his elbow. "Because I knew there was no possible way I could participate in the reconstruction of this country without standing side by side with its citizens during this time of testing."

"I guess you regret doing that." Knobloch leaned his elbows on the table.

Dietrich shook his head. "I don't actually. I did what the Lord willed me to do, and I trust that His will shall continue to be done in future days."

"Even here?" A thoughtful expression owned Knobloch's face.

Dietrich smiled. "Even here. Not to say I don't hope for a quick release. I do. But I know I can await whatever happens with confidence." He looked down at his watch, the memory of Maria's gentle fingers around his wrist still fresh in his mind. "I think I'll go back to my cell now. I want to write to a few people yet this evening."

Knobloch escorted him back, his footsteps soon reverberating down the empty hallway. Dietrich sat on the little stool beside his desk, his gaze taking in the four walls surrounding him.

The books Maria had given him sat on his desk, along with the Daily Texts from Eberhard, who'd visited on the twenty-third in an hour filled with so much friendship and renewal of ideas. Above his desk hung the picture of Maria, and beside it one of Eberhard and Renate. The candles Maria sent waited to be lit, next to the gloves she'd knitted him. Warm, the stiches slightly uneven, but the love she'd poured into the project emanated like a glow.

They were with him, these loved ones of his, in spirit if not in presence. His parents, siblings, Eberhard and Renate.

Maria most of all. She was all around him in his cell wherever he looked.

And he missed her. He tried to suppress the emotion, subdue the longing, but it rose now, sharp and sudden. He who provided strength for many, who tried valiantly not to worry anyone, who offered comfort—he needed her.

Dietrich suppressed a sigh. The action did not speak of gratitude, which he assured himself he did feel, but the wretchedness of depression.

That night he dreamed of her. They were married. She walked down an aisle strewn with rose petals, a vision in her flowing dress of white. He waited for her at the other end, smiling . . . everyone smiled, his parents, the Bethges, Sabine and Gerhard, home from England at long last.

Joy, such joy, a glorious day.

"Frau Maria Bonhoeffer," he whispered, as they stood on the steps of the church, his arm around her waist, well-wishers clustered near.

She laughed, the sound like music, sunlight raining down upon her hair. Everywhere, sunlight. "I love the sound of that."

"I love you more." He wanted so much to kiss her, but he'd wait, wait until they were alone and a kiss could become so much more.

They raced down the steps and into the waiting carriage, everyone clapping. Eberhard bounced a fair-haired child in his arms—a little boy. His parents stood beside their grandchildren, their gazes clear and free from worry. Hans and Christel, arm in arm. Christel wore flowers in her hair, and she and Hans couldn't stop smiling.

Inside the waiting carriage, he slipped his arm around Maria's waist and finally, finally kissed her, knowing beyond a shadow of a doubt that, this side of heaven, he had everything he could ever desire.

Only when he woke, did the truth crash down upon him. Hard. Cold. Solitary.

Reality.

Chapter Thirty-One

Only a Gestapo officer could make a casual invitation sound more like a threat. Maria shivered, gooseflesh pricking her exposed skin. She'd been visiting Berlin and the Bonhoeffers, staying at her aunt's apartment. Herr von Scheffler had arrived when she was the only one home and invited her to dinner. She'd refused, saying she'd already promised herself to the Bonhoeffers for the evening.

"How is your dear fiancé?" He'd leaned toward her, and she smelled *bier* on his breath. The look in his eyes—like a smoldering coal ready to burst into full flame—knotted her stomach.

"Fine." She took a step back.

"Let's hope it stays that way." He smiled, speaking the words almost cheerily, then repeated his dinner invitation.

Herr von Scheffler was no kind family friend. He lived for what he desired, and right now that seemed to be her attention. She'd wanted nothing more than to slam the door in his face. But she couldn't. He said he still worked on Dietrich's behalf, and she couldn't afford to anger him. She needed his help, and he knew it.

"You can pick me up at seven," she said softly.

The place he took her—a brightly lit club filled with jackbooted officers and women in sleek evening gowns—wasn't what she'd expected. Upon arriving, Herr von Scheffler ordered a massive quantity of food and proceeded to bolt it down with relish. Across from him at the candlelit table, Maria picked at her own plate, stomach soured by the suggestive song and dance a heavily made-up actress performed on the stage to great applause. Her own dress, a plum-colored floor-length gown, though modest, exposed far more of her than she wanted him to view.

"Why did you bring me here?" She leaned toward him, trying to direct his attention from his plate. "I don't think my vater would approve."

He raised his brows, still chewing. She sat, hands in her lap, waiting until he'd finished and wiped his mustached lip with a napkin. "It's a perfectly respectable establishment. And besides, your vater isn't really in a position to object, now is he?"

Maria didn't answer.

"But if you are not pleased with it, we can go just as soon as we've finished our meal." He put down his fork, reached a hand across the table—ostensibly to reach for the salt. His fingers brushed hers, voice low and silken smooth. "I've a bottle of wine in my apartment."

Fear, harsh and hot, bubbled in her chest.

She shook her head and forced a smile. "I'm very tired."

"All the more reason to join me." His fingers tightened around hers. She avoided his *bier*-sated gaze. Her heart thudded.

At nearby tables, male laughter mingled with feminine giggles, conversations Maria didn't want to hear. "Now that we've rid ourselves of the *Juden*, victory will come even more easily!"

"Maria?" Herr von Scheffler's tone commanded an answer. She looked away.

"Please . . . excuse me." The close-together tables, the stench of cigarettes, the singer's provocative lyrics made her head spin. She stood and picked her way through the smoke-filled room crowded with too many bodies.

She should have found some way to refuse. But desperation had dug its claws in deep. An ugly thing—mad desperation.

For Dietrich, she told herself. She'd done it all for him, submitted to Herr von Scheffler's visits and roving eyes, the way his hand frequently brushed her knee.

Her stomach churned.

She found the washroom at the back of the building and locked herself in. Bracing both hands on the sink, she stared at herself in the mirror. Wide eyes looked back at her, her breath coming fast from parted lips. A simple silver pendant shaped like a heart, a sixteenth birthday present from Max, dangled at her throat.

The last place she belonged was here.

She sucked in a breath, letting her eyes fall closed.

I feel so alone, Lord. I know it sounds selfish, but I want this all to end. I want to see Dietrich for more than an hour every month. I want to feel safe, instead of afraid. I want . . .

Opening her eyes, she splashed water over her hot cheeks and dried her hands on the towel. She'd return to the table, tell Herr von Scheffler she was sick, and convince him to drive her home.

Squaring her shoulders, she opened the door.

And came face-to-face with a tall, mustached man dressed in the uniform of a high-ranking officer, blocking the door. Light from the washroom blended with the darkness of the corridor.

Her heart flailed in her throat.

"Maria?" The man's brow creased.

"Cousin Fabian! I didn't recognize you at first. I didn't know you were in Berlin."

Fabian von Schlabrendorff nodded, gaze probing. "What are you doing here? I don't think your mutter would approve."

She hugged her arms around herself. "I wish I hadn't come. I came with a . . . friend." She didn't dare say Herr von Scheffler's name.

Fabian tensed. "I'm taking you home. This is no place for you. Did you bring a coat?"

She shook her head. She'd been tense at the thought of seeing Herr von Scheffler and had forgotten it at her aunt's.

"We'll leave by the back entrance." He led her through a narrow hallway that smelled of grease and sour *bier* and out into the crisp, cold air. She drew in a breath of it, freeing her lungs from the smoke. Stars sprinkled the sky. "My car is this way." They walked down the empty street until he stopped at a black motorcar. He opened the passenger seat door, and she climbed in.

In less than a minute, he'd jumped in and started the engine. They motored down the street. The car smelled of leather and cigarettes.

She turned to him, blinking in the semidarkness. "What were you doing there?"

"Meeting friends." His answer came smooth and easily, but somehow she sensed there was more to it than that. Fabian was involved in the conspiracy—whatever remained of one. His gaze bespoke burdens much masked and long carried.

"How is your fiancé?" He held the steering wheel in an easy grip, as if not a care in the world rested on his shoulders. Practiced acting. They all were practiced actors, lying to the government, to themselves.

"Still in Tegel." She stared at her hands, pale against the silky sheen of her skirt. Then angled her jaw to look at him. "Do you think it will all last much longer?" She held her breath. He glanced at her in the murky light, eyes serious, penetrating. The rumble of the engine filled the stillness.

"I don't think so," he said slowly.

"We're losing the war, and still it continues." She clenched her hands into fists on the leather seat. Snow drifted. They passed another car, nightfall—and air-raid time—closing in. "So many innocent lives. So many injustices. Christel von Dohnanyi told me about some of them." A shiver crawled up her spine. Christel hadn't exactly told her; she'd overheard a conversation between her and Ursula Schleicher. Though the Bonhoeffers and their kin welcomed her, it wasn't easy to become one of them, privy to all their secrets.

"You don't need to know about any of that," Fabian said, a firm, hard edge in his voice. They turned a corner.

"But there is something?" She whispered the question, willing him to answer and fill the gaping silence. To tell her the conspiracy still thrived, that there was still a chance of awakening from the nightmare their country had been steeped in for endless years.

He didn't look at her. Didn't answer.

But his silence spoke for him.

March 25, 1944
Bundorf

If Maria had become adept at anything over the past months, it was living a nomadic existence. As she traveled from Berlin, to Pätzig, to filling in for the mathematics teacher at her younger sister's boarding school, Maria's belongings seemed perpetually consigned to a suitcase. Thankfully, she'd finally found a place to settle for a time, tutoring her cousin Hesi's two oldest children—the youngest, Hanns Martin, spent his days toddling and cooing as she worked on studies with Hans-Christoph and four-year-old Cordula.

The village of Bundorf and the house itself looked as if they came from the days of knights and damsels. High stone walls, turrets, twisting staircases that led to secret passageways. The castle—nestled in the middle of a wooded valley, surrounded by whitewashed, age-old cottages—was the opposite of Berlin in every way. No bombs fell here, people only talked of them—of the big daylight air raids now decimating Berlin.

Here, one could feel safe.

But she didn't want to feel safe, not by herself. She missed Dietrich, and since he was in Berlin, she missed it too. But for now, she'd continue to help her cousin, surrounded by children noisy enough to crowd out the gigantic space within her heart. Almost.

Lessons finished for the day, she headed up to Hesi's sitting room. Her capable cousin had her hands full running the house, caring for the bomb refugees who had moved in, and keeping her children in line. Maria was grateful to be of use in any of those three capacities, the busier the better. A smudge of paint from their art lesson dotted her worn skirt, and her brown sweater had a hole in the elbow. She looked nothing like the woman who'd dined with Oskar von Scheffler, a night she'd tried to forget.

The wood floors creaked beneath her feet. These floors, and this house, had witnessed the lives of centuries of family ancestors. Even the air seemed to harken back to days gone by, though not in a fragile, whispery kind of way. Everything in the house had been built Spartan and sturdily. A good thing, too, since the family had two children already noisy and mischief-making, and one soon to become so.

Maria knocked.

"Come in." Hesi's girlish voice drifted out.

She opened the door. Her cousin sat on a window seat, a gigantic basket of mending at her feet. As was her habit, Maria took out a piece—today, one of Cordula's pinafores with a large tear down one side, and sank into the nearby armchair.

"How were lessons today?" Hesi didn't look up from her mending.

"Cordula's finally catching on to basic mathematics." Maria licked her thumb and threaded a needle. "And Christoph managed to get through a chapter in his grammar book. We're making progress."

"You don't know how thankful I am for you, coming here to help us out." Hesi looked up from her sewing, her plump face framed by pinned-up braided hair. "You've done wonders with the children."

"I'm happy to be of use to someone." Maria pieced the ripped edges of the pinafore together with pins.

"You say that like one who doesn't feel very useful." Hesi's brown-eyed gaze seemed to sift through every thought in Maria's mind. Most of which she'd rather keep to herself.

Maria sighed, the turmoil inside her kept silent for months, begging for release. "I feel useful to you. It's just . . ."

"Dietrich?" Hesi watched her knowingly.

She nodded, the words she'd managed to contain for so long, spilling out. "It's so hard. We see each other once a month for an hour at a time. We're forced to talk about things that don't truly matter to either of us, because we can't speak of anything else with others present. Sometimes, our visits are quite normal, and it seems like we're close. Other times . . . there's a distance between us. And how could there not be?" She pricked her finger with the point of her needle in the middle of taking a stitch. A bead of bright red blood rose to the surface of her skin. But the pain inside her far outweighed the physical. "We know each other so well yet don't know each other at all. I thought it would all be over by now. But still it goes on and on, this endless, maddening waiting with no end in sight." She wiped her finger on her maroon skirt.

The blood blended into the fabric, red against red. Like loss. With countless men dying on the battlefields daily, people scarcely bothered to grieve the loss of one. It just blended in with the rest.

Blood against blood.

Hesi sighed. "I'm probably the wrong person to advise you. I can't help but find the idea of you, a girl of nineteen, engaged to a man of thirty-eight who's spent the past year in prison, however undeservedly, not as it should be, even in these times. With all you've been through, you need someone who can be a constant presence. Who can help you, instead of bringing more distress." She tilted her head, gaze pressing into Maria. "Have you considered breaking off the engagement? I only ask this for your good, you understand."

Maria shoved her needle into the fabric, as if with the motion, she could reject Hesi's words and the truth they held, however much she wanted to deny them. Love was like a cord of rope, or the thread in her hands. It wasn't until that cord was pulled tight and tested that its strength became known. She'd entered into her engagement with Dietrich without having tested the cord binding them together. Now, she must learn the strength with which it had been wrought.

"I can't do that to him." She stared down at her stitches, voice empty. "How could I?"

"That's a question only you can be the one to answer," Hesi said softly. "None of us can choose for you. Only you know your heart." She withdrew an envelope from her apron pocket. "This came for you while you were teaching the children."

Maria recognized the writing instantly.

A letter from Dietrich. She stood and took it, movements wooden. Once, a letter from him would have thrown her into a state of giddy joy. But what could be said between them that hadn't already been? More talk of literature, the family? Words of love that went only as far as the paper they were penned upon and the hour a month they had together?

Paper words. That's all they were. Paper words that did little to assuage the ache in them both.

"I'll come back later." Maria left the room, steps slow and tired. She wanted to feel more, for a spate of energy to flare within her. Instead, dead emptiness pressed over everything.

Once inside her room, she closed the door and seated herself beside the tiled stove that took up a quarter of the space in her chamber. She stared down at the envelope, the weight of it resting featherlight in her hands. She bit her lip. Something about the packet seemed different. Almost civilian, as if it had not come from Tegel at all.

She slit the top and pulled out the pages, unfolding them in her hand.

> *My dear, dear Maria,*
>
> *It's no use. I have to write you at last and talk to you with no one else listening. I have to let you see into my heart without someone else, whom it doesn't concern, looking on. I have to talk to you about that which belongs to no one in the world but us, and which becomes desecrated when exposed to the hearing of an outsider. I refuse to let anyone else share what belongs to you alone; I think that would be impermissible, unwholesome, uninhibited, and devoid of dignity from your point of view.*
>
> *The thing that draws and binds me to you in my unspoken thoughts and dreams cannot be revealed, dearest Maria, until I'm able to fold you in my arms. That time will come, and it will be all the more blissful and genuine the less we seek to anticipate it and the more faithfully and genuinely we wait for each other. When you were here with your mutter the time before last, and I saw you for only a minute and lost you again, I thought I couldn't endure it anymore, but there were other people present and our time of fulfillment was still to come; I had to wait once more and keep my precious treasure safely hidden away.*
>
> *Do you think it was easy? If I would liken that treasure to anything, it would be far more like dynamite or radium than gold or pearls—and you know how carefully one has to handle such things if one isn't to provoke a disaster. How utterly impossible it is for me, speaking in a voice of the regulation volume, sitting at the regulation distance from you (so that everything can be supervised by a third party!), to tell you what I can only whisper to you at very private, precious, heaven-sent moments: that I love you as you are and for what you are—young, happy, strong, good, proud—and that I love you as my very own. Don't hear these words, Maria, hear only what underlies them and yearns for you and our future together; don't look at the sterile handwriting, look beyond it—I beg you—and see a heart that is often mistaken and selfish, inept and*

weak, but which believes that it can only find peace on earth if your own heart opens for it.

    Let us be quite frank with each other, dearest Maria. There are times when we find it hard to believe that we really, truly love each other. We know each other so little. And yet, whenever doubt begins to gnaw at me, I banish it and drive it away. How could you love me after all that has happened? Yet in some strange way it's true and will become steadily more so in the future! It's a growing seed. It may lie longer and deeper in the soil and need more time to develop into visible beauty, but it will be all the stronger and more lasting.

Maria lowered the letter, tears stinging her eyes. She didn't deserve him. Somehow he'd sent this letter to her without passing it through the censor and poured out so much of himself onto the page. How could her own emotions be so weak and traitorous, vacillating from one extreme to the other? It was shameful really, her lack of strength.

She reread the letter, drinking in every word. Here there were no empty topics. Here in these lines, on these pages, was the man she'd fallen fiercely in love with.

If only she could be with him while he sat alone in that barren cell. Her gaze took in the walls surrounding her. Small and cramped and empty, compared to her room at Pätzig.

She pulled a piece of chalk from the satchel where she kept her teacher's things. She stood, surveying the room with an architect's eye. Envisioning Cell 92 at Tegel Prison instead of the cozy room at her cousin's house. Her hand shook with some indefinable emotion as she carefully traced a rectangle shape on the floor, outlining the space her bed, desk, and chair sat in. Carefully copying the dimensions of his cell.

Equally sized spaces, equal loneliness.

She sat down in the middle of it, arms around her knees, staring out the window, the gray light of evening stretching before her.

April 11, 1944
Tegel Prison

His release wasn't coming anytime soon. He'd just received a coded message from his parents, saying he shouldn't expect a trial for some time. The eminent Dr. Roeder had lost jurisdiction of his case some months ago, replaced by a new, hopefully less stringent prosecutor. Dietrich hadn't met the new man in charge yet. It seemed the forces outside—Canaris and the others still in power at the Abwehr—were trying to keep his and Hans's trials concurrent. And Hans, a mere shell of the vital man he'd been, was too ill right now for a trial to go forward.

Their best hope was in the conspiracy outside and Hitler's demise. Or the end of the war, whichever came first. Both long overdue.

Dietrich pulled off his spectacles, rubbing a hand across his eyes. He set the spectacles on his desk atop a stack of books. The days spent and the days awaiting him stretched out. A long, dark tunnel, with him in the middle of it, not a speck of light on either side.

Only with Your help can I endure this, Lord.

From outside in the prison yard came the music of a thrush, chorusing its springtime song. Was it the same thrush that had sung to him this time last year when he'd first come to Tegel? A distant cousin, perhaps? If the thrush family was anything like the Bonhoeffers, there'd be relatives aplenty.

Enough about birds. He'd time ahead of him, time he wouldn't have after his release, when rebuilding all that Germany had lost in the church and beginning a new life with Maria took precedence. Perhaps this delay was God's way of giving him space to work on a new project.

He took out a fresh piece of writing paper, laying it atop the desk. The blank sheet beckoned to him as a slate for his ideas for the first time in a long while. He'd begin by penning a letter to Eberhard—thankfully Knobloch still smuggled regular epistles. Sometimes sharing his thoughts with his friend seemed to be what kept him sane.

But that wasn't true. Even if he could no longer write to Eberhard, Maria, or anyone else, he would not be alone.

He looked at the pictures hanging above his desk, his gaze falling upon the one of Baby Dietrich—his godson and namesake. The cherub cheeks and toothless grin of Eberhard's son made him smile. How proud Eberhard and Renate must be to be parents of such a fine boy.

His favorite picture, the one his eyes returned to time and again, hung next to the one of his parents. Maria's Christmas photo, the light in her eyes meant for him alone.

She'd responded to the smuggled letter, fully assuring him she echoed his thoughts and hopes for the future and that she understood entirely. It had been a relief to write that letter. So many of the others he sent, though not a lie, seemed false in many ways. They needed open honesty, both of them.

He would do it again from time to time, write to her in secret. For now, he'd begin work expanding upon ideas he'd so far only pursued in thought.

One of which revolved upon a new idea of Christianity. Not a religious kind in the typical sense of the word, but something deeper. Where the gospel permeated every aspect of one's life, beyond the rote practice of going to church on Sunday morning. Christ shouldn't be pigeonholed, as the Reich church wanted to do. God should be more than the Lord of sin and hidden thoughts. Not given just a bit of space, a designated slot of time, but as Lord over the whole. Humanity wasn't unspiritual, nor should one's daily life be dismissed as such. Instead, the whole of it—work, family, marriage— should be given over to God in its entirety.

As afternoon faded into twilight, Dietrich picked up his pen and began to write.

Chapter Thirty-Two

"*A uf Wiedersehen, Dietrich.*"

Sixteen reunions. Sixteen goodbyes. Sixteen hours of cramming a month's worth of conversation into sixty scant minutes. An embrace. A kiss. And she left him. Every time she left him.

Alone in the semidarkness of his cell, Dietrich pressed his hand into his forehead, the beating of the vein in his temple pulsing against his fingers. Maria's face engulfed his mind, the tears in her eyes as she pressed her lips against his before hurrying out the door, accompanied by the guard. As if she couldn't bear to let him see her cry.

He didn't want her to hide her tears. He wanted to hold her while she shed them. Wanted that Pätzig wedding in her little village church, to watch their baby play with Eberhard and Renate's son, to grow old with her beside him.

Drawing in a breath, he stared at the blank page. He'd planned to work on another chapter of his book.

Instead, he let his feelings flood the page, pen scratching against the paper, the voices of Tegel—footsteps of the guards, the stirring of the prisoners in neighboring cells, and the stillness in his own—surrounding him.

> *You went, beloved happiness and much-loved sorrow.*
> *What shall I call you? Misery, life, bliss,*
> *part of myself, my heart—the past?*
> *The door slammed shut;*
> *I hear footsteps slowly recede and die away.*
> *What is there left for me? Joy? Anguish? Desire?*
> *This only do I know: you went—and all is gone.*
> *Just as a puff of warm breath*

dissolves in cool morning air,
so does your image melt away
until I see your face, your hands, your form
no more.
A smile, a glance, a word comes back to me,
but all disintegrates,
dissolves,
is desolate and remote,
is destroyed,
is solely in the past.

He paused, pen lingering on the final word, past, present, and future blurring into one. Prison was more than the walls surrounding him. Prison was a place inside oneself, invisible manacles around the heart. He wouldn't blame Maria if she thought him a sort of pillar saint. He'd not tried to hold himself aloof, but sometimes it was simply easier to write letters about books and music and family news than about the things that truly mattered. Scissors in his head censoring the words before he'd written them.

Here there would be no censors.

He bent his head, fingers clenched around the pen. And wrote.

Your nearness awakens and alarms me
at dead of night.
Have I lost you once more? Am I always to seek you
in vain,
you, my past, my own?
I stretch forth my hands
and pray,
and hear the new tidings:
The past will be restored to you,
as your life's most vital part,
by gratitude and penitence.
Take hold, in what is past,
of God's forgiveness and grace.
Pray that God may preserve you,
today and on the morrow.

In his days as a student at Union Theological Seminary, he'd have laughed if someone told him he would someday sit in a prison cell and write a poem rife with longing. But as he poured himself onto the page, relief flooded him at the act of giving his emotions release and simply being who he was—a Christian, but also a man. One weak, flawed, and, though whole, also shattered.

He set down his pen and shook out his fingers, cramped from tightly gripping the pen. Here on these pages lay his feelings for the woman he loved. Feelings he must share with her. But how was he to send them? Would their fervency alarm her? Instinctively he sensed she'd understand. But she already carried so many burdens, and he didn't want to add to them by revealing the rawness he admirably concealed.

He'd send it to Eberhard first and ask his advice.

Without the usual knock, his door opened. Dietrich tensed. Knobloch stood in the doorway, panting as if he'd sprinted a kilometer.

"What?" Dietrich hid the poem beneath a stack of books and stood, the wooden legs of his stool scraping against the cement floor.

"You won't believe this." Knobloch's mouth angled to one side. A stir of anticipation replaced the tension inside Dietrich. It had to be good news.

"Tell me." Instinctually, he grabbed the suit coat lying discarded on his cot. Here, they summoned one for the most important things with the least amount of notice. Call him an upper-middle-class dandy, but looking decent always gave him a measure of confidence.

"General von Hase is here. And guess who he wants to see? You! Maetz is scraping and bowing like a condescending dog. You are to be left alone with him for as long as he wishes. Maetz sent me up here to fetch you."

"Uncle Paul is here?" Dietrich fumbled to redo his tie. His uncle's position as the city commandant had lent itself to much of the good treatment he'd received while in prison. But to show up at Tegel? Something must be shifting.

Knobloch laughed. "Uncle Paul! *Ja,* he's here. And you'll never guess what he's brought. Four bottles of champagne. I haven't seen that many since my cousin's wedding in '38."

"We'd better not keep him waiting." Dietrich followed Knobloch out of the cell. What was the cause of this bold move?

He'd been in Tegel fifteen months, each much the same in their stretching lack of real activity, real news. This visit had to be the herald of something important.

An underling hauled away a broom and mop, soapy water sloshing over the sides of the bucket, as if they'd given the visitor's cell a spit and polish shine on the double. Dietrich smiled at the elderly cleaner as they passed.

Uncle Paul sat inside the cell, all six feet of him encased in his pressed uniform, chest be-medaled with markings of rank. Beneath his thick, bristly mustache, his lips turned up in a smile.

"Nephew!" He stood, his frame, though lanky, filling the cell with an aura of power. "It's wonderful to see you." He grasped Dietrich's hand in a strong grip.

"Likewise, Uncle." It wasn't until Dietrich glanced behind him that he realized they were unguarded. How strange it would seem to those outside, this marveling at being alone with a relative.

"Sit, sit." His uncle gestured to the second chair. The bottles of champagne Knobloch had so exclaimed over rested on the table, along with two glasses. They were indeed a sight, one harkening back to prewar days and rooms without blackout curtains.

The two men regarded each other, his uncle with scrutiny, as if seeking reassurance that his nephew had indeed been well treated. Dietrich tried to read the man's expression.

"You gave my young corporal friend quite a shock." Dietrich smiled, running a hand across the back of his neck. "He was quite taken aback that anyone should possess that many bottles of champagne. He's been especially kind to me, so I'll take him a glass, if that's all right with you."

His uncle pushed his chair back from the table, stretching out his legs. "Take as much as you want. Shall we have a glass now? One of these bottles is for Maetz, who bowed and scraped quite admirably, if I do say so." The bottle opened with a festive pop as Uncle Paul uncorked the top. "Frankly, I don't much care for the stuff. But I thought it would make an impression. I figured on saving these until the end of the war, but then I thought, why wait?" He poured the light, fizzing liquid into one of the glasses and passed it to Dietrich. Filled his own glass, and held it aloft.

"What shall we toast to?" The coolness of the liquid seeped through the thin glass. The last time he'd held a glass of wine had been Vater's birthday celebration. How far away that day seemed now.

"Friends in high places?" His uncle quirked a graying brow. "Although since you're a pastor, you're probably primarily concerned with a Friend in high places."

"I'm genuinely grateful for all you've done for me," Dietrich said quietly as they clinked glasses. His uncle took a sip with a wrinkle of his nose. Dietrich savored the liquid. It really was high-quality champagne.

Uncle Paul set his glass on the table. "I didn't come here just to bring you champagne."

Dietrich glanced surreptitiously behind him. No one remained in sight. Although that didn't always mean no one was listening.

"Why then?" He lowered his voice, keeping it light, offhand, as if they talked of family ties and happier days.

Uncle Paul leaned closer. "Talk loudly over me. And I'll tell you."

Dietrich rattled off the latest family news—his parents were well, they'd moved all their paintings into the air-raid cellar.

"The coup is imminent," he whispered. "Plans are underway. It'll be a couple of weeks, at the most."

Dietrich sucked in a breath, keeping his expression neutral, as he spouted nonsense about how worried he was for his prized paintings. His heart raced. Only weeks. This time, they'd surely succeed. He'd be released, and the war would end. At long last, he and Maria could be together. Tegel would soon be a memory. Adolf Hitler . . . extinct.

Hope. He scarcely dared let it fill him.

"They're under new leadership." Paul shifted forward, arms folded on the table. His shadowed eyes blazed with anticipation. "Claus von Stauffenberg's in charge. He's smart. And determined. Determined not to fail."

———————

July 5, 1944
Bundorf

Nature surrounded Maria with sweet stillness, her skirt fanned out across the stone bench, a summer breeze warming her cheeks.

Nature was fortunate. At least today it stilled. Her own mind was a wreckage of chaos, as she read again the poem and letter.

In these penned words, Dietrich had given her his heart more completely than he ever had before. The lines were plea and declaration intermingled. A response to the letter she'd written. One where she'd shared more openly than she'd done before about her weakness, how it often tormented her to think of him, how she sometimes wondered how long she could go on in this separation. Even how she sometimes questioned the depth of what they shared. She shouldn't have sent it. It was a worry he didn't need, and she'd been selfish to burden him. Today, she'd received two letters. One contained the poem. In the other, he'd answered her concerns.

> *None of what you wrote surprised or dismayed me. It was all more or less as I thought. What entitled me to believe, when we've seen so little of each other, that you can love me at all, and how could I have failed to rejoice in the smallest token of your love? . . . Our love was destined to begin just*

when we parted . . . You felt you "couldn't go on." So tell me, <u>can</u> you go
on without me? And if you feel you can, can you still do so if you know
that I can't go on without <u>you</u>?

Sunlight dappled the carpet of green at her feet, but Maria scarcely heeded the surroundings of the grounds at Bundorf. She'd come to Hesi's to escape; there was no use denying it any longer. Here with her cousin and children, she could make herself useful and try to pretend she was still the hopeful girl who'd written her first letter to a man in prison, fully assured of his speedy release.

Months had worn away that hopeful girl, stripping her away in layers. Leaving her a pitiful barren wasteland. She shamed even herself with her desperation, her longing for peace and quiet. An end to these days of war and heartache. Each time she traveled to Berlin and to Tegel, it struck her fresh and fiercely. She hated seeing him in that gray prison, locked in a cell no matter how bravely he endured it. She wasn't as strong as he.

So she'd written Dietrich that she intended to stay away. For only a little while, she promised herself.

What should I do, Lord? I've never been so bewildered. Why has this happened? What purpose has it served? Was this truly best for our love?

Picking up a fallen twig, she broke it into tiny pieces and hurled each as far as she could. She needed to make a decision. Either hold fast to the promise she'd made and wait with him as long as it took, or drift into the background, his fiancée but only in title.

I can't go on without you . . .

She hated herself for even considering this question. How could there be any answer but one?

How could there not be? She'd waited with him and for him, a year and a half. When she'd first given him her yes, she'd never bargained she'd be saying yes to this.

She buried her face in her hands, tears spilling over her knuckles. A gust of wind snatched the pages filled with everything he had to give her and scattered them across the carpet of grass. She lifted her face and watched them fall, hands limp in her lap. How long she sat, she didn't know. Time held no consideration when it came to the workings of the heart. Hadn't Dietrich once said that there were some things one must work out for oneself, alone?

What cost would she be willing to incur for this man? Their love wasn't easy, Dietrich had once written. It was never meant to be so. They'd been destined to find each other directly before being separated.

Their love wasn't easy. But it was *theirs*. Hers.

She stood.

Slowly, resolutely, she bent to pick up the scattered pages, pressing each against her heart.

Chapter Thirty-Three

July 6, 1944
Tegel Prison

B ombs rained from the heavens.

Dietrich's feet pounded the hall as he ran, unlocking cell after cell. Knobloch took one side, Dietrich the other. Regulations had relaxed, and he wouldn't stand on procedure. No man should be left trapped in his cell in case of a hit. He'd grant them that much freedom.

An explosion pummeled the earth, shaking the prison building. Dust and debris rained from the ceiling.

"Get down!" Dietrich shouted to Knobloch. He flung himself to the ground in the middle of the hall, covering his head, tasting grit and dust. Something warm and shaking moved beside him—another prisoner. Dietrich met the man's terror-streaked gaze, body flush against the grimy floor. The middle-aged man whimpered like a child.

"Dear God, save us!" the man blubbered.

"Don't worry. It'll be over in ten minutes," Dietrich whispered. Now wasn't the time for a sermon.

"You're . . . so . . . calm." The prisoner's teeth chattered. "Who are you that you seem to fear nothing?"

The roar of the planes' engines overhead drowned out any answer Dietrich could have conjured. He stood, keeping his body low, and darted down the hall, freeing more of the prisoners.

"Danke!" they called, as they fled from their confined spaces to take cover. "Danke, Herr Pastor!"

As he worked, sweat from the stifling July heat soaked his shirt, drenched his face. The prisoners' words filled his ears, as he comforted those in the sick bay, administering what sedatives he could, working alongside the orderlies.

Who are you?

Who was he? It wasn't the first time he'd been asked that by a scared prisoner or an incredulous guard, wondering why the middle-aged man in the neat suit seemed to exert such a measure of control over his own emotions. And why was that?

Words strung themselves together in his brain, melding with his movements through the sick bay. Tend. Console. Encourage.

> *Who am I? They often tell me*
> *I would step from my cell's confinement*
> *calmly, cheerfully, firmly,*
> *like a squire from his country house.*

"It's over now," Dietrich addressed the head orderly. "Can we distribute anything? Something cool to drink, perhaps?"

The orderly nodded. The man's eyes were bloodshot, his clothing filthy, but he smiled slightly. "I'll see what I can find."

> *Who am I? They often tell me*
> *I would talk to my warders*
> *freely and friendly and clearly,*
> *as though they were mine to command.*

"Better now?" Dietrich stopped beside the bed of a young man who'd almost gone into convulsions during the bombing. Usually one of the brave ones, he'd just received word of his entire family's death in the last daylight air raid.

Slowly, the young man nodded, lying back against the threadbare pillow. Dietrich placed a hand on his shoulder in a brief gesture of comfort. "Much better, Herr Pastor. Danke."

> *Who am I? They also tell me*
> *I would bear the days of misfortune*
> *equably, smilingly, proudly,*
> *like one accustomed to win.*

Dietrich crossed to the window, pulling back the blackout curtain a bare amount, gazing across the total darkness of Berlin. Somewhere, his family was out there. His parents unprotected in their house. Hans languishing with sickness in prison. Eberhard fighting far away in Italy. Maria at Bundorf, distant.

> *Am I then really all that which other men tell of?*
> *Or am I only what I know of myself,*
> *restless and longing and sick, like a bird in a cage,*
> *struggling for breath, as though hands were compressing my throat,*
> *yearning for colors, for flowers, for the voices of birds,*
> *thirsting for words of kindness, for neighborliness,*
> *trembling with anger at despotisms and petty humiliation,*
> *tossing in expectation of great events,*
> *powerlessly trembling for friends at an infinite distance,*
> *weary and empty at praying, at thinking, at making,*
> *faint, and ready to say farewell to it all?*

Dietrich turned. Someone had lit a few candles, casting shadows upon the faces of the orderlies silently distributing a bucket and dipper. The light glimmered on an object Dietrich hadn't noticed before. Above the bed in the farthest corner, someone had nailed a rough-hewn crucifix, two pieces of wood tied together with twine. He stared at it, remembering the many churches he'd sat in, in Europe and beyond. The cathedrals, the makeshift chapel of Finkenwalde. The old letters from men now fallen, telling him they still continued the practice of daily meditation and prayer, even on the battlefield.

He blinked, a final stanza filling his mind.

> *Who am I? This or the other?*
> *Am I one person today, and tomorrow another?*
> *Am I both at once? A hypocrite before others,*
> *and before myself a contemptibly woebegone weakling?*
> *Or is something within me still like a beaten army,*
> *fleeing in disorder from victory already achieved?*

He breathed a sigh, rubbing a hand across his unshaven jaw, fingers coming away sweaty and begrimed. Again, his gaze found the crucifix.

> *Who am I? They mock me, these lonely questions of mine.*
> *Whoever I am, thou knowest, O God, I am thine.*

———

July 21, 1944
Tegel Prison

Blackout curtains were impervious to the changing sun. Though early morning, the prisoners in the sick bay were already awake. Dietrich entered the long room lined with beds, a book from the prison library in hand to give to the man so fearful now of the air raids. Adalbert Stifter's *Witiko* was a large volume, but it wasn't as if the prisoner had more pressing demands on his time.

The more than eight-hundred-page tome weighed heavily under his arm, as he moved down the line of beds, greeting the men. The sole orderly on duty stood at a tray of medical supplies, putting things in order. Head bent, the orderly barely acknowledged him. Things had relaxed over the months of heavy air raids. Dietrich found himself in the position of all-around assistant, as well as prisoner, able to move about at great liberty.

"Turn on the radio, will you?" one of the men called. "Maybe they'll be a concert on or something."

Setting the book on a table, Dietrich moved to the tiny radio on its stand, still functioning despite the raids. He crouched down, fiddling with the dial. A concert would be nice. Though it was still early for one. Occasionally, they'd been able to get a few classical pieces—

Dietrich turned the dial, slowly, station by station. The airwaves crackled. His hand stilled.

"This is a personal message from the Führer. Aired last night, it will be rebroadcast again." The announcer spoke in clipped, guttural tones.

More crackling. Then the Führer's voice.

"If I speak to you today, I do so for two special reasons. In the first place, so that you may hear my voice and know that I myself am sound and uninjured, and in the second place, so that you may also hear the particulars about a crime that is without peer in Germany."

Dietrich stared at the radio. Every drop of warmth seemed to drain out of his body. Utter silence, save the voice of Germany's dictator, reigned in the sick bay.

"An extremely small clique of ambitious, conscienceless, and criminal and stupid officers forged a plot to eliminate me and, along with me, to exterminate the staff of officers in actual command of the German Wehrmacht. The bomb, which was planted by Colonel Count von Stauffenberg, burst two yards from my right side. It injured several of my colleagues; one of whom has died. I myself am wholly unhurt. The clique of usurpers is an extremely small band of criminal elements who are now being mercilessly exterminated."

Dietrich turned off the radio. The men in the beds stared at him, faces studiedly blank. No one said anything.

There wasn't anything to say. No words could erase what had been done.

He stood and left the sick bay. He didn't need a guard to return him to his cell. His steps echoed on the hard floor. He walked the whitewashed halls, nodding to the guards he passed, just as he'd once nodded to fellow seminarians on the Berlin University campus.

Inside his cell, he shut the door and sank onto his cot, staring at the bricks in the wall he'd traced with his gaze innumerable times.

Stauffenberg . . . Determined . . . Won't fail.

His uncle's words reverberated, melding with the Führer's harsh voice.

A clique of officers . . . Mercilessly exterminated . . .

Mercilessly. Though none of the conspiracy's previous attempts had been successful, not a one of them had been discovered. The Führer romped along like a carefree child, unaware of the attempts upon his life. The Stauffenberg plot left him ignorant no longer.

The romping child would turn to savage beast.

Hitler would hunt them down, every last one of them. It was only a matter of time.

Alone in his cell, Dietrich laughed softly. How calm he felt. Not for the others, Stauffenberg and their friends—for them, he ached, but for himself.

Yesterday he'd read Psalm 20:7.

"Some trust in chariots, and some in horses: but we will remember the name of the Lord our God."

It was what it all came down to in the end. He wanted to live, to see his parents and marry Maria, but ultimately it wasn't about him. It was about submitting to the will of One greater than himself, seeking that will more than he sought anything else. *Valued* anything else.

Even his own life.

He stared out the high window, sunlight streaming through the dirty panes. Light filtering through gray.

He'd lived with uncertainty so long he'd ceased to be sensible of it. It was simply there, as present as these four walls that held him in, the bars that kept him from leaving this building and going to those he loved.

For a time, he'd been certain of Hitler's demise. After all, he'd reasoned as Stauffenberg and the rest had, they must succeed with one of their attempts. They'd planned so carefully; there was no reason for the plot not to prevail.

Yet they'd failed.

Ultimately it wasn't they who had control. Dietrich stood, then knelt on his cot, lifting his face toward the sun, drawn by some unexplainable need to be close to the light.

He wouldn't go so far as to say God had stopped the conspirators from succeeding. But God held the future of each of them, if they belonged to Him.

He bowed his head, swallowing hard.

Their lives, his life, were in God's hands.

And no one, not even Adolf Hitler, had the power to snatch them from His grip.

Chapter Thirty-Four

August 9, 1944
Berlin

O ne had not been destroyed.
So countless others had been lost.

The stories filtered through from Hesi's husband, Dietz. Uncle Henning, instead of allowing himself to be handed over to be interrogated under torture, had taken his own life. Claus von Stauffenberg, shot on the night that should've been a celebration of victory, along with his adjunct Werner von Haeften, a friend of the Bonhoeffers. Cousin Fabian taken into custody, facing torture, or worse. Then yesterday, Paul von Hase, Dietrich's uncle, had been hanged at the Plötzensee Prison, sentenced by the same judge who had done away with the Scholl siblings.

Maria shuddered.

Last month, Dietrich had been the star prisoner, relative to a general. Now in the eyes of the Reich, that general had become a traitor.

Dietrich had been part of the conspiracy. Perhaps not as actively as her uncle and cousin, but the Gestapo wanted anyone dead who bore even the slightest whiff of the stench of treason.

Not only wanted, demanded.

The train jolted to a stop, with a screech of whistles and grinding of gears. Crushed between a wall and her seatmate, Maria watched as passengers around her began to disembark. She twisted her faded handkerchief beneath gloved hands. She wore cream-colored gloves and a cobalt hat pinned to her curls, a light veil dusting the top half of her face. A trim suit to match. Heels. Lipstick. She'd borrowed all but the last from Hesi.

On such an errand as hers, she needed to look the part of confidence. These days, few bothered to wear nice things or curl their hair. Survival took up too much energy to spare.

Maria joined the rest of the passengers thronging off the train. She left the station, heels tapping against asphalt, and entered a decimated and destroyed Berlin. Once it had been a city of architecture, arts, and culture. Now scarcely a building did not bear the marks of bombs, many demolished altogether. A sticky breeze stirred her hair as she walked, wilting her curls in the humidity. A gaunt-faced adolescent rode by on a bicycle that hadn't seen a new coat of paint since the Führer became chancellor. Ragged children played amid a demolished building near the train station. Two women clutched marketing baskets close against themselves, as if fearful they'd be snatched at any moment.

With hunger raging rampant, it was not an unreasonable fear.

The longer she walked, the worse her feet ached, subjected to the rigors of fashion in the two-sizes-too-small heels. She checked street signs against the address written on the back of an envelope, the last traces of the setting sun fading, leaving the sky gunmetal gray.

Finally she reached the flat. The exterior of the building reminded her of the favored child, protected when no one else was. No bombs had fallen upon this brick building; no rubble lined the sidewalk.

Of course it would belong to Oskar von Scheffler. The favored one.

Inside, she climbed the steps, reaching the third floor. The numbers on the door matched the address in her hand. She smoothed her curls, pressed her lips together. Lifted her fist to knock.

She knew what she was about to do. On the train ride to Berlin, she'd rehearsed it in her mind over and over.

Let him be home. And let him have some power to save Dietrich.

She hadn't meant it as a prayer exactly. But it took on the cadence of one as she knocked twice, then stepped back to wait.

Minutes passed. Three maybe. Footsteps on the other side before the door opened.

Herr von Scheffler held the door with one hand. The other fumbled to fasten the ties on a quilted dressing gown. Maria flushed at the sight of his bare chest. What should she have expected? She hadn't phoned to tell him of her arrival.

Nor had she spoken to him since the evening she'd walked out on him at the restaurant. Such behavior had doubtless infuriated him. Still, he smiled upon seeing her.

"Maria. What a surprise! As you can see, I wasn't expecting company." He gestured to his attire.

"I brought you something." She opened her handbag and pulled out two expensive cigars. A prewar variety that couldn't be bought for love or money unless one was someone important. She'd bartered them for a month's butter ration from one of Hesi's air-raid refugees.

He smiled and took them, hand brushing hers. "Danke. Do come in. If you were so kind as to walk here in the heat, the least I could do is offer refreshment." He held the door.

A short hallway led into a living room decorated in a modern style—a sleek black leather sofa, a large radio, matching dark wood furniture.

"If you'll wait here a moment." He motioned her to the sofa, then strode down the hall. Even in slippers, an officer of the Reich didn't shuffle.

Maria removed her hat and gloves and set both on the table covered with party newspapers. She took the far end of the sofa. As she sat, her fingers brushed something on the arm. She picked it up, staring at a yellow dressing gown. The silk fabric slipped through her fingers, the scent of cheap perfume heavy on the garment.

This was the man she'd chosen to throw herself on the mercy of. It scared her. But Dietrich in the custody of the Reich scared her more.

He returned, carrying a tray. He set it down, pushing aside the newspapers. Two glasses accompanied a decanter of amber liquid.

"There we are." He undid the stopper and poured. The liquid swirled into the glasses. He handed her one, took the other himself, and joined her on the sofa. He'd changed out of his dressing gown into a white button-down shirt, but had only fastened half the buttons. Unlike the rest of Germany, instead of growing thinner during this time of rationing, he'd put on weight. He looked older too. A middle-aged man with a paunch, as the Reich he served gasped out its dying breaths.

The sofa creaked as he settled himself into its depths and crossed his legs. He picked up one of the cigars, holding it between his fingers.

"How long have you been in Berlin?" He took a swallow from his glass.

"I just arrived." She set her own drink on the table, not about to partake of it.

"And you came all this way in this heat to bring me cigars." Warmth entered his smile. "That was thoughtful of you."

"I . . . I thought you'd like them."

He chatted smoothly of family acquaintances, the latest war news. Maria did her best to keep up her end of the conversation. As he talked, he seemed to shift positions, moving closer to her. She scooted away. But there was only so far she could go on the sofa.

He finished two glasses of amber liquid, smiling at her over the rim of his glass as he took the last drink. "I know you came for more than cigars, Maria."

"*Ja*," she said quickly. "I did."

"You left that night at the club." His tone was smoother than the liquid that had been in his glass. Smooth and almost inhumanly calm.

"I'm sorry," she murmured. "I was very tired."

"So what can I do for the Fraülein Maria?" He spread his hands in a dramatic gesture. "How may I be of service?"

Her throat went dry. She grabbed her glass and gulped a sip. It burned going down. Wetting her lips, she faced him. "I need to know the status of Dietrich's case. I want him released. Surely, by now, the court sees he's innocent."

He leaned back against the sofa, arms folded, an amused lift to his brow. "And why should I help you? Hmm?"

Her heart thudded. "Because you're a kind person." He wasn't. But she said it anyway. "And because of our friendship."

He leaned forward toward her. His alcohol-scented breath wafted onto the air. "Our friendship," he murmured. "*Ja*, that might be a good reason." He reached out, placed his hand on her knee. His hot, strong fingers closed around her kneecap, moving higher.

She tensed, perspiration trailing down her spine. She forced a smile. "You'll help me then?"

"I might." He reached up with his other hand and ran it along her jawline. "With a bit more persuasion first. Perhaps you might . . . persuade me."

Her breath came out jagged through parted lips.

"I'd be happy to extol the virtues of my fiancé, if that would convince you." The words sounded like a lame attempt, even to her own ears.

"That's not what I meant, Maria, and you know it. You've toyed with me long enough. It's time you paid up." He leaned over her, pinning her against the back of the sofa with a grunt. His arms braced against the sofa, as he moistened his lips.

Her mouth went dry. She was trapped. If she didn't act now, she'd not get out of this unscathed. In a swift movement, she pushed against him, wresting herself from his grip, and bolted from the sofa, stopping only when she reached the living-room door. Her back bumped against the closed entry point. He stood, his large frame filling the space. Took a slow step closer.

"How dare you!" Her heart banged against her rib cage. "I came to ask a favor from you. Whatever you imply, rest assured, I meant nothing of that. I'm an engaged woman. And it's on behalf of my fiancé that I am here."

He laughed. "Your fiancé is a traitor, my innocent one. I've never understood the affection you claim to have for him when you could have an officer of impeccable bloodline. You needn't worry you'll be tied to him long. If the events of these past days have taught you anything, *Mein Liebe*, let it be this. We deal with traitors in the Führer's Germany." He bridged the distance between them in two strides, grasping her waist in his meaty hands. He stared down at her. She struggled to get free, but it was as if her body was mired in quicksand.

"Shall I educate you further on our treatment of traitors?" He trailed a finger down her jaw, fingers curling the side of her neck. She couldn't breathe. "We have many, many ways. We beat nails into their bodies with truncheons." He ran his hand along her arm. "We break their fingers. And finally, when they've no longer become useful to us, we put a bullet through their skulls. Let their conspiratorial brains get what is due them. Ah, the beauty of justice."

Her entire body trembled. Not with fear, but fury. "All this time, you haven't been helping me. Have you?"

He shrugged. "I didn't think your fiancé was worth the trouble. I knew you'd come to your senses and see what a real man can offer you is a hundred times more than anything you'll ever have with that pathetic wreck."

"You swine," she uttered the words through gritted teeth. "You think you're big and powerful. But you're small and weak."

Anger flashed in his eyes. But she wasn't about to wait for it to erupt. She shoved her knee, hard as she could, into the doughy flesh of his stomach. He stumbled back, pain and outrage flashing in his eyes.

"Dietrich Bonhoeffer is doomed." His voice thundered through the building. "And I'm securing the evidence myself!"

Heart aroar in her chest, she turned.

Ran, flying down the stairs and into the street, Hesi's hat and gloves left behind. With each pounding step, the words tore through her mind.

"We deal with traitors in the Führer's Germany."

Her breath came in burning gulps. She tripped on a loose stone, ankle twisting painfully. She stopped, Herr von Scheffler's house a speck in the distance, and collapsed against the side of a building. Her hair straggled against her sweaty cheek. She fought for air.

In the eyes of the Reich, Dietrich was a traitor. She didn't know the extent of his involvement, but any connection to the conspiracy had cost scores of lives over the past weeks.

If they discovered the truth, they'd kill him without mercy. So far, he'd remained safe.

But for how long?

And Dietrich? Dietrich knew this.

We don't know how often we shall see each other again in this life, the
times being what they are, and it depresses me a great deal to think that
we may later reproach ourselves for something irremediable.

Whatever came, she didn't want to live with the pain of reproach. Dietrich
was the man she loved, however unworthily. He needed her.

And she wasn't leaving his side ever again.

September 8, 1944
Tegel Prison

Knobloch spoke of escape.

"It's all over, Pastor." Shadows crouched in the corners of Dietrich's cell
as Knobloch settled onto the cot, Dietrich beside him. The guard shouldn't
be here at this hour, not at night. But Dietrich didn't fear for Knobloch. So
many had sought Dietrich for pastoral help of late that Knobloch's presence
could easily be explained away.

The men leaned closer, voices whispered, the dim bulb suspended from
the ceiling flickering.

"You think I don't know this." While acting as liaison for the smuggled letters, Knobloch had gotten to know the Bonhoeffer family. He'd visited them in late August, returning to Dietrich's cell with the dismal news.
Uncle Paul had been hanged. And as a result of the July 20 plot, Hans had
been transported to Sachsenhausen concentration camp. Their involvement
hadn't yet been proven, but that didn't stop the Gestapo.

Everything was unraveling, like threads coming loose from a coat and
being snipped off. One by one. Snipped off.

It was only a matter of time before orders came to transport Dietrich to
a camp. Where, like millions of others, he'd simply . . . disappear.

Escape from Tegel was his only option.

Or so Knobloch told him.

"It'll be easy to get you out. We can get you a mechanic's uniform, give
you a box of tools to put in your hand. When I finish my shift at the end of
the day, we can walk out together. Simple as that."

Dietrich rubbed a hand across his forehead. "It's anything but simple. I'll
need a way to get across the border into Switzerland. Once they find out I'm
gone, they'll come after my parents, asking questions."

"We'll hide you in a garden shed, on the outskirts of Berlin. You can stay there undetected for weeks while we figure out a way to leave the country. We can smuggle you food, blankets. And your parents"—Knobloch swallowed hard—"they want you to take the risk. Your brother-in-law is as good as lost. Hans's health won't withstand much more, even if they don't hang him. Don't you think that after this is all over, your mutter and vater will need you more than ever?"

Dietrich nodded, absorbing the words. It was a hard way to look at things. Hans couldn't be saved, but Dietrich could, so they must try. Cold and hard and necessary.

Somewhere nearby came the low moan of an air-raid siren. Berlin's whippoorwill.

"What of Maria? She's with my parents now, working for my vater as his secretary. What if they question her?"

"She's a smart girl. And I doubt they will. Your brother Klaus and your sister's husband Rüdiger will take the questioning. Rüdiger is a lawyer. They'll suspect him first." In the dim light, Knobloch's eyes flashed with an intensity Dietrich had never seen him own. "You've got to try, Dietrich. If you don't do it for yourself, do it for her." His words came fast, passionate. "I've watched you two for months. The way you greet each other and the way you say goodbye. How she's visited you month after month, sending you letters even before you could reply. Yours is no common love. For her sake and the sake of your future, you've got to try. To live."

For long minutes, Dietrich stared down at his hands. It would be a risk. But it would be a greater one still to remain at Tegel. They'd hung Uncle Paul, taken Hans away. He'd be next. Should he simply accept it as his fate? Was it wrong to want to live? To go on, even after others could not?

Knobloch was right. His parents would need him after the war. For them, he must take this chance.

And for Maria. A final fight for a future beyond letters sent from Cell 92.

He lifted his gaze, meeting Knobloch's.

"To escape then?" Knobloch held up his hand as if raising a glass.

Dietrich nodded, the gesture outwardly firm, belying his inner uncertainty. "To escape."

Chapter Thirty-Five

September 23, 1944
Berlin

Restoring order. To Karl Bonhoeffer's desk, at least. Maria swiped the dust cloth in even motions.

She could do little about the chaos in her own life. It couldn't be swept away with a swirl of a cloth, a rearranging of papers. Her life consisted of helping Dietrich's parents, performing secretarial work for his vater . . . and planning her fiancé's escape out of Tegel Prison.

The last was responsible for the dark circles around her eyes that greeted her every time she looked in a mirror—which wasn't often.

Maria picked up the wastepaper basket and hefted it in one hand. She glanced toward the window overlooking the street.

A figure hurried up the path. Christel?

Setting aside the wastebasket, Maria moved out of Karl Bonhoeffer's consulting room to the foyer. In the month she'd spent at the Bonhoeffer home, the house had become as familiar to her as her own. Stripped bare of the family valuables—moved to the country or to their air-raid shelter—the place resembled nothing so much as a genteel woman bereft of the adornments that gave her luster, but still refined, even without them.

She opened the door before Christel could knock. Strands of windblown hair frizzed around her cheeks, a faded gray sweater several sizes too large wrapped her gaunt shoulders.

And worry. Worry lived in her eyes, in the set of her frame.

Maria ushered the woman inside, closing the door firmly. Neither spoke until they'd entered the living room, drawn the curtains, and taken seats on the sofa.

Christel's hands shook. In and of itself, that was enough to raise a stir of alarm. Though concentration camp gates held her husband and the sole care of her three children rested on her shoulders, Christel kept her emotions under firm guard.

"Tell me." Maria pressed a hand over Christel's work-roughed fingers. Blue veins stood out against her clammy skin.

The woman looked up. "They've found the dossier."

Maria sucked in a breath. She'd learned of the Chronicle of Shame—Hans von Dohnanyi's meticulous records detailing the horrors of Nazi rule, moved to the Abwehr archives in Zossen for safekeeping. Meant to be used to make a case to the Allies about the conspirators' motives and the hell Hitler had unleashed upon Germany, the evidence inside those inconspicuous black files would damn each and every conspirator not already done away with. Lists. Names.

Dietrich's name.

"How? When?"

"I don't know." Christel expelled a reedy sigh. "A man came up to me on my way to market. I've never seen him before. It's best we don't know the names of those still active in the resistance. Those who remain alive. He handed me a note. It said the files have been found. That's all I know."

It was enough. Just the mention of those files in the hands of the vultures intent on picking apart every last piece of their prey was enough.

"We've got to go forward with the escape plan. Before it's too late." Maria's words tumbled over each other. Action. They needed action. Now, this very second.

Christel nodded.

"I've already got the uniform. Mutter Bonhoeffer and I have been scrambling to get food coupons and money." They'd met with little success. Food coupons were a priceless commodity, and despite dipping into their own allotments, they'd only procured enough for four days. By then, Dietrich and Corporal Knobloch must be well out of the country.

Head bent, Christel unclasped her purse. Maria stayed her hand. "We won't take anything from you. You're already starving yourself to send extra to Hans. We'll manage."

Christel reclasped her bag, eyes a study in weariness. "When does he plan to . . ."

"Soon. Tomorrow the Schleichers will deliver the things to Corporal Knobloch at his home."

Christel nodded. "Good. The sooner he's out of the hands of the Gestapo, the better for him. At least he still has a chance."

Hanging unspoken in the air was what she thought but didn't say—*Hans no longer has anything.*

"Shall I tell the Bonhoeffers?" Maria stood and paced the worn carpet, hands forming fists. She wasn't as strong as Christel. But oh, she was trying. Fighting with everything in her to save the man she loved.

Fighting to keep alive the flame their world seemed to drench at every turn. Hope.

"*Ja*, but quietly. Make sure no one is listening. The Schleichers should know too. And Klaus. Their names . . . their names might also be listed." Christel stood. "I have to get back to the children. It's not safe to leave them alone. Who knows what might happen."

Maria walked her to the door. Before turning the knob, the woman pierced her with a glance. Strength sparked beneath the exhaustion in Christel's eyes.

"Be careful, Maria. You're one of us now. A resistance woman, as much a wife to Dietrich as I am to Hans. Just be careful." She reached out, gave Maria's hand a quick squeeze.

Maria nodded. "I will. Take care of yourself."

Christel hurried down the path, sweater wrapped tight around her shoulders as autumn wind gusted the air. Maria watched her go until the woman's thin, determined frame faded from view.

Then she turned back into the house, jaw set. She didn't have time to worry.

Only action could help them now.

September 30, 1944
Berlin

Clutching the small loaf of rye bread wrapped in a towel, Maria hurried next door to the Schleichers' just as evening traced twilight across the sky. Her feet crunched against the path, gravel mixing with dying leaves. She opened the gate. A car sat in the Schleichers' driveway. Whom did it belong to? Autumn's breath stirred her skirt.

She knocked on the front door. Time stretched. She glanced, once and quick, at the desolate street. Someone was obviously home. Why did no one answer?

Finally, Ursula opened the door a crack, hands curling around the door's edge. Maria held out the bread. A cover, in case anyone overheard their conversation.

"We had extra and thought you could use it."

Ursula ushered her inside. The door clicked shut. Tension tightened the woman's face. "Paul von Hase's wife arrived this afternoon. Since her husband's death as a traitor, none of her relatives will take her in. I couldn't refuse her. She's upstairs, resting now. The bread will be helpful." She took the loaf, holding it close.

Maria pulled her sweater around herself, arms hugged across her chest. "Is that her car?"

"Nein. Klaus is here too. Rüdiger and Renate are gone. Can you stay?"

"Of course. Has something happened? Why is Klaus here instead of at home?" Maria pulled off the faded blue headscarf holding back her hair. Limp strands fell around her face. Even that had lost its luster.

Scant light filled the narrow hallway, casting shadows across Ursula's lined features. "He was driving home after work. As he reached his street, he noticed a car parked in front of his house. He thinks it was the Gestapo. He can't stay away forever, but I'm keeping him here tonight."

The Gestapo had come after Klaus. Who would be next? Maria swallowed. The control the conspiracy had maintained for years was slipping, sliding, too fast . . .

It was all happening too fast.

Ursula set the bread on the hall table. Dust coated Ursula and Rüdiger's wedding photo. It sat, crooked in its silver frame. "It's been absolutely hectic. At the same time Klaus arrived, Corporal Knobloch showed up."

"I came here to meet him. Has he left? We're arranging for Dietrich's flight out of Germany. A false passport." The secrecy of it all had turned her stomach into a roiling ball of knots.

A nod. "Klaus thought Dietrich should know about the Gestapo." Ursula clutched a faded shawl around her shoulders. "Corporal Knobloch went back to Tegel to tell him."

A vice cinched Maria's throat. "He shouldn't have done that. Now, more than ever, we must act. There must be no more delays." The sand was slipping from their hourglass. If they didn't act now, smuggle him out of Tegel, their chance wouldn't hold out forever.

Ursula's mouth tightened. "Right now, we need to think about Klaus." Ursula steered her toward the dining room. "Come. I need you to help me make him see reason."

"Reason?"

The woman's gaze bore into Maria, eyes glittering with intermingled panic and determination. "He's considering suicide."

Maria gasped. "Why?"

It was a stupid question, one flung forth in the moment. Why had Uncle

Henning, and others, chosen that path? When one fell under custody of the Gestapo, it meant torture, the likes of which those on the outside couldn't begin to fathom. No one, at least few, had the strength to withstand. The Gestapo wanted names, information. They wouldn't choose the merciful route and simply end the prisoner's life. They'd inflict horrific pain until the captive gave way and confessed. To avoid the risk of giving information under pressure, some simply ended their lives. But Dietrich's brother couldn't do that . . .

Ursula placed a hand on Maria's shoulder, bony fingers tightening. "You must help me, Maria." The words were a breath of desperation.

Maria nodded. *"Ja."*

Their footsteps echoed through the too-quiet house.

Klaus sat at the dining-room table, an empty cup at his elbow. Haggard shadows fell upon his face in the gray light.

"Hello, Maria." He gave her a smile, an almost gallant gesture.

"Klaus." Maria returned the smile.

"I've told Maria everything." Ursula sank into a chair.

"You mustn't do this." Maria pressed her palms against the table, glancing behind her. Had the Gestapo seen Klaus and followed? Were they even now striding out of their black cars, sidearms strapped to their waists, jackboots marching toward the house? Demons, roaming to and fro about the earth, seeking whom they may devour. "You don't know what they'll do to you."

Klaus made a noise of disgust. "Don't I? The dossier has doubtless been shown to the Führer himself, who will stop at nothing to rid the country of every last one of us. The only reason we haven't all been taken to some pit and shot is because first, they want to squeeze out every scrap of information they can. By whatever means."

"But what if there's still a chance?" Though Ursula's tone stayed low, the fierceness in her eyes shouted as if she'd done so verbally. "They might not take you. That might not have even been a Gestapo car . . ."

"Don't delude yourself. It was a Gestapo car."

"Could we get him out?" Maria ventured.

"Tonight? We'll be lucky if you manage to orchestrate Dietrich's escape." Klaus shook his head. "I know what I'm up against. There's no way I could leave the country. I can either allow myself to be taken into custody, or . . . or take a cyanide capsule." He paled, making his dark eyes stand out sharply in his face. The resemblance between him and Dietrich wasn't strong, but they shared the same set of the chin, the same broad foreheads and blue eyes. Dietrich wasn't here to speak words of wisdom to his brother.

But she was.

"What of Emmi and the children? What would they say if they heard you talking like this?" She kept her tone brisk. He was sinking. Lapsing into a place where he'd make good on his threat and end his life in an upstairs bedroom. She couldn't, wouldn't, let him go there.

"Emmi and the children are in the country to be away from the bombings. I can't get a message to her." Klaus's shoulders slumped. He pressed his fingers against his eyes. War had turned the most robust of them into sunken, aged humanity. With his bent shoulders and sallow face, Klaus looked older than his own vater.

Maria rounded the table and knelt, placing her hands on his wide shoulders. He kept his head bent. "Klaus, listen. Think of your children. What would they say if they heard you talking like that?"

"Don't you think you owe it to them to make some attempt, at least, to live?" Ursula was begging now. At one end of the room, the clock ticked rhythmically. Another sign they were running out of time.

Klaus lifted his gaze. Raw emotion showed in his eyes. Indecision. Despair. He swallowed, Adam's apple jerking. A long exhale deflated his chest. "You know, Maria, I've never shared Dietrich's faith. When I first heard he was planning to study theology, I'm afraid I gave him a pretty hard time about it. Throughout the years, he never tried to push his beliefs on me, but he did share them. Perhaps now I should revisit all he told me. I don't see there ever being a more opportune time." He gave a short laugh. "All right, Ursula. I won't do it. I don't hold out much hope for living either way, but if I let them take me, I suppose I'll learn the measure of my strength."

"You don't know what they'll do to you," Maria whispered. "They don't torture everyone."

"Perhaps." Klaus stared down at his folded hands.

"I'll make you something to eat." Ursula stood. "You should get some rest tonight."

Klaus nodded. Maria followed Ursula into the kitchen, the room barren and clean. She opened the cupboard, her face away from Maria. When she turned, Maria glimpsed traces of moisture in her eyes.

"Did I do right?" Ursula set the small bag of flour onto the empty counter. "Tell me, Maria, did I do right?" The words pled for reassurance. But Maria could only offer truth. False security was a lie none of them believed in anymore. For a world of fairy tales. Not nightmares.

She pressed her lips together. It was the question they all asked. Did they do right? In a world of choiceless choices, how could any of them be sure?

What was left to them but to throw themselves and their decisions upon the mercy of God?

That alone held steadfast.

"You did what you thought was right." Maria laid a steady hand on Ursula's shoulder. "That's the main thing."

Chapter Thirty-Six

October 1, 1944
Tegel Prison

A whisper could fill a room louder than a scream.

"They've arrested Klaus." Fault of the dossier hidden in the archives at Zossen. Hans had wanted the files destroyed before this, but Oster had urged them kept. Now they'd fallen into the hands of those determined to strangle the conspiracy until its dying breath.

Knobloch nodded, shifting his position on Dietrich's cot. His eyes spoke of a sleepless night. And worry. Much worry. "And Frau Schleicher says they hold out little hope that Rüdiger will remain free for long. We've got to get you out of here, Dietrich. Today."

Dietrich drew in a breath. "Nein," he said quietly, shaking his head.

"What do you mean nein? Are you crazy? Don't you know what this means? They'll take you somewhere that'll make Tegel look like a seaside resort. They'll—"

Dietrich held up a hand, halting Knobloch's words. "I know. But I can't leave. They'd try to get information about my whereabouts from Klaus." He pulled off his spectacles and scrubbed a hand over his eyes. "They'd take Mutter and Vater and Maria. They're ruthless when they think they've been thwarted. I won't risk it."

Knobloch heaved the sigh of one who knew logic but didn't like it.

"I'm sorry for you, my friend. You went to such trouble . . . planned to go with me." Showing a faithfulness and loyalty Dietrich had never reckoned on meeting behind prison walls, Knobloch had risked his own life by smuggling letters, planning the escape.

"Don't even think about me," Knobloch said fiercely. "I just want to try to change your mind."

Dietrich shook his head. "Can't be done, I'm afraid." He crossed to his desk and took his book of Daily Texts from the top of the stack. He held out the volume to Knobloch. Perhaps the last gesture of friendship he'd ever be able to give to the man who'd done so much for him during the eighteen months he'd spent at Tegel.

"It isn't much. But the daily verses have always been a comfort to me. It would make me happy to know that . . . after I'm gone, you'll read them."

"Danke. I'll do that." Knobloch took the book and stood. He moved toward the door, one hand resting against it, cap crooked upon his close-shaven hair.

For a long moment, he regarded Dietrich, a sad smile of resignation on his lips. He shook his head, a sheen in his eyes . . . though he'd never have owned it. "Blast it all, Herr Pastor! You're . . . I've never met anyone like you."

"Auf Wiedersehen, my friend." Dietrich kept his smile in place as Knobloch relocked the cell door. Until his footsteps echoed down the long corridor.

He sank down on his cot, staring down at his empty hands.

Now what? Since the Zossen discovery, there'd been no outward alteration in his circumstances. This present semblance of peace, this lack of apparent interest toward his case, that would soon change.

Was he ready to face whatever awaited him?

He didn't want this. Hadn't set out to arrive at this place when he'd first joined the conspiracy. But he'd known the risks. Been prepared. Or had he?

"I'm only human, Lord," he whispered into the silence. "Everyone thinks I'm some sort of saint, but I'm just a man like any other. I want to live. To marry Maria and hold our children in my arms. I want life. But it isn't to be. I'm not stupid. I know what the Nazis will do to me." He lifted his gaze toward the window, looking out at a freedom he'd refused. Audacious sunlight streamed through his grimy window. For once the sight filled his heart only with loss.

What was left for him but to wait for the end to come, wherever and however it would?

"Tell me, Lord." The words echoed through the four walls of his cell of solitude. "What is left to me?"

But he already knew the answer, and it came to him again, if not vanquishing the ache, at least filling it. Hadn't he been the one to preach and write about it?

He still had what he'd always had. Hope. Not in the fragility of the world, but in the solidarity of God. And until the end came, whether it pleased God for it to be tomorrow, or forty years from now, he would continue to live unreservedly. Taking seriously not his own sufferings, but those of God in the world. Abandoning all attempts to make something of himself and his life, knowing that though to live was Christ, to die was gain. Casting himself at the feet of God, and in doing so, embracing all of life's duties, problems, failures, joys, and perplexities.

That was faith. That stood fast, even when nothing else did.

The road he'd taken had not been easy, but necessary. Had he ignored the call of God on his life to speak out in the face of evil, had he lived ensconced in comfortable Christianity, it would never have shown him the cross. Only through the path he'd traversed had he gained this gift. And a gift it truly was, even if it found him sitting in a cell in a military prison, awaiting his fate.

Only he didn't. His fate, his final hours, had already been determined by God.

"Everything." A smile edged his lips. "Everything is left to me."

October 4, 1944
Berlin

Rain fell, a symphony of tears, as the Gestapo took Rüdiger away.

Maria stood on the sidewalk, her hand on Ursula's arm, watching the black Mercedes drive away, Ursula's face awash with bitter despair.

Silence fell as the two women climbed the front steps of Ursula's home, save for the gentle fall of the rain against the ground.

Standing on the top step, Maria stared out at the street as Ursula closed the door behind her, weary footsteps reverberating through the hall. Hans. Klaus. Rüdiger.

Dietrich.

What would become of them all?

Maria needed to go inside, tend to her sister-in-law, but Renate was already with Ursula, and Maria's own thoughts begged for quietude. Tugging the edges of her sweater tighter around herself, she started down the street, passing a shell of a house, blackened timbers and crumbling stones marks of devastation that had left few untouched. Wind pulled at the strands of hair not confined in her kerchief, swirling them around her face. Rain splattered her, soaked her, but she didn't care.

Images spun through her mind. A walk through a garden on a summer's eve. The laughter in a blue-eyed gaze as his fingers teased American tunes from the keys of her grossmutter's piano. Kindness in his eyes at the hospital, a balm to her heart roughened after Vater's death. Always with this man there had been kindness. In each letter, as he'd understated his own problems and sought to soothe hers. Holding hands on the bench in the visitor's cell with a guard looking on. He'd held her hands hungrily, as if to imprint her touch upon his heart. In every kiss, each one they'd shared sealed within her memory.

Tears spilled down her cheeks, silent grief given voice through droplets of pain.

She needed him. Safe and whole and by her side.

Now the possibility reared its ugly head. It might never come to be. Knobloch had given them the news that Dietrich had decided against escape. Too much of a risk for his family, the corporal had said. *Take the risk. Take it for me*, she'd wanted to scream. But Knobloch had been firm. Dietrich had made the decision to remain at Tegel and await whatever happened. He wouldn't be swayed, even by her.

Why, God? Haven't I lost enough? Will You not give him back to me?

She stared up at the slate-gray sky through a blur of tears. How fully she loved him, with every ounce of her passionate self. Only she couldn't go on loving him . . . unless she was equally prepared to relinquish him.

Dietrich didn't belong to her. He never had, much as she wanted to cling to him and keep him with her after every aching farewell. He was God's. God had only gifted her with the blessing of being able to share in his life. His future didn't rest with her, but with Him.

She chafed against it. Once Dietrich had written that it was an easy thing to say *Lord*; the difficulty came in saying *dear Lord* with all one's devotion. Never had she felt it more than now.

A youth pedaled past on a bicycle, splashing through puddles. She continued down the street, as aimless in her walk as she was within.

Could she trust God to do what He would with Dietrich's life? With her own? Trust that He had a plan far greater than the finite mind could comprehend?

"I can't do it in my own strength. If You can help me, then I can . . . try." She breathed the words, as a tiny flame sparked in her heart. Trust? Perhaps.

God had a plan for Dietrich Bonhoeffer. Whether or not his future included her, she'd been privileged to share a little of his present. A remarkable man, a once-in-a-lifetime kind of person. He'd given others so much.

He'd given her so much.

No matter what the days ahead would bring, she wouldn't exchange those spent while loving him.

Overpowering urgency stole her breath. She needed to visit Tegel. She'd avoided applying for a visitor's permit while they were planning his escape. But she needed to do it now.

She might not have always been the fiancée she wanted to be, but she could give him a memory to store within himself.

She turned toward the Schleichers, more determined with each step. Rain had ceased to fall, leaving her wet and chilled, but purpose warmed her more than sunlight.

She'd once promised to teach him to dance, imagined them in their little home, the strains of a record player filling the room. He'd misstep, laugh at himself, her with him. They'd kiss, long and lovingly, together at last.

It was a dream she'd received nourishment from during many a starving moment of deprivation.

But the future was not guaranteed. Freedom wasn't a certainty.

And there was no better moment than the present to show Dietrich how completely her heart belonged to his.

Chapter Thirty-Seven

October 6, 1944
Tegel Prison

"W*ait on the Lord: be of good courage, and he shall strengthen thine heart: wait, I say, on the Lord.*"

"Amen. Let it be so with me, Lord." Exhaling a peaceful sigh, Dietrich turned the page in his Bible. As he did so, the volume fell open to the front cover. A faded photograph, edges creased from the many times his fingers had closed around them, fell onto his cot. He picked it up, a wistful smile edging his lips.

"My beloved Maria." He brushed a finger across the picture-Maria's hair. Flat and paper-like. Not soft as an Alpine mist. His chest wrenched. "What I wouldn't give to see your face again. Hear your beautiful laugh. Have I told you lately, dearest one, how much I love you? Have I, Maria?"

Silence was his only answer. He returned the picture to the front page of his Bible, closing the cover. He couldn't continue to gaze at her picture and remain a sane man.

Longing. One could only take so much of it.

He stood and began his daily regimen of pacing back and forth across his cell. Whether he wanted to or not, he forced himself to do two kilometers per day.

Back and forth. One step. Three—the gray walls of his cell the only vista for his morning ramble. He imagined a meadow in Pomerania. The sharp scent of pine. Blooming flowers. A summer-day breeze.

And a girl on his arm with a smile to rival it all, roses intertwined in her windswept hair.

Back and forth. Marching in time.

How accustomed he'd become to the companionship of his thoughts. How easily they could lead him astray if he did not govern himself. Today, he let them wander where they would, imagining what Eberhard might be doing at the moment, wondering how Renate and baby Dietrich were spending the day—how large his godson must be growing. Thinking of and praying for his parents, for Hans and Christel.

Though he couldn't see their faces, he nonetheless lived these days with them beside him.

By powers of good he was wondrously sheltered.

A noise. The grinding of the bolt on his cell door.

Dietrich stopped pacing and waited, eyes on the door. A new guard—severe-faced for one so young, stood outside.

"Prisoner Bonhoeffer . . ."

"Ja?" If this was the end, he gave thanks that no fear leapt in his chest.

"You have a visitor."

A visitor? But one didn't ask questions, not with this guard. He grabbed his coat, shrugging into the sleeves as he followed the guard. He wouldn't get his hopes up.

Their steps echoed through the prison walls as they passed cell after cell. Some empty, some not. Here, as in the outside world, the stories of humanity played out. Someday would someone tell them? Tales of courage and cowardice. Of life . . . and death.

Down the flight of stairs, he followed the guard's brisk pace.

Foolishness. It would be foolish to hope.

Even he could only take so much disappointment.

The door to the visitor's cell stood ajar. Dietrich tried to peer over the guard's shoulder.

"In you go." The guard jerked his head toward the door but made no move to enter.

"Aren't you coming too?"

The guard shook his head. "Orders from the captain. You're to see this person alone."

Dietrich took a step toward the door. Curiosity warred with confusion. Since his uncle's execution, he'd been kept under more vigilant guard. Who would they allow to visit him alone?

A slight figure stood facing the window. Hair fell in loose waves over her shoulders, face tilted toward the sky.

Maria. His Maria.

His heart beat, a renegade drum inside his chest.

She turned, standing beside a sizable object covered with a cloth. Wearing a red coat. Smiling, her eyes softly aglow.

The guard shut the door behind them.

What a moment. Alone, for the first time since their engagement. Really and truly alone. His gaze settled on her, her beautiful face, those Danube-blue eyes.

"I don't understand. How did you manage this?" He could scarce trust his voice to utter rational words, his mind a coherent thought.

"I managed it." She stepped toward him, taking his hands in hers and looking up into his face. "I thought it was high time my fiancé and I were without a chaperone. Don't you agree?" She smiled at him, a trace of the playful girl who'd so beguiled him at her grossmutter's sparkling in her eyes. "They've promised us an hour," she whispered.

"How's the family?"

She pressed her lips together. "Rüdiger was arrested two days ago. He and Klaus are at the same prison."

Dietrich sighed, aching for Emmi and Ursula and all they would be enduring on their husbands' accounts, and for his brother and brother-in-law, penned in places far worse than Tegel. "And my parents?"

"They're fine. Worried, of course, but determined to keep their spirits up."

"Any word from Hans?"

Maria shook her head. "Christel's trying with all her might to see him, but so far, no success. Still, we're all well."

"Eberhard and Renate too?"

She nodded. "You should see baby Dietrich. He's so happy all the time and getting so big already. He brings us all such joy." She encircled his hand with her fingers. "Just like his namesake."

He kissed her, lost in the wonder of her touch. The softness of her skin, the sweetness of her fragrance, and the rightness of her lips against his.

"I wish I could marry you this moment." His hand lingered against her cheek. They'd grown together these past eighteen months. Perhaps not as they might have once wished, but the two of them had become stronger, better. No longer was she the innocent girl who'd first stirred his heart but a woman, brave and capable.

He loved them both. The woman and the girl.

"I wish you could too." She gave a shaky laugh. But this hour was too precious to be spent wishing. Reality was all they had. "But I have other plans for our hour together." She moved to the table and pulled the cloth off the object with a flourish.

"My gramophone?"

She nodded. "Remember when I promised to teach you to dance?"

"After we were married?" He watched as she positioned a record on the turntable.

"What better time than the present?" She tilted her head.

What was faith if it was not living fully and completely in all of life—its joys and sorrows, burdens and blessings? Taking hold of what one was given, instead of fearing what may come. The promise of a future was too feeble to be certain.

All they could be sure of was that they were in this moment. Together.

"Then Maria von Wedemeyer." He held out his hand, as she set the needle on the record. "May I have the honor of this dance?"

She nodded, placing her hand in his, as a soft, slow melody drifted from the gramophone.

"I've never danced before." He placed one hand around her waist and took hers with the other. "I probably have two left feet."

"Nonsense," she said softly. "It's simple. One, two, three. And again. One, two, three. There. That's it." She smiled up at him.

He didn't know the first thing about dancing. But he'd dreamed about a moment like this, holding her in his arms. He misstepped. She laughed.

"You're doing great."

He smiled. "You're kind to say that."

They moved closer together. She leaned her head against his chest. They continued to turn in a slow circle in the tiny cell, their surroundings vanishing. The music played on, soft and crackly.

"In all the times we've been together," he began slowly, needing with everything in him to say this to her, "I've had a difficult time telling you all that is in my heart. I'm a private man, Maria, and with others present, I couldn't bring myself to—"

"Tell me what?" She looked up at him.

He swallowed. Hard. "I meant every word I wrote in that poem and more. I love you in a way I've never loved another on this earth, and I will love you from this moment until my last breath. You have been light to me in this place of darkness, and for that . . . for that I thank you. I've given you so little, but if my unending love is worth anything, then it is yours. Know that whatever comes, it is and will always be . . . yours."

She stilled, as if absorbing, cherishing his words. "What an engagement we've had." She smiled through a sheen of tears. His own eyes burned. He blinked the tears away. "But then you never were an ordinary man."

"I'm not extraordinary, Maria." He sighed. "Anything but that."

"Oh, but you're wrong." She clasped his hands. "You've always been extraordinary to me."

He kissed her again. There should have been a million things said between them, but each one of them faded. The heart did not always need words to communicate, and in this kiss, he told her all.

Banging on the door caused them both to start and pull away. The door opened.

"I'm sorry, Fraülein, but you'll have to leave."

Maria nodded. She turned to him, pressing both her hands along the sides of his face. Her eyes fell closed, as if she were committing him to memory.

He pulled her into his arms, holding her fiercely, as if that alone could join them together far beyond this moment. Heedless of the guard, he kissed her again, soft and slow.

Making memories enough to fill the void of separation.

"Auf Wiedersehen, meine Geliebte." My beloved.

"I love you." He couldn't bring himself to say goodbye.

The guard hefted the gramophone. Hands at his sides, Dietrich watched her turn away. His mutter's face rose before his mind, as she ran along the train platform, sending his brother Walter off to a war from which he would not return, hands outstretched, reaching for his. In his memory, Dietrich heard her shouted words, as each step Maria took carried her from the room.

She glanced over her shoulder, her gaze finding his one last time. He smiled.

Though she left, he held her still. She would always be with him, deep inside his heart, no matter what future befell their earthly love.

As the cell door slammed, shutting her from sight, Dietrich whispered into the silence.

"Always remember. It is only space that separates us."

Epilogue

November 2, 1977
Boston

Memories visited her today. They called often, but she usually shoved them aside. Focused on the next task. It was easier that way. To forget.

But Maria always remembered.

Urgency heightened as her strength waned. If she wanted to give herself over to remembrance, it would have to be now. Here in this sterile hospital, surrounded by nurses and machines. Lacking the stamina to leave her bed unaided. Soon the capacity for thought would leave her too.

Maria leaned back against the pillows, running her hand along the white sheets, the scent of drugs and antiseptic heavy in the air. Since the diagnosis of cancer four months ago, this hospital room had become her vista, and she'd made it her home, putting pictures of her children—Paul and Christopher, both successful young men starting their own families—beside her bed, making sure there were flowers. Much as Dietrich had, she imagined, putting things around his cell to remember his family by.

A few days after her last visit, Cell 92 had emptied. Dietrich had been taken away. First, to the Gestapo prison on Prinz-Albrecht-Strasse where, she learned later, he'd brought hope to the inmates held for interrogation and torture in the underground cells. Her cousin Fabian von Schlabrendorff had been among them, and once he'd spoken to her of the courage Dietrich's presence instilled in them all. During the air raids, the most horrific Berlin had seen yet, he'd stood in the shelter, calming the others without showing the slightest flicker of fear for himself.

In early February 1945, his parents had trekked across the wasteland of smoke and ashes that was Berlin in an attempt to get to the prison to deliver a parcel of food, only to discover Dietrich had been moved. As soon as she'd helped spirit her family away from Pätzig and the fast approaching Red Army, she'd set off to find him.

Though decades had passed since then, she could still remember the feel of that suitcase in her hand, how her fingers ached and her feet throbbed as she approached the gates of Flossenbürg. Above all, that memory stood out.

Because it was there Dietrich would eventually arrive. On the evening of April 8, two months after she'd moved on to search other concentration camps, he'd been brought there. And the next morning, April 9, just as dawn streaked the sky, the Nazis had ended his life by hanging.

Nein, not the end, she reminded herself, but the beginning. Dietrich's final words, passed from a British prisoner who'd been with Dietrich to the last, on to Bishop Bell in England. His gift to them all, a parting reminder that this life was only a passage on the journey to freedom.

She'd grieved his loss. But in those days, they were all grieving losses, those days after the war when a defeated Germany sought to find its place again.

And she'd moved on. To study in America and gain a master's degree in mathematics. She'd married, first to Paul Schniewind in 1949. Together, they'd become parents of two sons. But as the years passed, their relationship, which had never been strong, foundered, no longer able to withstand the strain of their differing personalities. She married again, an American businessman, Barton Weller. He already had two children, and together they'd made a family of six in the small town of Easton, Connecticut. Until, despite their best efforts, that marriage too ended.

Her job at Honeywell Computers, where she became head of her department developing software for the new minicomputers, provided her enough income to purchase a house. A house beside the sea, directly overlooking the waves. Her ocean, she called it. Her children grew and thrived and went on to college. While she worked and poured herself into their lives and served the needy of Boston through her church.

Dietrich had been a part of her life. Though sometimes, working late at night in her office at Honeywell, she wondered if it had all been just a dream. Those years in Berlin, those hours with him. They'd so rarely been alone. When she'd first heard of his death, it had been hard to believe. As if it was just another separation, another period of waiting before a visit instead of the final separation.

A knock sounded on the door. Maria looked up. Her sister Ruth-Alice had traveled to America for an extended stay. She entered the room with a smile. She'd grown to look so like their mutter and still dressed like the daughter of a Prussian officer, her graying hair swept up with pins. Maria had always favored shorter, practical styles. They made her feel freer, more modern.

"Did you find somewhere to have lunch?" Maria asked as her sister set down her purse and pulled up a chair.

"The traffic was awful, so the driver took me to a café only a few blocks from here. I don't know how you've stood it, living in the city all these years." Ruth-Alice took off her coat and scarf.

"Boston has become my home. The world of Pätzig, our childhood, no longer exists," Maria said quietly. The Russians had burnt down the home of her girlhood as the Red Army surged across Germany. The flames had claimed everything. Almost.

Ruth-Alice sat down. The door was closed, leaving them alone, though the noise of busy nurses, visitors, and patients still managed to filter in.

Somewhere out in that hall was there a bench just right for two?

The thought came as unbidden as the rest of the memories.

It strengthened her resolve as she reached for the box beside her bed. She cradled it in her hands, gently lifting the lid. Inside lay so much more than letters.

It was their love story. She had no ring, no token to remind her of the man called Dietrich Bonhoeffer. Just these letters. She'd opened them only a couple of times throughout the years. Many had urged her to share them, as Eberhard Bethge had done with the volume *Letters and Papers from Prison*, detailing his own correspondence with Dietrich. That book had revealed to the world the thoughts and theology of a remarkable and original man. It challenged all who read it. Inspired them to stand for conviction and live in freedom, even in the most horrifying of circumstances.

Her own letters she'd shared with no one. She'd written one article for a theological journal and included a few excerpts. That was enough, she'd decided, after she'd sent in the article. These letters had not been written for the eyes of others.

But now she passed the box to Ruth-Alice, catching a fleeting glimpse of what her sister would see. Neatly stacked envelopes, faded and aged. Some more worn than others, carried in her skirt pocket during the years she'd received them—her girlhood self holding on to the only tangible link she possessed of their love.

Ruth-Alice took the box, recognition gaining in her eyes. "You brought them here?"

Maria nodded. Pain throbbed through her body. But the girl who'd arrived at Flossenbürg on foot was a fighter still, and she smiled in spite of it.

"What are you going to do with them?" Ruth-Alice asked. She picked up one of the envelopes, holding it in her hand.

Maria swallowed. Her days were numbered. And she didn't need the letters. She kept them inside herself, had always done so. It was time. "I'm giving them to you."

"Why?" Questions spun through her sister's eyes.

Drawing in a breath, Maria went on. "It's time they were published. And I want you to do it. It's time the world discovered the other letters and papers from prison. Learned that as well as being a theologian, Dietrich Bonhoeffer was also a man."

"You want me to publish them?"

She nodded, once and firmly. "Not right away. Wait a little while. And be sure when you compile the volume that you put a good commentary in with it. Some of the letters . . . people could misunderstand." Energy slowly ebbed from her body. She'd said what she needed to say.

She could only fight so long.

Ruth-Alice gazed down at the small box in her lap. "It will seem strange to read them after all these years. So much has happened since . . ."

Maria reached across the space between them and squeezed her sister's hand. "I know. But I want to know it will be done. That my addition to all that's been said and written about Dietrich can help people gain a new perspective about the time he spent in Tegel." She laughed softly. "Some of the things he wrote . . . people may be a bit shocked."

The world knew Dietrich Bonhoeffer. But they did not know him as she had. No one else did. Together, they had shared the most earthly and the most ethereal of emotions.

Love.

During a time history would remember as horrific, they'd experienced moments of beauty and joy. She smiled, resting her head against the pillows. Remembering December, laughing as she introduced a Christmas tree to Tegel Prison. Kissing him in the dingy visitor's cell. Living and loving for all they were worth during the brief time they'd had together.

She tucked her hand beneath her cheek, shifting onto her side to face her sister. Ruth-Alice continued to look down at the letters, picking one up, turning it over in her hands.

Ruth-Alice glanced up, a faint glow in her eyes as if she too remembered those tumultuous years. "He loved you."

Maria nodded, smiled, seeing not her sister's face but his. Faded perhaps with memory and time but, in that moment, vivid and mesmerizing as ever.

"He did," she whispered. "He really did."

Author's Note

Many world leaders, pastors, and individuals have been impacted by the legacy of Dietrich Bonhoeffer, but few know of Maria von Wedemeyer—the love of his life and the fiancée whose letters and visits infused hope into the long months of imprisonment. It is my earnest prayer that I have honored their story through these pages.

Almost every event in the novel actually occurred—from Dietrich and Maria's first meeting in June 1942 at her grandmother's home in Pomerania, Dietrich and Hans von Dohnanyi's trips to Sweden and Rome for the purpose of bringing word of the conspiracy to the British government, the deaths of Maria's father and brother, Maria's grandmother's matchmaking and Maria's mother's reluctance to allow the engagement, the failed attempts on Hitler's life in March 1943, the arrests of Dietrich and Hans on April 5, 1943, and their subsequent interrogation and imprisonment for months on end.

Blending fact with fiction presented a unique challenge, and though I did my best to remain true to what we know about Dietrich and Maria during the time line of this story, I took a few fictional liberties in my portrayal of certain elements. One of these included the omission of two of Dietrich's siblings—his oldest brother, Karl-Friedrich, and youngest sister, Susanne. Since I already had an extensive cast of characters to incorporate, I chose not to mention these two siblings. I also chose to place Maria at the home of the fictional Vogels for her term of national service.

Maria visited Dietrich a total of seventeen times during his imprisonment. According to *Love Letters from Cell 92*, their last visit took place on August 23, 1944. For the sake of my story, I gave them one final visit on October 6, 1944, two days before Dietrich's transfer to the underground

Gestapo prison at Prinz-Albrecht-Strasse, where he was held for four months. During his time at Prinz-Albrecht-Strasse, he was permitted a limited number of parcels and letters but, despite the valiant efforts of his family and friends, no visitors.

Oskar von Scheffler and his relationship with Maria is entirely of my own invention. I based Oskar on real-life Gestapo Criminal Commissar Franz-Xaver Sonderegger, who worked with Manfred Roeder during the interrogations of Dietrich Bonhoeffer and Hans von Dohnanyi. In September 1944, Sonderegger discovered the Chronicle of Shame hidden in the Abwehr archives in Zossen, information which led to the executions of Dietrich Bonhoeffer, Hans von Dohnanyi, Admiral Wilhelm Canaris, General Hans Oster, Klaus Bonhoeffer, Rüdiger Schleicher, and others.

In portraying the thoughts, dialogue, and actions of the characters, I relied upon extensive study of the letters of Dietrich Bonhoeffer, Maria von Wedemeyer, and other family members and friends, along with biographies, documentaries, and research materials detailing life in World War II Germany. Many of the letters interspersed throughout the novel are actual correspondence, used with kind permission, along with the inclusion of two poems written by Bonhoeffer. Though I used an abridged version of his poem "The Past," I encourage you to read the work in full. It's truly a beautiful and heartrending testament to love and longing.

Readers may be left with the pressing question of what happened to certain characters after the novel's conclusion. I've provided a brief description of the fate of major players below (for more detailed information, see the further reading section).

Hans von Dohnanyi—Though suffering both mental and physical anguish, Hans endured the grueling interrogations he was subjected to during his time at Sachsenhausen Concentration Camp and Prinz-Albrecht-Strasse Prison without giving Gestapo authorities a shred of information about the conspiracy. In the cellar at Prinz-Albrecht-Strasse, despite rigorous security, Dietrich managed to find ways to care for his partially paralyzed brother-in-law. On April 5, 1945, Hitler was shown the Chronicle of Shame and, in a burst of murderous outrage, ordered the immediate execution of every person listed in the dossier. Before the so-called "trial," a kind doctor dosed Hans heavily with painkillers, sparing him the pain of submitting to the farce of Nazi legal justice. On April 9, he was carried half conscious on a stretcher to the place of execution and hanged. His beloved wife, Christel, remained a source of strength for her children and aged parents in the years following the war. She never remarried and died in 1965.

Klaus Bonhoeffer and Rüdiger Schleicher—Klaus and Rüdiger were held in Gestapo custody from October 1944 to April 1945. Though there is no indication that Dietrich was ever tortured, both Klaus and Rüdiger suffered brutal beatings during their interrogations. For the rest of her life, Ursula Schleicher reproached herself for preventing her brother from committing suicide before he was taken into custody. On April 23, 1945, in an abandoned courtyard, Klaus and Rüdiger were executed by machine pistol.

Karl and Paula Bonhoeffer—Due to the chaos following the end of the war, the Bonhoeffers did not learn of Klaus's and Rüdiger's deaths until June 1945. For weeks after, they clung to the hope that Dietrich might still be alive and trying to return to them. But on July 26, they heard from a friend that a memorial service for Dietrich was to be broadcast on the BBC the following day. After the war, when asked about the loss of his four sons and sons-in-law, Karl Bonhoeffer said, "We are sad, but also very proud." Karl died in 1948, and Paula in 1951.

Eberhard Bethge—After being liberated by Soviet troops, Eberhard returned to Berlin and his young wife and baby. Following the war, he and Renate moved to London, where he pastored a German-speaking congregation for many years. The couple had two more children. It is to Eberhard and Renate that we owe much of our knowledge of Bonhoeffer's life and theology. During the harrowing days after the failed July 20 plot, Renate buried the bulk of her husband's correspondence with Dietrich in gas mask cans in the Bonhoeffers' back yard. These later formed the bulk of *Letters and Papers from Prison*. As they once joked about, Eberhard indeed became Dietrich's biographer. The over one-thousand-page volume is recognized as the definitive Bonhoeffer biography. Throughout his life, Eberhard worked tirelessly, editing and compiling Dietrich's unfinished book *Ethics*, along with the correspondence he and Bonhoeffer exchanged throughout their friendship. He generously answered every Bonhoeffer-related letter sent to him. Eberhard passed away on March 18, 2000. He was ninety years old.

Maria von Wedemeyer—Before her death, Maria informed her family of her decision to entrust her sister, Ruth-Alice von Bismark, with the task of publishing her correspondence with Dietrich. *Love Letters from Cell 92* was first published in German in 1992. Except for one interview for a television documentary and an article for Union Theological Seminary's *Quarterly Review*, Maria spoke little about Dietrich during her lifetime.

She passed away on November 16, 1977, after a four-month battle with cancer. She was fifty-three years old.

Though Dietrich Bonhoeffer's physical life ended on the morning of April 9, 1945, he left behind an incredible legacy. His example of living fully devoted to Christ and taking responsible action against a godless government has been a challenge and inspiration to millions. I am no exception. Though he left behind a grieving family and fiancée, I can't help but wonder if, had he survived the war, he would be as well-known and remembered today.

Studying the life of Dietrich Bonhoeffer has caused me to ponder questions such as "How does a Christian behave when earthly authorities are going against everything the gospel stands for?" and "What is God asking me to surrender for His glory?" Bonhoeffer famously said that Christians are not to simply bandage the wounds of victims beneath the wheels of injustice but are to drive a spoke into the wheel itself. Reading the words of a man living in Nazi Germany and prayerfully pondering them as they apply to life in the twenty-first century has taken me on a journey of growth that continues to challenge and enrich my faith. I pray you discover the same!

Blessings,
Amanda

For further reading, I highly recommend the following:

Love Letters from Cell 92 by Dietrich Bonhoeffer and Maria von
    Wedemeyer, edited by Ruth-Alice von Bismarck and Ulrich Kabitz
Letters and Papers from Prison by Dietrich Bonhoeffer
The Cost of Discipleship by Dietrich Bonhoeffer
Bonhoeffer: Pastor, Martyr, Prophet, Spy by Eric Metaxas
Dietrich Bonhoeffer 1906–1945: Martyr, Thinker, Man of Resistance by
    Ferdinand Schlingensiepen

p. 18, **The thought that you are concerned**: Dietrich Bonhoeffer
and Maria von Wedemeyer, *Love Letters from Cell 92: The
Correspondence Between Dietrich Bonhoeffer and Maria von
Wedemeyer*, ed. Ruth-Alice von Bismarck and Ulrich Kabitz, trans.
John Brownjohn (Grand Rapids: Zondervan, 1995), 203.

p. 39, **I haven't written to Maria**: Bonhoeffer and von Wedemeyer, *Love
Letters from Cell 92*, 330–31.

p. 105, **Dear Fraülein von Wedemeyer**: Dietrich Bonhoeffer, *Conspiracy
and Imprisonment, 1940–1945*, ed. Lisa E. Dahill and Mark
Brocker, Dietrich Bonhoeffer Works 16 (Minneapolis: Fortress Press,
2016), 366–67.

p. 127, **Fundamentally, you and I**: Bonhoeffer and von Wedemeyer, *Love
Letters from Cell 92*, 333.

p. 128, **But only from a peaceful**: Bonhoeffer, *Conspiracy and
Imprisonment*, 370–71.

p. 158, **We have been silent witnesses**: Dietrich Bonhoeffer, *Letters and
Papers from Prison*, trans. Reginald Fuller and Frank Clark (New
York: Touchstone, 1997), 16–17.

p. 165, **I've known, ever since arriving home**: Bonhoeffer and von
Wedemeyer, *Love Letters from Cell 92*, 338.

p. 166, **Dear Maria, may I simply tell you**: Bonhoeffer and von
Wedemeyer, *Love Letters from Cell 92*, 339–40.

p. 167, **Don't say anything**: Bonhoeffer and von Wedemeyer, *Love Letters
from Cell 92*, 340.

p. 222, **Dearest Dietrich, has something bad happened**: Bonhoeffer and
von Wedemeyer, *Love Letters from Cell 92*, 347.

p. 248, **Dear, beloved Dietrich, your mutter . . . without my writing them
down**: Bonhoeffer and von Wedemeyer, *Love Letters from Cell 92*,
22–23.

p. 301, **My dear, dear Maria, it's no use**: Bonhoeffer and von Wedemeyer,
Love Letters from Cell 92, 199–201.

p. 305, **You went, beloved happiness**: Bonhoeffer and von Wedemeyer,
Love Letters from Cell 92, 248–51.

p. 309, **None of what you wrote surprised:** Bonhoeffer and von
Wedemeyer, *Love Letters from Cell 92*, 254–55.

p. 314, **Who am I? They often tell me . . . O God, I am thine:** Bonhoeffer,
Letters and Papers from Prison, 347–48.

p. 324, **We don't know how often we shall:** Bonhoeffer and von
Wedemeyer, *Love Letters from Cell 92*, 256.

Winner of the 2021 Christy Award for Historical Fiction

"That rare and powerful story that rips your heart apart at the same time that it inspires you to live for something greater. . . . A beautiful masterpiece of a novel!"

—Heidi Chiavaroli, Carol Award–winning author of *Freedom's Ring* and *The Tea Chest*

KREGEL
PUBLICATIONS

Get ready for a very *marry* Christmas!

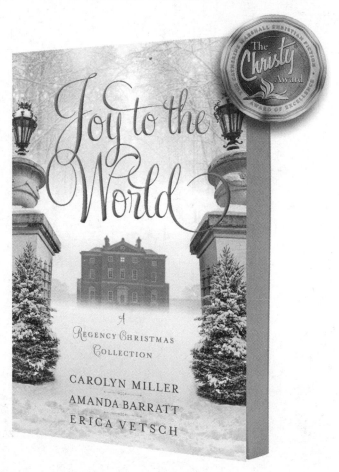

Depth, faith, and satisfying stories of love—you'll fall for this heartwarming collection of holiday Regency romance from three popular inspirational authors!

CAROLYN MILLER—"Heaven and Nature Sing"
AMANDA BARRATT—"Far as the Curse Is Found"
ERICA VETSCH—"Wonders of His Love"